A REASON TO DIE

A PERLEY GATES WESTERN

A REASON TO DIE

A PERLEY GATES WESTERN

WILLIAM W. JOHNSTONE

with J. A. Johnstone

PINNACLE BOOKS
Kensington Publishing Corp.

www.kensingtonbooks.com

PINNACLE BOOKS are published by

Kensington Publishing Corp.
119 West 40th Street
New York, NY 10018

PUBLISHER'S NOTE
Following the death of William W. Johnstone, the Johnstone family is working with a carefully selected writer to organize and complete Mr. Johnstone's outlines and many unfinished manuscripts to create additional novels in all of his series like The Last Gunfighter, Mountain Man, and Eagles, among others. This novel was inspired by Mr. Johnstone's superb storytelling.

All Kensington titles, imprints, and distributed lines are available at special quantity discounts for bulk purchases for sales promotions, premiums, fund-raising, educational, or institutional use. Special book excerpts or customized printings can also be created to fit specific needs. For details, write or phone the office of the Kensington sales manager: Kensington Publishing Corp., 119 West 40th Street, New York, NY 10018, attn: Sales Department; phone 1-800-221-2647.

PINNACLE BOOKS, the Pinnacle logo, and the WWJ steer head logo are Reg. U.S. Pat. & TM Off.

ISBN-13: 978-0-7860-4219-7
ISBN-10: 0-7860-4219-2

First printing: September 2018

10 9 8 7 6 5 4 3 2 1

Printed in the United States of America

First electronic edition: September 2018

ISBN-13: 978-0-7860-4220-3
ISBN-10: 0-7860-4220-6

CHAPTER 1

"It's a good thing I decided to check," John Gates said to Sonny Rice, who was sitting in the wagon loaded with supplies. They had just come from Henderson's General Store and John had wanted to stop by the telegraph office on the chance Perley might have sent word.

Sonny was immediately attentive. "Did he send a telegram? Where is he?"

"He's in Deadwood, South Dakota," John answered. "He said he's on his way home."

"Did he say if he found your grandpa?"

"He said he found him, but Grandpa's dead. Said he'd explain it all when he gets back."

"Well, I'll be . . ." Sonny drew out. "Ol' Perley found him. I figured he would. He usually does what he sets out to do."

John couldn't disagree. His younger brother was always one to follow a trail to its end, even though oftentimes it led him to something he would have been better served to avoid. He laughed when he thought about what his older brother, Rubin, said about Perley. *If there ain't but one cow pie between here and the Red River, Perley will most likely step in it.*

It was a joke, of course, but it did seem that trouble had a way of finding Perley. It was true, even though he would go to any lengths to avoid it.

"We might as well go by the diner and see if Beulah's cooked anything fit to eat," John casually declared, knowing that was what Sonny was hoping to hear. "Might even stop by Patton's afterward and get a shot of whiskey. That all right with you?" He could tell by the grin on the young ranch hand's face that he knew he was being japed. As a rule, Sonny didn't drink very often, but he would imbibe on some occasions.

Thoughts running through his mind, John nudged the big gray gelding toward the small plain building at the end of the street that proclaimed itself to be the Paris Diner. He was glad he had checked the telegraph office. It was good news to hear Perley was on his way home to Texas. He had a long way to travel from the Black Hills, so it was hard to say when to expect him to show up at the Triple-G. His mother and Rubin would be really happy to hear about the telegram. Perley had been gone a long time on his quest to find their grandpa. His mother had been greatly concerned when Perley hadn't returned with his brothers after the cattle were delivered to the buyers in Ogallala.

John reined the gray to a halt at the hitching rail in front of the diner, then waited while Sonny pulled up in the wagon.

"Well, I was beginning to wonder if the Triple-G had closed down," Lucy Tate sang out when she saw them walk in.

"Howdy, Lucy," John returned. "It has been a while since we've been in town. At least, it has been for me. I don't know if any of the other boys have been in." He gave her a big smile. "I thought you mighta got yourself married by now," he joked, knowing what a notorious flirt she was.

She waited for them to sit down before replying. "I've had some offers, but I'm waiting to see if that wife of yours is gonna kick you out."

"She's threatened to more than once," he said, "but she knows there's a line of women hopin' that'll happen."

She laughed. "I'm gonna ask Martha about that if you ever bring her in here to eat." Without asking if they wanted coffee, she filled two cups. "Beulah's got chicken and dumplin's or beef stew. Whaddle-it-be?"

"Give me the chicken and dumplin's," John said. "I get enough beef every day. How 'bout you, Sonny?"

"I'll take the chicken, too," he replied, his eyes never having left the saucy waitress.

Noticing it, John couldn't resist japing him some more. "How 'bout Sonny, here? He ain't married and he's got a steady job."

She chuckled delightedly and reached over to tweak Sonny's cheek. "You're awful sweet, but still a little young. I'll keep my eye on you, though." She went to the kitchen to get their food, leaving the blushing young ranch hand to recover.

"She's something, ain't she?" John asked after seeing Sonny's embarrassment. "Can't take a thing she says seriously." He thought at once of Perley, who had made that mistake and suffered his disappointment. Further thoughts on the subject were interrupted when Becky Morris came in from the kitchen.

"Afternoon, John," Becky greeted him. "Lucy said you were here." She greeted Sonny as well, but she didn't know his name. "It's been a while since any of the Triple-G men have stopped in. Perley used to come by every time he was in town, but I haven't seen him in a long time now. Is he all right?"

"Perley's been gone for a good while now," John answered. "I just got a telegram from him this mornin' from Dakota Territory. Said he's on his way home."

"Oh, well, maybe he'll come in to see us when he gets back," Becky said.

"I'm sure he will." John couldn't help wondering if Perley had taken proper notice of Becky Morris. Shy and gentle, unlike Lucy Tate, Becky looked more the woman a man should invest his life with. He might be wrong, but John suspected he detected a wistful tone in her voice when she'd asked about Perley.

Before they were finished, Beulah Walsh came out to visit. John assured her that her reputation as a cook was still deserved, as far as he was concerned. He paid for his and Sonny's meal, and got up to leave. "We've gotta stop by Patton's before we go back to the ranch. Sonny's gotta have a shot of that rotgut whiskey before he leaves town."

"I never said that," Sonny insisted. "You were the one that said we'd go to the saloon."

"Don't let him bother you, sweetie," Lucy said and gave him another tweak on his cheek. "I know how you heavy drinkers need a little shooter after you eat."

"What did you tell her that for?" Sonny asked as soon as they were outside. "Now she thinks I'm a drunk."

"I doubt it," John replied.

Moving back down the short street to Patton's Saloon, they tied the horses to the rail and went inside.

Benny Grimes, the bartender, called out a "Howdy" as soon as they walked in the door. "John Gates, I swear, I thought you mighta gave up drinkin' for good."

"How do, Benny?" John greeted him. "Might as well have. We ain't had much time to get into town lately. Ain't that right, Sonny?"

"That's a fact," Sonny agreed and picked up the shot glass Benny slid over to him. He raised it, turned toward John, and said, "Here's hopin' Perley has a safe trip home." He downed it with a quick toss, anxious to get it over with. He was not a drinker by habit and took a drink of whiskey now and then only to avoid having to explain why he didn't care for it.

"Well, I'll sure drink to that," John said and raised his glass.

"Me, too." Benny poured himself one. After they tossed the whiskey down, he asked, "Where is he?"

"Way up in Dakota Territory," John said, "and we just got word he's on his way home, so we need to let the folks hear the news." He had one more drink, then he and Sonny headed back to the Triple-G.

* * *

The man John Gates had wished a safe trip home earlier in the day was seated a few yards from a crystal-clear waterfall. It was a good bit off the trail he had been following, but he'd had a feeling the busy stream he had crossed might lead to a waterfall. As high up as he was on the mountain, it stood to reason the stream would soon come to a cliff. It pleased him to find out he had been right, and it had been worth his while to have seen it. It was a trait that Perley Gates had undoubtedly inherited from his grandfather—an obsession for seeing what might lie on the other side of the mountain. And it was the reason he found himself in the Black Hills of Dakota Territory on this late summer day—that and the fact that he was not married and his brothers were. It didn't matter if he rode all the way to hell and who knows where. There wasn't any wife waiting for him to come home, so he had been the obvious pick to go in search of his grandfather.

His grandfather, for whom he was named, was buried in the dark mountains not far from where Perley sat drinking the stout black coffee he favored. He felt a strong kinship with him, even though he had not really known the man, having never met him until a short time before he passed away. Even so, that was enough time for the old man to determine that he was proud to have his young grandson wear his name, Perley Gates. The old man had been one of the lucky ones who struck it rich in the Black Hills gold rush before an outlaw's bullet brought his life to an end. Determined to make restitution to his family for having abandoned them, he hung on long enough to extract a promise from his grandson to take his gold back to Texas.

The gold dust had been right where his grandfather had said it would be. Perley had recovered four canvas sacks from under a huge rock before he'd been satisfied there were no more. With no scales to weigh the sacks, he guessed it to be ten pounds per sack. At the present time, gold was selling in Deadwood at a little over three hundred and thirty dollars a pound. If his calculations were correct, he was saddled with a responsibility to deliver over thirteen thousand dollars in gold dust to Texas, more than eight hundred miles away. It was not a task he looked forward to. The gold rush had brought every robber and dry-gulcher west of Omaha to Deadwood Gulch, all with an eye toward preying on those who had worked to bring the gold out of the streams. Perley's problem was how to transport his treasure without attracting the watchful eye of the outlaws. It would be easier to convert the dust to paper money, but he was not confident he would get a fair exchange from the bank in Deadwood, because of the inflation there.

To add to his concerns, he had accumulated five extra horses during his time in the Black Hills and he didn't want the bother of driving them all the way to Texas with no one to help him. With forty pounds of dust to carry, he decided to keep one of the horses to use as a second packhorse. His packhorse could carry the load along with his supplies, but with the load divided onto two horses, he could move a lot faster in the event he had to. His favorite of the extra horses would be the paint gelding that his grandfather had ridden. The old man had loved that horse, maybe as much as Perley loved Buck, so he didn't feel right about selling it.

With Custer City and Hill City reduced almost to ghost towns, he decided to ride back to Deadwood to see if he could sell the other four. Deadwood wasn't a good market for selling horses. Cheyenne would be a better bet, or maybe Hat Creek Station, for that matter, but he figured he hadn't paid anything for them, so he might as well let them go cheap.

With that settled, he packed up and started back to Deadwood.

"Evenin'. Looks like you're needin' to stable some horses," Franklin Todd greeted Perley when he drew up before his place of business.

"Evenin'," Perley returned. "Matter of fact, I'm lookin' to sell four of 'em if I can get a reasonable price. I'm fixin' to head back to Texas, and I don't wanna lead a bunch of horses back with me."

Todd was at once alerted to the prospects of acquiring four horses at little cost, but he hesitated for a moment, stroking his chin as if undecided. "Which four?" he finally asked.

Perley indicated the four and Todd paused to think some more.

"I really ain't buyin' no horses right now, but I'll take a look at 'em." Todd took his time examining the four horses, then finally made an offer of ten dollars each.

Perley wasn't really surprised by the low offer and countered with a price of fifty dollars for all four.

Todd didn't hesitate to agree. "These horses ain't stolen, are they?" he asked as he weighed out the payment.

"Not till now," Perley answered.

With an eye toward disguising four sacks of gold dust, he left Todd's and walked his horses past a saloon to a general merchandise establishment.

"Can I help you with something?" the owner asked when Perley walked in.

"I'm just lookin' to see if there's anything I need," Perley answered and quickly scanned the counters and shelves while taking frequent glances out the door at his horses at the rail. In the process of trying to keep an eye on his horses, his attention was drawn to several large sacks stacked near the door. "What's in those sacks?" He pointed to them.

"Probably nothing you'd be looking for," the owner replied. "Something I didn't order. Came in with a load of merchandise from Pierre. It's about four hundred pounds of seed corn. I don't know where it was supposed to go, but it sure as hell wasn't Deadwood. There ain't a level piece of ground for farming anywhere in the Black Hills. I tried to sell it to Franklin Todd at the stable for horse feed. Even he didn't want it."

Perley walked over to an open bag and looked inside. "I might could use some of it. Whaddaya askin' for it?"

Too surprised to respond right away, the owner hesitated before asking, "How much are you thinking about?"

Perley said he could use a hundred pounds of it.

The owner shrugged and replied, "I don't know. Two dollars?"

"I could use some smaller canvas bags, too, four of 'em. You got anything like that?"

With both merchant and customer satisfied they had made a good deal, Perley threw his hundred-pound sack of seed corn across the back of one of his packhorses and started back toward Custer City. Although already late in the afternoon, he preferred to camp in the hills outside of Deadwood, considering what he carried on his packhorses.

He rode for a good nine or ten miles before stopping. When he made camp that night, he placed a ten-pound sack of gold dust in each of the twenty-five-pound sacks he had just bought, and filled in around it with seed corn. When he finished, he was satisfied that his dust was disguised about as well as he could hope for, and the corn didn't add a lot of weight with the amount necessary to fill the sacks.

He downed the last gulp of coffee from his cup and got to his feet. "Well, I can't sit here and worry about it all night," he announced to Buck, the big bay gelding grazing noisily a few yards away. "You don't give a damn, do ya?"

"That horse ever answer you back?"

Startled, Perley stepped away from the fire, grabbing his rifle as he dived for cover behind a tree, searching frantically for where the voice had come from. It didn't sound very far away.

"Whoa! Hold on a minute, feller," the voice exclaimed. "Ain't no need for that there rifle."

"I'll decide that after you come outta your hidin'

place," Perley responded and cranked a cartridge into the cylinder of the Winchester.

"Hold on," the voice came back again. "I didn't mean to surprise you like that. I shoulda sang out a little sooner. I was just passin' by on the trail up there on the ridge and I saw your fire, so I thought I'd stop and say howdy." A short pause followed, then he said, "It always pays to be careful to see what kinda camp you're lookin' at before you come a-ridin' in. I'm comin' out, so don't take a shot at me, all right?"

"All right," Perley answered. "Come on out." He watched cautiously as his visitor emerged from the darkness of the trees above the creek, alert for any sign of movement that might indicate there were others with him. When he felt sure the man was alone, he eased the hammer back down, but still held the rifle ready to fire. Leading a dun gelding with a mule following on a rope, his surprise guest approached the fire. "You're travelin' these back trails pretty late at night, ain'tcha?" Perley asked.

"Reckon so," the man replied, "but with all the outlaws ridin' these trails lookin' for somebody to rob, it pays for a man alone to travel some at night." He looked around at the loaded packs and the horses grazing close by. "Looks like you're gettin' ready to travel, too, from the looks of your camp. I smelled your fire from the ridge back there. Thought maybe I might get a cup of coffee, but I see you're 'bout ready to pack up."

"I was thinkin' about it," Perley said. "Where you headin'? Deadwood?"

"Nope, the other way. I've seen Deadwood. I'm ready to go back to Cheyenne."

Perley studied the young man carefully for a few moments. A young man, close to his own age, he figured. There was nothing unusual about him, unless you counted the baggy britches he wore, that looked to be a couple of inches short, and the shirt that looked a size too big. Perley decided he was no threat. "Well, I've got plenty of coffee, so I reckon I can fix you up with a cup. What about supper? You had anything to eat?"

"As a matter of fact, I ain't. I had that thought in mind when I caught sight of your camp. I'd be much obliged. My name's Billy Tuttle."

"Perley Gates." He waited for the man to ask the name again, which was the usual response. When he didn't, Perley said, "Take care of your animals and I'll make us a pot of coffee. It's kinda late to go any farther tonight, anyway, so I think I'll just stay here. You like venison? 'Cause that's what I'm cookin' for supper."

Billy said that would suit him just fine. He'd been living on sowbelly and little else for the past couple of days.

Perley soon decided there was nothing to fear from his surprise guest. As he had said, he was focused on getting back to his home in Cheyenne.

Perley guessed the young man was also short on supplies. "You any kin to Tom Tuttle there in Cheyenne?"

"He's my pa," Billy replied. "You know him?"

"I've done some business with your pa," Perley answered. "Matter of fact, I sold him a couple of horses when I stopped at his stable one time. He's a good man."

It didn't take long before Billy told the story of his attempt to make his fortune in Deadwood Gulch, a story that left him headed for home with empty pockets. It was a story all too common in boomtowns like Deadwood and Custer City.

"So you partnered up with a couple of fellows and they ran off with all the gold the three of you found?" Perley summed up.

"That's a fact," Billy confirmed. "It wasn't but about four hundred dollars' worth. Wouldn'ta paid us much when we split it three ways, but it was still a helluva lot more than I came out here with."

"I swear," Perley commented. "That's tough luck, all right. Did you know these two fellows before you partnered up with 'em?"

"No, I just ran up on 'em one mornin' and they looked like they could use a hand, so I went to work with 'em, building a sluice box. Wasn't long before we started strikin' color, and it wasn't long after that when I woke up one mornin' and they was gone. Cleared out while I was asleep."

It was hard for Perley not to feel sympathy for the unfortunate young man. He couldn't help thinking that Billy's experience sounded like the kind of fix that he carried a reputation for. He thought of his brother Rubin saying *If there wasn't but one cow pie on the whole damn ranch, Perley would step in it.* He had to admit that sometimes it seemed to be true.

Maybe he and Billy had that in common. "So whaddaya plan on doin' now? Go back and help your pa in the stable?"

"I reckon," Billy replied, then hesitated before going on. "Pa ain't gonna be too happy to see me come home. I think he was hopin' I'd stay on out here in the Black Hills."

That was surprising to Perley. "Why is that?" Tom Tuttle impressed him as a solid family man. He had to admit, however, that he had only a brief acquaintance with him.

"The woman Pa's married to ain't my mama," Billy said. "Pa married her when my mama died of consumption. She's my stepmother and she's got a son of her own about my age. She's talked Pa into turnin' his business over to her son when Pa gets too old to run it, and I reckon I'm just in the way."

Perley didn't know what to say. In the short time he had dealings with Tom Tuttle, he would not have thought him to be the type to abandon his own son. He had compassion for Billy, but all he could offer him was common courtesy. "Well, I'm sorry to hear you have troubles with your pa, but if it'll help, you're welcome to ride along with me till we get to Cheyenne. I'm guessin' you ain't fixed too good for supplies."

"You guessed right," Billy responded at once. "And I surely appreciate it. I won't be no bother a'tall. I'm used to hard work and I'll do my share of the chores."

"Good," Perley said with as much enthusiasm as he could muster. Truth be told, a stranger as a traveling companion was close to the last thing he wanted, considering what he was carrying on his packhorses. He didn't intend to get careless, even though Billy seemed forthright and harmless. Close to Perley's age, Billy might come in handy if they were unfortunate enough to encounter outlaws on the road to Cheyenne.

After the horses and Billy's mule were taken care

of, the two travelers ate supper, planning to get an early start in the morning.

"Here," Billy insisted, "I'll clean up the cups and fryin' pan. I've got to earn my keep," he added cheerfully. After everything was done they both spread their bedrolls close to the fire and turned in.

Perley was awake at first light after having slept fitfully, due to a natural tendency to sleep with one eye open, even though he felt he had nothing to fear from Billy. He revived the fire and started coffee before Billy woke up.

"Here I am lyin' in bed while you're already at it," Billy said as he rolled out of his blankets. "Whatcha want me to do?"

"Just pack up your possibles and throw a saddle on your horse," Perley said. "We'll have a cup of coffee before we get started, eat breakfast when we rest the horses."

It didn't take long for Billy to load the few items he owned on the mule, so when he finished, he came to help Perley. "What's in the sacks?" He saw Perley tying two twenty-five-pound sacks on each of his pack-horses.

"Kansas seed corn," Perley answered casually. "I found a store in Deadwood that had about four hundred pounds of it. Ain't nobody in Deadwood wantin' seed corn, so I bought a hundred pounds of it at a damn good price. Gonna take it back to Texas and start me a corn patch. If I'd had a couple more horses, I'd a-bought all he had." He made a point then of opening one of the sacks and taking out a handful to show Billy. "You can't get corn like this in Texas."

Billy nodded his head politely, but was obviously unimpressed, which was the reaction Perley hoped for. Packed up and ready to go, they started the first day of their journey together, following the road toward Custer City, heading south.

The second night's camp was made by a busy stream halfway between Hill City and Custer. By this time, Perley's supply of smoked venison was down to only enough for another meal or two. Then it would be back to sowbelly, unless they were lucky enough to find some game to shoot. Perley was not inclined to tarry, considering the gold he was transporting. As somewhat of a surprise to him, he found Billy just as eager to put the Black Hills behind them, considering what he had said about his father.

Curious, Perley asked him, "What are you aimin' to do when you get back to Cheyenne? You think your pa really won't be happy to see you back?" He couldn't believe that Tom Tuttle would kick his son out.

"Oh, I ain't worried about that. I don't wanna work in the damn stable, anyway. I've got a few ideas I'm thinkin' about."

"What kinda ideas?" Perley asked.

"Yeah, what kinda ideas?" The voice came from the darkness behind them. "Maybe stealin' gold from your partners, stuff like that, huh, Billy?"

"Don't even think about it," another voice warned when Perley started to react.

He had no choice but to remain seated by the fire.

A tall, gangly man stepped into the circle of fire-light. He was grinning as he held a double-barreled shotgun on them. "Come on in, Jeb. I've got 'em both covered."

In another second, he was joined by a second man, this one a bull-like brute of a man. "Hello, Billy. I see you got you another partner already. It took me and Luke awhile before we tracked you down. Seems like you took off so quick, you must notta realized you took all the gold, instead of just your share."

"Whoa, now, Jeb," Billy exclaimed. "You know I wouldn'ta done nothin' like that. Luke musta buried it somewhere else and forgot where he put it." He looked at the lanky man with the shotgun. "What about it, Luke? Ain't that what musta happened? You were awful drunk that night."

His question caused Luke to laugh. "I gotta give you credit, Billy, you can make up the damnedest stories I've ever heard."

Jeb, who was obviously the boss, said, "We'll see soon enough when we take a look at the packs on that mule." He stared hard at Perley then. "Who's this feller?"

"His name's Perley Gates," Billy said, causing both of the outlaws to laugh.

"Pearly Gates," Luke echoed. "Well, ain't that somethin'? Looks to me like he's carryin' a helluva lot more than you are. Maybe ol' Pearly struck it rich back there in the gulch and now he's packin' it all outta here."

Perley spoke then. "If I had, I reckon I'd still be back there in the gulch, lookin' for more." Angry that he had been taken so completely by surprise, it didn't help to learn that Billy had fooled him, too. Not only was he a thief, he had brought his troubles to roost with him.

"Damn. He talks," Luke mocked. "We'll take a look in them packs, too."

"You're makin' a mistake, Jeb," Billy said. "Pearly ain't got nothin' in them packs but supplies and some kinda fancy seed corn he's fixin' to plant. If you think I stole your gold dust, then go ahead and look through my packs."

"Oh, I will," Jeb replied, "you sneakin' rat. Luke, go through the packs on that damn mule. There's five pounds of dust in 'em somewhere. That oughta be easy to find." When Billy started to get up, Jeb aimed his pistol at him. "You just set right there and keep your hands where I can see 'em."

Caught in a helpless situation, there was nothing Perley could do but sit there while Luke rifled through Billy's packs. When he glanced at Billy, he saw no sign of concern in his face. Maybe he really hadn't stolen their gold, but it sure seemed like his former partners were convinced that he had.

"Ain't no need to make a mess of my stuff just 'cause you was wrong," Billy complained when Luke started throwing his possessions around in frustration.

"Shut your mouth!" Jeb yelled at Billy. "Look in his saddlebags," he said to Luke then.

"I told you I ain't got your gold," Billy argued. "Looks to me like maybe you oughta be askin' Luke where that dust is. All I wanted was to get the hell outta that creek after you shot that feller. I figured you and Luke could have my share."

Jeb shifted a suspicious eye in Luke's direction. "I don't reckon somethin' like that mighta happened, could it, Luke? I mean, we was all drinkin' kinda heavy that night. Last thing I remember before I passed out was you holdin' that sack of dust and talkin' about what you was gonna buy with your share. When I woke up the next mornin', you was already up and Billy was gone."

"Hold on a minute!" Luke blurted out. "You're lettin' that lyin' son of a bitch put crazy ideas in your head. Me and you been ridin' together long enough for you to know I wouldn't do nothin' like that."

"You looked through all his packs and there weren't no sack of gold dust," Jeb reminded him. "Whaddaya suppose happened to it?"

"How the hell do I know?" Luke shot back, then nodded toward Perley, who was still a spectator at this point. "Most likely it's in his stuff. Billy musta put it on one of his packhorses." He turned and started toward Perley's belongings, stacked beside his bedroll.

"This has gone as far as it's goin'," Perley said, getting to his feet. "You've got no call to go plunderin' through my things like you did with Billy's. Billy just hooked up with me last night and he wouldn't likely just hand over five pounds of gold dust for me to tote for him, would he? You can take a look at what I'm carryin', but I'll help you do it, so you don't go tearin' up my packs like you did with Billy's."

His statement caused them both to hesitate for a moment, surprised by his audacity. Then they both laughed at his obvious stupidity.

"Mister," Jeb informed him, "you ain't got no say in what we'll do. It was bad luck for you when you joined up with Billy Tuttle. I'm tired of jawin' with both of you." Without warning, he said, "Shoot 'em both, Luke."

"My pleasure," Luke said and raised his shotgun to fire. Before he could cock the hammers back, he was doubled over by a .44 slug from Perley's Colt.

Jeb's reaction was swift, but not fast enough to draw his pistol before Perley's second shot slammed into his chest. He was already dead when his weapon cleared the holster and fired one wayward shot in Billy's direction.

Billy howled, grabbed his leg, and started limping around in a circle. "Damn, damn, damn . . ." He muttered over and over as he clutched his baggy trouser leg with both hands.

Perley holstered his .44 and moved quickly to help him. "How bad is it? Let me give you a hand."

"It ain't bad," Billy insisted. "I can take care of it. You make sure them two are dead. I'll take care of my leg."

"They're both dead," Perley said. "Now sit down and I'll take a look at that wound." He paused then when a peculiar sight caught his eye. "What the—" was as far as he got before he saw a tiny stream of dust spraying on the toe of Billy's boot, not understanding at once what he was seeing. When he realized what it was, he looked up to meet Billy's gaze.

"Looks like I sprung a leak," Billy said, smiling sheepishly. "The son of a bitch shot a hole in my britches."

Perley said nothing but continued to stare in disbelief.

Billy tried to divert his attention. "Man, you're fast as greased lightning. You saved both our lives. I ain't never seen anybody that fast with a handgun." He was hesitant to move his foot for fear of causing the gold to mix in the dirt beneath it.

Perley's gaze was still captured by the little pile of gold dust forming on the toe of Billy's boot. "You caused me to kill two men you stole gold from," he said, not at all pleased by the fact.

A little more apprehensive now that he had seen Perley's skill with a gun, Billy countered. "Let's not forget that they was fixin' to shoot us. There weren't no doubt about that. I saw 'em shoot a man at a placer mine and take that little five-pound sack of dust. That's when I decided that weren't no partnership for me."

"So you cut out and took the gold with you," Perley reminded him. "Looks to me like they had good reason to come after you."

"Well, they didn't have no right to the gold," Billy said. "'Specially after they killed him for it." When it was obvious that Perley was far from casual when it came to the taking of a man's life, Billy tried to change his focus. "I reckon you've earned a share of the gold, and I don't mind givin' it to you. I figure I've got about sixteen hundred dollars' worth. That 'ud make your share about eight hundred."

When there was still no positive reaction from Perley, Billy tried to make light of the situation. "And that ain't countin' the dust runnin' outta my britches leg." He hesitated to make a move, still not sure what Perley had in mind. "All right if I see if I can fix it?"

"I reckon you might as well," Perley finally said, not really sure what he should do about the situation he found himself in. He was still feeling the heavy responsibility for having killed two men, even knowing he had been given no choice. The one called Luke had been preparing to empty both barrels of that shotgun. There had been no time to think.

"I don't want any share in your gold," Perley said. "Go ahead and take care of it."

Billy's expression was enough to indicate that he was more than happy to hear that. He immediately unbuckled his belt and dropped his britches to reveal two cotton bags, one hanging beside each leg from a length of clothesline tied around his waist. Perley could hardly believe what he saw. Jeb's wild shot had drilled a hole straight through Billy's trouser leg and the cotton bag hanging inside.

"What about their horses and guns?" Billy asked as he transferred the remaining dust in the damaged bag into the other one.

"What about 'em?" Perley responded, still undecided what he should do with Billy.

"I mean, hell, you killed 'em, both of 'em. I reckon you'd be right in claimin' you own all their belongin's." He glanced up quickly. "I sure as hell ain't gonna give you no argument."

While Billy was busy trying to recover every grain of dust that had poured through the hole, Perley took an extra few minutes to think it over. He had to admit that he didn't know what to do about it—

a thief stealing from another thief. The part that worried him was the killings he had been forced to commit, and he blamed Billy for causing that. One thing he knew for sure was that he'd had enough of Billy Tuttle.

He told Billy, "I ain't ever operated outside the law, and I don't reckon I'll start now. Those two fellows were outlaws and you were ridin' with 'em, so I reckon whatever they done, you were part of it. You're sure as hell an outlaw, too. I reckon this is where you and I part ways. You take your gold and the horses, and anything else on those two. If your daddy wasn't Tom Tuttle, I might be inclined to turn you over to the sheriff back in Deadwood, but your pa doesn't need to know you got on the wrong side of the law. If you'll go on back to Cheyenne and start livin' an honest life, he'll never hear from me about you bein' mixed up with these outlaws. We'll go our separate ways and forget about what happened here. Can I have your promise on that?"

"Yes sir, you sure do," Billy answered in his most contrite manner. "I 'preciate the chance to get myself right with the law. I've sure as hell learned my lesson. If it weren't for you, I'd most likely be dead right now, so you have my promise." He hesitated for a few moments, then said, "I don't see no use in us splittin' up, though. It looks to me like it'd be better for both of us to travel together for protection. Whaddaya say?"

"I don't think so, Billy," Perley answered. "At least for me, I'll be better alone. Good luck to you, though."

CHAPTER 2

As Perley had insisted, they parted company, Billy to continue along the Cheyenne–Deadwood Stage Road, while Perley followed a trail leading west. He knew that it was less than a full day's ride in that direction to be out of the mountains and back in Wyoming Territory, so he intended to turn back to the south once he cleared the mountains. That way, Billy should be well ahead of him on the stage road to Cheyenne. In the long run, it would delay him on his trip back to Texas, but only for half a day or so of the two and a half to three weeks he figured to take.

His thoughts kept returning to Billy and the situation he had been caught in. Before they parted company, Billy had sworn that he had learned his lesson, and he was going to follow the straight and narrow from that point on. Maybe he would. It was hard to say, but Perley preferred to let Billy deal with his conscience by himself. He was already involved in the mixed-up young man's life far more than he had expected when Billy first rode into his camp.

Since Perley was not really familiar with the

country he was riding through, he was dependent upon no more than a sketchy knowledge of the heavily forested mountains. For that reason, when he came upon a busy stream that appeared to head in the right direction, he followed its course down from the mountains. Luck seemed to be with him, for it eventually led him down through the hills and into the flatter prairie west of the Black Hills. He decided it best to camp beside the stream that had led him out of the mountains, and set out on a more southeasterly course the next morning. It would be an uneventful ride of a day and a half before he struck the Cheyenne stage road just north of Hat Creek Station.

"Well, if this isn't a fine surprise," Martha Bowman said when she saw him walk in the door of the hotel dining room at Hat Creek Station. "I thought you'd be back home on that Texas ranch by now."

"I'm on my way," Perley responded. "Just thought I'd stop in for one of those good suppers you folks fix."

She followed him over to the end of the long table in the center of the room. "Are you staying in the hotel?"

"Not this time," Perley said. "I'm puttin' my horses up at the stable for the night and I expect I'd best sleep with them."

She stepped back, pretending to be offended. "Was the hotel bed so bad last time you were here that you'd rather sleep in the stable?"

He laughed and replied, "No, ma'am. It's just that Buck, my horse, is feelin' kinda puny, so I'd best keep an eye on him." Martha was a friend, and he trusted her completely, but he didn't think it a good idea to tell her he was more concerned about the four bags of seed corn in his packs.

"There you go, ma'aming me again," she scolded. "I thought we settled that last time you were here."

"Sorry, I forgot . . . Martha," he quickly corrected himself. "I wasn't sure you'd be here. Thought maybe you'd be married and gone."

She chuckled at that. "I've been too busy to even think about that. Besides, I thought I told you I'm particular about the man I marry, and he hasn't showed up yet."

He had never stopped to analyze his relationship with Martha Bowman or given thought to the fact that he was so free and easy around her. As a rule, he was shy around all women, especially one of Martha's beauty and grace. But Martha was different. He was comfortable in her presence and free from getting tongue-tied, as he often did when talking to any woman outside a saloon.

He was brought back from his thoughts when she asked if he wanted coffee. "Yes, ma'am," he replied, then quickly corrected himself. "Yes, Martha."

She left to fetch the coffeepot, shaking her head in exasperation. "I'll get a plate for you," she called back over her shoulder.

He was working on a slice of apple pie when Martha found the time to sit and visit with him for a while. "I'll have a cup of coffee while I've got a chance," she said. "Is that pie any good?"

With a mouthful of it, he answered with a satisfied nod.

"I haven't tried any, myself," she continued. "Gotta watch my figure."

"Me, too," Perley said. "What's goin' on here at the ranch?" He was interested, since the ranch foreman, Willis Adams, had at one time tried to hire him.

"Nothing new that I know of," she answered. "There's hardly anybody staying in the hotel. A man and his wife waiting to catch the stage to Deadwood, and some man on his way to Cheyenne."

That caught Perley's interest. "Who's the fellow goin' to Cheyenne? Has he been here long?"

She shrugged. "I don't know. Young fellow. Checked into the hotel this morning. He's not waiting to ride the stage 'cause he's got some horses with him."

That was not good news to Perley. It could be a co-incidence, but there were better odds that it could be Billy. Martha said he'd checked in that morning.

Why would he want to stay over another night here? Unless he just wants to enjoy some of that money he stole. Or maybe he's got something else in mind. That's a possibility. Billy already demonstrated a potential to bury himself in deep trouble. And since he stumbled into my camp, he seems to want to share it with me. Perley glanced up to find Martha staring at him.

"Where did you drift off to? I think I lost you there for a minute," she said.

"I reckon my brain ain't caught up with me since I left Deadwood," he joked. "I have to stop and wait for it once in a while." He couldn't help thinking he'd stepped in another cow pie. He wasn't even sure the man Martha was talking about was, in fact, Billy Tuttle. He didn't ask her if she remembered the

man's name because he didn't want to hear her say
Billy Tuttle.

At any rate, if it was Billy, he had a room in the
hotel while Perley would be sleeping in the stable. If
he was careful, there shouldn't be any occasion for
Billy to know he was even there unless he bumped
into him in the dining room.

"Well, I reckon I'd best get outta here and let you
get back to work," Perley announced.

"Yeah, I guess I'd better, if I don't wanna lose
my job."

"That's a fact," he said, knowing she was joking.
Her father owned the hotel, so he was not likely to
fire her.

"You gonna be back for breakfast?"

"I ain't sure. Depends on how early I get started in
the mornin'." Any other time, he wouldn't have
missed the opportunity to see her again.

He paid for his supper, said good-bye, and hurried
out the door, unaware that she stood watching him
until he disappeared around the corner of the building. The only thing he was thinking at that point was
that maybe he shouldn't have left his packs unguarded in the stable for so long. Then he reassured
himself that he had been right to not show any undue
concern over the packs he had left in a corner of the
stall. Besides, Robert Davis was the man responsible
for watching the stable, and he was as trustworthy as
you could ask for.

As Perley had figured, his packs and possessions
were undisturbed when he got to the stable and
Robert Davis was still there to keep an eye on things.

He said he had a few things he wanted to take care of before he retired to his room on the back of the barn.

"I'll not hold you up any longer," Perley said.

"Well, I reckon you can just make yourself at home," Davis said. "I put fresh hay down in the other corner and you know where the water is. I'll see you in the mornin'."

After Davis left for the night, Perley spent a little time making sure his horses were all right. Then he arranged the hay in the corner opposite his packs and spread his bedroll on top of it, making a soft, comfortable bed. He could hear the loud voices coming from the saloon fifty yards away, but they were not enough to delay his falling asleep almost immediately.

Billy looked at the big clock behind the bar in the tiny Oasis Saloon, which anchored the hardware store, separated by a common wall. It was getting late and there were few customers left to work on Ernie Dykes's supply of rye whiskey, and Billy was beginning to become discouraged. He'd thought for sure Perley Gates would show up there before turning in for the night, but he was damn-sure taking his time about it. Billy had gambled on Perley stopping at Hat Creek Station, so much so that he spent some of his ill-gotten gold dust to take a room in the hotel for the night. He was confident that his gamble had paid off when he bought a drink for one of the wranglers at the station, who told him that a fellow had ridden in that evening. He said he was riding a bay horse and leading two packhorses, one of which was a paint. Maybe Perley took a bottle up to his hotel room, or maybe he just wasn't a drinker. Whatever the reason, Billy was tired of waiting for him to show up. His plan had been to take another try at talking Perley into riding to Cheyenne together. He figured that somewhere between there and Cheyenne, he might get a chance to take a closer look at those sacks of seed corn. Perley struck him as more of a cowhand than a farmer, and with the way he handled that Colt .44 he wore, he might not be either one.

The more Billy thought about it, the more impatient he became, until finally he convinced himself that Perley was holed up in the hotel. When he gave it more thought, that was actually the best place for him. His horses were in the stable and he wasn't likely to carry all his packs to the hotel. *I ain't known for my smarts,* he thought, *but I sure as hell should have thought of that before now. I'm wasting my time sitting here. I'd best go take a look in the stable.* He settled up with Ernie and walked out of the saloon.

A bright three-quarter moon was climbing high overhead that cast a silvery light upon the side of the barn next to the stables. Billy walked past the blacksmith shop across the street, then paused to watch the barn for a few minutes. No sign of anyone around. At the rear of the barn, he saw a lantern shining through the single window of a shack built onto the back. Figuring that was the stable man's shack, it appeared that he was in for the night.

Billy moved quickly across the open street to the shadow of the barn. When there was still no sign of anyone about, he cautiously tried the door. It was barred on the inside, which was no surprise, but it was worth a try. Not discouraged, he moved around the side to what he guessed was the tack room window. It was shuttered, but upon trying it, he found it to be unlocked. All he needed was something to stand on. Looking around him, he spotted a half-keg filled with water. *Perfect,* he thought. After tipping it over to empty out the water, he rolled it under the window, turned it upside down, and climbed up on it.

He took a cautious look inside to make sure no one was there, then easily pulled himself inside the dark room to sit on a workbench built under the window. Waiting only a few seconds to adjust his eyes to the dark interior, he scrambled off the bench and started searching the tack room. There were saddles, bridles, and various tools and supplies, but nothing that looked like Perley's packs. *Of course,* he thought. *They're in the stall with his horses.*

Leaving the tack room, he paused to make sure there was no one in the barn then walked through to the stables. The first two stalls he passed held his three horses and his mule, so he continued toward the back stalls, checking the horses in each one. At the very last one, he found the big bay Perley called Buck. There in a corner of the stall, he saw the packs piled, waiting for him.

For fear he might cause the horse to get nervous, he patted it on the neck and whispered, "Easy there, easy." When the horse showed no signs of resistance, he pushed on past and went to the packs, feeling smug when he saw the four seed sacks. Taking the first one, he hurried to untie the strings, and when he opened it, it appeared to be filled with corn. About to dig down into the corn, he suddenly froze, stopped by the distinct sound of a hammer cocking.

"You took an interest in growin' corn, Billy?"

Shocked because he had assumed Perley had a room in the hotel, same as he had, and terrified because he remembered the efficiency with which Perley had gunned down Jeb and Luke, Billy was unable to move a muscle. To do so would surely mean his death. He stood in the dark stall, desperately trying to come up with a believable story to explain his presence.

After what seemed a long moment of hesitation, he managed to find his voice and came up with the first thing he could think to say. "This ain't w-what it l-looks l-like," he stuttered.

"That so?" Perley responded. "I'm glad to hear that 'cause I'll tell you what it looks like to me. It looks like you were fixin' to steal some of my seed corn, and I told you how hard that corn is to come by in Texas."

Desperate to think of something to save his life, Billy swallowed hard and blurted, "I was only gonna take a handful. Just to see if it would grow in Cheyenne. I didn't think you'd notice a handful missin'." He knew without a doubt that Perley was hiding something in those sacks of corn, but he was afraid to say so. It might mean his instant death.

"If you'da asked me for a handful of corn, I mighta gave it to ya," Perley said, still playing the charade that the sacks contained nothing more than valuable seed corn. "But I can't abide a lowdown thief." Grabbing a coil of rope hanging on a peg in the wall, he stepped up behind Billy and ordered him to unbuckle his gun belt. When Billy did so, Perley ordered, "Turn around. Put your hands together."

"Whatcha fixin' to do?" Billy complained when he

turned to face him. "I wasn't gonna take nothin' but a handful of corn."

"Put 'em together," Perley barked and raised his .44 to point at Billy's nose.

"All right, damn it!" Billy yelped and clasped his hands together. "Don't go shootin' off that gun."

Before Billy could pull them apart again, Perley quickly looped the rope around his wrists, and with the same speed with which he could draw a weapon, took a couple of turns of the rope and tied a knot.

"What the hell?" Billy blurted and started to raise his hands, but Perley suddenly looped the rope around Billy's chest, continuing to use up all of the coil of rope as he tied Billy's arms down tightly to his body.

"All right," Perley said. "Start walkin'." He gave him a shove and started him out of the stalls and into the barn. Curious, Buck plodded along behind his master.

"If you're thinkin' 'bout takin' me to the sheriff," Billy said, "there ain't none at Hat Creek. Me and you might as well join up. I'll split my gold dust with you and you split whatever you've got in those sacks with me."

"I told you, there ain't nothin' but seed corn in those sacks," Perley said again as he grabbed another coil of rope he saw hanging on a post in the barn. "And stealin' a man's seed corn is a hangin' offense."

"What the hell are you talkin' about?" Billy exclaimed, thinking Perley must surely be insane. With his arms pinned tightly to his crotch, his only option was to run, so he bolted toward the barn door. Expecting as much, Perley was right behind him. He kicked Billy's boot, causing his feet to tangle and Billy to trip. He landed heavily on the barn floor with no way to catch himself. Perley was on him at once, looping the rope around Billy's boots. Then he pulled the rope up to take a turn around the rope wrapped around Billy's chest. With Billy bound like a mummy and helpless to resist, Perley pulled his bandanna from his neck, and when Billy started to protest, Perley shoved it in his mouth. With nothing else to use, he took his own bandanna off and used it to secure the gag in Billy's mouth.

With the would-be thief lying helpless on the barn floor, Perley dragged him underneath a crossbeam and threw the loose end of the rope over it. "I reckon we're ready for the hangin'," he announced. "You got any last words?"

Billy attempted to protest, but could not talk.

Perley concluded, "No? Well let's get on with it. Come here, Buck." When the bay gelding came to him, Perley looped the end of the rope around the big horse's withers and hauled Billy up to the beam. Billy was not a big man, but his weight was enough to cause Perley to strain when he took the end of the rope off Buck and managed to loop it around a support post quick enough, so Billy dropped only about a foot. Perley stepped back and appraised his work, satisfied that Billy was hanging upright but helpless, looking pretty much like a cocoon dangling from a web.

With an idea toward putting some distance between himself and Billy, and perhaps discouraging any further contact with him, Perley saddled Buck, loaded his other horses, and led them out of the barn. "It's still in the middle of the night," he said to Billy as he went past. "Robert will likely be in early to cut you down, but you oughta have enough time to make up a good story to explain what you're doin' here. I expect it'll be a real interestin' story, but I ain't gonna hang around to hear it. I don't expect to see you anymore after tonight." He sincerely hoped that would be the case.

In the quiet of the moonlit night, he guided Buck toward the Cheyenne-Deadwood Stage Road once again. His horses were rested, and the well-traveled road was easy to follow with the help of the moon, so he planned to make the most of it to put some distance between Billy and himself. According to his railroad watch, he should have about four hours' head start before Robert Davis came to the stable. He could only speculate what Davis would do when he discovered Billy hanging in his barn. From his brief exposure to the young thief, Perley figured that Billy was not especially bright, but he was determined as hell. Allowing for the possibility that he would still try to follow him, Perley planned to follow the stage road until daylight, then leave it to take a more easterly course and ride till he struck the North Platte in Nebraska Territory. If he was careful about it, and Billy wasn't too skilled at tracking, maybe Perley could lose him for good.

When the moon sank below the horizon, chased away by the early appearance of a lightening of the dark sky, Perley figured he must have ridden close to twenty miles. Riding to a sizable stream cutting across the road, he decided it was time to rest his horses and cook a little breakfast for himself. The stream was wide enough to allow him to guide Buck up the middle of it, so as not to leave tracks for anyone to follow. After following the stream for a few hundred yards, he left the water when he reached a place that offered a small patch of grass in the middle of a stand of cottonwoods. He decided to stop well off the road, hopefully far enough for his fire not to be seen by anyone passing by.

After leaving his camp by the stream, he traveled for the next two days through a land of rolling, seemingly empty plains, with no sign of animal or human life. This part of the plains was new to him, and his natural sense of adventure would have welcomed the journey had it not been for the gold his packhorses carried. The task he had set for himself was to deliver his grandfather's legacy safely to his family, as he had solemnly promised the old man. It was more responsibility than Perley enjoyed.

At the end of the second day, he was relieved to strike a river, which had to be the North Platte. Although he was still not in country he was familiar with, he knew that he could follow the river east to reach Ogallala. From there, he would travel trails that he had traveled before. He had no idea how far it was to Ogallala, but he guessed it to be no farther than a day and a half, possibly two days.

It was at that point that his sorrel packhorse decided to slow him down.

When he stopped to make camp by the North Platte and turned his horses out to graze, he noticed the sorrel favoring its right front leg, almost to the point of limping. "Come here, boy." Perley took him by the bridle, wondering how long the horse had been suffering an injury. "Let's take a look at that."

He lifted the sorrel's hoof to discover the shoe was missing. "How long have you been walkin' without a shoe?" Perley asked, as if expecting an answer from the horse. He looked over at Buck. "Why didn't you let me know we were workin' a lame horse?" He examined the hoof and decided there was no injury to it. "Ain't nothin' I can do for you now. You just threw a shoe back there somewhere. You're gonna have to wait till we get to Ogallala before I can get you a shoe." He stroked the patient horse's face. "I'll throw most of your load over on the paint. Ain't neither one of you totin' that much. He can handle it for the rest of the way to Ogallala."

He took the occasion to check the hooves of his other two horses and determined that the sorrel was the only one needing a blacksmith right away, although it wouldn't be too long before the others were about due.

Perley was underway again early the next morning, following the river east along a well-traveled road, setting a pace to suit the comfort of the sorrel. When he deemed it time to rest the horses and cook some breakfast for himself, he began watching for a good place to stop. Approaching a sizable stand of cottonwoods close by the water's edge, he turned Buck's head toward them.

Buck's whinny and snort alerted him to the presence of other horses even before he entered the stand of trees.

Perley immediately reined the big bay to a halt while he was still in the cover of the trees and drew his rifle from the saddle sling. He heard an answering whinny from a horse down near the water's edge, but still could not see it. Nudging Buck gently, he moved slowly forward until he spotted the horses through the trees. Looking farther down the bank, he saw a wagon parked on a shallow bluff and smoke from a campfire rising up from the water's edge below it. He turned Buck and circled around closer to the wagon, while still using the cover of the trees, thinking that it might possibly be his best decision to ride quietly back to the road and find another place to stop. About to act on that option, he hesitated when he heard the voices of two small children playing in the shallow water.

That made up his mind for him. "Hello the camp," he called out, convinced there was no danger there. "Can I come in?" His greeting caused an immediate panic among the two adults tending the campfire and he could see the woman and the man scrambling to take cover, calling the children to them. In a moment, he saw an arm reach over the side of the wagon to grasp a shotgun, before ducking back down below the bluff.

Perley called out again. "I don't mean you any harm. I was just fixin' to stop to rest my horses. It looked like a good spot, but I didn't know you folks were down here till I rode through the trees. There's plenty of other good spots, though, so if you don't want any company, I'll just ride on down the river. Just say the word."

There was no answer for a long moment, but Perley

could see the barrel of the shotgun under the bed of the wagon, the man was evidently lying behind the wagon wheel. Perley couldn't fault the man's caution.

After another moment with no response, Perley called out again. "I'll ride on then, and wish you folks a good day." He wheeled Buck around to leave.

"Hold on, there, mister. There ain't no use in you goin' to look for another place. Come on in and share some food with us."

When Perley turned Buck around again and rode down to the bluff, the man got to his feet and stood by the wagon tongue. "I hope you'll pardon my lack of hospitality, but I declare, I've got to where I'm mighty cautious."

"It's a good way to be," Perley said. "Can't tell who you're liable to run into these days." He pulled Buck up at the wagon and stepped down. "Howdy. My name's Perley Gates."

His greeting was met with a look of astonishment, then a broad grin, a reaction Perley was accustomed to.

"How do, Pearly. I'm Lawson Penny." He turned and called behind him, "Jenny, come on up and say howdy to Pearly Gates."

In a moment, a tiny elfin woman with braids hanging down below her waist, climbed out from behind the low bluff where she had sought to hide.

"This is Pearly Gates," her husband said, still all smiles.

His comment caused her to smile as well as she looked at Perley. "Welcome to our camp, Mr. Gates. We've got coffee on the fire and some sowbelly to share, if you're hungry." She was almost knocked off balance then when two small children bumped into her legs, eager to see the stranger. "This is Luke and Mary," Jenny said.

"Well, I'm mighty proud to meet you," Perley said and extended his hand, which the young boy grasped and shook up and down like a pump handle exactly two times, while Mary preferred to hide behind her mother's legs. "I appreciate your hospitality," Perley said, looking back at Jenny. "I've got some food I can offer, if you'd like some smoked deer meat. I reckon that's what I was fixin' to cook."

"That would surely be welcome," Penny said. "We don't get that very often, do we, Jenny?" He waited for her smile in response, then turned back to Perley. "Pearly Gates, that's a right interestin' name. I guess I oughta explain why it caused me to grin like I did. You see, I just left Blue Creek yesterday, where I was pastor of a new church. It ain't nothin' but a tent, but we had hopes of buildin' a real church with the help of some of the settlers there. It's a long story, but what came of it was things didn't work out to support a church. So I decided we had to leave town and look for another place to live. Now when a man comes along with a name like Pearly Gates, right when I had given up, it must be a sign that me and my family were doing what God intended, and He wants a church in Blue Creek."

Perley listened politely but was not convinced the preacher was reading the signs correctly. Perley could never imagine he might be used to carry any spiritual messages. "I don't know if it makes any difference or not, but my name ain't spelt the same as those gates up in heaven. It just sounds the same."

"Sometimes a sign from the Lord can be mighty subtle," Penny said. "It's up to man to recognize one when it's given, and I think I just got one when you showed up right now. I think it was more than coincidence when you picked this very spot to rest your horses."

"Let the man take care of his horses, Lawson," Jenny Penny interrupted. "You can see he wants to let them drink." She smiled at Perley. "My husband can get carried away sometimes. You do what you were fixin' to do and I'll start some fresh coffee. We can talk when we're eatin' that venison you offered."

Perley turned to lead his horses down to the river, but she added one more thing. "I can sense that you've had to explain your name every time you meet somebody new. I can appreciate how you feel. I've got a silly name, myself. *Jenny Penny*. I almost didn't marry Lawson because of it." She laughed and gave her husband a playful punch on his shoulder.

He responded with a grin, having heard it many times before.

CHAPTER 3

"Where is Blue Creek?" Perley asked as he sat by the fire with the Reverend and Mrs. Penny. "I can't say as I've ever heard of it."

"I don't wonder," Penny replied. "It ain't been but about a year in the makin'. About seven miles downstream from here, Blue Creek empties into the river. Three miles up that creek is the town of Blue Creek. Some years back, an Indian village set on the spot. They had some trouble with the army and the soldiers wiped the village out. Settlers are moving in around there now, enough of 'em that a little town started to grow. There's a post office, a general merchandise store, a livery stable, and of course, a saloon. That's what brought me and Jenny to Blue Creek. We figured if they were goin' to have a representative of the devil, they needed a representative of the Lord, too. Problem is, ain't nobody able to help out much, and nobody's got money to spare to build a church. They're too hard up against it trying to get their farms goin'. But I know in my heart that if there was a building, a solid church, instead of a tent, it'd be enough to get the support a community needs. They need a rock to stand on and the church would grow from that."

When the preacher finally paused to take a drink of coffee, Perley took the opportunity to ask a question. "What about cattlemen? Any trouble between the farmers and the cattlemen? Blue Creek ain't very far from Ogallala and the railhead of the Union Pacific. I'd a-thought there might be some trouble with cattlemen. My family's in the cattle business, and I helped drive a herd up from Texas durin' the first part of summer, myself."

"No trouble so far," Penny replied. "There's a couple of cattle ranches east of the town, but they're closer to Ogallala than they are to Blue Creek." After a short lull in the conversation, he said, "But enough about us and Blue Creek. You never said where you're on your way to."

"Texas," Perley answered. "I'm on my way back home to Texas. I'm needin' to find a blacksmith pretty quick, though. One of my horses threw a shoe. But when you were talkin' about Blue Creek, I didn't hear you say a blacksmith was there."

"There sure is," Penny was quick to reply. "I guess I did forget. Leonard Porter, he's a dandy blacksmith and a fine fellow. He'd treat you right." When he saw that Perley was giving that some consideration, he asked, "Why don't you ride along with us to Blue Creek? We'd be glad to have you join us, unless the wagon would slow you down too much."

"That suits me just fine," Perley said. "I ain't movin' very fast, anyway, since one of my horses is limpin'. I expect I'd best take the closest blacksmith I can find."

"Good," the preacher replied. "We'll enjoy the company, won't we, Mother?"

His wife smiled broadly in response.

When the camp was dismantled, the wagon hitched up, and Perley's horses ready to go, Perley started to Blue Creek with his new friends, and eight-year-old Luke riding behind his saddle.

"How far is Ogallala from here?" Perley asked when they reached the point where Blue Creek flowed into the North Platte River.

"Close to thirty miles from right here," Penny answered. "Leonard Porter's blacksmith shop ain't but three miles that-a-way, though." He pointed up the creek, thinking that Perley might be changing his mind about going to Blue Creek. "There'll still be plenty of daylight left when we get there. You can camp with us at our old spot while you're waitin' for Leonard to shoe your horse. Maybe Jenny will whip up some biscuits for supper. If nobody ain't moved in our old place, there's a good oven I built in the ground that bakes 'em dang-nigh as good as an iron oven."

"That sounds to my likin'," Perley said, then turned to the young boy riding behind his saddle. "How 'bout you, Luke?"

"Yes, sir," Luke replied and kicked his heels against Buck's sides. "Giddyup!"

The big bay turned his head to look back at the boy, but didn't move until Perley nudged him forward. He was already getting a feeling that he had been adopted by the family. *Another soul to save,* he thought might be Penny's intention, *but probably just friendly hospitality.* His recent experience with Billy Tuttle had left him with a natural suspicion of anyone's motives. He reminded himself that Penny had shown no interest at all in what he carried in his packs.

Three miles up the creek they came to the first of the collection of frame buildings, just as Penny had said. It was a stable with a barn and corral. Penny said the man who had built it was Frank Mosely. He walked out front to hail the wagon when he spotted them passing his stable, and Penny pulled up to speak to him.

"Well, howdy, Reverend, Mrs. Penny," Mosely greeted them. "I thought you folks had decided to leave us. You comin' back?"

"That's a fact," Penny replied. "Got to thinkin' it over and decided I was givin' up too quick." He chuckled and added, "You sinners in Blue Creek deserve savin'."

"Don't know about that, but I'm sure we *need* savin'. I'm mighty glad you changed your mind. I was afraid we might end up with a town as wild as Ogallala. Who's this you got ridin' with you?"

"Perley Gates," Penny answered with enthusiasm, "and he's needin' to have Leonard take a look at one of his horses . . . if he ain't already gone to the house for supper."

"Glad to meetcha, Pearly," Mosely said, then turned to Penny again when Perley nodded in response. "I expect he's still there. I saw him a few minutes ago out in front of his forge."

"We'll get on down there, before he decides to go

home," Penny said. "See you in church on Sunday?" he asked as he pulled away.

"Reckon so," Mosely replied, knowing his wife would give him little choice. "You gonna need some help puttin' your tent back up?"

"No, thanks just the same. Jenny and I took it down. Maybe Perley will help us set it up again."

"Well, your cook shed is still there," Mosely said. "Least it was this mornin'. I don't reckon anybody bothered it."

While Mosely stood watching them, he thought, *Pearly Gates, now how the blue hell did Penny come up with a man named Pearly Gates?* "Maybe I'd better go to church," he muttered.

Aware now that he was expected to pay for the supper Jenny promised by helping erect a large tent, Perley shrugged. He was not surprised. Penny and Jenny seemed like really nice folks, though. He should be glad to help out. It might help to get him in good with the Lord.

Perley's thoughts were interrupted by a sudden shout from Luke behind him. "Howdy, Mr. Porter!"

"Howdy, Luke," Porter replied with a great big grin for the boy. "Whatcha doin' ridin' that big bay horse?" He didn't wait for a reply from Luke, but called out a greeting to his father. "Reverend, I thought you'd left us."

"I did, but I got called back," Penny said, then went through the same explanation he had just covered with Mosely. When he finished, he introduced Perley and told Porter that Perley had need of his services.

"That so? Let's have a look." The blacksmith lifted

the sorrel's hoof and inspected it. "Shoe's gone, all right, but the hoof looks like it ain't in bad shape. I can fit you a new shoe." He dropped the hoof and squinted at the sun sinking closer to the western horizon. "You gotta have it tonight?"

"I reckon not," Perley answered. "It's gettin' along toward sundown. I expect I'd best go on and make camp tonight, unload my horses, and bring the sorrel back in the mornin'." He was thinking about the time he was going to spend helping Penny and Jenny get settled, and that was most likely not going to happen tonight. On the other hand, Porter might do a better job if he wasn't trying to hurry in order to get home to supper.

"That's a good idea," Porter was quick to agree, obviously relieved. "I'll look for you in the mornin'."

Penny urged his team of horses on again. Perley held Buck close beside the wagon seat, the better to hear Penny's rambling introduction of the fledgling town as they rolled past each business.

"This is Willard Spence's general store. Willard's wife, Ellie, helps out in the store. Fine people. The Blue Creek Saloon," he continued as they passed the only two-story building on the short street. "A fellow from Omaha, named Jim Squires, built it." Next came the tiny post office and Penny said, "John Blessing is our postmaster."

Perley couldn't help but wonder if Blessing wound up there because of his name, like he did—divine coincidence in Penny's mind.

"That's the sheriff's office next to the post office," Penny continued. "The town council hired a young

man named Marvin Kelly to be sheriff. He was a
deputy over in Ogallala and he moved his wife and
three children up here when he heard we were looking for a sheriff. He ain't called upon to do much
beyond haulin' in a drunk once in a while to sleep it
off in his jail cell."

They continued out the north side of town until
Penny turned toward the creek on a couple of ruts
that served as a wagon road.

"It doesn't look like anybody's been here," Jenny
said when they came to a small clearing in the trees
that lined the creek. "The cookhouse looks just like
I left it."

Perley followed her gaze to a small three-sided
shed, approximately eight feet square, with a stovepipe protruding through the roof. Evidently, that
was where she did the cooking, but he saw no stove
connected to the stovepipe. Maybe they were hauling
it in the wagon.

He found out soon enough that she had no stove.
The canvas-wrapped object he had glimpsed in the
wagon and thought to be a stove, was, in fact, a small
organ. She cooked over a fire pit, fashioned with
rocks, and the stovepipe merely served as her chimney. He, of course, helped to pitch their tent, which
wasn't as much a job as he had anticipated, having
expected a large tent big enough to hold a whole
congregation of people. In contrast, it turned out
that the tent was to house Penny, his wife, and their
two children, and was no bigger than an army squad
tent. When he held church services, they were con-
ducted out in the open.

No wonder their major concern is a building, Perley

thought. *Especially when cold weather is not that far away.* The preacher and his family needed not only a church, they needed a house.

When the Penny family at least had a canvas shelter over their heads, Perley helped Penny unload the organ and set it up inside the tent.

With time to finally see to his own needs, he moved a few dozen yards downstream to make his camp. Of major concern, as usual, were the four sacks of seed corn he packed, but there seemed to be little chance anyone might raid his camp. There appeared to be no threat in the small community where everyone knew everyone else. He decided the best thing to do was not to demonstrate any concern for his packs. He didn't plan to spend much time with his hosts after supper was finished, anyway, so he wouldn't be away from his camp very long.

The supper hour lasted a good bit longer than Perley had expected, due primarily to Lawson Penny's enthusiasm for what he was convinced was his calling—to bring the Word of God to the people of Blue Creek Valley. Contributing to Perley's extended stay were the biscuits Jenny had baked in the oven Penny had built in the ground.

After listening to the preacher's dreams of building his church, Perley had to ask the question obvious to him. "You figure you can raise the kinda money it'll take to buy the lumber and such for your church? I didn't see but four or five businesses when we rode through town."

"I know it doesn't look possible when you just look at the town," Penny replied. "But what you don't see are the folks workin' farms around the county.

Jenny'll tell you, we were already gettin' a lot of those folks at my Sunday services, and they were helpin' out as best they could when the collection plate was passed." He looked toward his wife and she confirmed with a nod.

"As they grow and the town grows," he went on, "there'll be more businesses and more folks. They'll want their church for themselves and their children."

"Maybe you're right," Perley said. "Least I hope so." He had his doubts, however, but didn't express them because Penny believed it so passionately. Glancing at Jenny while her husband was talking, Perley could see the same light of faith in her face.

It was going to take a hell of a lot more than what little bit the congregation could spare in the collection plate for the lumber and carpenters to build his church, however.

The doubt must have been on Perley's face, causing Penny to grace him with a patient smile. "It'll happen. The Lord's given me enough signs to tell me that. You came along, bringin' me a message that I oughta stay right here."

Perley wasn't quick enough to hide the skepticism on his face.

Penny said, "The messenger don't always know what's in the message." He smiled and continued. "Day after tomorrow's Sunday. We got back before most of our people even know we had gone."

"That is a fact," Perley replied, thinking about his unguarded camp. "I expect I'd best get on back to my horses. I enjoyed havin' supper with you folks. Except you," he added and playfully tousled Luke's hair.

The young boy had rarely left his side during the supper hour.

"Can you come to church Sunday?" Luke asked. "You can hear Papa preach."

Perley couldn't remember the last time he had been to church. He'd prayed plenty of times, but seldom inside a building built specifically for that purpose. "I reckon I'd best get along toward Texas. I'm already gonna lose half a day tomorrow while I get my horse some shoes." There was no chance of missing the disappointment registering on Luke's face.

"Luke's got a good idea there," Penny said. "I'd consider it a real honor if you would stay over one more day and join us for church. How 'bout it, Perley?"

"Yes, Perley," Jenny chimed in. "Won't you stay over?"

Perley didn't know how to tell them that he'd rather take a whipping than go to church, even one that didn't have a roof. He had a small fortune he was anxious to transport safely to his family in Texas and had already lost two days on the trail. They seemed so genuine in their hope that he would stay, however, that he found it difficult to turn them down.

Finally, he relented. "I reckon it wouldn't throw me too far behind to stay here one more day, but I'll expect some powerful preachin' outta you."

His decision was met with an almost joyous response from all. Little Mary even smiled—Perley had thought that she never did.

"I'll be packin' up all my possibles and ridin' into town in the mornin'. I'll put my horses up at the stable and sleep with them tomorrow night."

"We'll be expecting you for dinner on Sunday," Jenny said.

"Ah, n-no, ma'am," he stammered. "I don't wanna put you out no more 'n I already have. Besides, I don't wanna cost you any money you might be savin' to build that church."

"No need to worry your mind about that," Jenny said. "Our congregation always brings a chicken or two, sometimes a ham or some vegetables. There'll be food enough."

Little Mary spoke up then. "Maybe he'll just ride outta town when his horse is fixed and not even come here on Sunday."

That was what I was thinking about doing, until you said it, Perley thought. "Why, that wouldn't be a very polite thing to do, would it? I'll be here. I wouldn't miss hearin' your daddy preach."

Perley was waiting in front of the stable when Frank Mosely showed up the next morning.

"Well, good mornin'," Mosely greeted him. "You're up early this mornin'."

"Mornin'," Perley returned. "I'd like to leave my horses with you for a couple of days, and if it's all right with you, maybe leave my packs somewhere where they'll be out of the way."

"Why, sure," Mosely said. "Glad to have the business. Did you catch Leonard in time yesterday?"

"Yes, sir, I did, and as soon as I get 'em unloaded, I'm gonna take the sorrel over to his place."

"Come on," Mosely said. "I'll show you which stalls

you can use and a room for your saddle and packs. You need help unloadin' your stuff?"

Perley said he didn't, so Mosely led him past some stalls and pointed to the ones he should use.

Mosely then continued beyond them to a door at the back of the stable. "This is sort of a catchall room, odds and ends—mostly stuff that's been takin' up room in the tack room." He opened the door. "There ain't much in here right now, so you're welcome to use it."

"'Preciate it," Perley said. "This'll do just fine and it'll get my stuff out of the way. After I've unloaded my horses, I'll turn 'em out in the corral."

"I'll leave you to it," Mosely said. "I've gotta go throw down some more hay." He left to do his morning chores, showing no interest in what Perley had in the packs.

With his seed corn bags in a pile under his cooking pan and coffeepot, his supplies and extra clothes, ammunition, and smoked venison, Perley left Buck and his late grandpa's paint gelding in the corral and led the sorrel down to the blacksmith shop. As he had at the stable, he caught Leonard Porter just coming to work.

"Mornin'," Porter greeted him. "Pearly Gates, right?" he asked as if not certain he had heard right when Lawson Penny had introduced him the day before.

"That's right," Perley answered, "just like the gates in heaven, only it ain't spelt the same."

"Well, let me get my fire goin' and I'll have another

look at that hoof," Porter said. "It won't take long, once I get my forge heated up."

"Take your time," Perley said. "I'm gonna be in town all day. Come to think of it, you might take a look at the other three hooves while you're at it."

"Be glad to," Porter responded. "I gave 'em a quick look yesterday and they seemed all right, but I'll look a little closer. How'd you meet up with Reverend Penny?"

Perley told him about the chance meeting with the preacher and his family when they had happened to pick the same spot to camp.

"Well, I know I ain't the only one glad to see him and Jenny come back home," Porter said. "Folks in Blue Creek know we need a strong church if we're gonna be a town that lasts. Wonder what changed his mind about leaving?"

"I ain't got any idea," Perley replied with no intention of telling him that Penny decided that their coincidental meeting was a sign from God. Ready to change the subject, he asked, "Anyplace here where a man could get some breakfast? I didn't take time to cook any myself this mornin'."

"Yeah, you can get something to eat in the saloon. It ain't fancy, but Jim Squires has a woman workin' for him that'll cook up something for you that'll stick to your ribs. Right now, that's the only place to eat, but it won't be long before somebody comes along and builds a diner. We'd like to see a hotel in town, but I don't look for that to happen anytime soon. Blue Creek ain't really on the way to anywhere." Porter looked up as if to apologize for rambling on about the town. "Anyway, we'll get there now that

Lawson Penny has decided to stick it out till we can raise enough money to build that church. Now, I'd best quit talkin' and get to work. You go on over to the saloon. Gussie'll fix you something to eat."

Perley took his time to walk the short distance down the street to the saloon. He had only met a couple of people in the fledgling community, but he already had the impression that everyone saw the importance of a church. In his opinion, they were going to be a long time in building one.

The saloon was open, but there were no patrons that early in the morning. The owner, Jim Squires, was seated at a table near the kitchen door, eating breakfast. He called out a greeting to Perley when he hesitated at the door. "Good mornin', stranger. Come on in. We're open." He got up from the table and started toward the bar. "What's your pleasure?"

"I was just hopin' I could find some breakfast," Perley answered.

"You came to the right place." Squires looked toward the kitchen door and yelled, "Gussie!"

After a moment or two, a short red-haired woman appeared in the doorway.

"Fellow, here, is lookin' for some breakfast."

Gussie cocked an eye at Perley standing there, then looked back at Squires. "What does he want for breakfast?"

"I don't know," Squires answered, then looked at Perley. "What do you want for breakfast?"

"I don't know," Perley replied, not expecting to have a choice. He had assumed the cook probably mixed up some kind of mush to dish out for those hungry enough to eat it. "Can I get something like eggs and maybe some ham?"

Squires started to repeat the question to Gussie, but she interrupted him. "I heard him. I've got eggs, ham, and fresh-baked biscuits, too. Is that what you're lookin' for?"

"Yes, ma'am. That 'ud be more than I expected. If there's some coffee to wash it down, I'd be plum tickled."

She spun on her heel and disappeared into the kitchen, leaving him to pick a table to seat himself.

"Why don't you join me?" Squires invited. "This must be the first time you've been in Blue Creek. I never saw you before. Passin' through, or are you gonna be here for a while?"

Perley pulled a chair back and sat down. "Passin' through. Least I was till I promised Lawson Penny I'd hang around to hear him preach tomorrow. I had to get one of my horses shod and that's the reason I ended up in Blue Creek."

"You a friend of the preacher's?"

"Not till I met up with him about seven miles up the river. We'd both picked the same place to camp. I needed a blacksmith and he knew where one was."

"Last I heard, Penny packed up his tent and left town," Squires said. "You sure he said he was coming back here?"

"He's already back," Perley answered. "I ate supper with him and his wife last night."

They paused when Gussie came out holding a cup and a large gray coffeepot. She poured a cup for Perley and warmed Squires', then she backed away as if waiting for her boss to ask the question.

He didn't disappoint her. "You ridin' with a fellow named Wick Bass?"

"Nope," Perley replied. "I ain't ridin' with anybody. I'm on my way home to Texas."

His answer was enough to satisfy Gussie. She promptly turned and went back to the kitchen.

"Well, welcome to Blue Creek," Squires said, extending his hand. "I'm Jim Squires. This is my establishment. Glad you stopped in."

Perley shook his hand. "Perley Gates."

"Say what?" Squires replied, not understanding.

"My name's Perley Gates."

"The hell it is," Squires responded with a chuckle. Then realizing that Perley was serious, he quickly apologized. "No offense. I'm pleased to meet you, Perley."

He was saved from further embarrassment when Gussie arrived with a plate of ham and eggs, two large biscuits riding shotgun. She remained long enough to see Perley's reaction to her cooking. When he showed obvious satisfaction after a couple of bites, she returned to her kitchen.

When Perley finished eating and asked how much he owed, Squires said, "We charge twenty-five cents for breakfast and twenty-five cents for coffee." He waited then for Perley's complaint. When there was none, and Perley reached into his pocket for the money, Squires thought to mention another accommodation. "You say you're stayin' overnight in Blue Creek. I've got a couple of rooms for rent upstairs."

"I reckon I'll be sleepin' with my horses." Perley was thinking the price of breakfast was high enough, although he had not complained. The price of a room might be comparable to that for the food.

Not one to give up on a customer who appeared to have a little money on him, Squires was quick to offer further inducement. "Gussie ain't only a good cook. For a little extra, she can see that you have an enjoyable night with us." When Perley showed no interest, he sought to entice him. "Gussie may be a little older than you, but sometimes a little experience can make a world of difference. It'd be like havin' your mother tuck you in tonight."

Perley was afraid that would be exactly what it would be like, so he quickly declined. "I'll just finish my coffee and be on my way. Mr. Porter oughta be about through with my horse."

Squires had to get up and tend the bar then. Someone had walked into the saloon, so Perley took his time with his coffee.

"Won't be long," Leonard Porter sang out when he saw Perley returning from the saloon. "You were right to have me check all the shoes. A couple more of 'em were a little loose."

"Like I said, I ain't in a hurry."

"Did Gussie fix you up with a good breakfast?"

"That she did. I didn't expect to get ham and eggs."

"Gussie can cook up a storm," Porter commented. "She offers other services, too, but I wouldn't go so far as to recommend 'em." He started to comment further, but stopped before he got the next word out.

Perley turned to see what had captured his attention and saw that he was staring at three men on horses, just pulling up to the saloon.

"Damn . . ." Porter drew the oath out softly, talking

more to himself than to Perley. "I was hopin' to hell they were gone."

When Porter continued to stare at the three men until they disappeared into the saloon, Perley asked, "Somebody you know?"

"Somebody this town don't wanna know," Porter replied. "They showed up here day before yesterday, ridin' up and down the street like they were lookin' the town over. I told Frank Mosely it's a good thing we ain't got a bank 'cause it seemed like they were lookin' for one to rob. Jim Squires said they sat around his place, drinkin' whiskey and askin' him all kinds of questions about the town. He said the few regular customers he had left when those three started gettin' too loud, but he said he didn't try to tell 'em to leave. He was scared they'd tear his place up. They rode outta town and we didn't see hide nor hair of 'em yesterday, so we figured they'd moved on to raise hell where there was better pickin's." He made a violent shake of his head as if trying to clear them out of his brain. "And, damn, here they are back again. I don't know what they're lookin' for. There ain't nothin' in Blue Creek to attract men like that. If they're lookin' for a wild town, they oughta go on down the river to Ogallala."

Perley could see how someone like the three men described could worry the merchants of a little settlement like Blue Creek, where the main focus at present seemed to be to build a church. He felt sorry for honest hard-working folks like Leonard Porter, but it was not his concern. That was a job for the sheriff. He would have been back on the trail to Lamar County, Texas, this afternoon, if he hadn't promised to go to church in the morning. "Maybe they'll see this ain't a regular cow town like Ogallala or Dodge," he offered. "Then they'll move on to somewhere else."

"I hope you're right," Porter said as he hammered a horseshoe into shape on his anvil. "A couple of us went to talk to Marvin Kelly about 'em, but he said there wasn't anything he could do about 'em. He said they ain't broke no laws."

CHAPTER 4

It was halfway to noon when Perley paid Leonard Porter and led his sorrel back to the stable, where he turned it into the corral with the other horses. He had a few minutes' conversation with Frank Mosely, then checked to see how Buck and the paint were getting along. There was nothing else for him to do, and he was already regretting his commitment to Lawson Penny. He remembered something then that he could do to help pass the time. He needed a new bandanna. The last time he had seen his old one, it was stuffed in Billy Tuttle's mouth as Billy was swinging from a crossbeam in the stable at Hat Creek Station.

Before he left, he took a quick look in the storeroom where his belongings were piled to make sure nothing had been disturbed. He trusted Mosely, but he didn't know who else might have reason to be in the room. Nothing seemed to have been disturbed, so he walked back toward the other end of the short street where a sign proclaimed BLUE CREEK MERCHANDISE.

Inside, he was greeted by a heavyset man with gray

hair and a bushy gray mustache to match. "Howdy, neighbor. What can I help you with?"

"Howdy," Perley returned. "I'm wonderin' if you've got some bandannas for sale. Mine got chewed up a while back and I ain't ever had a chance to find a new one."

"I'll say I have," the man behind the counter said. "Down at the end of the counter, there's a whole box of 'em. Any particular color?"

"I'm partial to red," Perley replied.

"Well, there's two or three different red ones." He looked Perley over as he walked to the end of the counter. "You're new in town, ain'tcha?" When Perley said that he was, the man asked if he was riding with Wick Bass, the same question Jim Squires had asked.

"Nope," Perley answered. "I don't know anybody by that name."

That seemed to put the merchant at ease. "Well, welcome to Blue Creek. My name's Willard Spence. This here's my store. 'Preciate you stoppin' in. You gonna be with us a while, or are you just passin' through?" Perley started to answer, but Spence suddenly turned around to face the front door when it opened and two men walked in. Forgetting Perley, Spence hurried to the other end of the counter to meet them.

"We come to collect some money," one of the pair announced.

"What money?" Spence replied at once.

"The money for protectin' your store," his partner replied. "Wick told you how much it was gonna cost to protect your business."

"He said I had till Monday to decide," Spence said.

"I ain't got that kinda money layin' around. It takes me a while to earn that much in the store."

"Things have changed," the other man said. A tall, dark-complexioned man, thin as a knife blade, wearing a Colt .45 in a cutaway holster, riding low and tied to his thigh. His line of business was obvious. "Your insurance payment is due today."

Uh-oh, Perley thought, *that doesn't sound good.* He continued to sort through the different colors of bandannas in the box, pretending not to notice. He soon became aware that the partner of the one doing the talking was eyeballing him. *I swear,* Perley thought, *it seems like my brother's right, I always manage to land in the middle of trouble. And it ain't got nothing to do with me. I just want to buy a bandanna.* He stole a glance at Spence.

The store owner showed signs of anger more than fear of the lethal-appearing man confronting him. "I told your boss I didn't make enough money to buy your so-called insurance. I've never heard of anybody buying insurance on anything in this part of the country. I told him I'd discuss this business with the rest of the town council and let him know Monday."

"Like I said, things have changed. We want the money now, or you're gonna be without insurance to make sure nothin' bad, like a robbery, happens to your store. You ain't thinkin' too smart if you ain't got somebody to protect you."

"That sounds like a threat," Spence said.

"It's more like a prediction," the man said, a thin smile forming on his unshaven face. He cut his eyes over toward his partner and winked.

"That's right, Blackie, more like a prediction," his partner said.

"If somebody robs me, I'll let the sheriff take care of it," Spence said. "That's what we pay him for. Why should I pay you?"

"'Cause when you pay me, we keep you from gettin' robbed in the first place," the man called Blackie replied. "Pay me and your store, here, won't catch on fire and burn down. How's your sheriff gonna keep that from happenin'?"

Uh-oh, Perley thought.

Spence's wife Ellie came in from the back room of the store at that moment. Recognizing the two men from a couple of days before, she stopped in the doorway in time to hear her husband's response to his unwelcome guests—that he would talk to the rest of the town council, but he felt sure nobody was going to pay for insurance. "I think you gentlemen have your answer," Ellie said with authority.

"Lady, we're talkin' business here. You best go on back in the kitchen where you belong."

Perley saw Spence's jaw tighten up in anger. He knew the shop owner was about to be provoked into an altercation with the two gunmen, a fight he was bound to lose, and it was too late to go for the sheriff. "The red one," Perley suddenly blurted out and walked up to the counter, stepping between the two gunmen, waving a bandanna back and forth. "How much is this one?"

"What the— Who the hell are you?" Blackie demanded and shoved Perley aside, causing him to bump into the tall thin gunman.

"I wanna buy this bandanna and I was here before

you and your impolite friend barged in here talkin'
all that insurance nonsense," Perley insisted. Creating
confusion was the only way he could think of at the
moment to keep Spence, and maybe his wife, from
getting shot.

"Why you dumb son of a bitch!" the thin man exploded. "I'll kick your ass from here to Sunday." His
hand dropped to rest on the handle of his Colt .45.

"Seein' as how tomorrow's Sunday, you wouldn't
be kickin' it very far, would you?" Perley goaded. "We're
gonna have to ask you and your friend to leave now.
Your language ain't fittin' in the presence of a lady."
He was counting heavily on confusing the gunman to
the point where he would be undecided what to do
and to whom. It seemed to be working. Blackie and
his partner had turned their attention to him. The
only problem with that was how to get out of the trouble Perley had invited upon himself.

As soon as their attention was diverted from the
shop owner, Perley noticed that Spence whispered
something to his wife and pushed her toward the
door. She slipped out the door unnoticed by Blackie
and his friend. Perley hoped she was going for the
sheriff.

"Mister, are you lookin' for somebody to settle your
hash for you or are you just plain dumb as you look?"
Blackie demanded. "I'll tie that damn bandanna
around your neck tight enough to shut your mouth
for good."

"'Preciate the offer," Perley replied, "but I don't
need any help with it. What's the name of that insurance company you work for?" he asked, hoping to
further confuse the gunmen.

It seemed to serve the purpose, but it also served to infuriate Blackie even more. "None of your damn business," he replied. "Now, if you don't get the hell outta here, I'm gonna blow a hole through your head."

Stalling for time and hoping the sheriff was on his way, Perley backed a few steps away in case he was forced to defend himself. "There ain't no call for you to get upset about it. Matter of fact, I ain't got any insurance a'tall, and I was thinkin' maybe you could give me some information about insurance."

Blackie's partner, Red Johnson, gaped at Perley, fairly astonished. "This fool's a bona fide idiot. We'd do him a favor if we put him outta his misery." He reached for his pistol.

Before he had time to draw it, he was stopped by a command from the front door. "Just hold it right there!" Sheriff Marvin Kelly ordered as he charged through the door, holding a double-barreled shotgun.

Blackie turned, his hand poised to draw, but froze when he saw Perley's .44 already in his hand. A moment later, Spence held his own shotgun from under the counter. Obviously outgunned, the two outlaws raised their hands.

"What's goin' on here, Willard?" Sheriff Kelly asked. "Ellie said there was a holdup."

"They want money to protect my store," Spence exclaimed. "That's sure as hell a holdup, and they're threatening to burn it down if I don't pay."

"That's a damn lie!" Blackie bellowed. "We never made no damn threat."

"He called it *insurance*," Spence said. "Insurance

against robbery or fire. If that ain't a threat, I don't know what is."

Kelly wasn't sure what he should do. He'd never heard of anybody trying to extort money by calling it insurance. He looked at Perley, standing out of the way, his .44 back in his holster. "Who's this? Is he with them?"

"No," Spence quickly responded. "That's Perley Gates. He's just a customer, tryin' to help out." Spence suddenly realized he might have been on the verge of being shot if Perley hadn't stepped in with the bandanna. With a few minutes to think, he wondered if Perley had had that in mind. Maybe he wasn't the bumbling fool Blackie thought he was.

"Did they pull their guns and demand money?" Kelly asked Spence.

"Well, no," Spence said after hesitating a moment, then pointed at Blackie, "but he was just fixin' to."

"Me and Red was fixin' to leave," Blackie said. "That's all we was fixin' to do. He already admitted I didn't pull my gun. There weren't no reason to call you up here."

"He's got a point there," Kelly said to Spence. "I can't see that a crime was committed. Just two men arguing is what it looks like."

"Damn it, Marvin," Spence complained. "He was fixin' to pull his gun on me and that's why Ellie ran to get you. I was just lucky you got here when you did."

Still undecided, Kelly turned to Perley. "What did he say your name was?" When Perley repeated it, Kelly paused a moment to make sure he heard right. "Perley Gates, huh? How 'bout it? Did it look to you like this man was gettin' ready to pull his gun?"

"Yes sir," Perley answered. "There wasn't any doubt in my mind that if you hadn't got here when you did, there would have been some shootin'. That feller was reaching for that Colt he's wearin' when you came in the door."

Blackie's cruel lips parted slightly to form the sinister smile he had confronted Spence with before. "Can't hardly arrest a man for thinkin' about shootin' somebody, can you, Sheriff? If you could, I expect you wouldn't have a jail big enough to hold 'em all."

"I reckon you're right," Kelly felt obligated to say, "but I might arrest you for disturbin' the peace. I think it'd be a good idea if you and your friends would move on to some other town. Blue Creek ain't got nothin' for men like you. This town was built by honest, hard-working folks, and it ain't a good place for drifters that didn't come here to work and build the community. So you two get along now. I want you out of town before sundown. If you ain't, you'll be spendin' the night in jail."

There was no reaction from either of the outlaws right away. Then Blackie's sarcastic smile returned to his face. "That was a right pretty speech, Sheriff. Me and Red will leave the store and we'll go tell our partner we've gotta be outta town before sundown. I doubt if he's gonna like that."

"No, he ain't gonna like that." Red snickered.

"Come on, Red," Blackie said. "We don't wanna cause these hard-workin' folks no trouble." They filed out of the store, but with a defiant swagger that promised trouble to come.

When they had left, Spence turned at once to the sheriff. "Damn, Marvin. How can you just let those two walk away like that? You shoulda locked both of 'em up."

"I didn't have any real reason to lock 'em up—not for just gettin' into an argument with you—but I ran 'em outta town. That's better 'n havin' to feed 'em for a couple of days in my jail. That comes outta the town budget, and you folks ain't been too anxious to pay for any of my expenses."

"*Maybe* you ran 'em outta town," Spence came back. "We'll see if they're still here after sundown, won't we? All I know is I'd better sleep here in the store tonight in case they decide to come back with a torch."

"I'll be keepin' an eye out for any trouble," Kelly said. "I think they'll move on out. There ain't nothin' here to make 'em wanna stay." He nodded politely to Ellie then and walked out the door and stood watching the two outlaws until they went into the saloon.

"How much?"

"What?" Spence muttered, suddenly rocked from his intense speculation on the possibility of harm yet to come for him and his wife.

"The bandanna," Perley replied. "How much?"

"Oh," Spence responded, just then remembering Perley was there. "I usually get fifty cents for one like that." Remembering then how Perley had luckily blundered into the middle of his argument with Blackie, he said, "But I'll let you have it for a quarter."

"You can have it for nothing," Ellie spoke up. She gave her husband a look of exasperation. "Twenty-five cents off for saving your life isn't much reward, Willard."

"That's all right, ma'am," Perley said. "A quarter's

a more than fair price for a bandanna like this one. I like it better 'n my old one and I paid a dollar for it."

"Ellie's right, Perley. You mighta kept me from gettin' shot, whether you know it or not. That snaky lookin' outlaw was fixin' to pull his gun. I won't ever forget the look in his eye. It was like lookin' in the eyes of a dead man. Yes, sir, you take that red bandanna and I hope it does the job for you."

"Well, I surely appreciate it." Perley nodded graciously to Ellie Spence and left the store, tying his new bandanna around his neck as he walked past the saloon on his way to the stable.

Wick Bass reached for the bottle and poured himself another drink of Jim Squires' rye whiskey. "I'm thinkin' it don't make good sense to let you two wander around without somebody to watch you. Whose idea was it to tell Willard Spence he needed insurance?"

"It was my idea," Blackie confessed. "I thought it was a pretty good idea, Wick. I never thought that fat store owner had the sand to tell me no. Things just went wrong all of a sudden. I was fixin' to see if he still said no with a gun lookin' him in the eyes, and some damn lunatic walked right in between us, wavin' a red bandanna. Next thing I know, there's a shotgun and a handgun leveled at me and Red, and the sheriff comin' in the door with another shotgun aimed at us."

"I swear," Wick fumed, "you just made our job a helluva lot harder than it oughta be. What the hell were you and Red doin' in the store, anyway?"

"I needed some cigarette papers," Blackie said. "And by the time the sheriff run us outta there, damned if I didn't forget 'em."

"You ain't told him the good part," Red spoke up. "That sheriff told me and Blackie to get outta town before the sun sets." Knowing Wick's temper, he was eager to hear his reaction. He wasn't disappointed.

"You two ain't got the brains it takes to pour piss out of a boot," Wick roared. "I wasn't ready to let the sheriff know what we're fixin' to do. Now, thanks to you two jackasses, he's tipped off that somethin's gonna happen in his peaceful little town."

"Are we gonna get outta town, like he said?" Red asked. "I reckon he just meant me and Blackie, though. He didn't say nothin' about you."

"No, you damn fool," Wick exploded. "Ain't none of us gonna leave town. I told you when we rode in here that I plan to own this town. I wanted to find out if there's anybody here that could stop us, and we'd take care of him first off. Now, after you two warned the sheriff that we're fixin' to hit all the businesses in town, we're gonna have to take care of him before we do anything else."

"How we gonna do that?" Blackie asked. "Call him out in the street and settle it between him and me?" He naturally assumed that, since he was faster than Wick or Red.

"Nope," Wick said. "We're gonna set right here in this saloon and let him come get us. We'll see if that sheriff has the guts to come in here and arrest anybody. I'm bettin' he ain't, and he ain't got nobody to help him against three guns."

On their first day in town, the three of them had

scouted every business to see who ran it and how much trouble it would be to rob it. In every case, they found the business owned by one family and operated by one person in that family. In some cases, like the general store, a family member worked in the business to help the proprietor. In Spence's case, that was his wife, who posed no threat at all. It was the ideal setup. Wick had always had dreams of robbing an entire town, and Blue Creek was just made for it.

Then he remembered something Blackie had complained about. "What about this other feller you were talkin' about? The one wavin' the bandanna."

"I wouldn't worry about him," Blackie replied. "Tell you the truth, I ain't sure he had brains enough to know what was goin' on, him hollerin' about a bandanna."

"Yeah," Red agreed. "Then he wanted Blackie to tell him what insurance was." He chuckled while recalling it. "He ain't nothin' to worry about."

"I thought you said he had his gun out," Wick reminded him.

"Well, yeah, he did," Red allowed, "but that was after the sheriff came in with his shotgun."

"Then the feller backed up like he didn't want no part in it," Blackie added. "I wouldn't be surprised if he ain't already hightailed it outta town. The sheriff didn't know him, so he don't belong around here."

"All right, then," Wick announced. "We'll set right here and see if that sheriff's got the guts to come in to get us." He yelled to Jim Squires, who was standing behind the bar. "Hey, Squires, tell that woman to get us some supper out here."

Squires didn't answer, but went into the kitchen to tell Gussie to fix three plates of food for them.

"I heard him," Gussie said before Squires opened his mouth to speak. "Them three bastards have run all our regular customers off and left me with a pot full of stew I'm gonna have to throw to the hogs. Why don't you tell 'em we don't serve no supper? Maybe they'll hurry up and get outta here."

"They know better 'n that," Squires said. "Hell, they ate supper here two nights ago."

"Well, I druther throw it all to the hogs before I serve it to the likes of them. They're cookin' up trouble for Blue Creek. You don't have to be smart to see that. They ain't nothin' but common outlaws."

"I reckon you're right about that," Squires admitted. "I've been thinkin' about tellin' the three of 'em to get out. They've been drinkin' my whiskey ever since this afternoon and I ain't seen a dime of their money yet."

"I swear, I can't believe I have to tell you this, Jim, but you ain't gonna see any of their money. They're fixin' to hold us up for certain."

He knew she was right. He had just been reluctant to admit it. "Well, I reckon I've had about enough of it. I'm gonna run 'em outta here. It might be a good idea if you slip out the back door and go fetch Marvin Kelly."

"You sure?" Gussie asked. "There's three of 'em, you know, and they look like they ain't no strangers to trouble."

"They won't be expectin' me to come outta here with a loaded shotgun," Squires assured her. "They'll know the first one that makes a move will get cut down. If they try to bluff it out, I oughta be able to hold 'em till you get back with Marvin, so hurry."

"I will," she said and headed for the back door.

He waited for a few minutes to give Gussie some time to reach the sheriff's office before he picked up his shotgun, broke it to make sure it was loaded, took a deep breath to steady his nerves, then went back into the barroom.

Busy planning how they were going to rob each business on the street, before the next on the list was aware of what was happening, they paid no attention to Squires holding the shotgun until he spoke.

"It's time for you three to leave my saloon," he announced, catching them by surprise as he had expected.

"What the hell are you talkin' about?" Wick replied.

"I'm talkin' about the three of you sittin' around here all afternoon, drinkin' my whiskey and ain't paying a penny for it. You've run off all my regular customers tonight, so I'm tellin' you to get out, plain and simple."

"Well, I'll be . . ." Wick started, frankly astonished. He hadn't figured the man had it in him. "And what if we don't, Squires?" he asked calmly. "You gonna shoot us?"

"If I have to," Squires answered.

"I'm right sorry to hear you say that. We was just talkin' about how much we appreciated the hospitality you was showin' us. Weren't we, boys?" Wick glanced at Blackie and winked, causing Blackie to smile, for he knew what Wick had in mind.

"We was even plannin' on rentin' a couple of those rooms upstairs," Wick continued. "But if we ain't welcome, I reckon we'll have to get out." He got up from his chair. "Let's go, boys. Just don't crowd me."

His mind gripped by anxiety for the task he had set himself, Squires found the remark an odd thing to say. Too late he realized the three outlaws were purposely spacing themselves apart while taking their time heading for the door. Finding it difficult to cover all three, he started shifting his aim from one of them to the other in a panic.

"Squires!" Wick suddenly yelled, and the saloon owner swung his shotgun around to aim at him.

It was plenty of time for Blackie to draw his Colt and send a .45 slug into Squires' chest. It was followed a second later by a shot from Red that tore into Squires' gut. He was already dead when his finger squeezed the trigger and sent a load of buckshot through the front window.

"Hot damn!" Red sang out. "I felt the wind of them buckshot when it flew between us."

"So did I." Wick laughed. "He damn-near got one of us after he was dead." He walked over to stare down at the body, then he shifted his gaze to the kitchen door, his gun in hand. From his brief acquaintance with Gussie Beatie, he half expected the cantankerous cook to come through the door with a gun in her hand. When she did not, he told Red to look in the kitchen for her.

In a minute, Red came back and reported that the kitchen was empty. "She musta run when she heard the shootin'," he surmised. "But at least she didn't run off with the stew pot," he added with a grin.

"Ain't no doubt everybody heard the shots," Wick said, "so I reckon we can get ready for the sheriff's visit pretty quick now. Red, throw the lock on the kitchen door. I'll make sure the bar is on that hallway door in the back. Then I reckon we'll just set back and wait for Sheriff Kelly to make a call."

"That's right," Blackie said. "It's gettin' along about sundown, time for him to run me and Red outta town." That brought a laugh from his two partners. "I think I'll dip me out a bowl of that stew Gussie left on the stove. We might get busy later."

"That's a good idea," Red decided. "I think I'll join you."

The incident was taking on the air of a wild party. The presence of the body sprawled on the barroom floor added to the fun.

"How 'bout it, Wick?"

"I'm gonna see how much money ol' Squires left in the till for us," Wick answered. "He's most likely got his big money hid somewhere in this place. I ain't seen no safe."

"You want me to throw that bar on the front door?" Blackie asked.

"No," Wick answered. "We ain't gonna lock the door. I want that sheriff to feel welcome to walk right in."

"What are we gonna do about the horses?" Red asked. "We need to take 'em to the stable if we're gonna hole up here."

"We will," Wick said, "but right now we need to wait to see what the sheriff's gonna do about the shootin'. After we take care of him, we'll do whatever the hell we wanna do."

* * *

Sheriff Marvin Kelly sat at his desk in the cramped two-room building that served as Blue Creek's sheriff's office and jail. In his early thirties, he had taken on the job in the fledgling farming settlement mainly because there seemed no likelihood of any real trouble for a law officer. Drifters, cowhands whooping it up at the completion of a cattle drive, and outlaws of all kinds would be attracted to Ogallala, over thirty miles away. Until today, that had proven true.

He looked at the clock on the wall, which seemed to be hurrying toward sundown. He got up from his desk and went over to the door to take a look at the setting sun, knowing he was going to have to see if his orders to the two drifters had been obeyed. About to open the door, he stopped short when he heard the shots. *Two revolver shots*, he thought, *and one shotgun*. He jerked the door open to discover Gussie Beatie running toward him.

"Gussie!" he exclaimed. "What is it? What's the matter?"

"I'm afraid they mighta shot Jim!" she cried out. "He was gonna run 'em out of the saloon, so he sent me to get you. I just heard shots!"

"Who's in the saloon?" Kelly asked. "Is it the same three drifters that were here? All three?" he repeated, knowing the answer before she nodded excitedly. The two he had ordered out of the general store had not left town as he had told them. He looked down the street and saw three horses still tied at the rail in front of the saloon.

"It's the same three," Gussie said. "Whaddaya gonna do?"

"I reckon I'll go down there and order 'em out of

there. Maybe you better stay here." He stepped back inside to get his shotgun, wishing like hell that he had been out of town, hunting or fishing, but knowing he had to go. It was a matter of pride at that point.

Perley was feeding Buck a portion of oats when he heard the shots from the saloon.

A few minutes later, Frank Mosely walked in from the barn. "Did you hear those shots?" When Perley said he had, Mosely said, "Sounded like they came from the saloon."

They walked outside the stable and looked toward the saloon. Already a few people were gathered across the street from it, also curious to see the cause. Perley saw the sheriff walking toward the saloon, carrying a shotgun. He didn't have to be told who was causing the trouble.

"It was just a matter of time," Mosely said. "Those three jaspers spelled trouble as soon as they hit town."

"I don't know what the sheriff's gonna do," Perley commented. "But if he's fixin' to take those three on, he'd best deputize a couple of fellows to help him."

"Come on," Mosely said. "We can't see what's goin' on from here at the stable." He didn't wait for Perley and headed up the street at a trot.

Perley caught up with him after a few yards. "Are you one of his deputies?"

"Hell, no," Mosely answered. "I just wanna see what's happenin'."

They arrived to stand with the other spectators a few seconds after the sheriff arrived at the front of the saloon and in time to hear Kelly's ultimatum.

Standing by the three horses at the hitching rail, Kelly shouted to the three inside. "All right, in there. You were told to get outta Blue Creek, so it's time for you to leave. Come on outta there with your hands up."

"I'll tell you what, Sheriff," a voice came back. "Why don't you come in and get us?"

Kelly hesitated, not knowing what to do. He stepped closer to the horses tied at the rail, thinking that they might not take a chance on hitting their horses should they suddenly open fire. "Is Jim Squires in there?"

"Yeah, Jim's in here," the jeering voice answered.

"Well, let him walk out here. You got no reason to hold him in there."

"Jim don't look like he could do much walkin' right now," Blackie answered. "But if he can get up and walk out, we won't try to stop him." His words were followed by the sound of chuckling from Blackie and Red.

"Or you can come in and get him," Wick said.

Leonard Porter stepped up close to the sheriff. "Whaddaya gonna do? They've done shot Jim."

Kelly clearly didn't know what to do. To walk into the saloon would be certain death. "I don't know," he confessed while he tried to think of any option left to him. "I'm gonna need some help from some of you fellows if we're gonna get 'em outta there."

"If you're thinkin' about walkin' in there to arrest 'em, you can count me out," Porter said. "I ain't walkin' in there. That's just what they want you to do."

"Maybe we could get in the back door. How 'bout it, Frank?" Kelly said, looking at Mosely.

Mosely quickly let him know where he stood. "They can stay in there till the place falls down, as far as I'm concerned. It sounds to me like Jim Squires is dead, so there ain't nothin' we can do for him now. And I sure as hell ain't plannin' to join him."

Porter was quick to agree with him. "Leonard's right. Come to think of it, we ain't too smart, standin' around here. They might start pickin' us off anytime now."

"You might be right," Kelly said. "Maybe we'd best back up and take cover behind your forge." He moved toward the forge.

Immediately, the spectators also retreated across the street, seeking protection behind the blacksmith's forge and workshop.

All except one.

As anxious as the other gawkers, Perley watched the standoff, too, but when the others backed away, he calmly stepped up to the hitching rail and untied the three horses. Taking the reins of all three, he led them away from the rail and walked them down to the stables. He figured it wouldn't hurt to have something for the sheriff to bargain with.

"What the hell's he doin'?" Kelly blurted.

Inside the saloon, the same question occurred when Red Johnson, peeking out the corner of the broken window, announced, "He took our horses!" He turned to Blackie and Wick. "That crazy bastard with the red bandanna just walked away with our horses!"

It occurred to all three at that moment that they hadn't thought about their horses.

"I shoulda shot the son of a bitch, but I didn't know what he was doin' till after he did it," Red complained.

After a short pause, Wick commented, "It ain't gonna do 'em no good. When we're ready to leave, we'll just take our horses, same as we're gonna take everything else we want."

"What's to keep 'em from surroundin' the saloon and waitin' for us to come out, then shoot us comin' out the door?" Blackie asked.

"There's enough food and stuff in here to last a good while," Wick said. "There ain't enough men in this little town to stand guard on this place for very long. As long as we sit tight, there ain't nobody gonna try to come in and get us. It don't matter 'bout the horses. We was gonna put them in the stable, anyway."

"What if they decide to burn us out?" Red wondered. "We could come out shootin', but without our horses out front, we'd have to run down the street to the stable. Everybody with a rifle would be shootin' at us."

"They ain't gonna wanna burn the saloon down," Wick said. Even when he said it, he wasn't sure they wouldn't. After all, the owner of the saloon was lying dead on the barroom floor. It was becoming painfully clear to him that his plan might not be as smart as he had first thought. It also occurred to him that one of the three of them would have to stand guard every night, as well. He wished that they had ridden in, struck the saloon and the general store, and ridden out again. He couldn't admit his error to his two partners, however.

Across the street, Sheriff Kelly was still pleading for recruits to help him set up a guard around the saloon. When Perley returned from the stable, Kelly approached him. "What the hell were you thinkin' when you took their horses? You mighta got yourself shot."

Perley shrugged. "I reckon if the shooting was to start, I just didn't want those horses to get shot."

"I'm needin' men to keep a constant guard on the front and back of the saloon," Kelly said. "Can I count on your help?" He knew Perley was just passing through town, but if he was dumb enough to walk up to the rail and take their horses, he might agree to help out.

"I reckon," Perley answered. "Seems to me those fellows holed up in there have got as big a problem as you have, though. We can't get in, but they can't get out. If I was you, I'd offer to give 'em back their horses if they agreed to ride on outta town and not come back."

"I can't do that," Kelly replied at once. "They've killed Jim Squires. I can't just let 'em go."

"I never said you should let 'em go," Perley said. "I said you could tell 'em you would. There ain't no sin in tellin' a lie if it's in a good cause."

"We're talkin' about three pretty mean gunmen," Kelly insisted. "They ain't likely to surrender peacefully. Somebody's liable to get shot."

"How 'bout if I can fix it so you and I can handle the arrest without endangerin' any of the town's citizens?"

"How you gonna do that?" Kelly was desperate enough to listen to any solution for his problem.

"First, you gotta tell 'em you'll give 'em their horses back and won't try to stop 'em if they'll agree not to shoot anybody else and just ride outta town." Perley went on to explain his plan in detail, and when he was finished, Kelly was not absolutely convinced it would work.

"Well, that's the best I can come up with," Perley concluded. "You got any ideas?"

"No, I reckon not," Kelly confessed. "Let's give her a try." He turned to the spectators hiding behind every solid object they could find in Porter's shop. "Folks, you're gonna have to get on up the street now, toward Leonard Spence's store. There's liable to be some shootin' and I don't want nobody else hurt."

One by one, they started to back away, not willing to chance getting shot, but still wanting to witness the standoff.

Kelly called out to the men in the saloon. "You in there. Enough bloodshed. I don't know how Jim got shot, maybe he brought it on himself. But right now, I just want the three of you out of Blue Creek. If you and me can make a deal, there won't be nobody else gettin' shot, and you can go free."

"You must think we ain't got no brains a'tall," Wick called back.

"Hear me out," Kelly replied. "You've got me over a barrel. I can't rush in there without gettin' shot. And if you try to make a run for it, I've got your horses and everything you left on 'em. Like I said, all I want is for you to get outta this town. I'll give you your horses and hold my fire if you'll agree to jump on 'em and ride. Whaddaya say?"

"And every man in town with a rifle shootin' at us,"

Wick came back. "That don't sound like no good deal to me."

"Look out the window," Kelly said. "I've already sent everybody to the other end of town. There ain't gonna be nobody left but me and one man. I need him to bring up your horses."

"Is that so?" Wick returned. "Who's the other man?"

Kelly pointed to Perley, standing behind him.

"That's that crazy fool with the red bandanna," Red whispered, standing at the other side of the window. "He won't cause no problem."

"Whaddaya wanna do?" Wick asked, turning to consult with his partners. "We might be able to hole up here for a long time."

"I'd just as soon get the hell outta here," Blackie said. "I don't like bein' boxed up like this."

"I reckon that goes for me, too," Red followed.

"All right. We'll take our chances," Wick said, then called out to the sheriff again. "All right, Sheriff. We'll go peaceful, but I wanna see those three horses standin' right there in front of the saloon. I don't wanna see a damn soul on the street but you and that feller with our horses, and I wanna see that shotgun on the ground behind you. Is that agreed?"

"That's agreed," Kelly said. "I'll send Perley to get your horses."

Wick watched as Perley trotted back toward the stable. He told Blackie and Red to get ready to make a dash for the horses on his signal. When they were all set, he said, "I aim to put a bullet into that fat sheriff as soon as I'm in the saddle."

In a few minutes, Perley appeared, leading the three horses up from the stable. He positioned them right in front of the saloon and walked over to stand beside the sheriff.

"It's all clear," Kelly sang out and laid his shotgun on the ground behind him.

Very cautiously, Blackie opened the door and stood just inside while he looked up and down the street. He told his partners that there was no one in sight but the two standing across the street, so they eased out the door to join him.

"Don't shoot till we're in the saddle," Wick reminded them. "You ready?"

He got two ready responses.

"All right. Go!"

They charged toward the horses, all three leaping into the stirrups on the run only to land violently on their backs when the saddles slid upside down and ended up under the horses' bellies. The frightened horses bolted wildly, causing more confusion as Perley and Kelly drew their pistols.

"All right!" Kelly barked. "On your feet and hands in the air!"

Stunned from the surprise, all three outlaws took a few moments to collect their senses before slowly getting up from the ground.

"Better do as he says, boys," Wick said. "Looks like we've been double-crossed. Just don't crowd me."

Recognizing his signal to spread out, Red and Blackie climbed to their feet, stepping to the side as they raised their hands in the air.

The sheriff walked around behind them to relieve them of their weapons, leaving Perley to watch them.

Nothing could have pleased Blackie and Red more, having already formed an opinion of the fool who had waved the red bandanna in the general store. Adding to their confidence, it was three against two, in their favor. Almost as if on signal, both reached for their weapons when Kelly stepped behind Wick. With reflexes quick as a rattlesnake, Blackie reached for his Colt .45, his target Perley. Red spun around to draw on Kelly.

It was over in a fraction of a second with Blackie dropping to his knees, a bullet in his shoulder, his pistol on the ground, and Red collapsing with one round in his side. His pistol had never cleared the holster.

It was debatable who was the more shocked, Wick or the sheriff.

While they recovered, Perley picked up the .45 Blackie had dropped, then drew Red's pistol from his holster. "Better take his gun," Perley reminded Kelly, whose hand was still hovering over the weapon in Wick's holster.

Coming out of his shock then, Kelly took Wick's pistol, still cocking an eye in Perley's direction, not sure what had just happened, since he had not been in a position to witness it.

"You gonna lock 'em up?" Perley asked, since Kelly had still not spoken.

"Yeah, I'm gonna lock 'em up," Kelly replied, his mind finally in the present. "Those two are gonna need some doctorin', though." He looked at the two wounded men, concentrating on Red. "Him, especially. It's a good thing Reverend Penny decided to come back."

Misunderstanding, Perley said, "I don't think he's

hurt that bad. I didn't have much choice when he turned sideways to shoot you."

"No, I didn't mean that," Kelly quickly informed him. "We ain't got a doctor yet. Jenny Penny can do a little doctorin' if it ain't too serious." He paused to think a moment, remembering Jim Squires inside the saloon. "We ain't got an undertaker, either."

Now that the shooting appeared to be over, a few spectators began to emerge from the various points of refuge they had taken minutes before. Soon there were plenty of hands willing to help the sheriff transport his prisoners to the single cell behind his office. It would be their home for the long wait before a U.S. deputy marshal could be summoned to come take them to trial. Kelly sent a young boy to ride out to tell Jenny Penny she was needed.

With plenty of people to help the sheriff, Perley went to round up the three horses that had bolted. All three had stopped at the upper end of the street and were standing calmly. They came willingly when Perley took each one by their reins and righted the saddles.

During his directing of the volunteers, the sheriff managed to cock an eye in Perley's direction, watching as Perley righted the saddles on the horses and tightened the cinches. He couldn't help a moment's speculation as to what kind of man Perley Gates really was. Still somewhat confused by the incident that had just occurred, the only explanation was the wounding of the two outlaws had been done by Perley's hand. Marvin Kelly had heard a saying once. *You can't judge a book by its cover.* He had read very few books in his life, but he understood the meaning of the quote, and it certainly applied to Perley Gates. Kelly was sure of one thing—that he might not be alive had it not been for Perley.

Before turning to follow the crowd to the jail, he couldn't resist calling out to him. "Don't forget to tighten up those cinches."

"I won't," came the reply. Perley tightened the cinch straps and led all three back to the saloon.

CHAPTER 5

Since Blue Creek had not developed to the point where it had an undertaker, Frank Mosely and Leonard Porter volunteered to dig a grave for Jim Squires on a shallow rise east of the town. Perley offered his services as well, and a handful of folks—Jim had no family that anyone knew about—attended Jim's burial Sunday morning before church. No one actually said anything over the body, but Reverend Penny said that he would devote a good portion of his sermon to remembering the saloon owner. Among those at the actual burial, the most concerned appeared to be Gussie Beatie, which seemed natural to Perley. She would be the one most directly affected. Her concern was her livelihood, and from her point of view, she was the logical person to inherit the saloon.

After Squires was retired to his final resting place, she announced the new management of the saloon and a name change to *Gussie's*. The only question came from Porter and his concern that Gussie didn't have the financial means to run the saloon after its present supply of libation was spent.

"Don't you worry yourself about that," Gussie assured him. "My financial situation is in fine shape, and I plan to hire a cook and bring in a couple of ladies to please the customers." No one raised any more questions. The general consensus was that she would try and ultimately fail, then someone would take it off her hands.

After the altercation with Wick Bass and his two partners the evening before, a party of the town's merchants, led by Sheriff Kelly, searched the saloon from top to bottom. The purpose was to find any operating cash Squires might have hidden away in the building somewhere. The search was fruitless. There was no money to be found and no hidden safe. Gussie participated in the search, often complaining of damage to the premises in some cases when it became too aggressive.

Acting in his official capacity, Sheriff Kelly decreed, "All right. We'll turn the deed over to you and let you run it. But if it gets run down, we'll close you down."

"Fair enough," Gussie replied. "That's all I ask." She had operating capital that no one suspected.

Working for Jim Squires for the past year, she had become quite attuned to his habits and tendencies, one in particular. She noticed that he'd had a tendency to develop a case of the trots every time a large shipment of whiskey came in. She had found it unusual that it struck him every single time, so, being naturally nosey, she decided to see for herself.

When a shipment arrived one day from Ogallala, she'd waited until Jim excused himself to visit the outhouse, then snuck around behind the toilet. Peeping through a crack between the boards, she'd seen him remove one of the boards in the outhouse seat and take out a metal box hidden there. On her next visit to the outhouse to satisfy her own urges, she'd pulled the box out and discovered a great sum of money.

Knowing that money was there, she was more than confident that she could operate the saloon. There would be no more cooking for her, and no more wrestling with unwashed cowhands. She decided to find a new place to hide her money, however, in case anyone else was prone to peek through the outhouse cracks.

When the burial was over, Lawson Penny invited everyone to attend his church service to follow in an hour. Most of those who came to see Jim Squires put in the ground assured him that they would be there. Perley, having already promised he would come, also told Penny that he'd be there.

Since he planned to start out for Ogallala as soon as the service was over, he went directly to the stable to saddle Buck and load his two packhorses. Anxious as always when he had to leave his packs unguarded, he was relieved to find his belongings undisturbed. He was about to leave the stable when Marvin Kelly came by, riding a gray horse.

"You gonna go to church?" Kelly asked when he pulled up beside Buck and the other two horses.

"Yep," Perley answered. "I told the preacher I'd be there."

"Looks like you're loadin' up for a trip a lot farther than the church," Kelly said.

"Reckon so," Perley replied. "I plan on startin' out for home as soon as Penny says the final amen. I'da been gone yesterday if I hadn't promised I'd go hear him preach." He tightened the rope holding the pack on his grandpa's paint pony and retied it. "How 'bout you? You goin' to church?"

Kelly shook his head thoughtfully. "I reckon not. I've got prisoners to watch, and with almost everybody goin' to church, I'd best stay and keep an eye on the town." He smiled. "With the new owner of the Blue Creek Saloon openin' up today, I wouldn't want her to get robbed on her first day."

"I got an idea that Gussie's got starch enough to operate that saloon," Perley said.

"You know, Perley, this town is raw as a newborn calf right now, but it's growin' faster 'n a puppy on buttermilk." Kelly got around to the real reason he had sought Perley out. "There's already eight farms within five miles of Blue Creek, and there's gonna be more merchants comin' in to take care of their needs. And there's gonna be a need for more 'n one man to maintain the peace." He paused, then went on. "After the way I saw you handle that .44 you're wearin', I know I could sure use a man like you as my deputy."

The offer took Perley by surprise, and he had to pause a few moments to think how to respond. "I really appreciate the offer, Sheriff, but I'm already overdue back home in Texas, and I expect the family's beginnin' to wonder if I've met with bad luck. Besides, all I've ever known is workin' cattle and I reckon that's my callin'." He said that even though he would be happy if he never roped another cow for the rest of his life. In one sense, he was not that anxious to get back to Lamar County, Texas, but he knew Blue Creek was not the place he was meant to land. Besides, he was saddled with the responsibility of transporting forty pounds of gold dust to the Triple-G.

Kelly nodded his understanding and reached down to extend his hand. "Thanks again for your help and good luck to ya."

Perley shook his hand and replied, "Same to you, Sheriff, and good luck to Blue Creek."

Kelly wheeled his horse and called out in parting, "If the preacher ever raises enough money to get that church of his built, maybe we'll attract more Christian folks."

The Sunday service went a little longer than Perley expected, but then they always did, as far as he was concerned. It was different, since it was outdoors under a partly cloudy sky, but Jenny played her organ and Penny led the singing. Perley, using an overturned bucket behind the congregation for a seat, tried to join in but could never find the right key. It seemed the hymns were either too high or too low, but every once in a while the tune would pass through his range. When it did, he'd hit it hard for the few notes he could reach, till it passed on through. Nobody seemed to notice.

Sitting behind the worshippers, he was surprised to see several farm families in attendance as well as Leonard Porter and his family, Willard and Ellie Spence, and the postmaster and his family. Perley had to admit, it was a spirited meeting, but at the end of it, no collection plate was passed around. Contributions were left on a small table beside Jenny's organ. When Perley went up to shake Penny's hand and say good-bye to him and his wife, he realized the congregation was generous in their offerings. Although there was only a pitiful bit of money, the table was overflowing with vegetables, hams, a couple of chickens, eggs, meal, and other edibles. *Lawson and Jenny shouldn't starve*, he thought. But it looked doubtful if they could ever raise enough money to build a church.

"Look around you, Perley," Penny said. "These are solid people, good, God-fearin' folks. We'll build this town and we'd like to have young men like you to help us build it."

"'Preciate what you're sayin', Reverend, but I reckon my callin's back home in Texas, and I expect I'd best get started in that direction."

They walked with him back to the clearing where his horses were waiting with the other horses and wagons.

As he stepped up into the saddle, Jenny thanked him for showing up at that campsite on the North Platte. "You're the reason Lawson and I came back to Blue Creek, and in spite of what you say, I believe you're more of an angel than you let on."

Unable to hide the embarrassment her comment caused him, Perley mumbled a quick good-bye and wheeled Buck back toward the little town. The couple stood and watched him for a few moments before turning back to the tent.

"Too bad he couldn't stay for supper," Jenny said.

Later, when the sun was setting close to the horizon and the last of the people had started toward home, Lawson and Jenny took stock at the table of offerings.

"The folks have been mighty generous, just like always," Penny said as he poked through the food left for them. "Two dollars and twenty cents," he announced after counting the cash. "It ain't much, but it'll go to the buildin' fund. Sometimes there ain't any money." He paused then and asked, "What's that in the cloth next to that ham?" He picked it up, surprised by the weight. Untying the corners of the cloth, he stared, confused by the little pile in the middle of the cloth. "What in the world?" It suddenly struck him. "Honey," he exclaimed. "Bring that lantern!"

Caught in his excitement, she hurried to him, holding the lantern. "What is it?"

"It's gold!" Penny cried, "pure gold dust! Look at that!" He pulled the corners of the cloth together again and hoisted it. "It must weigh four or five pounds." He looked at his wife, whose eyes were bigger than saucers, and announced, "It's our church!"

"But, who?" Jenny could not believe it. "And why didn't they say anything about it?"

"I don't know." Her husband laughed. "The Lord moves in mysterious ways." He grabbed her by her hands and began to dance around in a circle. "I ain't one to question good fortune, but I ain't sure there ain't an angel by the name of Perley Gates."

Feeling none too angelic, the angel Perley made his way along the North Platte river trail. In fact, he was suffering a twinge of conscience for spending part of his grandpa's fortune that wasn't his to spend. It was thirty miles to Ogallala and he was getting a late start. Still, he planned to reach the thriving cow town in time to get supper at Ogallala House, the town's fancy hotel. The hotel's dining room was famous for its fine food, and he felt that he deserved one good meal before the long ride home to Texas. Although it troubled him that he had given Lawson Penny about four pounds of the family's gold dust, he justified the gift as one that his grandpa would have approved. It was a small portion of the approximately forty pounds, and since he was the only one who knew how much was in the original treasure, they'd never know the difference. It seemed of small importance to the Gates family in the long run, but it was enough to build Lawson Penny's church and then some. He could imagine the smile on Penny's face when he saw his church rise up from the ground. The thought brought a smile to Perley's face, as well.

When he reached the river crossing that Frank Mosely had told him to look for, he stopped to rest his horses for a while before riding the short distance left to Ogallala. If he was on the right trail, he would leave the North Platte there and strike the South Platte in about ten miles and the town of Ogallala beside it.

While it was still early in the evening, he followed the trail up from the river. He could hear the noise of the wild cow town well before he reached it. It was late in the summer for cattle herds to still be arriving. He had not expected the town to be as busy as it apparently was.

Coming to the one short street of Ogallala, he turned Buck toward the Ogallala House, which was the last building on the street. He thought of Billy Fowler as he slow-walked Buck past the Cowboy's Rest Saloon. One of the few people he knew in Ogallala, Billy was the bartender in the saloon, but Perley didn't plan to stop to visit. He only wanted to stop in town long enough to enjoy a good meal, then be on his way and camp outside of town. There was no use taking any chances with the load he was packing on his horses.

He pulled Buck up before the hotel, looped his reins over the rail, and walked in the front door. The last time he and his brothers had delivered a herd to Ogallala, they had planned to dine at the hotel, but ended up eating supper at the Cowboy's Rest instead. There was no one at the front desk, so instead of ringing the bell, he walked to a door he guessed might lead to the dining room. His hunch was correct. He stepped inside to make sure it was still open and was greeted by a pleasant-looking woman, who invited him in.

"Yes, ma'am," he responded. "I just wanted to make sure I wasn't too late to get some supper. I'll be right back." His real purpose had been to locate any windows in the dining room.

Having done so, he went back outside and moved

his horses around to the side of the building near a window. The short street was crowded with people, horses, wagons, even oxen, and the saloons were all plenty busy. He didn't feel comfortable leaving his horses out of his sight for very long.

Back inside, he didn't wait for the lady to show him to a table, but went directly to one by the window. Satisfied that he could enjoy his supper while keeping an eye on his horses, he waited to be served.

Assuming he was one of the cowhands from the last herd to hit town, Evelyn Rooney greeted him again. "You eating all by yourself or will someone be joining you?"

"Just me," Perley answered. He looked around him at the few people in the room. "Looks like I mighta missed out if I had gotten here a few minutes later."

"Plenty of time," she said. "We stay open for another hour. What would you like to eat?"

"Whatever you're servin'," he answered, surprised by her question.

"You have a choice," Evelyn said. "Tonight it's beef stew or lamb. Maybe you didn't notice it written on the board by the door." She was not really surprised, accustomed as she was to so many cowhands who couldn't read.

"Oh," Perley replied. "You're right. For a fact, I didn't see it. I reckon I'm partial to beef stew." He had been too intent upon seeing where the windows were to notice the board. In addition to that, he wasn't accustomed to eating in dining rooms where you were given a choice of meals.

She left to get him some coffee, pausing on her

way to the kitchen to say something to a man and woman seated at a table near the door. Moments later, the couple got up and left the dining room.

When Evelyn returned with his coffee, he saw fit to comment. "Looks like I'm your only customer left. I hope I didn't run 'em all off."

"Oh, no," she said, forcing a laugh for his remark. "There'll be one or two more before we're closed. I'll be right back with your supper."

"Is that the cook?" Perley asked, when she returned, noticing another woman standing just inside the kitchen door. It seemed to him that both women tended to stare at him. "If she's wonderin' about the food, tell her it looks like a feast fit for a king."

"I'll tell her." Evelyn returned to the kitchen, and the cook followed her back inside.

The stew was good, with generous chunks of beef and biscuits still warm from the oven. Perley gave it his full attention, barely glancing up when another patron came inside and took a seat at a table directly across the room from him. When his coffee cup was empty, it occurred to him that he hadn't seen Evelyn in a while, so he looked around the room in case she was cleaning tables near the front. He didn't see her, but he noticed the man who had just come in wasn't being served, either. "Don't know what happened to the lady," he said. "Maybe she'll be back in a minute."

"Maybe so," the man replied.

Perley noticed he was wearing a badge on his vest. "I could use a little more coffee, myself," he remarked before taking another glance out the window to make sure no one was snooping around his horses.

"Evelyn," the man called loudly, "man out here needs some more coffee!"

In a minute, Evelyn appeared with the coffeepot.

"'Preciate it," Perley said.

She responded with a brief nod, then returned to the kitchen without a word to the lawman.

Reckon he didn't come in to eat, after all, Perley thought, while the lawman continued to sit there, evidently waiting for someone . . . or something. In a few minutes, another man came in the dining room and the lawman got up to meet him, then suddenly, they both approached Perley, guns drawn.

"Keep those hands up on the table where I can see 'em," the second man ordered. "I'm Sheriff Dan Wheeler and I'm placin' you under arrest. Cliff, take his pistol."

The deputy walked behind Perley's chair and drew the .44 from its holster.

"Now, get on your feet," the sheriff commanded. "Make it easy on yourself. Just do like I tell you."

Taken completely by surprise, Perley could only do as he was told. It was obvious that the sheriff meant business. "Hold up a minute, fellows. If I was supposed to leave my gun outside, I swear I didn't see the sign. Hell, I didn't even notice the sign about the choice of suppers, either. Ask that lady. She'll tell you that."

"I expect you'll be Ben Mather," the sheriff said, "and you're under arrest for robbin' this hotel and murderin' Jim Goodman. By God, we heard you had a helluva lotta nerve, but I didn't expect you to show up here again."

"Whoa," Perley responded. "I see what the trouble is. I ain't this Ben Mather fellow you think I am. My name's Perley Gates, and I sure ain't ever robbed this hotel."

There followed a moment of silence, then both lawmen laughed.

"Perley Gates, huh? Well, that's a good one all right, ain't it, Cliff?"

"Sure is," Cliff replied. "What's the matter, Mather? Didn't you get enough the first time?"

"You're makin' a big mistake," Perley protested. "I ain't the man you're lookin' for. I'm Perley Gates and this is the first time I've ever set foot in this hotel." He couldn't believe this was happening to him, and with his horses standing outside, packed with just under twelve thousand dollars in gold dust. "You fellows gotta listen to me, I'm not your man," he pleaded as the deputy clamped handcuffs around his wrists.

"Is that a fact?" Wheeler replied. He turned and yelled back toward the kitchen door. "Hey, Evelyn, come on in here. He's under control." When she came from the kitchen, he asked, "Is this the man who stuck a gun in your husband's face and ran off with the cash box?"

Evelyn took a long look at the man handcuffed and standing in her dining room. She had been at the front desk, waiting for her husband to finish for the evening, when the holdup had taken place. Looking at Perley now, she was not certain. The robbery and the killing of Jim Goodman, who had attempted to stop the robber, had occurred over a week before.

"Well," she hesitated, "it looks like the same man,

and he's got that red bandanna he wore over his face. It looked like it was pretty new, just like that one he's got around his neck now." She studied Perley carefully. "He's wearin' the same flat-crowned hat. At least, it looks like the same hat. He was wearing a rain slicker, so I don't know what kind of shirt or vest he mighta been wearing."

"Well, there you go, Ben," the sheriff crowed. "Too bad you kept that bay you're ridin' in Walter Bray's stable. Else we wouldn'ta knowed your name. When we wired Omaha about you, we found out what a busy man you've been all summer."

Perley could see that Evelyn was having second thoughts about her memory and he looked her straight in the eye. "Ma'am, you're makin' a big mistake. I might look like that fellow, but I never set foot in here before tonight."

The sheriff noticed it as well, and decided to march Perley out of the diner before Evelyn might think to retract her identification. "Come on, Mather. You're wastin' my time." He gave him a shove toward the door.

"Wait a minute, Sheriff," Perley pleaded. "I've got my horses to take care of. Whaddaya gonna do with my horses?"

"You mean them three you tied up beside the buildin'?" Cliff responded. "The ones you've been peepin' at through the window? I'm kinda interested in seein' what you're carryin' on them two packhorses, ain't you, Dan?"

"I'd have to say so," Wheeler agreed. Then to Perley, he said, "We'll take your horses to the stable and Walter Bray will take care of 'em till the judge decides what to do with you. If I was you, I wouldn't worry too much about your horses 'cause you'll be swingin' on a rope for killin' Jim Goodman.'"

Surely he was in a dream. That just could not be happening, but the cuffs on his wrists felt very real, and the two gruff lawmen were deadly serious about their business. If he didn't wake up from the nightmare pretty soon, he was going to jail and the fortune in gold riding on his packhorses would be lost. He started to protest again, but the deputy gave him a hard shove toward the door and he felt the barrel of a pistol between his shoulder blades. Evelyn and the cook watched anxiously as he was hustled out the door. Evelyn looked as if about to apologize, but turned away.

Outside, Sheriff Wheeler marched Perley around beside the building where his horses were waiting. "I'll lock Mr. Mather up," he told his deputy. "You take these horses down to Walter's stable. Tell Walter to take care of 'em and I'll handle the bill. Remind him that everything in the packs and saddlebags belongs to the court and isn't to be tampered with till the court says what to do with 'em after the hangin'." He glanced at Perley and smiled. "I mean, *trial*."

Cliff nodded and took the bay gelding's reins in hand.

When he started to place his foot in the stirrup, Perley warned him. "You'd best lead him down to the stable."

The deputy paused. "Oh? Why is that?"

"Buck won't let anybody ride him but me," Perley said.

"Is that so?" Cliff responded, not at all concerned. "He looks peaceful enough to me."

His comment caused the sheriff to chuckle. "Maybe you'd best listen to the man, Cliff," he joked.

"Damn," Cliff scoffed and proceeded to step up in the stirrup, swung his leg over, and settled his considerable bulk in the saddle.

The sheriff then handed him the lead rope for the two packhorses. The deputy gave Perley a smug grin before giving Buck a kick with his heels.

The bay took about half a dozen steps before erupting like a four-legged volcano to rid itself of its rider. Cliff found himself sitting in midair, about ten feet above the ground, with no horse under him. Seconds later, he landed rudely on his backside, and to his credit, still holding the lead rope in his hand. He remained sitting there for a long moment, unable to utter a word, with the two packhorses staring at him patiently.

He finally forced out a painful grunt. "Damn!"

"You all right, Cliff?" Wheeler asked, not sure whether to laugh or not.

"Damn!" Cliff repeated, still sitting there. "Damn! I think I broke my back."

"Like I said," Perley advised, "it'll go easier if you lead him."

Free of his rider, Buck padded softly back to stand beside Perley.

"Better listen to the man," Wheeler said to Cliff. "Best lead the horses down to Walter's." He paused before adding, "If you can still walk." He waited to see that his deputy was able to get on his feet and take Buck's reins again.

When he walked away, leading all three horses, Wheeler tapped Perley on the shoulder with his pistol barrel. "Now we'll walk up the street to my office and put you in a cell. Make no mistake. One wrong move from you and I'll shoot you down right here in the street. Do I make myself clear?"

"Sheriff, I ain't the man that robbed the hotel," Perley said. "Evidently, the only thing I'm guilty of is lookin' like some fellow named Ben Mather. That don't hardly sound like a hangin' offense to me."

For a brief moment, Wheeler almost believed him. Nothing about his prisoner even resembled the rough-edged sinister bearing of a man who would wantonly commit murder. A thin smile crossed his lips then as he reminded himself that vicious men come in all shapes and forms. "If you don't give me any trouble," he informed him, "you'll get your chance in court."

Perley looked out the one small window in his jail cell at the busy street that never seemed to settle down, even with night rapidly approaching. It had been almost an hour since Cliff had led his horses to the stable. Picturing him ripping open his packs to find what was hidden inside made Perley feel sick. His anxiety was intensified when he heard the deputy come into the sheriff's office downstairs.

Anxious to hear the conversation between Cliff and Wheeler, Perley got on his knees and held his ear to the floor. He found he could almost hear them, enough to realize someone else was with them, but he couldn't make out what they were saying.

In a few minutes, he heard footsteps on the stairs, then the door opened and Wheeler, his deputy, and another man walked into the cell room. They stood before his locked cell, still talking.

"You say he's carryin' somethin' interestin' in those packs?" Wheeler asked. "Money?"

"It ain't money," Cliff answered. "There was some money in his saddlebags, about ninety dollars, but no money in his packs."

"Well, what was in the packs?" Wheeler asked, impatient with Cliff's stalling.

Cliff chuckled. "Corn. Ain't that right, Walter?"

Busy staring at the man inside the cell, Walter said that it was.

Cliff continued. "He's got supplies and ammunition, a good Winchester rifle, and some other things anybody would need. But he's got four sacks he's totin' on his packhorses. I opened every one of 'em and they're full of corn."

"Corn?" Wheeler asked. "You mean corn whiskey?"

"No," Cliff answered, still finding it amusing. "I mean corn."

"Seed corn," Perley quickly explained. "It's a special seed corn. I was takin' it back to Texas to try plantin' it down there."

"Seed corn," the sheriff repeated, scratching his chin thoughtfully. He was about to ask another question when Walter Bray interrupted.

"That ain't the man who told me his name was Ben Mather," Walter announced, which immediately caught their attention. "And those three horses Cliff brought me, ain't any one of 'em like that gray Mather rode." His proclamation left the two lawmen speechless, stunned.

Wheeler finally spoke. "Are you sure, Walter? I thought you said Mather was ridin' a bay. You sure this ain't the man callin' himself Ben Mather?"

"That's what I'm tellin' you," Walter answered calmly. "I ain't ever seen this man before, and like I said, Mather was ridin' a gray."

"Thank you, sir," Perley said. "I've been tryin' to tell him that." He looked toward the sheriff. "Now, how 'bout lettin' me outta here?"

"Just hold your horses," Wheeler replied, not yet ready to accept the fact that he had locked up an innocent man. He still had a witness that identified Perley as the man she had seen hold up the hotel. "Evelyn Rooney said you're the man that took the cash box and shot Jim Goodman on your way outta the hotel."

"She just made a mistake," Perley argued. "I don't think she's dead sure of what she saw in the first place."

"I'm gonna get to the bottom of this," Wheeler insisted. "We can start by you tellin' me what your real name is."

"Perley Gates," he answered.

"If you're really innocent," Wheeler came back right away, "you're just makin' it hard on yourself if you don't tell me your name."

With his frustration rising to a boiling point, Perley became desperate to think of some way to convince Wheeler he had the wrong man. He had nothing but his word to prove his name and that obviously was not enough to satisfy the sheriff. Then a thought occurred to him. "Sheriff, my brothers and I brought a herd of cattle up from Texas a few weeks back. We spent some time in the Cattleman's Rest. I think the bartender might remember me from then. We talked for a pretty good while that night."

"Cliff, go get Billy Fowler," Wheeler said at once, eager to get any information he might have. "Bring him up here and don't tell him the prisoner's name." When Cliff went out the door, Wheeler turned back to Perley. "It still might not prove you didn't kill Jim Goodman, even if Billy does know you."

It was obvious that the sheriff was more concerned about letting a guilty man go free than he was about hanging an innocent man. So Perley was still unable to gain much confidence in how much good it would do if Billy remembered him. With the number of cowhands that drank whiskey at the saloon, it was unlikely Billy could remember them all. Wheeler and Walter went back downstairs, leaving Perley to worry about his fate until Cliff returned with Billy.

Interested in how it was all going to turn out, Walter remained to talk to Wheeler. They headed downstairs to wait until Cliff returned with the bartender.

"Howdy, Sheriff," Billy said when he walked in. "Cliff says you want me to look at a prisoner you got locked up."

"That's right," Wheeler replied. "Just wondered if you remember him bein' in the saloon before. Did Cliff tell you his name?"

"Nope, just that you wanted me to see him," Billy answered.

"Good. Come on upstairs." Wheeler led him up the steps, followed by Cliff and Walter. At the top, Wheeler opened the door and stepped aside.

Billy walked into the cell room and as soon as he saw the man behind the bars, he exclaimed, "Perley Gates! What the hell are you doin' in there?" Billy looked back at Wheeler, questioning, then back at Perley. "What did you do to get arrested?"

"Looked like somebody else," Perley answered matter-of-factly.

The remark went right by Billy. "Did you find your grandpa?"

"I did," Perley replied. "I found him up in the Black Hills, but I'm sorry to say he didn't make it back with me."

"Well, now, that's a shame," Billy said, "but at least you found him and told him about your pa dyin' and all."

Wheeler interrupted then, having seen enough to know he had locked up an innocent man. Still, he was duty-bound to be convinced 100 percent before he let Perley go. "Come on back downstairs," he said to Billy. "I wanna ask you some more questions."

"All right," Billy said, then turned back to Perley again. "Come on by the saloon when Dan turns you loose and I'll buy you a drink."

"Much obliged," Perley said. "I'll do that." He was still not sure he'd make it, since Wheeler made no motions toward opening his cell door. His suspense lasted no longer than about half an hour, however, when Wheeler came back upstairs and unlocked the cell. "I'm free to go?" Perley asked.

"You're free to go," Wheeler confirmed. "And you have my apologies for the mix-up. But I swear, I didn't have much choice. I mean things happenin' like they did. Evelyn identifyin' you was what started the whole misunderstandin'. Billy told us about you and your brothers comin' in the saloon and talkin' about your grandpa. I'm just sorry we had to inconvenience you."

"Ain't no hard feelin's, Sheriff," Perley said. "I seem to find myself steppin' in a lot of stuff other people don't. I reckon I ain't surprised when I do." He grinned. "And my name don't help much."

Wheeler laughed. "Yes sir, I can rightly understand that."

CHAPTER 6

Downstairs in the sheriff's office, Perley found the deputy also waiting to offer his apology for the mis-understanding.

In return, Perley offered an apology on Buck's behalf for the sore backside Cliff suffered. "Buck ain't learned a polite way to say *get off.*"

Wheeler returned Perley's gun belt, then they all shook hands and Perley walked out. He went straight to the stable to check on his horses and his packs. It was almost too much to expect that Cliff and Walter had opened those sacks and hadn't discovered what the corn was hiding.

Walter greeted him when he came in the barn. "I'll bet you're mighty happy to be a free man again."

"That's a fact," Perley replied. "I reckon I'll take my horses off your hands now."

"You can leave 'em till mornin' if you want to," Walter said. "Sheriff Wheeler said he'd pay for stall and grain. Unless you're set on leavin' town tonight, you might as well stay over and go in the mornin'."

"I might at that," Perley said, after thinking about

it for a second. "I'll go take a look at my horses. Where'd you put my packs?"

"In an empty stall next to that bay." He led Perley back in the stable where Buck and his other two horses were. "Don't worry 'bout your possibles. Everything's just like you left it."

"Much obliged," Perley said, then went into Buck's stall and fussed with the big bay until Walter returned to the barn up front. As soon as he left, Perley went into the stall where his saddle and packs had been stowed. Much to his relief, the sacks holding the gold were undisturbed, although he could see that the strings had been retied. Cliff had evidently not been curious enough to see if anything was buried in the corn, or the idea hadn't occurred to him.

Next, Perley checked his saddlebags and found all his cash money still there. With everything in good order, he walked back to the front of the barn, where he found Walter throwing some hay down from the hayloft.

"I've got a couple of places I've gotta go before I turn in for the night," he said to Walter. "How much if I sleep in the stall tonight with my horses?"

"Nothin'," Walter answered. "I'll put it on the sheriff's bill. How late you think you're gonna be?"

Perley said he didn't anticipate being more than an hour or so, but if he was more than that, and it was time to close, to go ahead and lock up. "I've got money to buy a bed in the hotel if I miss you."

Leaving the stable, he decided he'd wait until later to have that drink Billy Fowler promised him. He walked on past the Cowboy's Rest and headed for the hotel. He figured he had something to settle there first.

"Can I help you, sir?" A man behind the front desk asked when he walked in the front door.

"I'm headin' for the dinin' room," Perley answered.

"The dining room's closed," the man said. "Won't open again till six o'clock tomorrow morning."

Perley hesitated while he decided what to do. "I'm lookin' to find the lady that runs it. I think her name is Evelyn."

"I'm her husband," the man informed him. "Maybe I can help you."

Before Perley could respond, a voice from the small office behind the front desk interrupted. "No, Sam. I think he needs to see me, and I don't blame him."

In a couple of seconds, Evelyn Rooney appeared in the doorway. "I can guess why you're looking for me," she said to Perley. "Before you say what you've come to say, I want to apologize for causing you so much trouble. Dan Wheeler came to tell us of the terrible mistake I made and I truly am sorry. Go ahead and speak your mind." She stood next to her husband while they both stared at a puzzled Perley Gates.

"I just came to pay for my supper," Perley said. "I didn't get a chance to pay you before the sheriff hustled me out the door.

His statement left them both astonished, Evelyn more so than her husband, for she had expected an angry tirade for his treatment at the hands of the law.

She stopped him when he took some money out of his pocket. Holding up her hand, she said, "Put your money away. I wouldn't think of charging you after the trouble I caused you."

Struck speechless by Perley's purpose for the visit, Sam spoke up then. "Where are you staying tonight? 'Cause, if you need a room, you can have one here for the night, no charge."

It was Perley's turn to be amazed. The thought of a free room had never occurred to him. "Well, I was plannin' to sleep in the stable with my horses," he responded after a long moment to decide if he should sleep close to his seed corn. "I wouldn't wanna cost you the rent on a room from a payin' customer."

Sam assured him they had several empty rooms that late in the season.

"Well, I'm much obliged then," Perley said. "I don't reckon my horse will miss me for just one night, but give me one of your cheapest rooms. No sense in givin' away one of your best ones."

With a key in his pocket for a room on the second floor facing the street, Perley returned to the stable to get his saddlebags and let Walter know he wasn't going to sleep there that night.

"Maybe Evelyn will give you your breakfast free, too, and you won't have to eat any of that corn you're totin'," Walter said. "You sure must love corn."

"That corn ain't fit to eat," Perley replied. "That's seed corn for plantin'."

"I was wonderin'." Walter walked out with him and barred the stable doors after Perley left, then went out the back after locking the padlock on the door.

Perley walked back toward the Cowboy's Rest, his saddlebags on his shoulder and his rifle in hand, reasonably sure his corn was safe for the night.

Billy Fowler called out a cheerful howdy to Perley when he walked in the Cowboy's Rest, then pulled out a bottle of the good whiskey and filled a glass more suited to hold beer.

"That's the expensive stuff, ain't it?" Perley asked. "I hate to see you waste it on me. I don't know if I can drink that whole glass and still walk outta here."

"Don't make no difference if you can't," Billy said. "Drink as much as you want. I'll pour what's left back in the bottle." He wanted to hear all about finding Perley's grandpa.

Perley told him the whole story, except the part about the gold dust in the sacks of corn. They talked through about half of the glass of whiskey, before Perley called it his limit. By the time he had satisfied Billy's curiosity, it was already later than he had planned to stay, so he thanked Billy for the whiskey and headed to the hotel, with one intermediate stop at the outhouse.

When he got to his room on the second floor, he found a note on his pillow, inviting him to have breakfast in the morning at no charge. *Can't pass that up*, he thought, considering his room and board for the night had come at a mighty inconvenient price.

Aided by the alcohol he had consumed, he slept solidly through the night, waking at five o'clock, which was later than he had anticipated. He planned to get his horses before he ate breakfast, since the dining room didn't open until six. He climbed into his clothes as fast as he could, left his room key on the desk as he passed by, then hurried down the street to the stable.

Walter opened up at five-thirty, surprised to see

Perley waiting by the back door. He helped Perley get his horses ready to travel, including his packsaddle. "You best be extra careful on your trip," he advised as he lifted one of the sacks and handed it to Perley. "They could cause you some trouble you don't want."

Perley paused to look at him.

Walter continued. "Cliff's young and always in a hurry. He didn't take the time to see if there was anything else in these bags besides corn. Me being older and maybe a little more nosey than him, I couldn't resist diggin' down in one of these bags to see if there was somethin' you might not want everybody to see. I figured I oughta tell you to be careful where you leave your horses. Lots of folks are nosey, but all of 'em ain't as honest as me. I'm fessin' up to this in case you wanna check those sacks to make sure there ain't nothin' missin', so when you get on down the road, you'll know you had it all when you left here."

Dumbfounded for a moment, Perley was stunned to know his treasure could have been in peril when he had figured it to be safe. At the same time, he was relieved to find an honest man in Walter Bray. He thanked him and took the time to tell him of the series of events that had led to the finding of his grandfather, and his grandfather's wish that the gold he had come by should be given to his family. "I reckon it's up to me to get it back to Texas." He paused to shake his head. "And I damn-near lost it at the first town I hit."

"I'd advise you to skip the towns on your way home," Walter said, "and sleep with one eye open."

"That sounds like good advice to me," Perley agreed. He had been lucky when he left his packs in the stable at Hat Creek, too. Like Walter, Robert Davis was an honest man. It might be that the third time was the charm. He shook Walter's hand and thanked him again. "I've got some money of my own. I can at least pay you for takin' care of my horses."

"No such a thing," Walter insisted and refused it. "You take care of yourself, son. Good luck on your way home." He stood watching as Perley rode toward the hotel, thinking the guileless young man was going to need it.

When he got to the hotel, Perley rode around to the side and tied his horses beside the dining room windows as he had done before.

Inside, he found Evelyn waiting for him. "Good morning," she greeted him. "I was afraid you'd left without having breakfast with us. Sam found your room key on the desk and figured you'd gotten an early start." She placed her hands on her hips in mock impatience. "And after Beatrice make flapjacks this morning, especially for you."

"No, ma'am," Perley insisted. "I wasn't about to miss a good breakfast before I left town." He then proceeded to a table by the window where he could keep an eye on his horses. Once he sat down, the food never seemed to stop coming. It would be a breakfast he would not soon forget. When he could eat no more, he insisted that he had to get started back to Texas. "I expect I won't have to eat anything else before I get through Oklahoma," he joked.

"No hard feelings, I hope," Evelyn said when he finally said good-bye. "You think you'll ever be this way again?"

"Most likely next spring," Perley said. "When the Triple-G drives another herd of cattle up here."

"Well, we'll be expecting you to come back to see us."

Much later than he had expected, he climbed up into the saddle, wheeled Buck back toward the street, and led his packhorses out the south end of town, with no thoughts that anyone might be trailing him.

More familiar with the prairie he now rode across, Perley followed the obvious trail left by the thousands of cattle driven up from Texas. It was a long ride to Dodge City, which he intended to bypass, heeding Walter Bray's advice about staying clear of big towns. The wide expanse of open, rolling prairie emphasized how small and insignificant he and his horses must seem to the Maker of this broad land. He thought of the many days ahead of him before he would reach the Red River and home. Anxious to be free of the responsibility for the small fortune in gold dust he was bound to deliver, he preferred, by far, to return to the carefree way of life he was accustomed to. "There ain't much I can do about it till I get it home," he sighed as he approached one of the many small creeks along his path. "I expect you're about ready for a rest," he said to Buck.

As was his custom, the big bay didn't answer.

Perley pointed the horse toward a scattering of small trees and bushes on the bank that promised the possibility of some grass. Guiding Buck down through the trees, he was suddenly startled when the branch of a chokecherry tree suddenly snapped in two about a foot from his head. It was followed within a couple of seconds by the report of the rifle. Reacting immediately, Perley gave Buck his heels and the big horse knew what to do.

At a full gallop, they raced along the creek with rifle shots snapping through the bushes on both sides of them. His first thought was that someone back in Ogallala must have found out what was in those sacks of seed. Possibly Cliff wasn't as careless as he'd pretended, or maybe Walter Bray had told someone. Perley didn't figure Walter to be that kind of man, however. Whoever it was, it appeared there was no mistaking their intentions.

Afraid that at any moment one of those slugs might find him or his horses, all Perley could do was run. With no time to wonder about who or how many, he drove Buck and the packhorses on toward a low rise that formed a high bluff along the creek. He pulled him to a sliding stop at a spot where the bank rose high enough to shield them. Rifle in hand, he was out of the saddle in an instant. After a quick check to make sure his horses were protected behind the creek bank, he scrambled up to the edge in an effort to see where the shots had come from. Looking back toward a prairie of low, rolling, treeless hills, he could only guess.

In his haste to save his hide, he couldn't say how many bushwhackers there were. Indians? Outlaws? One man or many? While he'd been running, it had seemed like more than one shooter, but it was possible that one man could shoot and reload that quickly. *I need to find out for sure,* he thought as he quickly looked upstream and down, promptly deciding that he didn't have much cover from either side.

With nothing he could do but sit tight, he checked the loads in his rifle and handgun while keeping a sharp eye on the line of low hills before him. *Landed in another mess,* he thought. *At least, I can hold them off as long as I'm behind this bank. That is, if there ain't enough of them to come at me from the sides.* With his foremost thought to keep his head down in case their shooting improved, he drew his skinning knife and began to dig a small trench at the edge of the bank to lay his rifle in to shoot from.

After a long period with no more shots fired, he began to wonder if the bushwhackers had given up. To find out, he stuck his hat on his rifle barrel and walked it along the bank, just high enough for most of the crown to show. He hadn't moved it more than a couple of feet before a single shot rang out and kicked up dirt several inches from his hat. When he repeated the test in the other direction, he again attracted a single shot from the low hill. It kicked up dirt no closer to his hat than the first shot had. *It ain't but one man,* he thought, *and he ain't that good a shot.* Perley had presented him with two targets and the shooter had missed both times.

No telling when he might get lucky and hit something, however. On the other hand, maybe the shooter was an Indian, and not after Perley's gold at all. Maybe the shooter was trying not to hit the horses. That made sense if the horses were what he was after. He might be on foot.

Perley looked up at the sky. It was still early in the afternoon and he had planned to ride at least twenty miles farther before making his camp. *I can't sit on this creek bank all day, waiting for him to make some kind of move.* He looked back at the line of hills, straining to see some movement that would indicate his attacker was thinking of circling around to one side or the other. Anxious to get out of the standoff with what he was convinced was an Indian horse thief, Perley decided the Indian was on foot. He would rest his horses for a short while longer then make a dash along the creek bank, hoping the Indian's marksmanship hadn't improved. If he was right, and the Indian was on foot, he should be out of range in a very short time. It was a plan, not a very good one, but it was all he could think of. The alternative was to sit there behind that creek bank all afternoon and wait for the Indian to sneak up on him that night.

The afternoon wore on and Perley never took his eyes off the line of treeless hills from which the shots had come. He could see the entire slope, from the eastern end to the western end, and he constantly scanned the hills. There was no chance anyone could approach his position by the creek without his seeing them.

Finally deeming it time to ride, he climbed into the saddle, and with a firm nudge of his heels, signaled Buck to spring into a lope along the edge of the creek. He picked a spot to cross the creek some thirty yards or so past the point where he and his horses would be exposed to the would-be horse thief. As he'd expected, he was once again under fire as several shots rang out. By the time he heard the third shot, he knew he was in the clear, but he held Buck and the packhorses to the pace until he had left the creek far behind him.

Reining the bay back to a fast walk, he cut back more to the east, since his dash up the stream had taken him off his intended course.

When he came to a series of rolling hills, he rode to the top of the tallest and paused to look over his back trail. For as far as he could see, there was no sign of anyone following him. That seemed to confirm his thought that his bushwhacker might be on foot, but he was not content to count on it. He wheeled Buck and the packhorses and loped down the grassy hill, determined to put as much distance as possible between himself and whoever the shooter might be.

Even though his horses had not rested as much as he normally would have rested them, he held them to a steady pace until it was almost dark. When he came to a small creek, he decided to make his camp there, afraid he might not come to another one all night. After his experience at his previous stop, he thought it best to set up a mock camp, just to be cautious. Unlike his last stop, there were no trees of any size on either side of the creek, but random clumps of small wild cherry trees and thick berry bushes provided some cover. After unloading his horses, he built a fire to make some coffee and fry some bacon. His distraction at the last creek had caused him to go without anything since breakfast. *It's a good thing that one was a good one,* he thought, *else my belly would have rubbed a blister on itself.*

He felt reasonably sure that he had left his assailant behind, but thought it common sense to assume the opposite. After satisfying his hunger, he added wood to his fire and made a decoy with his rain slicker, the hide from the last deer he had killed, and his saddle as a pillow. As another precaution, he hobbled the two packhorses to prevent them from wandering very far.

He took his blanket behind a clump of the berry bushes, where he could guard his horses. Thinking to put the gold he transported to good use, he made his bed with the four sacks situated around him. *Maybe that gold will slow a bullet down.* He'd been protecting it all day. It might return the favor by protecting him at night. When he felt he had taken all the precautions he could, he crawled into his gold-lined breastworks, his rifle close beside him, and tried to sleep.

It didn't come easily, but sleep finally overtook him, accompanied by the singing of the night critters that called the creek home. Sometime in the wee hours of the morning, the sounds of the insects ceased, replaced by a whinny from Buck.

It was enough to cause Perley's eyes to flicker, accustomed as he was to the big bay's warnings.

In a minute, he realized he was awake, unaware that Buck had alerted him. Perley listened for a few moments, but hearing nothing, he turned on his side, hoping to go right back to sleep. A few moments later, his eyes snapped open when he heard Buck whinny again, registering that something was wrong. He raised up on one elbow to look toward his campfire, no more than glowing embers. A dark shadow approached the lump that Perley had fashioned to resemble a sleeping body. Before moving, Perley looked all around the creek bank to see if others were closing in on his camp.

Sure there was but one, he silently rose to his feet.

In the darkness, he could determine that it was not an Indian as he had assumed, and he had caught up to him pretty fast, too fast to be on foot. He was undecided what to do until he determined the man's intention. That only took a moment, however, for the intruder slowly raised a pistol and fired it into the dummy, cocked it, and fired a second and third time. He stood there, staring down at what he thought was a body, until he heard the unmistakable sound of Perley's Winchester as he levered a cartridge into the cylinder. He whirled around, only to feel the impact of the .44 slug before he was able to raise his weapon. He staggered backward, dropping his pistol as he went to his knees.

Perley cranked another cartridge into the cylinder, ready to fire again, but his would-be assassin could not reach the weapon he had dropped.

In obvious pain, and helpless to defend himself, he started whimpering, "I'm done for," he pleaded. "Don't kill me."

"Billy?" Perley gasped. "Billy Tuttle?" He was stunned. "It was you takin' potshots at me today?" He shook his head, amazed. "And now, you just murdered me in my sleep, so you thought."

"I never meant you no harm," Billy wailed. "I just wanted to take a look in them bags you're totin'."

Even more amazed, Perley responded. "You never meant me no harm? Billy, you walked into my camp and pumped three rounds into what you thought was me. That qualifies as *harm*."

Billy groaned, supporting his right arm with his left hand. "I reckon you could look at it that way, but I'm willin' to let bygones be bygones, long as nobody died."

Obviously, he was an imbecile.

Even knowing that, Perley was finding it hard to believe Billy's logic. The question was what to do about it. He would be perfectly within his moral and legal rights to finish his assailant and be done with it. But somehow it didn't feel right to simply put Billy out of his misery like you would a crippled horse or a wounded deer. From Billy's response, Perley wondered if he was that simpleminded, that he really thought his attempt to murder could be forgiven.

Perley reached down and picked up Billy's pistol while he wrestled with the decision he had to make. "There ain't no *bygones be bygones* when you set out to murder somebody in their sleep. You gotta pay for what you tried to do."

"Oh, me," Billy moaned. "I think I'm bleedin' out pretty fast. I reckon I couldn't blame you for leavin' me here to die."

"Nice try, but you ain't hardly wounded that bad," Perley said. "You just ain't gonna be usin' that shoulder for a while." Still uncertain what to do with him, he couldn't let Billy go free to come after him again.

"If you're fixin' to kill me, please tell me one thing before you do it. What's in them four sacks?"

Perley shook his head, perplexed. "Seed corn," he answered, still unwilling to give Billy the satisfaction of knowing he had sniffed out a big prize.

Perley decided then what he would do. It would delay his journey even more, but he was unwilling to execute him, partially because it was not in his nature, and partially because Billy's father was a good man.

Since it was out of the question to leave Billy to recover and stalk him again, he decided to take him to his father's home in Cheyenne. He would turn Billy over to Tom Tuttle and let him decide what action to take with his son.

With that settled, he tied Billy hand and foot, ignoring his painful protests when he pulled his wrists behind his back. With his prisoner hog-tied, he then examined the bullet wound in his shoulder. "It's in pretty deep. I think it's best to leave it till a doctor can dig it out. I'll stuff something in your shirt to slow the bleedin' down. Where's your horse?"

"Back yonder on the other side of the creek," Billy answered. "There ain't but two of 'em. I sold the dun and that mule I had. These ropes are painin' me somethin' awful. They're pullin' on my wound too much. Can't you ease up on 'em a little bit?"

"Reckon not," Perley answered. "I want you to be here when I come back."

"I give you my word, I won't try nothin'."

"Well, now, that makes me feel a lot better," Perley said. "I can take a handful of that sand by the creek and mix it up with your word, and I expect I'd end up with a handful of sand. You just sit tight and I'll be right back."

Lying there, his shoulder throbbing with the pain of the bullet lodged deep in the muscle, Billy could only blame himself for one mistake. He hadn't thought Perley would suspect someone was trailing him. Billy had been careful. Leaning against a post at the railway depot, he had watched Perley ride out of town, leading the two packhorses. "Well, it took you long enough," he remembered mumbling to himself, having waited the whole time Perley was eating breakfast. He had remained against the post until Perley put a safe distance between them before climbing into the saddle and starting out after him. He had been careful to stay far enough behind to keep Perley from spotting him.

What he had in mind was going to be done at long range.

Having seen Perley's skill with the .44 he wore, Billy knew he was no match for him close up. Convinced that if there was nothing hidden in those bags of corn, Perley would not have objected to letting him see, Billy was more determined than ever to empty them. He figured since Perley was on his way back from Deadwood, it was most likely gold he was hiding. He had shot Luke and Jeb down to keep them from opening those sacks. Billy had been more than willing to bushwhack Perley to get a look inside them.

He thought about the hours he had spent hanging helplessly from the beam in the barn at Hat Creek until Robert Davis found him the next morning. He wasn't sure Davis believed his story about having been jumped by a would-be horse thief when he'd slipped into the stable to check on his horses. Since none of the station's horses were missing, Davis had had no real reason to detain him.

Billy had been confident that he would kill Perley. All he needed was a clear open shot with his rifle, and he had been patient enough to wait for the opportunity. He had thought that luck was riding in his favor. He believed that because it had been luck when he'd stumbled upon the tracks that told him where Perley had left the road to Cheyenne and headed up a wide stream to camp. He had found that camp and the tracks that led off toward the southeast, and not toward Cheyenne. It was luck again when he'd decided that if Perley wasn't going to Cheyenne, then he was likely headed to Ogallala. After riding his two horses half to death, he had finally caught up with him. It was hard not to believe that luck was on his side, even finding himself in the position he was currently in.

With no thoughts of going back to sleep that night, Perley found Billy's two horses, tied Billy to the base of a large bush, and revived his fire. It was still a couple of hours until first light, so he decided to make some breakfast. By the time they finished eating, it should be time to load the horses and turn back toward Cheyenne.

When the coffee was ready, Perley served up a fresh cup and a couple of thick slices of fried sowbelly to chew on. He even untied Billy's hands so he could feed himself while sitting across the fire with Perley's pistol leveled at him.

When he was finished, Perley tied him up again then packed up to get underway.

"I reckon you know you whupped me," Billy confessed. "I won't try to give you no trouble. Hell, I can't. My shoulder's so bad I can hardly move it. I know I was wrong comin' after you, but I was really just wantin' to partner up with you. We'da made a helluva pair, but I'm done. I'm ready to pay for my crimes."

"I'm glad to hear it," Perley said, thinking Billy had a strange way of partnering up with someone. Having already decided that Billy was operating with some loose screws in his head, Perley was still reluctant to execute him. With a shake of his head, he surrendered to his prior impulse. "I'm takin' you back to Cheyenne and turning you over to the sheriff. It'll be up to him what he wants to do with you. Your daddy's a friend of the sheriff. Maybe they can work something out for you."

"That sure-enough sounds like a good idea," Billy said. "Maybe he'll work out some way that I can get my good name back again. You reckon?"

"Maybe so, if you convince everybody you're on the level," Perley answered

"By crackee, that's what I'll do, and I've got you to thank for it. I'm a new man. Let's get started back to Cheyenne. I'll make my old man proud of me yet."

Billy's enthusiasm seemed genuine, but Perley wasn't ready to accept his word that he would behave on the long ride to Cheyenne. It did relieve Perley of his guilt for not going for a kill shot, however, when Billy had turned to shoot at him. "All right. We'll start back, but you're gonna be ridin' with your hands tied behind your back and I'm keepin' my eye on you the whole time."

"Right!" Billy exclaimed, enthusiastically. "That's the way I want it. So you'll see I'm a changed man. I've been rattlin' some sinful thoughts around in my head for a spell now. Thanks to you, I see where I was travelin' down the wrong road. I aim to get myself on the right trail from now on."

Used to hearing Billy speak out of both sides of his

mouth, Perley took the declaration with a grain of salt. "I reckon that'll make it easier on both of us. Let's get mounted and we'll start out for Cheyenne." Before helping him up in the saddle, Perley took the horse's reins and tied them around a stout branch of a chokecherry tree. "I wouldn't want your horse to bolt before you got yourself in the saddle and hurt that shoulder. I'll tie your hands after you pull yourself up."

"I 'preciate it, Perley. My shoulder has started achin' somethin' fierce." He paused before lifting his foot to the stirrup. "Let me get my breath for a minute, then I'll be all right." He seemed to be holding on to the saddle for support, so Perley waited for him to recover.

By the time Perley realized Billy was actually fumbling with the flap on his saddlebag, it was too late to stop him. Already in his grasp was the extra pistol he carried there and he spun around to fire it.

Perley's natural reactions took over and he dropped to his knee. They fired at almost the same time. Billy's shot snapped a foot over Perley's head, while Perley's slammed Billy in the chest. Fatally wounded, Billy squeezed the trigger again, sending one shot into the ground beside him before he sank to his knees, then keeled over onto his side. Perley went quickly to him and took the pistol from his hand.

Billy made no effort to resist. "Damn you," he rasped. "You've kilt me."

"You shouldn't have reached for that gun," Perley said. "I didn't plan to kill you. I was gonna take you back to Cheyenne, to your pa. I didn't think about you keepin' a spare gun in your saddlebag. I shoulda checked it."

Billy coughed feebly, causing blood to run from the corner of his mouth as he grew visibly weaker. His eyelids flickered uncontrolled for a few moments before his face relaxed as if seeing Father Death coming for him. Apparently finished, his eyelids flickered half open again and he whispered. "There's more 'n seed corn in them damn sacks, ain't there?"

"Yeah," Perley replied softly. "There's a ten-pound bag of gold dust in each one of 'em."

A hint of a smile appeared on Billy's face. "I knew it," he barely managed, then his face became a blank mask in death.

Perley sat back on his heels and stared at the body of the perplexing young man, half expecting him to come to and start yakking away again. He reprimanded himself for his carelessness. When he had killed the two men who had come after Billy, he had wanted no part of their possessions. He should have remembered that Billy came away from that fight with not only two horses, but also several weapons, as well. "There's most likely another .44 in the other saddlebag," Perley mumbled. "Careless!"

After a while, he got to his feet, trying to decide what to do. Tom Tuttle, Billy's father, was a good man, and maybe Perley owed him the courtesy of telling him what had happened to his son. But Cheyenne was a hell of a trip out of his way. It was also a little difficult to go tell a man, "By the way, I killed your son." He would have to think about that.

For the time being, he figured he owed Billy a decent burial instead of leaving him for the buzzards and wolves to dispose of. Also to consider was the matter of Billy's two horses, with saddles; the weapons and ammunition; not to mention what was left of five pounds of gold dust. All of that Billy stole from his former partners. Perley paused, undecided if it should go to Billy's father.

"Hell," Perley expressed to Buck. "None of that stuff belonged to Billy in the first place." He looked again at the corpse lying at the foot of the berry bushes. "Feedin' the buzzards is the last chance Billy's got to do something useful. I ain't got a shovel, anyway."

He packed up his camp, rigged a line to lead four horses, then stepped up in the saddle and headed south again. He had a long ride before he would reach the Red River and Texas.

CHAPTER 7

Leading four horses, it took three days of hard riding before Perley sighted the buildings of Dodge City standing stark against the vast openness of the prairie. With no wish to endanger his sacks of gold dust, he was inclined to pass the wild town by, even though he knew he'd have an opportunity to sell horses there. He had two more than he wanted to bother with but decided to heed Walter Bray's advice and steer clear of towns like Dodge City. He rode past the town, striking the Arkansas River a few miles west, where he made his camp for the night.

The next morning, he headed in a more south-easterly direction. Leaving the cattle trail he had been following, he rode a good thirty miles or so before striking a wide creek bordered on both sides with cottonwoods and thick bushes. His horses were due a rest, and he was due some breakfast, so he picked a small clearing in the midst of a stand of cottonwoods hugging the banks, planning to give them ample time to water and graze.

He still had plenty of coffee beans, but wondered

if he should have ridden into Dodge City and bought some beans and hardtack. He was riding through country he was not familiar with and hoped he would come to a town or trading post in the next few days. He had a supply of bacon, but nothing to go with it. "Damn," he swore. "I'm sick of bacon. If I don't find something to hunt pretty soon, I'm gonna turn into a hog."

While his horses were drinking, he walked along the bank of the creek, picking up dead limbs for his fire and scouting for tracks left by any animal. *This country should be good for deer or antelope,* he was thinking. But he could find no sign of either. Resigned to his salt pork diet, he carried his firewood back to his camp and prepared to build a fire. *Could have bought some more matches, too,* he thought as he started a flame under the dead grass and leaves he was using for kindling. It was then that he sensed he was being watched.

He immediately became tense as his kindling began to catch fire. Moving very slowly, he reached for the Colt riding on his hip and eased it up out of the holster, cocking the hammer back as he did. His senses told him that the danger was to his left, somewhere on the bank, so he slowly turned his head in that direction. Seeing no one, he continued to turn until he was looking almost directly behind him before he discovered his observer. A large rabbit sat watching him, curious no doubt as to what strange creature had invaded his world.

Damn, Perley thought and shot the unfortunate visitor to his camp. "You gave me a fright there for a minute, but you're surely welcome. There'll be no salt pork for breakfast this mornin'."

The .44 slug had almost torn the head off the rabbit, but the meat had not been damaged. Perley skinned it, gutted it, and soon had it roasting over the fire. It was a welcome change from the bacon he had planned to cook. It was a sizable rabbit, but he had no intention of saving any of it for later. He ate the whole rabbit, washed down with a couple of cups of coffee, the effect of which made it inviting to take a little nap.

"What the hell was that?" Blanche Dickens exclaimed, looking around her cautiously for the source. She hurried up from the edge of the water where she had been rinsing out her cup and plate. "Did you hear that?" she asked Dolly Rich.

"Yeah, I heard it," Dolly replied. "It was a gunshot, a pistol, sounded like to me." She walked up to the top of the high bank of the creek and peered upstream, but the trees along the banks blocked her line of sight. "Maybe somebody huntin' up that way."

"With a pistol?" Blanche questioned. "More like somebody shootin' somebody else. Just what we need right now."

"Maybe not," Lucy Butcher said. "Maybe it's somebody who can give us some help." She looked back at the carcass of the old horse where it had fallen, still hitched up to the wagon, which was only partially out of the water. "We damn-sure need some help."

"Lucy's right," Grace Belcher said. "We need help. The four of us women can't get that wagon outta the creek, and even if we do, I don't think any of us can bring a dead horse back to life. I don't know about the rest of you, but I don't wanna walk all the way to Dodge City and leave my trunk with all my belongings here in this creek." Her comments were met with uncertain expressions, but it was obvious the other three felt the same.

"It sounded like it mighta been a half mile or more back up that way," Lucy said, pointing upstream. "Instead of just settin' here talkin' about it, I think we oughta go find out who did the shootin'. They might be comin' this way. I'd rather see them before they see us." When her three companions just looked at each other, still uncertain, she volunteered. "Hell, I'll sneak up the creek to find 'em. I'll take the shotgun with me. Anybody else wanna go with me?"

No one did.

Blanche summed up the reason pretty accurately. "Honey, if I was as young as you, maybe I'd go with you, but if I was to get caught in those trees and had to run, I couldn't." Dolly and Grace nodded in agreement.

Lucy shook her head as if disgusted. "Just as well. If I have to run for my life, I'd just as soon not have to herd one of you old women ahead of me." She picked up the shotgun they had rescued from the wagon earlier and set out along the bank.

When she was out of their sight, Grace posed a question. "What are we gonna do if she runs into some Indians or outlaws? We might lose her and the shotgun." She shook her head slowly at the thought. "We've got no business out here in the middle of nowhere with no protection and a dead horse. Whose idea was this, anyway?"

"Yours," Blanche answered.

"Huh," Grace grunted. "Well, it was a good idea. Dodge City's about the only hope left for us since the ranch at Fort Supply dried up. It wasn't my idea to buy that damned old horse, though." She pointed a finger at Dolly. "And if you knew how to drive a horse and wagon, we wouldn't be stuck here with the damn thing half outta the water."

"You coulda took over anytime you thought you could do better," Dolly replied in her defense. "Besides, all three of you helped pick that place to cross."

While the argument over who was to blame for their predicament continued, Lucy was making her way through a stand of cottonwoods about a mile upstream. Preparing to circle around a clump of bushes that extended out over the water, she stopped in her tracks, afraid to take another step. In the small clearing she was about to cross, she discovered several horses grazing. She dropped to one knee and clutched the shotgun while she decided what to do. When it appeared no one had seen her, she scanned the creek bank in search of anyone, but saw no one. She saw a campfire, but no people. Her eyes swept across the creek bank again, then stopped and went back a few yards when she spotted someone lying flat on his back. Thinking he was probably the victim of the gunshot they had heard, she quickly looked around the clearing for his assailant. No sign of anyone else.

Where could they be? Were they hiding, perhaps having seen her approaching? Maybe they were circling around behind her. In a state of panic, she could feel her heart beating against her breast. Her next thought was to turn and run, but looking behind her revealed no sign of anyone. Still afraid to move, she remained there, stone still, until she realized that if there was anyone else, they would have surely attacked her already. Returning her gaze to the body lying on the ground, it occurred to her that the man may have shot himself, either accidentally or on purpose, and *that* was the gunshot they had heard. Thinking that explanation a possibility, she felt emboldened to the point where she was determined to find out.

Ready to flee at any time, should she have to, she approached the body, walking as quietly and carefully as she could manage, her shotgun held at the ready. She paused only once when the big bay horse grazing nearby whinnied and snorted a couple of times. With still no sign of life from the man sprawled on his back, she inched closer until she could see him clearly. He was a young man. His eyes were closed, his face relaxed as if in peace, but she saw no sign of a gunshot wound.

Suddenly, his eyes opened. She started, but was too stunned to move.

Perley was looking at the business end of a double-barreled shotgun inches from his face. Too startled to think, he realized that one wrong move might cause him to have his head blown off. He took his eyes off the two dark tunnels that threatened him and looked beyond the barrels of the shotgun to focus on the terrified face of a young woman. For a long moment, they looked each other in the eyes, both parties afraid to make a move, lest it might ignite an explosion.

Finally, Perley spoke. "I made some coffee. You want a cup?"

Startled, Lucy hesitated before she answered, her shotgun still inches from his face. "I don't know. Yes, I guess I would enjoy a cup of coffee if you have plenty to spare."

"If you don't mind, I'll move this outta my face." He slowly raised his hand and gently moved the double barrels of her shotgun to point away from him. When she made no effort to resist, he took the weapon from her and placed it beside his saddle on the ground.

She took a step back and looked around her.

He sensed what she was thinking. "Ain't nobody but me. Were you fixin' to shoot me with that shotgun?"

Aware now that he was not a threat to her, she began to recover her composure. "I mighta if I'd had to. Tell you the truth, I thought you were already dead."

"I thought I was, too, when I woke up and saw that shotgun in my face."

"We heard a shot," she went on. "Who got shot?"

"Him," Perley answered and pointed to the rabbit pelt hanging on a bush on the other side of the fire. "If you'da got here a little while ago, I coulda offered you some."

She nodded slowly, seeming still to be somewhat in a fog. He went to his packs to find his extra coffee cup. After he filled it, there was a little left in the pot, so he emptied the rest into his cup. She took the cup when he offered it.

Finally, he asked, "Where'd you come from?"

She took a couple of sips from the cup before answering. "Back there, about a mile or so downstream." He was about to ask for more information than that, but she continued. "Four of us. Our wagon's stuck in the creek and our horse died tryin' to pull it out."

"There's four of you?" Perley asked. "Family?"

"No, just four of us women."

"Four women?" he couldn't help asking in surprise. "Where were you goin'?"

"Dodge City."

Four women alone on their way to Dodge City. It was an easy assumption to make that they were "sporting ladies," but he asked anyway. "Whaddaya gonna do in Dodge? You know folks there?"

"We're gonna do what we always do," Lucy replied. "We just need to get someplace that ain't dyin' out like the one we just left."

When Perley asked where that was, she told him they'd worked on a ranch at Fort Supply.

"I thought that old army post was shut down," he said.

"It might as well be. That's why we're goin' to Dodge City." Rapidly becoming impatient with the man's polite conversation, she finally asked her question. "Can you help us get there?"

"I reckon I can try," Perley answered. "I'll have to break camp first."

She said again that they were only about a mile from the wagon and asked why he had to pack up everything to go that far.

"Because I need to keep an eye on my possibles. Ain't likely to run into anybody out here, but I ran into you, so it's best to keep 'em where I can watch 'em."

"I'll help you," she said. "I don't wanna be gone so long my friends will think something's happened to me."

"'Preciate it." Perley quickly unhobbled his horses and got them ready for the trail while Lucy rinsed his cup and put out the fire.

Then she helped him load his horses. "What's in the sacks?"

"Which ones?" Perley replied. "Those hangin' on the saddle of that one horse is holdin' all my cookin' stuff and my clothes. Those on the horses with the packsaddles are totin' seed corn." As he expected, she asked why so much seed corn and he told her the same story he had tried to convince Billy Tuttle with.

She only shrugged and commented, "It must be really special corn, since you've got so much of it."

"There ain't none like it where I'm from," he responded. "It's a real money crop."

Ready to go, he helped her up to ride on Billy's horse and they headed downstream.

"She's been gone a helluva long time," Dolly Rich declared, a worried frown on her face. "What if she ran into some trouble? We'd never know it until it was too late."

"We ain't heard no gunshots," Grace said, "so nobody shot her. 'Course, they mighta just grabbed her and now they know we're here." She looked around her frantically as if searching for something. "We oughta be thinkin' about protecting ourselves."

"How?" Blanche spoke up. Older than the other three, she was usually the one who made the decisions. "Lucy's got the only damn gun we brought with us. There ain't nothin' much we can do except wait and see what happens."

"You don't reckon it's Jake, do ya?" Dolly was the first to come out with it, but it was clearly on the minds of all three.

Blanche started to answer, but Grace interrupted her. "Why don't you ask Lucy? Here she comes now."

A moment later, Lucy came out of the trees astride a horse, and a man on a horse followed along behind her. He was leading three more horses. The first question that came to mind was the one Dolly had just asked, but they could see right away that it was not Jake Barnes. There was still the question of whether or not Lucy was riding in under her own free will or if she was being herded back under threat.

Moments later, they were relieved when Lucy pulled up before them and slid off the horse.

"Look what I ran into," she sang out cheerfully. "I got us some help. This is—" She paused abruptly and turned toward Perley. "I swear, I didn't even ask your name, did I? Or tell you mine, for that matter."

"Perley Gates," he replied as he dismounted, his attention immediately drawn to the horse's carcass hitched up to the wagon. Ignoring the usual facial reactions upon introducing himself, he was first prompted to ask, "Where's your other horse?" The dead horse was hitched up to the side of the wagon tongue.

"There weren't no other horse and there weren't no other wagon," Blanche answered, "so we hitched him up to the side. He was doin' fine till we got stuck in the water. Is that your real name?" In her business, she had dealt with many men going by names other than the one their mama and papa had given them.

Perley smiled patiently. "Yes, ma'am. What's yours?"

"Blanche Dickens," she replied. "You already met Lucy, and this is Dolly and Grace. We're obliged for your help."

He could pull the wagon out of the water, but it was obvious to him that it wouldn't do them much good without a horse, or horses, to pull it. He stood there for a long moment, staring at the dead horse, while the women stood staring at him. They needed two horses and he had two he didn't need. It would seem like the perfect twist of fate that had caused the two parties to meet, and in the middle of the prairie where there was no wagon road to anywhere.

Not even an Indian trail or a game trail. What in the world are they doing out here?

Somehow, he didn't imagine they had any money to buy two of the horses from him, so he didn't bother to ask. *Stepped in another cow pie.* He couldn't leave them without the horses to get them to Dodge City. From the hopeful expressions on all four faces, he knew they were thinking the same thing. He was reminded of four puppies begging at the kitchen table for scraps.

"First thing is to pull your wagon outta the creek,"

he finally commented, and went at once to unhitch the dead horse from the wagon tongue.

The women gathered around to watch him as he freed the harness from the carcass. Using the lead rope from his packhorses and Buck's horsepower to roll the carcass on its side, he managed to separate the unfortunate nag from the traces. "How long has he been lyin' here?" he asked as he labored.

"Since yesterday mornin'," Blanche answered. "We were thinkin' about butcherin' him and eatin' him before much longer if we didn't get outta here."

"We didn't know how long he could set there before he started gettin' rank," Grace commented. "But we were gonna use up all the bacon and jerky before we started in on him."

"I expect he'da let you know before very much longer," Perley said.

"I feel real bad that we killed him pullin' that wagon," Lucy said.

Perley took another look at the carcass. "I expect he'da died of old age by the time he got to Dodge, anyway." With the wagon free now, he pushed it back into the water just far enough to allow the wheels to turn and miss the carcass.

It was a simple task for Buck to pull the wagon out of the water and up onto the creek bank. The women cheered when the wagon rolled up on dry ground. Then the hopeful puppy-dog faces returned as they gathered around Perley.

"Are you by any chance headed for Dodge?" Blanche asked.

"I just came from Dodge," Perley said. "I'm headin' south. Got a long ride ahead of me to Texas." He hated to say the words, but knew he had no choice. "I reckon I can go back to Dodge and lose another day or two, so you nice ladies won't have to pull a wagon there."

His declaration was met with a joyous cheer from all four.

"Hallelujah," Dolly exclaimed. "I knew anybody named Perley Gates had to be an angel!"

"We'd offer to buy a horse from you," Blanche said, "but we ain't hardly got the price of a good horse between the four of us. We spent most of what we had to buy that one you see layin' there, but we can pay you for usin' one of your horses to take us to Dodge. 'Course, that's if you're willin' to take it out in trade."

He didn't have to take any time to consider that proposition. "Why, no, ma'am. I wouldn't take any money for escortin' you nice ladies that little distance. I'm just glad I happened to come along when you needed help. Tell you what, though, I'll hitch two horses up to your wagon, so it won't be so hard on just one. And we'll get ready to roll. It's already past noon."

That set the four in motion, gathering up the few cooking things they had removed from the wagon and their bedding from the one night spent sleeping on the ground. Perley watched them scurrying around to leave, all the while wondering why he always seemed to find himself in scenes such as this.

"Is it very far from here to Dodge?" Grace asked.

"It's a little over thirty miles, I'd say," Perley replied. "Day and a half in that wagon. We'll go back the way I just came. I know a good spot to camp tonight."

The two saddle horses were not too enthusiastic about being hitched up to the wagon, causing Perley to have to work with them a little before turning the reins over to Dolly. When they settled down, Perley led his party away from the creek and started to retrace his tracks from that morning. Spirits were high among the four women in the wagon because it seemed their journey was nearing an end. There was much speculation about the Good Samaritan who had happened upon them.

Dolly insisted he really was an angel. "That's the reason he ain't interested in Blanche's offer of our services. Angels ain't interested in sins of the body."

"Hell," Grace snorted. "I think he's just bashful. Just plain innocent. Ain't ever been around women like us before."

"Whores, you mean?" Lucy asked as if offended.

"Yeah, whores," Grace came back. "You druther I call us ladies of the evenin' or angels of mercy? How 'bout what Jake Barnes thinks we are? *Hogs?* Ain't that what everybody called that place of his, a hog ranch?"

"If that's what you think you are, then that's what we'll call you," Lucy said.

"All right," Blanche interrupted. "You two are fixin' to get into a catfight if you don't shut up. That's the reason for this whole thing, ain't it? 'Cause we're tired of bein' treated like somebody owns us. Like hogs or those horses, right? When we get to Dodge City, we'll be our own bosses. We'll set ourselves up in a nice social club where we entertain our gentlemen and don't nobody own us." She didn't offer any means they possessed to accomplish that lavish plan.

Not one of the other three believed it could happen, but at that point, no one wanted to point it out to her. They had summoned the nerve to make their escape, so they had to believe something good would come of it.

Up ahead, the "innocent" cowboy was muttering under his breath about his natural tendency to find himself in the middle of somebody's problems. It reminded him that he had found himself in a similar situation with two whores on the way to Denver about a year before. That had turned into a gunfight before it was over. This time, there looked to be no problems beyond needing some horses. At least, there had been no mention of anything beyond that. He had to admit, however, that they had not had time to discuss their situation at any length.

After covering about ten miles, Perley decided it would be a good idea to rest the horses and stopped near a small stream that offered some grass as well as water.

Lucy strolled over to talk to him while he unloaded his horses. "Why are we stoppin' so soon?"

"Rest the horses," was his simple answer.

She nodded and thought about that for a moment. "We were drivin' our horse a lot farther than this before we met up with you, and that was just one horse pullin' the wagon."

"That so?" *Lucy*, he thought, recalling another girl named Lucy, a girl who once had him thinking he was in love. The trouble was so did every other bachelor back home in Paris. This Lucy was nowhere near the tease Lucy Tate was. He decided he liked this one a whole lot better. "Reckon you could go back to the creek and ask that horse how that worked out for him." When she shrugged as if indifferent, he asked, "Did you let him graze when you *did* stop?"

"We let him drink if there was water, but he had all night to graze when we stopped every night."

He didn't ask any more questions after that. He felt sorry for the old horse to have ended its days in the hands of the four women who obviously had no notion of how much rest and feed a horse pulling a wagon needed. At the same time, he couldn't really fault the women for their lack of horse sense. He suspected that the four sacks of seed corn were weighing more heavily on his mind than they were on his two packhorses, and that was the reason he couldn't feel more empathy for his new companions. He scolded himself for his attitude and decided he could be a more cheerful guide. None of the women but Lucy had shown even the slightest interest in what he carried in his packs, and she showed no more after he told her it was corn. He decided there was little need to worry about it, at least until they reached Dodge City.

When he deemed the horses had had enough rest, he loaded everybody up again and set out for the creek he had in mind for their stop that night.

CHAPTER 8

"Hey-yo the camp. Is that you, Blanche?"

Perley sat rigidly upright, almost spilling the coffee in his cup when he heard the deep voice calling from the darkness. He rolled out of the firelight and looked back at the four women, who were too shocked to move.

When none of the women answered, the voice came again. "I found your horse back yonder. Looks like you found yourself some help, but it wasn't such a good idea to take this little trip. It sure has cost me a lotta trouble."

Finally, Blanche found her voice. "You've got no business here, Jake. We don't work for you no more."

"Well, now, I reckon as how I see things a little different from you," Jake called back. "I spent a lotta money settin' you girls up in business and I ain't had much return on my investment. Tell you the truth, I wouldn't give a damn if it was just you that ran off, but you took three younger girls with you. Left me in a bind. So I've come to take my property back."

"We ain't your damn property!" Lucy yelled back.

"You didn't give us half of what you promised when you talked to us in Cheyenne."

"Sounds to me like you found some other sucker to take you in," Jake called out again. "Whoever you are, I don't expect those women told you they made a deal to work in my place. I'd best come on in and we'll talk this over."

"The hell you say!" Blanche responded. "You've got no business with us."

Caught completely by surprise, Perley could only listen in amazement. He realized he was involved in the trouble between the prostitutes and this Jake person who seemed to think he owned them. Cradling his rifle, Perley looked toward the fire and saw four anxious faces looking back at him. "All right," he answered. "You can come on in and we'll talk about it. You by yourself?"

"There's two of us," Jake called back.

"He's got Grady Short with him," Dolly whispered. "We're done for."

"He don't own us," Blanche complained to Perley. "He's got no right to stop us."

"Who's Grady Short?" Perley asked.

"He's a damn gunslinger that takes care of all of Jake's dirty business," Lucy answered. "Jake says he wants to talk, but he won't waste any time talkin'. I'm sorry we got you into this, Perley. I reckon the best thing you can do is just do whatever he says and maybe you won't get hurt."

"To hell with that!" Blanche growled. "He's gonna have to kill me. I ain't goin' back to that damn hog ranch."

Perley hesitated for a few moments, then decided

to try to settle the debate peacefully. "Come on in as long as you're peaceful," he yelled. Then back to the terrified women, he said, "We'll hear what he has to say. Maybe he'll listen to reason when you tell him what your complaints are."

Blanche glared at Perley, hopeless. "Perley Gates," she pronounced slowly. "You're a nice enough young man, but you ain't ever come up against the likes of Jake Barnes and Grady Short. They'll cut you to pieces. I'd advise you to run, but it's too late now," she said as the two men emerged from the darkness.

Perley stood up from the kneeling position he had taken when he heard the first shouts from Jake. He studied the two men as they approached the fire. There was no need for introductions, for it was easy to see which one was the gunslinger by the way he wore the cutaway holster low on his hip.

Jake wasted no time in addressing his problems. "Damn you, you old bitch," he started on Blanche. "You've cost me time and money. Did you think I wouldn't come after you?"

"This is my camp," Perley interrupted. "I thought you came to talk to *me*."

Jake cast a critical eye toward Perley, glaring at him for a long moment before asking, "Who the hell are you? These four women work for me. The best thing you can do is just keep your mouth shut and maybe you'll come outta this alive."

"Like I said, this is my camp and I invited you in to talk like civilized people, but it doesn't look to me like you're anything close to that. From what I've heard so far, it sounds like you think you own these ladies. Everybody knows that ain't true since the war some years back. It doesn't look like they wanna go back with you, so that pretty much ends the story, doesn't it?"

Jake and his partner were astonished by Perley's speech and swapped puzzled glances before Jake could summon words again.

"Mister, how the hell have you lived this long? What the hell is your name?"

"Don't say anymore, Perley," Blanche interrupted, feeling guilty for involving him. "You'll get hurt. Just let it be. This is between Jake and me. You shouldn't have even got mixed up in our problems."

"Perley?" Jake blurted. "Is that what she called you?"

"That's right. Perley Gates."

"Well, if that ain't—" Jake started, then both he and Grady Short burst into loud guffaws. "Perley Gates." He repeated it several times, laughing harder each time. "I swear, Blanche, you picked you a real stud horse to protect you this time." Turning back to Perley, he said, "I'll tell you what. I'm in a good mood tonight since I got my whores back, so if you pack up your possibles and ride on outta here, I'll let you go this time." He cocked his head in warning. "But don't ever cross my path again, or Grady, here, will write his initials across your chest with .44 slugs. You can take your packhorses, but leave the two you hitched to the wagon. I'm gonna need them. I'm pretty sure that's where Blanche got the horses, so to show you what a sport I am, I'll buy 'em from you. I'll give you twenty-five cents apiece for 'em. How's that? That's fair, ain't it? Twenty-five-cents and your life."

Perley waited patiently until Jake finished his rant before responding to the ultimatum. "The horses ain't for sale," he said calmly. "'Preciate the offer, though. Now I'd appreciate it if you and your friend would ride on back the way you came and leave us alone. The women don't wanna go with you, so I can't let you take them." He waited then, knowing what was coming, wishing that it wasn't, but knowing there was no choice.

"Mister," Jake fumed, "you're the dumbest jackass I've ever run into. You ain't leavin' me no choice. Cut him down," he yelled to Grady, reaching for his pistol as he said it.

Grady, anticipating the move, was fast enough to beat Jake to the draw, but his shot went into the ground at his feet when Perley's .44 slug split his chest. Stunned by the swift execution of his partner, Jake finished in third place when the second round from Perley's Colt doubled him over, gut-shot.

A stony silence fell over the creek following the sudden explosion of gunfire. Stunned immobile, by the unbelievable speed just witnessed, all four women could only stand and stare at the mild, unassuming young man.

Lucy uttered the first word after what seemed an eternity. "Damn!" That was all she could say.

Blanche, equally shocked, commented, "I think there's a lot more to Perley Gates than meets the eye. Here, I was afraid we were gonna hafta take care of you. You beat Grady Short," she said, as if he didn't realize what he had done. "Grady Short had a helluva reputation."

"Maybe so," Perley said at once, "but I don't want one. The less talk about what happened here, the better. I don't get any pleasure outta takin' a man's life, even one as bad as those two. I just wish they'd 'a talked it over with you women, but when he went for his gun, I didn't have any choice."

When the shock of the unexpected visit from Jake Barnes and Grady Short finally subsided, they were left with several somber decisions to be made. The unpleasant aspects of two bodies to dispose of would seemingly be left up to the man. At least, that was what Perley expected, but he was surprised to find all four women were more than willing to help put the two bodies in the ground.

In fact, Blanche, especially, seemed to be quite enthusiastic about it. When Dolly suggested dragging the bodies out of their camp and leaving them for the buzzards, Blanche insisted that she deserved the privilege of throwing a shovelful of dirt over Jake's face. "I figure I've got that comin' after all the hell I've put up with from him," she asserted.

Perley asked if there was anyone else involved in Jake's operation. She told him that Jake and Grady were the whole operation.

"Oh, there's two women still there that didn't wanna come with us," Blanche said. "I reckon it'll be up to them what they wanna do when they find out Jake ain't comin' back."

"Maybe you might wanna go back now," Perley suggested.

"Hell, no!" Grace responded before Blanche could. "That place is dead. There ain't nothin' there no more." The other three women promptly agreed.

"Well, you've picked up a couple of horses you didn't have before," Perley pointed out. "So I reckon you don't need mine anymore. And you've picked up some guns and ammunition, so you've got more than that one shotgun for protection."

"We've also got any money they're carryin'," Lucy declared. "It belongs to us, anyway 'cause every cent they've got came from what they made offa us." She made the statement even though she was uncertain whether Perley might claim some of the spoils since he'd done the actual shooting.

He staked no claims on any of their possessions. He had shot only to keep from being shot and he told them so. "After we bury 'em, I don't reckon you'll need me anymore. You've got your own horses and you ain't but a short day's drive from Dodge City." As soon as he said it, he saw concern on each of their faces.

Blanche confirmed it at once. "I ain't talked to the others about it, but I'd surely appreciate it if you'd ride along with us to Dodge City. I know you say we ain't far from there, but we wouldn't have been this far east if any of us had enough sense to know what direction we was drivin' in." The other three women were nodding their agreement, so she continued. "I know we're holdin' you up on your way to Texas, but we'd be glad to pay you a little for your trouble. Whaddaya say? It'll just set you back a day."

"Two days," Perley corrected her. He was thinking that he couldn't tell them he had avoided Dodge before because of his concern for what he was carrying in the sacks of corn on his packhorses. As he glanced from one of them to another, he saw a return of the childlike hopeful faces he had seen before. He wanted to say no and cursed himself for not being able to. "I'll ride with you to Dodge, but I won't take any money for it."

"I knew he wouldn't take any money," Dolly said, a wide grin adorning her ruddy face. "Angels ain't got no use for money."

"Angels don't go around shootin' people," Perley said, halfway convinced that the simple woman might be serious.

Grace got a lantern from the wagon and they walked down along the dark creek bank, looking for a spot where the ground might be a little easier to dig.

"Hand me that shovel and I'll get started," Perley said. He got a good start on a hole to bury the two victims in before Blanche insisted on taking over for a while.

Before the grave was deep and wide enough to hold both bodies, everyone had a chance to have a hand in it.

"That oughta do it," he decided and stepped up out of the rough hole. He waited then while the women stripped the two bodies of anything they could possibly find a use for. By the time they dragged them over to the grave, Jake and Grady were left to face their Maker in their underwear.

He was caught by surprise when Blanche suddenly started hiking her skirt up and he realized what the next part of the burial ceremony was going to be. "I reckon I'd best go check on my horses," he announced. He turned and walked down near the creek, only pausing to look after he was some distance away from the grave. "I reckon they really hated that man," he said to Buck as he watched their parting message to the departed.

In the glow of the lantern light, accompanied by a chorus of giggling, each one squatted on the edge of the grave to leave their final respects.

"I swear," Perley uttered. "I reckon we can cover them up now." He returned to the graveside when Blanche was already in the process of shoveling dirt on Jake Barnes's face.

It was virtually impossible for the women to get much sleep that night. Perley could hear them talking well into the wee hours. He finally picked up his bedroll and moved down the creek a few yards.

Up at daylight the next morning, he had a fire going and coffee working away before Lucy crawled out from under the wagon where she and Dolly had slept. Seeing that she was the first of the women to wake, she picked up the shovel and banged the side of the wagon with it. "Time to get up, lazybones!" Then she helped herself to a cup of coffee and sat down on the ground beside Perley. "What time do you think we'll get to Dodge City?"

"This afternoon," Perley answered, "dependin' on how soon we get started." He could see by her expression that she was giving the prospect serious thought, so he asked, "You ladies got any idea where you're gonna go in Dodge? You know anybody there?"

"We ain't got the first idea where we're gonna end up," she confessed. "None of us know anybody or anything about the town other than what we've heard. That it's a wide-open town."

"I was there a few weeks ago," Perley said. "Me and my brothers drove a herd of cattle through there and stopped for a couple of days on our way to Ogallala. And to tell you the truth, the crew said there wasn't no shortage of whores."

"I know," she said. "We've talked about that."

"Talked about what?" Blanche asked, having just returned from a trip to the bushes.

When Lucy told her, Blanche immediately responded. "We'll find us a spot to work out of," she said confidently. "Whatever it is, it'll be better 'n where we came from. Hell, if we have to, we'll work outta the wagon." She laughed and declared, "We could call it the Dodge City Hayride." She turned to Perley then. "Whaddaya think? Perley, you'd take a chance on a hayride, wouldn'tcha?" When he answered with no more than a shy grin, she chuckled delightedly. "I swear, Dolly might be right. Maybe you are a genuine angel. Most men would be wore out by now from takin' turns in the back of the wagon, especially if they didn't have to pay for it." Since the threat of pursuit by Jake Barnes was no longer an issue, she found herself in a much more playful mood, and Perley's obvious shyness around women made him the perfect target. "Ain't none of us got your blood stirred up yet?"

"Leave him alone, Blanche," Lucy scolded, noticing a slight blush creeping up from Perley's collar. "He's got his reasons. You keep pickin' at him and we'll be back tryin' to find Dodge City on our own again."

"I reckon I'd best go see to the horses if we're gonna get started anytime soon," Perley declared and got to his feet, ignoring the broad grin on Blanche's face.

Since they would make Dodge that afternoon, regardless of the time they started, he left it up to them to decide if they wanted to eat breakfast before starting or wait till they stopped to rest the horses. He was not surprised when they chose to eat first, so it was close to seven o'clock before they were all packed up and ready to roll.

Although he deemed it necessary to make a stop short of Dodge to keep the horses pulling the wagon fresh, they rolled into the town in the middle of the afternoon, just as he had promised. They were stopped almost immediately by a man wearing a badge as they passed the railroad station. Perley wasn't surprised. A wagon carrying four rather rough-looking women would catch the eye of a lawman.

"Afternoon," the lawman offered as he signaled Dolly to rein her horses to a halt. He waited then for Perley to dismount. "Where are you folks headed?"

He directed the question at Perley, but Blanche answered his question. "Nowhere. If this is Dodge City, we ain't goin' nowhere. We're here." She looked at Dolly beside her and they exchanged grins.

"New in town, huh?" He again addressed Perley. "There's some rules you need to know before you think about staying in this town, and if you don't obey 'em, I or one of my deputies will lock you up. Now, to start with, you're already looking at a jail cell for those weapons you're carrying." When Perley looked genuinely surprised, the lawman continued. "Since you say you're new in town, I'm gonna give you the benefit of the doubt. But if you're plannin' on staying here, you need to know there's a deadline that runs north of the railroad yards on Front Street. You are not allowed to wear or carry firearms north of that line. That's the commercial district, and I won't stand for any violence in that section." He glanced briefly at the four women staring at him. "There's plenty of saloons and brothels in the red-light district south of the deadline. I expect that's what you're looking for."

"And just who might you be?" Blanche enquired. "You the head of the welcomin' committee?"

"I'm Wyatt Earp, Chief Deputy Marshal," he said.

"Earp, huh?" Blanche grinned at Perley. "And you thought you had a funny name."

Perley quickly jumped in before she made any more smart remarks. "She don't mean no sass, Deputy, and I sure don't wanna break any rules."

Earp was in no mood for lip from a whore. He pointed toward a saloon south of the deadline. "Take your ladies down that way and stay out of trouble or I'll let you get acquainted with my jail. You obey my rules, and you'll get along just fine."

"I'll not trouble you a'tall, Deputy," Perley said. "I'll turn right around and head for Texas. I just led these women to Dodge. They were lost, so I brought 'em here. I'm sure they won't break any rules. They're just workin' ladies, tryin' to get ahead." He turned toward the wagon and said, "Good luck to you ladies. I hope you find what you're lookin' for. And you'd best behave yourselves. I believe this man means business."

"I'm gonna miss you, Perley," Lucy said. "I kinda liked havin' you around."

"I'm gonna miss you, too," Perley responded. "I'd

stick around to see how you ladies end up, but I expect the folks back home in Texas need my help. So take care of yourself and don't give the marshal here no trouble."

"It'll be hard to keep Blanche in line, but I'll try," Lucy said, then remembered. "What about your two horses? You have to wait till we get them unhitched."

"I'm gonna let you keep those two horses," Perley said. "Maybe you can sell 'em. You're gonna need a little startin'-up money." They had belonged to Billy Tuttle, anyway, and he was quite content to see the last of anything to remind him of Billy Tuttle.

They all said good-bye and thank you, and while Earp watched, Perley wheeled Buck and the pack-horses and headed south at a lope, anxious to leave Dodge City behind.

"What's his name?" Earp asked.

"Perley Gates," Lucy answered, "and he's the best man I've ever met."

"Perley Gates," Earp repeated. "Funny name." He turned and pointed toward the red-light district.

With no need for further directions, Dolly slapped the reins across the horses' rumps and the wagon jolted off toward their side of town.

"Wyatt Earp," Perley thought aloud. "Where have I heard that name?" He tried to recall, but gave it no more than a couple of minutes before he returned his thoughts to the trail ahead. He should have re-membered the rules about a deadline in the town, but he didn't. Maybe it was because he stayed with the cattle when they had stopped to rest the herd, but none of the men had mentioned it. Maybe this Earp fellow just got there.

Perley's chance meeting with the four prostitutes had delayed his journey at least two or three days. Maybe he should have sent another wire to Rubin when he was in Dodge City, but it hadn't occurred to him at the time. "Oh, well," he sighed to Buck. "We'll get there when we get there, long as we don't run into any more delays."

Buck whinnied, a response Perley thought appropriate. He had not let his horses rest before turning them around again, but the morning trip had not been that long. He figured he'd ride another ten miles before giving them a good rest. After that, he might try to put another twenty miles between himself and Dodge City. If his memory served him, he figured it to be around fifty or sixty miles from Dodge to the Oklahoma border. He'd know he was in Oklahoma when he struck the Cimarron River.

It felt good to be riding free and clear. He had run into more trouble on his journey to and from the Black Hills than any one man could expect. With nothing on his mind but to ride to Texas, he was determined to avoid any more towns unless he had to buy more supplies. Hopefully, he'd already had his share of trouble.

CHAPTER 9

After camping for the night at the Cimarron River, Perley packed up, saddled Buck, and with the packhorses, left the river, heading due south. His plan was to stop at a trading post sitting in the fork created by the confluence of the Beaver River and Kiowa Creek. It was owned by a man named Malcolm Drew. Perley remembered the store when on the cattle drive up through Oklahoma Territory in the past. He hadn't seen it on the drive just recently made that had ended with the search for his grandfather. They had driven the cattle over a little farther to the west than they normally did, but he assumed the trading post was still there.

From the Cimarron, it was a ride of no more than twelve or fifteen miles, so he had not ridden long when he saw the trees that bordered the Beaver River. And off to his left, he spotted a faint trace of smoke snaking its way up through the trees where he expected to find the store.

He guided Buck and the packhorses down through the trees that grew along the riverbank until stopping short when he neared the point where the creek joined the river. Immediately alert, he backed the bay gelding up to remain among the trees. The store was gone, replaced by a pile of burnt timbers, lying haphazardly around a stone fireplace and chimney. The smoke he had seen was still wafting up from some of the timbers, even though the fire had long since burnt out. Scanning up and down the river as far as he could see, he looked for signs of anyone, but saw no one. Still, he waited for a while, alert for any threat, until he decided no one was about. Then he nudged Buck, and the patient horse walked slowly down from the trees, and into the yard where Perley dismounted. *Indians?* he wondered. *Or maybe a lightning strike? Who could say?*

As he walked around the remains of the log structure, he confirmed that the fire in most of the timbers had gone out some time before his arrival. *I reckon Mr. Drew had some bad luck*, he thought as he approached what he guessed were the living quarters. He started to move on, but suddenly stopped when something caught his eye. He took a step back to be sure what he was looking at. Behind the chimney, underneath a half-burned ridge pole, he discovered a grisly scene. Two bodies, burned beyond recognition, were trapped side by side in the partial remains of a bed.

Mr. and Mrs. Malcolm Drew, I expect.

It must have been a lightning strike that killed them instantly, he figured, since they had not even had time to get out of bed. And the fire had gone out before it totally consumed the bodies.

"That's some bad luck," he murmured as he pulled

aside a piece of fallen rafter, held it for a few seconds before dropping it again, startled by what he discovered. Pieces of burned rope still bound the bodies to the bed frame. "Damn!" he gasped involuntarily. Drew and his wife had been murdered, tied to the bed and burned to death. Perley automatically brought his rifle up, ready to fire as he looked all around him, but there was still no sign of anyone. Yet, once again, he had a feeling that he was being watched. Another quick look around told him it was his imagination.

More attentive to any signs that could tell him more of the tragic story, he studied the tracks of horses and boot heels—enough to tell him there had been several horses, so that meant more than one assailant, no doubt with robbery as their incentive. A small barn had been left untouched and the gate to the corral was standing open.

This was bad business. Why couldn't they just have robbed the couple and left them alive?

He looked again at the bodies and decided the killing was not done by Indians. Even though the hair was burned off, there were no signs of a scalping knife. Also, he saw enough boot prints to indicate white men were recently there.

Perley felt sure the murderers who had done this evil thing were no longer anywhere around. He felt a Christian obligation to remove the bodies from the wreckage and give them a decent burial.

Since that was going to take some time, he first unsaddled Buck and relieved the packhorses of their burdens. "It ain't my idea of a pleasant place to camp," he said to Buck as he pulled the saddle off, "but it's the right thing to do." He looked in the barn and was pleased to find a shovel, since the only tool he carried that he could dig with was his knife. "We'll put 'em to rest up there on the bank," he said to Buck, who responded with nothing more than a curious eye. "But not too near those big cottonwoods. No sense in havin' to fight any big roots."

The spot he picked for the grave turned out to be a good choice because the ground was not overly hard. He decided on one big grave, thinking the man and his wife would want it that way. The digging was the easy part; moving the bodies out of the house was the unpleasant part of the job. When first he tried to pull one of the bodies from the house, it began to pull apart and he was afraid the legs were going to separate from the pelvis. He remembered seeing a piece of canvas in the barn, so he got that and rolled a body onto it, then dragged it to the grave site and rolled it into the grave. That worked pretty well, so he repeated the procedure on the second body. That worked well, too, except when he rolled it off the canvas, it landed facedown in the grave.

"Damn," he muttered.

They were supposed to lie side by side, and there was no room for him to get down in the grave to turn the body right side up. It was obviously the wife's body that had landed wrong. Since it was smaller than the other one, he was able to shift it around with the shovel until she was on her side, although with her back toward her husband.

"That'll have to do," Perley decided. He suddenly had another feeling that he was being watched. He looked around him again, but there was no one there. "Nobody'll know she's got her back to him," he said, thinking the corpses were far past caring. He spread the piece of canvas over them, then began shoveling the dirt back in, stopping once to pick up his rifle when Buck whinnied and snorted.

But, as before, there was no sign of anyone, so he continued until he finished filling the grave.

Ordinarily, he might have decided to cook himself some breakfast before he got his horses ready to travel again, but after having dealt with the two burned bodies, he was not in the mood for any bacon fried in the pan. In fact, the thought of it made him feel a little queasy. Deciding to crank up his coffeepot anyway, he built a fire with some small half-burned pieces of shingles then went down to the river to fill the pot. Again, he experienced the feeling that he was being watched. He recalled the day he'd had the same feeling and turned to find a rabbit watching him. He chuckled to remember the rabbit had ended up as supper and minutes later Lucy Butcher had showed up.

With his coffeepot full of water, he had turned to take it back up the bank when he experienced a distinct feeling that something was watching his every move. He sensed that it came from a gully half covered by a berry bush near the top of the bank. Rabbit, maybe, or muskrat. He couldn't be sure, but he was convinced something was in that gully, watching him.

He pretended not to notice the gully and started up the bank, aware of a slight rustling of the bush when he became level with it. Figuring he wouldn't get but one chance before the critter took off for the water, he slowly drew his pistol, ready to fire, and stopped beside the bush. A slight tremble occurred in the leaves of the bush, but he could not see into the gully beneath it. It dawned on him that it might be a bigger critter than a rabbit, and that maybe he might better be thinking about avoiding wrestling with a bobcat. Too curious at that point to leave the critter alone, he parted the branches of the bush with the barrel of his .44 to reveal a small boy huddled as far back in the gully as he could get.

"My God in heaven . . ." He exhaled.

Stunned, both man and boy continued to stare at each other, speechless for several long moments.

Although it was obvious to him, Perley finally asked, "Was that your mama and papa I just buried?"

There was no reply to his question. The terrified boy just continued to stare, his eyes wide with fright.

"It's all right, boy," Perley said, speaking as calmly as he could. "I ain't gonna do you no harm. You can come outta your hidin' spot now. Whoever did this is gone."

Still the boy crouched hard against the side of the gully.

After a moment, Perley tried again. "My name's Perley Gates. What's yours?"

Still no response beyond the boy's wide-eyed look of fear. Perley decided the boy was undoubtedly still in a state of shock, most likely from having seen his parents murdered. He was going to have to give him more time, but it would probably speed the process up if he could get him out of the gully.

"I'm fixin' to make some coffee and I always carry an extra cup just in case I have somebody to share it with. How 'bout it? You want some coffee?"

Again there was no sound out of the boy's mouth, but he saw a slight lowering of the child's chin, which he decided to take as a possible nod. "Maybe I can find you something to eat, too. You look like you ain't et in a while. Maybe I oughta fry up some bacon to go with the coffee. Whaddaya say?" With still no verbal response, Perley got to his feet. "I'll be over by the fire. You come on out when you feel like it."

He turned and walked back up the bank to his fire, which was showing a healthy blaze by then. He had lost his appetite for fried bacon after seeing the charred bodies of the boy's parents, but bacon was the quickest food he could fix for the boy. He got what was left from the side of bacon he had bought in Deadwood and sliced off some strips to fry. While it was frying, he went to his packs and got a plate and some hardtack to warm in the bacon grease then knelt beside the fire to tend the cooking. He turned partially away from the river, pretending to pay no attention, but he was able to watch the gully out of the corner of his eye.

In a little while, the coffee was ready and Perley made a big show of pouring a cup for himself, smacking his lips after taking the first sip. It seemed to make no impression on the boy hiding in the gully. Perley began to think he was going to have to drag the boy out of his hole. Just before he started to do just that, there was a definite rustle in the leaves of the berry bush.

Moments later, the boy crawled out of the gully, but stood by it, watching Perley, much like a stray dog or a wolf lurking around a buffalo hunter's camp.

Perley picked up his extra cup and held it up so the boy could see him fill it. "Get it while it's hot," he sang out.

There was still a moment of hesitation on the boy's part, but he finally came up from the riverbank and picked up the cup of coffee Perley had set on a piece of board.

"I'll have you some bacon in a minute." As soon as the meat was done, he put it on the plate, then soaked up most of the grease left in the pan with the hardtack, and handed it to the boy.

There was no hesitation then. Like he was afraid someone might take it away from him, the boy downed the bacon and hardtack almost without chewing.

Perley watched, amazed. "How long have you been hidin' in that gully?"

The boy just shook his head and continued eating. Perley guessed it must have been at least two days. They continued sitting in silence until the boy finished all the bacon and hardtack Perley had cooked. The terrified look had left the boy's eyes finally, replaced by a mournful gaze.

"I know it's mighty hard to wrap your head around something like you've just seen, but you've got to let that picture go. My name's Perley Gates. What's yours?"

The boy shook his head as if he couldn't remember.

"Are you Malcolm Drew's son?"

"Yes," the boy replied so quietly that Perley almost missed it.

"Good. I was afraid you couldn't talk, and I ain't so good at talkin' with my hands, like a lotta those deaf folks do. What's your name?"

"Lincoln," the boy answered.

"They call you Link, I reckon."

"Yes, sir," he answered with a little more strength.

"All right, Link, I expect we'd best decide what we're gonna do. You got any kin anywhere around here?"

When Link said that there were none he knew of, Perley asked if he knew of any kin anywhere, east or west, but Link gave him the same answer.

"Do you know the men who killed your mama and papa? You ever see 'em before?"

Link shook his head in response to both questions. Perley continued to press him until Link finally recovered enough to paint the whole picture for him. It was a grim picture, indeed.

Two days before, a gang had ridden into the yard a little before dark. When Perley asked how many, Link told him there were four men and one woman, but the woman rode and acted more like a man. He said he overheard his father tell his mother he didn't like the look of them, and he hoped they would do their business and move on. They wanted whiskey and Link's father told them he couldn't sell whiskey in Indian Territory. That made the men mad and they started tearing up the place, looking for whiskey.

"Papa told them to get out of his store, but they only laughed at him. Mama told me to go hide in the barn till they left."

While he was hiding behind some hay bales, he heard the gunshots from the house, accompanied by a chorus of wild laughter and shouting. When two of the men came outside and opened the gate to the corral, Link knew they would be in the barn next, so he wiggled through a hole in the back wall of the barn and ran down the riverbank. He hid in the gully while the gang stomped through the store and the house behind it, yelling and shooting their guns. He knew his mother and father were dead. His father would have fought to protect his wife and home.

"There were just too many of them," Link sobbed. "I shoulda helped my pa fight 'em."

"Your pa wouldn't have wanted that," Perley said. "You did the right thing when you stayed hid. Did you hear any of their names?"

Link shook his head, then said, "One, I heard somebody keep yellin' Brice, but that's the only one."

It was only after the gang took everything they wanted, including Malcolm Drew's horses, that Link heard them get on their horses and leave. He was aware that they had set the store on fire when the whole yard lit up with the flames. Afraid to leave his hiding place, he nevertheless ran to the house to find his parents. With the walls already being eaten up by the fire, he ran down the smoke-filled hall to his parents' bedroom. The horrifying sight that met his eyes was enough to send him screaming in shock. He tried to get to them, but he couldn't endure the intense heat, and he was finally forced to retreat to the yard. Unable to cope with the horrible scene he had witnessed, the only thing he could think of was to crawl back into the gully that had hidden him before.

Perley could not imagine a more terrifying scene to confront a young boy. When asked his age, Link said he was nine. He was four when his father built the trading post in Indian Territory, and he knew that they had come from somewhere in Missouri. Of the troubles Perley had encountered during the last year, this might prove to be the most perplexing—being charged with the care of a nine-year-old orphan. What was he to do with the boy? He had no ready answers for the question, but he knew for the time being, he had no choice other than to take him along. Further questioning only confirmed what Link had originally told him—he didn't know of any relatives and the only home he knew was now a pile of burnt timbers.

"Well," Perley concluded, "I reckon you're gonna go to Texas with me." With no sign in the boy's face showing feelings one way or the other about that prospect, Perley tried to paint a better picture for him. "You'll be right at home on the Triple-G. Fred Farmer's son works on the ranch. He's thirteen. My brother, Rubin, has two boys, one's six, the other one's eight, if I remember correctly. You'll fit right in." He paused for some kind of response, but all he got was the same baleful stare.

Reckon he just needs a little time.

They remained near the creek for the rest of that day before starting out early the next morning to strike the Canadian River. Perley planned to follow the Canadian down through Indian Territory until it reached a point where it turned in a more easterly direction and headed toward Arkansas. He would leave it to continue riding due south to Texas.

He transferred some of his packs from his grandfather's horse and let Link ride the paint gelding. The boy seemed quite at home on the horse's back, even without a saddle. Perley couldn't help wondering if Link would complain if he was in pain, for he never said a word unless he was asked something.

The first night after leaving the remains of the trading post, Perley heard Link quietly crying, but by the time they struck the Canadian, he seemed at peace, content to follow Perley to Texas. The brutal murder of the boy's parents by the gang of ruthless outlaws continued to trouble Perley as they followed the Canadian on its southern course. The outlaws should be punished for their evil work back at the fork of the Beaver River and Kiowa Creek, but he felt helpless to do anything about it. He had no idea where the gang was heading, only that they appeared to have ridden out on the same trail he was following. He thought to inform the Indian police of the slaughter, but didn't know where to find them. At that point, he was not certain that he was even in one of the five nations. He might still be in Osage Territory, where there were no established Indian police.

Four men and one woman, the boy had said, and all of them vicious cutthroats. Perley wasn't sure he could do much against those odds. Nothing to do but continue on his way home and take the boy with him. He imagined the response he might get when he rode into the Triple-G, bringing a young boy to raise. *It worked out all right for Sonny.* The young man had wandered onto the Triple-G when only a few years older than Link. Nathaniel Gates, Perley's father, had taken the stray in and made a ranch hand out of him. All the hands had had a part in raising Sonny, not just the family. *Maybe it'll work that way for Link.*

The tracks left by the outlaws entered the river after the second day of following them. Perley could see the tracks on the opposite bank where they came out. He figured it just as well. It was best for Link not to be reminded of them day in and day out.

Two days later, they were awakened by a small herd of deer crossing the river about thirty yards from where they'd made their beds. Perley was quick enough with his rifle to get a shot at a young doe, and the rest of that morning was spent butchering and feasting on fresh venison. It delayed the trip, but it seemed to cheer his orphan up a bit.

Riding on, Perley changed his course a little more to the southeast and headed toward Atoka in the Choctaw Nation. Up till then, he had made it a point to avoid towns of any size, still concerned about the sacks of corn he carried. That had not been difficult since there were no towns to speak of along the way they had come. However, the nights were getting a little colder with the arrival of autumn, and Link had no clothes other than the shirt and trousers he'd been wearing when his parents were killed. Perley knew there was a store in Atoka that sold clothes, so he'd decided they would go there and buy a coat for Link.

It was approaching the supper hour when they rode down the street in Atoka, past the railroad depot, heading for the general merchandise store.

"Evening," Tom Brant greeted them cheerfully when they walked in the door. "What can I help you with?"

"This young fellow needs a jacket," Perley replied. "Think you might have something to fit him?"

Brant looked the small boy up and down. "I might," he decided. "My wife knows more about the clothes." He called out, "Eva."

In a few seconds, a pleasant-looking woman appeared in the doorway from another room.

"Hon," Brant said, "this young gentleman is looking

for a jacket. You got anything in that closet that might fit him?"

Eva smiled as she gazed at Link. "I think so. We don't sell many children's clothes, but we have a few that might do the job if you ain't too particular." She led Link through the door she had just come from.

While Perley waited, Brant struck up a conversation with him. "I'm tryin' to remember when you were in here. It was a little while back, but you came in asking about somebody you were lookin' for."

"My grandpa," Perley said. "Perley Gates."

"That's right," Brant responded, remembering then. "I didn't think I'd forget the name. Did you ever find him?"

"Yes, sir, I did."

"I don't reckon that's him you're buying a jacket for, is it?" Brant joked.

"No, sir, my grandpa's dead."

"Oh," Brant reacted, and the broad grin disappeared from his face. "I'm right sorry to hear that. No offense."

"None taken," Perley replied.

A few minutes later, he and Link walked out of the store with Link sporting a new wool pullover sweater, his choice over a wool sack jacket, which was a bit too large.

Now that the boy had a sweater to keep him warm, Perley decided it would be a good idea to buy him a good supper, since they had lived off practically nothing but venison and coffee for the past few days. He remembered the one time he had been in Atoka before and had eaten at Mabre's, next to the hotel. The food had been good, so he was happy to try it again. In fact, he had promised Lottie Mabre that he would be back if ever in Atoka again. "Reckon you could eat some supper?" he asked Link.

"I reckon," the boy answered eagerly.

Perley rode up the street toward the hotel and reined up before the small building next to it with the sign proclaiming it to be MABRE'S DINER. Looking right and left, he saw very little activity on the quiet street, so he figured his packhorses were safe enough. Before going inside, he asked Link, "Can you read?"

Link nodded.

Perley continued. "Tell me what that sign says."

Link studied it for a moment, uncertain of the pronunciation. "It's says it's a diner. May-bers or something."

"May-*bree's* Diner," Perley sounded out, hoping Link might justify the embarrassing mistake he had made when he was here before. He had thought the sign said *Mable's* Diner and made a fool of himself when he thought Lottie Mabre's name was Mable. He hoped she might not remember the incident.

"Well, look who's back!" Lottie exclaimed when Perley walked in, followed by Link. "Mr. Gates, if I remember correctly.

Perley nodded with a polite smile.

"Mable ain't here, if that's who you're lookin' for." She chuckled heartily in appreciation for her humor.

Perley felt himself cringing.

"Who's this you got with you?" Lottie went on. "Is this your son?"

"Nope," Perley answered, ignoring her attempt at humor. "This is my partner, Link Drew, and I told him he could find some good chuck in here."

"Well, we'll try not to disappoint you, Link," Lottie said. "Why don't you and Mr. Gates set yourselves down at that end of the table and we'll get you started." Like Tom Brant, Lottie remembered that he had been looking for his grandfather when he had been there before, and asked if he had found him.

"Yes, ma'am, I found him," Perley answered and left it at that.

The supper was not a disappointment and the enthusiasm with which young Link attacked it was appreciated by Lottie. It was reassuring to Perley as well, for it appeared that, day by day, Link was recovering from the horror of witnessing his parents' murder. *The boy's going to be all right,* Perley thought, as he watched Link finish off a slice of pie. It was a thought that lasted only until they said good-bye to Lottie and left the diner.

"Come on and I'll give you a lift up," Perley said as he untied the horses from the rail, but Link didn't respond. Perley looked behind him to see why the boy hadn't hurried to be lifted up on his horse. He found Link standing rigidly, as if in shock, staring at a group of riders slow-walking their horses down the middle of the street. Perley was immediately alert. He counted the riders, five men, he thought at first, then decided that one of them was a woman, a heavyset brute of a woman. He knew at once they were the party who had murdered Link's parents.

What to do about it? He wasn't sure, but something had to be done. They were casually riding down the street, obviously looking the town over. Before taking any action, he thought to reassure the boy. "Link, I know who they are. Don't worry, I'm not gonna let them get near you." When no response came from the boy, Perley placed his hand on Link's shoulder.

Link jumped as if he had been shot.

Perley assured him. "Link, they're not gonna hurt you. We'll take care of 'em, but I've gotta see if we can get some help." He looped the horses' reins back over the hitching rail, grabbed Link by the hand, and pulled him back into the diner. Lottie and her cook were in the process of cleaning off the table, and they immediately saw the urgency in Perley's face.

"Is there any law in this town?" he asked frantically. "A sheriff or a marshal?"

Responding immediately, Lottie exclaimed, "There's a Choctaw policeman. That's all. What's wrong?" She looked at Link, who was obviously frightened, his eyes wide open in shock.

Perley didn't answer for a moment, trying to determine what options were available to him. A Choctaw policeman had no jurisdiction over white men. He would have to telegraph Fort Smith to get a deputy marshal and a posse sent to handle the problem, and there was no time for that. Something had to be done right now. Lottie pressed him for information.

"This whole town might be in trouble," Perley said, "and I'm trying to figure out what to do about it." When she was about to demand more information, he told her that the gang who had killed Link's parents and burned down their store were checking out her town.

"Oh, my Lord in heaven!" Lottie exclaimed. "Are you sure?"

"Pretty much," Perley replied as he watched the

riders out the window of the diner. "At least I'm sure it's the same bunch that killed his folks. He got a good look at 'em—too good a look, I'm afraid. I don't know what they've got in mind. Maybe nothin', maybe they're just needin' supplies. They pulled up at the general store."

"If they're lookin' for whiskey, they ain't gonna find any," Lottie said. "Tom ain't got any for sale. It's against the law in the Nations."

Another possibility occurred to Perley when he glanced at the railroad tracks. "What about the train? Is there one this evenin'?"

"Every evening," Lottie answered. "Usually about an hour from now."

"Does it usually stop in Atoka?"

"Most of the time," Lottie said. "Just long enough to drop off the mail or take on passengers."

"That just might be what those outlaws are thinkin'," Perley said. *And if they knew what I'm carrying in those canvas bags, they'll be after me,* he thought. *What the hell to do?* "We need to alert the other folks in town. Maybe we can get up a posse to stop 'em and hold 'em till they can get some marshals over here. We're gonna need some more help. There's five of 'em. One of 'em is a woman, but I'm countin' her as a man. Who can we count on for help? We have to let them know what's happenin'."

Lottie had to think for a few moments. "I'd say my husband, but he's not here. He's gone deer huntin' over in the Jack Fork Mountains." She paused again before continuing. "Well, there's Stanley Coons at the stable, and Garland Wilson, the blacksmith. That's two who can handle a gun, and there's Tom Brant."

"I reckon we can't count on him, since the outlaws are in his store right now. So that makes three of us." Perley still had not decided what to do, since the outlaws had not made any move to show their hand. As yet, he had no reason to believe they planned to harm anyone. They may have stopped to buy some supplies then planned to ride on out of town, but he didn't really believe that to be the case. The party of outlaws had already shown a pattern of plunder and murder, and if that's what they had in mind for Atoka, the whole town could suffer.

Finally, he decided. "Most likely this bunch is plannin' to rob the train. We need to get our guns and set up a welcomin' committee for 'em at the depot. Is anybody there now?"

"Elvis Farrier," Lottie answered. "He's the station-master and telegraph operator."

"Good," Perley said. "That gives us four. We oughta be able to handle the five of 'em if we get the jump on 'em before they know we're on to 'em."

Lottie had no objections or suggestions to add to the plan other than to ask, "What if they don't try to rob the train?"

"Then I reckon all this will be for nothin', and they'll ride on out of town and leave us lookin' silly, standin' at the depot. Unless they hold up Brant's store. Then I guess we'd have to be ready to help him. We need to stop 'em before they ride outta town, even if they don't do anything here. They killed Link's folks and burned his home to the ground." Perley shrugged, not able to think of any better plan.

Since it was less than an hour till the train was scheduled, Peggy, Lottie's cook, volunteered to take the message to Coons and the blacksmith, and tell them to meet Perley at the depot. She figured she wouldn't attract the outlaws' attention. The remaining concerns for Perley were Link and his seed corn, neither of which he could afford to lose.

Lottie offered to keep the boy with her. "And if you're worried about your horses, you're welcome to put them in the corral behind the hotel. My husband owns the hotel."

It was still a risk, as far as Perley was concerned, but it was a small risk.

She put her arm around Link and said, "Don't you worry, son. Ol' Lottie's gonna make sure you're safe."

Elvis Farrier looked up from his desk when Perley appeared at the window. "Can I help you with something?" He got up from the desk and walked to the window, preparing to take the message for a telegram.

Perley's first thought was that he might have been premature in counting Farrier as one of his vigilantes. The man was small in stature, and to make matters worse, was obviously crippled in one arm. *What the hell . . .* , he thought. To Farrier, he said, "Yes, sir, you can let me in. I'm thinkin' you're about to get robbed." Had he thought a moment before announcing it, he might have worded it differently.

The unimpressive little man reached under the counter with his good arm and came out with an army model Colt .45, which he stuck in Perley's face and cocked the hammer back.

"Hold on!" Perley blurted. "Not by me! I came to warn you!"

Farrier paused, but continued to hold the cocked pistol in Perley's face while he hurriedly told him of the impending danger to his train. "Peggy, over at the diner, is on her way right now to tell Stanley Coons and Garland Wilson to meet us here to make sure you don't get robbed.

Farrier considered the story for a long moment before finally lowering his weapon and releasing the hammer.

"I don't know for a fact that that's what they have in mind, but it's a good bet, just in case they do. And I know for sure that they murdered a man and his wife and burned their house down."

At last convinced that Perley was not making up a wild tale, Farrier stepped over and unlocked the door. Perley promptly changed his initial evaluation of the man's ability.

CHAPTER 10

"I'm not allowed to sell whiskey, even if I had some, which I don't," Tom Brant insisted. "You ain't supposed to sell it anywhere in the Nations. You fellows oughta know that." He glanced nervously at the somber man's companions, who were wandering about his store, aimlessly looking at things on the shelves, seeming to want to touch everything. One of them, a tall, stringy man, wearing a brown fedora, was behind the counter, fondling some brass belt buckles. Brant wanted to tell them to keep their hands off the merchandise, but he was afraid to. They were an evil-looking lot.

"Hey Brice," the tall man behind the counter blurted. "Look at this." He held up a fancy belt with a bull's-eye engraved on the buckle. "This is what you need. Give the marshals somethin' to aim at."

The man at the counter, talking to Brant, looked at him and grunted. "It'd look better on you, Shorty. Why don't you put it on, so we can see how good it works?" He returned his attention to Brant. "I know you ain't supposed to sell no whiskey, but I know damn well you've got some in this place somewhere that you sell to white folks. So suppose you fetch me a couple of bottles and quit wastin' my time."

"I swear, mister, I don't have any whiskey anywhere on the place," Brant said. "If I did, I'd surely sell it to you."

"Why, you lyin' son of a bitch," Brice growled and drew a long skinning knife from his belt. "I'm gonna cut you some new airholes in your throat." He grabbed Brant by the collar and pulled him halfway across the counter. About to slice Brant's throat, he hesitated when they suddenly heard a train whistle.

"Leave him be, Brice," Clementine Cobb said. "The train's comin' in, and we need to get up there to the depot." Stoic and gruff as a bear, the sullen woman had stood, silently watching the men. Apparently, she had no interest in the storekeeper's wares. "I believe he's tellin' the truth. You can come back and hassle him all you want after we meet the train." She turned and started for the door. When one of the others lingered over a barrel filled with dried apples, she snapped, "Get your sorry ass movin', Junior!" The lumbering brute grabbed a handful of dried apples and hurried out the door.

Tom Brant breathed a sigh of relief, happy to see them go. He rubbed his neck, not sure if Brice really would have cut his throat. His wife joined him now that the ruffians had gone. She was still holding the shotgun she had prayed she wouldn't have to use. They watched from the window as the outlaws crossed the street to the railroad depot.

"They're nothing but a bunch of animals," Eva said. She was especially shocked by the woman with them. "She looks older than the men, and just as rough as they are."

"You've got that right," Brant said, still gaping at the solid-looking woman dressed in men's trousers and boots, her hair pulled up under a gray Montana Peak hat. She wore a Colt .44 on her hip, and judging by the response of the four men, she was the boss. "They're fixing to make some trouble for somebody. She told the one about to slit my throat to stop, because they had to go to the train depot."

"You reckon they're thinking about robbing the MKT?" Eva asked. "Maybe we oughta try to warn Elvis!"

"Wouldn't surprise me none," Brant replied, "but there ain't any way to warn him. They're already at the depot." His main worry at the moment was what might happen after they robbed the train, if that's what they intended to do. The dour woman giving the orders indicated that Brice could come back and slit his throat after their business at the depot was finished. "I'm gonna lock up and stay right behind the counter and shoot the first one that tries to break in."

"I'm gonna stay with you," Eva said. "They're not taking our store without walking over our dead bodies." They exchanged expressions of determination. "I just wish Jim Little Eagle was here." The Choctaw policeman had gone to Muskogee that very morning. He held no jurisdiction over non-Choctaw outlaws, but he would have helped in a situation such as this.

* * *

Having answered the summons delivered by Peggy short minutes before, Stanley Coons hurried up the steps at the depot, where he found Garland Wilson huddled with Perley and Elvis.

"They're comin' this way!" Garland Wilson announced from his position just inside the door to the storeroom seconds after Coons walked in. "There's a big ol' horse-faced woman in the lead. Damned if she don't look scarier than the men, except maybe that big ox eatin' some plums or something."

Wilson's description of the gang they were set to apprehend did very little to boost the courage of the newly formed vigilantes. Standing behind him, they checked their weapons again.

"All right," Elvis Farrier said. "I'm gonna run back to the office and wait for them. We don't wanna go off half-cocked, so don't nobody do anything until we know for sure they've got robbery in mind. As soon as I know, I'll fire a shot."

Perley was quick to remind them that they had a duty to capture the gang whether they robbed the train or not. "This bunch has already murdered the mother and father of a nine-year-old boy that's over in the diner with Lottie. They burned his folks up in their store." His last words were followed by another blast of the train's whistle as it slowed for the station.

A few minutes later, Brice Cobb rapped on the window of the telegraph office. Elvis opened the small half-window and asked as calmly as he could affect, his good hand under the counter, resting on his revolver. "Can I help you, sir?"

"That train's fixin' to stop, ain't it?" Brice asked. "Do you need to get out here and flag it down?"

"No, sir. It'll stop. They have to pick up the mail." Elvis could see the other rough-looking men standing behind Brice and wondered if Perley hadn't gotten the men of Atoka into something that would turn out decidedly bad for them. He was thinking that maybe he should have signaled the train to keep moving.

The fact that the woman and the three other men were standing together on the platform behind Brice puzzled Perley. He would have thought if they were planning to take control of the train, they would have better positioned themselves to do so. Once the train stopped, they were going to have to move very quickly to cover the engine and the baggage car door. It wasn't a very professional job. He turned to look at the two men standing in the stockroom with him. The blacksmith was standing calm and ready. Stanley Coons was sweating profusely, in spite of the chilly day. Perley looked through the crack in the partially closed door of the storeroom, wondering if Elvis was sweating like Coons.

At that moment, it dawned on him that he had found himself in another of the awkward situations his brothers japed him about.

As the train pulled into the station and stopped, there was still no signal from Elvis. Perley was afraid the whole operation was going to fail. He was not about to let the killers of Link's parents simply walk away. Why didn't Elvis signal? The train was stopped, still the five outlaws were standing on the platform. On a sudden impulse, he pushed the door open and stepped out on the platform, ready to react. The party of outlaws paid him no mind as they peered at the slowly braking train.

Perley was still trying to decide what to do when Clementine Cobb cried out, "There he is!"

They all turned, including Perley, to see an old man getting off the train, three cars back. All five outlaws rushed down the tracks to meet him. Stanley Coons, already tense with uncertainty, accidentally pulled the trigger on his Henry rifle. The shot was wild, ricocheting off the side of a passenger car, but it triggered a chain reaction that sent everybody diving for cover. One of the gunmen, a willowy young man with coal black hair and mustache, wearing a quick-draw holster, spun around and fired three quick shots at the telegraph office in return. They were followed by a hail of gunshots from the outlaws, which forced Coons and Wilson to dive back into the storeroom at once. With no place to run, Perley rolled off the three-foot platform and used it for protection. *This ain't working out worth a damn,* he thought while several shots sent chunks of wood flying from the heavy platform planks.

With all the shots fired back and forth, it seemed a miracle that no one was hit in the confusion, until the old man slowly dropped to his knees.

"Papa!" Clementine Cobb cried out and ran to catch him before he fell over. Coon's accidental ricochet off the train car had caught the old man in the side.

"Kill 'em, damn it," she commanded. "Kill every one of 'em!"

The shooting increased in intensity in response, spraying the telegraph office wall and the open door of the storeroom with flying lead. There was no return fire from the storeroom, causing Perley to worry that Coons and Wilson had been hit. His concern was wasted, for both had squeezed through the small window in the back of the storeroom and retreated to the closest place of safety—which happened to be across the street in Brant's store.

Perley turned his attention to the telegraph office and Elvis Farrier's fate. Elvis had either caught a stray bullet or was hunkered down behind a desk in the office. At any rate, no gunfire was coming from the window. Perley, alone, was the only vigilante left to fight the outlaws, and his position under the edge of the platform was not a good one. He had to raise up to shoot, then quickly drop down again to keep from being hit. He had very little time to zero in on a target in the brief time his head was above the platform. And with no more shots coming their way, the outlaws were all focusing on his position at the edge of the platform. Like target shooting at a carnival, they waited for his head to pop up to see who could hit it. Perley knew it was only a matter of time before one of them won the prize. He looked around him, searching for an escape route, and the only thing that presented itself was to crawl under the platform. Maybe he could crawl until he was even with the train engine. Then maybe he could crawl out and make a dash to get on the other side of the train. He didn't hesitate to think it over. With no other choice, he turned around and started crawling as fast as he could.

Since it was dark under the platform, he had to guess when he had reached the telegraph office. It was easy to determine, however, when he saw a dark square extending down from the platform. Starting to crawl around it, he realized it was a trapdoor hanging open from the office above his head. *Well, I'll be gone to hell*, he thought. *It's an escape hatch in case there is a robbery*. He quit worrying about Elvis after that. Even in the dull light under the platform, he could readily see evidence of Elvis' exit. He followed, crawling even faster, his plan still to cross over the tracks and use the train for cover.

Finally, he came even with the engine and crawled over to the edge of the platform. As far as he could tell, the five outlaws were still near the back of the train. He crawled out from under the platform and sprinted across in front of the engine. With the train to provide cover between him and the shooters, he started trotting toward the rear of the train, planning to get behind the outlaws. If he could get the drop on them from behind, there was a chance he could force them to throw down their guns.

Behind the tender filled with wood, the engineer and his fireman were huddled in the cab of the train for protection. They had ducked down when the shooting started, but now that it had stopped, they weren't sure what to do.

The fireman peeped over the window of the cab in time to glimpse Perley run across the track. "They're gettin' on the other side of the train," he whispered loudly. "They're plannin' on comin' on board!"

"I'll be damned," the engineer swore. "Let's get the hell outta here." He reached up and threw the throttle forward.

With no more return fire from the station or the storeroom, Brice Cobb and his aunt Clementine figured they had won the day. They started toward the station platform with Junior and Shorty carrying Clementine's wounded father when the train started rolling.

"Keep a sharp eye," Brice warned. "In case they're playin' possum."

"Brice!" Slick Dorsey exclaimed in a whisper and pointed toward the wheels of the train.

Brice looked where he pointed and saw the legs of a man running toward the end of the train.

"You go on," Slick said. "I'll wait and give the son of a bitch a little surprise." He grinned at Brice and Brice nodded, knowing how much enjoyment the perverted gunman got from sending someone to hell.

As the train began to build up speed, Perley stopped, unaware that he had been seen, and thinking that all five of the outlaws were on their way to the telegraph office. On the opposite side of the train, Slick positioned himself to be ready and gleefully waited to surprise him. When the caboose finally rattled from between them, the two men suddenly found themselves facing each other across the railroad tracks. Both reacted instantly. Slick doubled over from the impact of Perley's .44 slug in his gut, a split second before he fired a wild shot in reaction. With his face a horrified mask of disbelief, he took a few steps backward before collapsing.

Perley turned at once toward the man's friends, but they had already gained the protection of the telegraph office after the oversized halfwit called Junior kicked the door open.

"He got Slick!" Shorty Hicks exclaimed in disbelief. "He's faster 'n Slick!"

"Nobody's faster 'n Slick," Junior insisted. "Slick musta not saw him."

"You damn ninny," Shorty insisted. "Slick was waitin' for him. Who is that feller?"

"Damn it, Shorty!" Clementine roared. "Shoot the son of a bitch!" She was concerned about her father and had no patience to waste on a man they had outnumbered four to one. "I need to find a doctor, if there's one in this town. Did anybody see a doctor's office?"

No one had.

She looked at the bullet hole in her father's side. "How you doin', Papa? I'm gonna get you some help. Maybe it ain't so bad."

"Helluva note," the old man gasped painfully. "Outta prison two days and get shot gettin' off the damn train. Who shot me? What was he shootin' at me for?"

No one realized that he had been hit with a bullet glancing off a train car.

"I don't know who the hell he is, Grandpa," Brice answered. "He just started shootin' when you got off the train. Whoever he is, he's faster 'n Slick. Maybe he's the sheriff here."

"He ain't no sheriff," Clementine said. "There ain't

no regular sheriff in any town in Injun Territory. All they've got is a Choctaw policeman and he ain't likely to come after us. They just police Injuns." She looked at Shorty Hicks, standing beside the shattered ticket window. "What are you waitin' for, Shorty?"

"I don't know where he went. I don't see him no more."

"Hell, there ain't no place he could hide," Brice said. "He's gotta be behind that shack where them other two jaspers were hidin' before they ran off. We never saw those two come out the door, so I'm thinkin' there's a back door or window they musta went out of. And if there is, I'll bet this feller went in the way they ran out."

"That makes sense," Clementine said. "He's in that storeroom and he's figurin' on shootin' at us when we come out the door. But he just mighta crawled into a trap, if we can hem him up inside that little shack." She went on to give them her plan of attack.

When they all understood their part, they launched it. Brice and Shorty swung the office door open and stepped out, blazing away with their six-guns into the open door of the storeroom. Under cover of their fire, Junior ran around behind the storeroom to keep Perley trapped inside.

It might have worked if Perley had crawled through the window as they had thought. Not comfortable with the idea of being trapped inside the small room, he had decided to take the low road again. He'd quickly run across the tracks and crawled underneath the platform to the same spot he had fired from when the shooting first started. He arrived in time to see Brice and Shorty open fire on the empty storeroom, and when Junior ran toward the rear of the shack, Perley fired a shot that caught him in the thigh. The huge man crashed hard on the platform. Perley's next shot struck Shorty in the chest when he and Brice turned in reaction to the shot that downed Junior. There was no time for a shot at Brice before he lunged backward into the office.

"The son of a bitch!" Brice blurted. "He runs around under that platform like a damn lizard."

"What about Shorty and Junior?" Clementine exclaimed. She went to the ticket window to peek out and saw them lying on the platform.

"They got hit," Brice answered, still gasping for breath. "I don't know, but I think Shorty's a goner. It looked to me like Junior got hit in the leg."

"Ain't neither one of 'em movin'," Clementine said.

"Junior's most likely playin' dead to keep from gettin' shot again," Brice said. "There ain't nothin' we can do for either one of 'em without gettin' shot."

"I've gotta get a doctor to take care of Daddy," Clementine fretted. "We can't stay bottled up in this damn train station."

Afraid she was going to become so frustrated that she might endanger him as well as herself, Brice tried to calm her. "There ain't nothin' we can do right now, Aunt Clem. If we set foot outside that door, we're done for. He's just hopin' that's what we'll do. Grandpa looks like he ain't no worse off than he was, so we've got time yet."

No doubt they were in a serious situation with no apparent way out. Their horses were tied at the rail in front of the general store, and that was too long a run, even if they didn't have his grandpa to carry.

With the old man, it was impossible. They were at a standoff with the lone gunman.

The lone gunman was of the same opinion. Perley knew he had them treed, but he didn't know what to do about it. He couldn't go in after them . . . or could he? He remembered the open trapdoor that Elvis Farrier had used for his escape. Even in the darkness, he could still see the door hanging open. Maybe it was in a closet or someplace where it was not obvious. Otherwise, the outlaws would surely have closed and latched it. He thought about the possibility of surprising them and it seemed a good risk. The downside was the possibility that they might decide to charge out the door while he was in the process of crawling under them. He decided he'd best do something rather than just sitting there, and he'd better do it quick before they took a notion to come out and maybe spray gunfire under the platform.

Soon after Garland Wilson and Stanley Coons had showed up at the door of Brant's store, they'd been joined by Elvis Farrier. Brant had gladly unlocked his door and let them in, anxious to have extra guns to help defend his store.

"Whaddaya reckon we oughta do?" Coons asked, standing at the edge of the window, peering out at the railroad depot across the street.

"I don't know," Wilson answered. "We sure as hell didn't do much when we were over there."

"We didn't have any choice," Coons was quick to reply. "They were shootin' that place to pieces. If we'da stayed in that shack, we'd be dead now."

"You shouldn'ta shot at 'em when they went to meet that old man on the train," Wilson said. "We was supposed to wait till they made some kinda move on the train."

"I didn't shoot at 'em," Coons insisted. "There's somethin' wrong with my rifle. It went off accidentally." He couldn't bring himself to admit that he had caused the rifle to fire because of his nervousness.

"Well, if they come back here looking for trouble," Tom Brant stated, "we'll give them more than they can handle." His courage had ramped up considerably with the three extra men now set to help defend any attack on his store.

"What happened to the other fellow?" Elvis Farrier asked. "What was his name? Purely?"

"Perley," Brant corrected him. "Perley Gates, like the 'Pearly Gates' up in heaven."

"Well, who is he?" Farrier pressed. "What has he got to do with any of this? I don't believe there was any trouble, except what he started. I think those men just came to meet somebody on the train, and he came in and got us all up in the air about a train robbery."

"He's been in town before"—Brant felt he should defend Perley—"looking for his grandpa."

"I remember him now," Coons said. "He came by the stable that day Tom's talkin' about. Perley Gates he said his name was and he was lookin' for his grandpa by the same name. Peggy said he knew who those five were. Outlaws, she said. They murdered a fellow and his wife at a trading post and left their son an orphan. The little boy is with Perley and identified the woman and four men as the ones that killed his folks. Lottie's keepin' the boy at the diner."

Farrier considered what they said about the man, but he still had some doubts. "Well, I'll admit I turned tail and ran when they started shooting up my office, but I never saw Mr. Perley Gates after the shooting started, either."

"What about the shooting that happened after all of us ran?" Wilson asked. "They mighta shot him. Maybe we oughta try to go back. We sure as hell didn't do much of a job of backin' him up."

"You'd be crazy to go back over there," Brant insisted. "They're probably waiting for you to try again. The best thing to do is to sit right here and wait for them to come get their horses. Then we can blast them out of their saddles. We pussyfoot around trying to arrest them, we're gonna end up with some of us dead."

"That makes sense to me," Coons said at once. "They ain't goin' nowhere without their horses, and we ain't got no jail. They'd hang for killin' that little boy's folks, anyway."

They talked it over briefly before everyone decided that was the thing they should do. It was true there wasn't any jail as such, but Jim Little Eagle often used an empty smokehouse to hold prisoners. Still the final decision was execution by gunfire when the outlaws came to get their horses.

While the would-be vigilantes were deciding to set up an ambush, Perley was staring up into the opening created by the open trapdoor. Since it was dark above him, he figured he'd guessed right. He was peering up into a closet or some small room. And since no one was above him peering back at him, he rose up enough to stick his head through the opening. Discovering that his head was the only occupant in the small enclosure, he turned all the way around to see all four walls and decided that he was in a records closet of some kind. Shelves filled with various-sized boxes occupied three of the walls and a closed door hung on the other.

Before going any farther, he paused to ask himself if it was a good idea to climb up into the closet. If he made any noise at all, it might cause a volley of gunshots right through the door, and as small as the room was, he was bound to get hit. In view of that, he deemed it too big a risk, but decided to do it, anyway. Very carefully, he laid his pistol on the floor then pushed up through the opening until he could sit on the floor with his feet dangling in the opening of the trapdoor. He was not as quiet as he'd hoped, however. He heard the old man's voice on the other side of the door.

"Clementine, I hear noises behind my head."

"Somebody is hidin' in that closet!" she exclaimed and got up from her father's side.

Brice turned at once. "Well, we'll fix that!" He emptied his gun, firing six shots through the door in a neat circular pattern, waist high.

Inside the small room, Perley had no chance to duck into the hole again as he heard the slugs pass over his head and embed themselves in the closet shelves behind him. With no time to think, he reached out beside him to a stack of boxes full of records and pushed them over, hoping the paper-filled cartons would give him some protection if the next shots were lower.

Hearing what sounded like a body hitting the floor, Brice bellowed, "I got him, Aunt Clem! By God, I got him!" He hurried to yank the riddled door open, only to confront Perley sitting on the floor, his Colt .44 aimed squarely at him. In the next instant, he was knocked backward by the bullet in his chest. As he fell to the floor, he pulled the trigger and heard the sound of the hammer striking an empty cylinder.

Perley quickly took advantage of the confusion caused by the unexpected incident. He scrambled the rest of the way out of the trapdoor opening and got to his feet, his six-gun ready to fire if Clementine made any move to draw the pistol on her hip. "There's already too many people killed, Clementine," he warned, having heard her father call her name. "If you go for that gun, there ain't gonna be anybody to take care of the old man there."

She thought about it for no more than a couple of seconds before raising her hands. "That's my papa. You shot my papa. Who the hell are you, anyway?"

"Just somebody who came along after you and your gang murdered that man and his wife at the fork of the Beaver River and Kiowa Creek, then burned his store down."

"We ain't never been there," she said. "We just rode over this way from Colorado Territory to meet my papa on the train, and you just up and shot him. Now you've killed my nephew." She glanced at Brice, slumped over against the front wall.

"You made a mistake when you didn't find their son," Perley said. "He saw you murder his folks, so I reckon you can save your breath on that story. Now, the best thing for you to do is unbuckle that gun belt and let it drop—with your left hand, if you please."

Not willing to see how fast he really was, she did as he commanded and dropped her gun belt.

"That's good. I don't like to shoot women. It makes me melancholy. Now, sit down in that chair." He pointed to Elvis Farrier's desk chair.

She sat down.

Still holding his gun on her, he looked through Farrier's desk drawers for something to tie her with. A ball of twine served the purpose. "Put your hands behind the chair." When she did, he tied them together, winding the twine numerous times to make sure it would hold her.

With the surly woman secured, he checked on Brice's condition, since he had shown no sign of life and no sound of suffering. He found that Brice was not playing possum. Perley's chest shot had hit him in the heart.

"Sorry about your nephew here," he said. "I didn't have time to take dead aim."

"You knew he emptied his gun through that door," she protested.

"That's a fact, but I didn't know if he had another one and was tryin' to shoot it." Next, Perley went to stand over the old man lying on the floor with a seat cushion under his head for a pillow. "How bad are you hurt, old-timer?"

He was gazing up, unblinking. "Kiss my ass."

"Not that bad then, I reckon. I'll just let you lay there for a little bit longer." Perley had not forgotten about the two men outside on the platform. One of them was seriously wounded, if not dead, but he had only shot the other one in the leg. It had not critically hampered him, evidently, for when Perley looked out the ticket window, the man was gone. *Damn. if my posse hadn't fled the scene, they might have stopped him. Nothing I can do about that now.*

Back to the woman then, he said, "When I see the telegraph operator again, I'll have him wire Fort Smith to send somebody to pick you up. Since I'm just passin' through here, I'll have to let some of the townspeople put you somewhere to wait for a deputy to come get you. And we'll see if there's somebody to take a look at your papa." Thinking about the gunman who had disappeared, he went back to the closet, closed the trapdoor, and latched it.

When he walked back into the room, Clementine said, "You ain't got no right to hold my father. He didn't do nothin' but get off the train. He ain't wanted for nothin'. He did his time in prison up in Kansas. He was just comin' home, and you shot him"

"Like I said, I didn't shoot your father and I don't know who did. I expect it was a stray shot that hit him. We didn't have any reason to shoot him. But maybe you're right. We don't have any right to hold him, so I reckon he's free to go, if he can make it without help. We'll see if anybody in town can do some doctorin', and after he's fixed up, why, hell, he's free as a bird."

"I'll need to take care of him," Clementine implored. "Why are you arrestin' me, anyway? The only reason I'm in this fix is because I came to meet Papa. I ain't got anything to do with whatever my nephew and his friends have been up to."

The sudden change in her attitude might have had a better chance of fooling him, had not Link witnessed her role in the slaying of his parents. Perley didn't bother to remind her of that. He told her that he was not arresting her, but was simply turning her over to the town of Atoka to charge her as they saw fit. "I'm a stranger here, myself. I'm just tryin' to see some justice for what your gang did to a nine-year-old boy's parents. We're gonna walk outta here now and go across the street where you left your horses. I'm guessin' that's where some of the posse is waitin'. You can tell them your story. Maybe they'll set you free to take your papa home."

After he picked up all the weapons, he rolled her chair over to the door before drawing his skinning knife and cutting her bonds. "Thought I'd best tell you, if you take a notion to run, I won't kill you, but I'll shoot you in the leg to slow you down." He glanced back at the old man on the floor. "You just rest easy. I'll get somebody to come help you."

"You go to hell," the old man called after him.

"He's got a kinda gentle nature, don't he?" Perley said to Clementine. "Must run in the family." He wasn't worried about leaving the old man alone, figuring that he was hurt too bad to run as well as the fact that he wasn't guilty of anything beyond fathering some rotten offspring.

* * *

"Well, I'll be. Look comin' yonder," Garland Wilson exclaimed.

The others went to the window to see.

"There's your Perley Gates. He ain't dead after all."

They watched for a few moments longer to see if anyone else was behind him, not sure at first if he was being marched out by one of the outlaws.

Realizing no one was behind Perley, Stanley Coons stated the obvious. "That's just the woman. What happened to the rest of 'em?"

Emboldened to leave the protection of the store, the four vigilantes hurried out to meet Perley before he crossed the street.

"We were gettin' ready to come look for you," Coons lied.

"What happened to the rest of 'em?" Garland Wilson asked. "It got too hot for me and Stanley to stay in that shack."

Perley told his sullen prisoner to stop and his newly motivated posse gathered around them. "This is Aunt Clementine. I don't know her last name. There's dead and wounded back there that'll need some help. One was her nephew. Her pa's lyin' in your office, Elvis. He got shot in the side when he got off the train. I don't know if they were plannin' on robbin' the train or not, but he didn't have anything to do with murderin' Link Drew's parents. I'm turnin' Aunt Clementine and her father over to you to do with as you see fit. I've already spent more time here than I intended to. I just wanted to stop long enough to get Link a sweater and eat some supper. I've got a ways to ride before I'll be across the Red to Texas."

"We can take control of the situation from here," Tom Brant blustered. "We damn-sure appreciate your help with this trouble, don't we, fellows?"

They all nodded vigorously.

"I'll lock Aunt Clementine up in my supply shed till Jim Little Eagle gets back from Muskogee," Wilson volunteered. "Then she can stay in his hoosegow till a deputy comes for her." He drew his pistol and leveled it at her. "Come on, darlin'. I'll make you nice and comfortable."

Beyond a defiant scowl, she made no effort to resist as he marched her toward his shop.

Now that Clementine was off his hands, Perley was most anxious to see how Link was doing. He returned to the depot with them only because his rifle was lying on the ground beneath Elvis's trapdoor. He retrieved it while they surveyed the damage. He was glad to see Tom Brant taking the leadership role as he directed Elvis and Stanley as to what should be done.

"There was one more that I don't see here," Brant said to Perley. "The big fellow, where is he? The woman called him Junior."

"That I don't know," Perley had to admit. "I put a bullet in him, but he must have run while I was under the platform."

That news was disappointing. "Too bad we didn't get every one of them," Brant said, "but we sure as hell stopped any mischief they had in mind for our town."

"Yeah, we sure did," Coons said sarcastically.

Eva Brant stood at the window and watched the prisoner exchange in the street until Wilson marched the woman away and the others went back to the depot. Relieved that it had all ended with none of the townsfolk harmed, she turned to go back to the counter, only to stop dead still, her heart seeming to stop for one horrible moment.

"You make a sound and I'll rip your head off," Junior Grissom threatened. Standing in the doorway to the back room with his trouser leg dripping blood, he seemed to fill up the entire door frame. "Come over here," he ordered, and when she was too frightened to move, he threatened again. "I ain't got time to fool with you, woman. If you wanna live, you'd best do what I tell you."

Terrified, she forced herself to move to the end of the counter where he'd pointed. It registered dimly in her brain that he was holding a bedsheet that he had picked up in the back room. Then while she watched, horrified, he unbuckled his belt and let his trousers fall to his boot tops.

He ripped the sheet in half and handed one half to her. "Here, wrap this around my leg," he said, pointing to the bloody patch in his underwear.

When she had tied the sheet firmly, he pulled his pants up, forcing them over the swath of bandage. Then, glancing out the window to make sure the men were still in the train station, he ordered her to fill a sack with dried apples and beef jerky. When she had done that, he took the remaining half of the sheet and used it to tie her hands behind her back. There wasn't enough left to reach her ankles, so he cut a long length of hemp cord from a spool on the counter and used that to tie her feet together. To make sure no one could hear her shout an alarm after he left, he picked her up and carried her into the back room, where he left her wide-eyed with fright.

Helping himself to a couple of boxes of .44 cartridges as he went back through the store, he hurried to the horses. With darkness rapidly approaching, few people were on the street to notice as he untied his horse and two others, which were as many as he wanted to fool with. He rode out the upper end of town at a lope, leading the two horses behind him.

CHAPTER 11

Sensing that the shooting had finally ended, the citizens of Atoka gradually returned to the street from the places where they had taken cover. Perley walked past them on his way to the diner.

"Looks like it's all over," Lottie sang out to Peggy and Link, who were in the kitchen. "Here comes Perley now." They came from the kitchen to join her as she opened the door for him. "We heard an awful lot of shooting," she commented when he walked inside. "I'm mighty glad to see you're still walking."

"Yeah, it turned out all right," Perley said. Looking at Link, he added, "We won't have to worry about that gang anymore. The only one left is that big woman, and she's locked up, waitin' for a deputy marshal to come get her. Three of the four men are dead. The other one got away, but he's wounded. He wasn't part of the family, so he's likely tryin' to get as far from here as he can. It ain't gonna make up for losin' your mama and papa, but you at least know they didn't get away with it without being punished."

He, Lottie, and Peggy all studied the young boy's

face while Perley gave him the news. It was difficult to imagine what Link was thinking. His expression never seemed to change from the stoic calm they had become accustomed to seeing.

When it became obvious he was not going to show any emotions, Perley finally asked, "How 'bout it, Link? Are you ready to get back on the road to Texas?"

"Yes, sir, I reckon I am," was Link's quiet answer.

"Let's go pick up the horses and we'll head down the trail a while before we make camp tonight." He turned to thank Lottie. "How much do I owe you?"

"Nothing."

He came back with, "How 'bout the horses ? Any charge for keepin 'em there at the hotel?"

"Of course not," Lottie replied, pretending she was offended. "After what you just did for the town? Besides, they didn't do anything for your horses but let 'em stand around in the corral. You just be damn sure you stop in to see us next time you pass though Atoka."

"You can count on that." He reached out and gave Link a tug on the shoulder. "Let's go, Link! As soon as we get home, I'm gonna see if we can find you a saddle. You're gonna need one if you're gonna be a real cowhand." He couldn't tell if that prospect excited him or not. The boy's noncommittal expression seldom changed.

Relieved to find his horses and packs just as he had left them, Perley got them ready to ride. He gave Link a boost up on the paint and said, "We oughta be done with all the fuss and excitement now and just have a nice ride home."

"How far is it from here to your home?" Link asked,

surprising Perley with the question. It was the first time he had shown any interest in caring where the road led.

"*Our* home," Perley quickly corrected. "I figure we'll be there in two days. We'll start out on the road to Durant till we strike Clear Boggy Creek, and make camp there for the night. In the mornin', we'll just follow Clear Boggy to the Red River. Once we cross the Red, we'll practically be in our front yard." Perley watched the boy's eyes as he followed his words, and decided that Link was finally thinking about what his life might be, now that his folks were gone. It was a good sign. "How 'bout it? That all right with you?"

"That's all right with me," Link said with a hint of a smile, the first Perley had seen on the boy's face.

"Let's go, then." Perley gave Buck a gentle nudge with his heels.

Thirteen-year-old Jimmy Farmer was perched on the top rail of the corral, watching John Gates work with a spirited buckskin gelding that had shown no interest in accepting a saddle. A couple of the men who rode for the Triple-G had given the buckskin a try, but no one had been able to take the cantankerous streak out of the horse. It was the kind of challenge John eagerly accepted, so he decided that today was the day he and the buckskin, appropriately named Sidewinder, would come to terms. John had hoped to saddle break the ornery horse before approaching suppertime, but had not yet imposed his will upon it.

Jimmy twitched and turned in unison with the horse's every maneuver to rid itself of the rider, traits that earned the horse its name. Sidewinder wasn't named for the rattlesnake. He was named for his method to shuck anyone off his back—dancing stiff-legged along the sides of the corral, bouncing against the rails, and trying to pin the rider's legs.

"They oughta named that cuss Devil Dancer," said Jimmy's father, Fred, as he walked up to watch with his son. He started to climb up beside him, but paused when he caught sight of some riders approaching from the north. "Look yonder. Who's that?"

Knowing his father's eyesight was not as keen as when he was a younger man, Jimmy turned to look. After a moment, he answered excitedly. "It's Perley! It's Perley, and it looks like he's got a little boy with him." It was enough to bring Jimmy down off the rail and deprive the bronc rider of his audience.

"Run to the barn and tell Rubin," Fred said, and Jimmy was off at once to deliver the message. Fred turned back toward the corral, but decided John was too busy to be disturbed at the moment as Sidewinder took him for another circuit of the corral rails. *They'll be mighty glad to see Perley,* he thought.

Both of the older brothers couldn't help but worry about him, in spite of the natural gift of speed and accuracy he was born with when it came to handling a firearm. It was the fact that he also appeared to have inherited an unavoidable tendency to draw trouble to him like a magnet. Fred stared at the approaching riders, eager to hear the circumstances that caused Perley to be arriving with a young boy in tow. He was joined a few seconds later by Rubin Gates.

"So the wayward son has come home," Rubin joked and peered out across the prairie, too. "I sent

Jimmy up to the house to let Ma and the other women know. Wonder who the hell he brought home with him?"

"I wonder," Fred echoed, and they both laughed.

Behind them, John, oblivious to the homecoming, had his hands full trying to keep Sidewinder off the rails.

By the time Perley and Link rode into the barnyard, Jimmy had come back from the house with Rubin's two sons and John's seven-year-old daughter trailing behind him. By the time Perley reined Buck to a stop, his sister, Esther, and his sisters-in-law had come to the welcome party.

"I swear," Perley said, "if I'da known we were gonna get such a big welcome, I'da stopped at the river and cleaned off some of this trail dust."

"Let's hear it," Rubin said abruptly, knowing there was a story waiting to be told.

His wife Lou Ann interrupted. "First, you should introduce the young man with you."

"You're right," Perley replied and stepped down from his saddle while Link threw his leg over the paint's back and slid off. "This is Mr. Lincoln Drew," Perley said with a flourish. "Better known to his friends as Link. He's come to stay with us at my invitation. Link, this shaggy crew is part of the Triple-G family. I can't vouch for their character. You'll have to decide that for yourself after bein' here a while." He then went down the line and introduced each one by name.

They all gave Link a warm smile with a few polite words of welcome, especially the women, for they knew there was bound to be a good reason Perley had brought him. They were also astute enough to know that the full details of Link's arrival would be forthcoming when they were no longer in the boy's presence.

"Well, I guess we'll need to decide where Link will bunk," Lou Ann said, "so we can help him put his things away. He can bunk in the house with my boys. There's plenty of room."

Perley could have kissed her for suggesting it. He hadn't decided what he was going to do, as far as Link was concerned. His first thought had been to give him a bed in the bunkhouse, but then he'd changed his mind when he realized Link was too young to be thrown in with a rowdy bunch of ranch hands, no matter how good their intentions. At the same time, he felt uncomfortable asking the family to accept him as a family member.

"Thank you, Lou Ann. That's a dandy idea. As far as his *things*, he's wearin 'em."

"Oh," she responded. "Then I suppose we'll have to do something about that, too."

"Well, you got here at a good time," Esther commented. "Supper's almost ready, so you'd best take care of those horses. Maybe Henry can show Link where to wash up."

Henry, her eight-year-old son, grinned and nodded to Link.

Content to let the women handle the situation with Perley's orphan, Rubin was a little curious about the sacks on Perley's packhorse. "What are you totin' in the grain sacks?"

"Oh, them," Perley responded. "That's seed corn. A special kind. I'm gonna set them on the front porch at the house for the time bein'." He handed his horse's reins to Jimmy Farmer. "Take ol' Buck to the barn for me. I'll be there in a minute."

"What? Are you thinkin' about takin' up farmin' now?" Rubin asked, knowing it was highly unlikely.

"I might," Perley answered, and started to hand Jimmy the paint's reins as well.

"I can take my horse." Link suddenly spoke up and took the reins from Perley.

"Right," Perley responded, surprised. "I sorta forgot what I was doin' for a minute there. You can take care of your horse. Just follow Jimmy, and I'll be there as soon as I unload this one." He led the packhorse up to the front porch and unloaded his four sacks of seeds just outside the door, then went to the barn.

Perley stuck his head inside the door to his mother's bedroom. "How you doin', Ma?"

Sitting up in bed with a stack of pillows behind her, Rachel Gates beamed with pleasure at the sight of her youngest son. "Perley," she pronounced softly. "I'm doin' all right, I guess, for a woman my age. I'm glad to see you back home, son. Come sit by me."

He pulled a chair up beside the bed and sat down, giving her hand a little squeeze. The Gates family had never been a hugging family, so she knew that gesture was meant to show his affection for her.

"I see Rubin and Lou Ann have moved in with you. Have you been doin' all right?"

"Oh, I've been having some spells of being dizzy-headed," she said. "Nothing that worried me. When you're as old as I am, you're supposed to be dizzy-headed. Anyway, they thought it would be best if they were here with me. So they moved out of their house and Fred and Alice and Jimmy moved into it." She smiled and squeezed his hand. "Don't worry. I told them your little room in the back is still yours."

"If they need more room, and they might, I don't mind sleepin' in the bunkhouse with the rest of the crew."

"Nonsense," his mother said. "This house is as much yours as anybody else's in the family." She gave his hand another squeeze. "Thank you for finding your grandfather, I'm sorry he didn't survive to make it back with you, but I'm glad you found him before he died. Your telegram didn't give a lot of details."

"Yes, ma'am, he was truly glad that I found him and he really wanted to make things right with the family. It didn't all turn out the way I wanted, but I think it turned out to suit him." Perley patted her hand. "Are you feelin' strong enough to make it to the table for supper?"

"I wouldn't miss it," she quickly responded. "I was just a little tired. Thought I'd rest a little before supper. I wanna hear all about your trip to Deadwood, but I'll wait till we all get to the table so you don't have to go over it twice. Get out and let me put my robe on."

He started for the door, but she stopped him. "Esther said you brought a little boy back with you."

"Yes, ma'am. His name is Link Drew, and he's in bad need of a family. I'll tell you all about it." He left her then to get dressed for supper.

The whole family gathered in the main house for supper, which was a combined effort of both daughters-in-law, as well as that prepared by Alice Farmer, Fred's wife, who normally did the cooking. It was a joyous homecoming for Perley and afterward, when the youngsters had left to show Link around the barn and stables, Perley told them how he happened to find Link after his parents were murdered. "He's got a lot of bad memories to try to forget, but I think he's gettin' better every day." He then recounted the story they were all eager to hear. When he finished, he summed it up with these words. "Grandpa gave his life to save mine. He wanted to make sure I got back home with those packs. I know he purposely drew on that man to make him shoot that shotgun, so I'd have time to get him. I promised Grandpa I'd bring his treasure back home for the family, and that's what I did."

There was a moment of silence afterward until Rubin, always the practical one, spoke. "Grandpa's treasure," he groused. "You risked your neck, and most likely that boy's, for four sacks of corn?"

"Not just corn," Perley replied with a wide grin, "seed corn. The kind that's hard to come by. Let me go get a sack of that corn and show you." He got up from the table and went to the porch. He came back with one of the grain sacks and dropped it in the middle of the dining room floor. Thoroughly enjoying the skeptical expressions on everybody's faces, especially the women, he proceeded to untie the sack and started pulling double handfuls of corn out and dumping them on the floor, until finally one of the women had to protest.

"Perley, really? In the middle of the dining room floor?" Esther sighed.

"I'm sorry. I reckon I coulda done this in the barn. I just thought you'd like to see it."

"I don't know who you think is gonna plant all that corn," Rubin said. "I thought you knew we're in the cattle business." He was about to say more but paused when Perley dug deeply into the sack and pulled out a smaller one.

"Come here and take a look at this," Perley said, dropping the sack to the floor and untying it. "This is what I risked my neck for." He stepped back then as Rubin and John both hurried to see.

"Good Lord in heaven," Rubin exclaimed upon seeing the contents of the sack.

John reached in and lifted a handful of the dust up for everyone to see. He looked at Perley. "How much of this stuff have you got?"

"Well, when I left Deadwood, gold was sellin' at twenty dollars and sixty-three cents an ounce," Perley said. "That's a ten-pound sack you're holdin' right there, which would make it worth about thirty-three hundred dollars. There's two more bags like that one and another one with about four pounds less." He had no intention of admitting that that particular four pounds went to the town of Blue Creek, Nebraska, for the construction of their first church. His family might likely be in favor of the donation, but if they didn't know about it, they wouldn't have to decide if they liked it or not. He had a strong feeling that his grandpa approved of it, and that was what counted most.

The table was deserted within a couple of seconds as they all gathered around the sack of gold dust.

"Somebody get a pencil and paper," John said. "I can't figure that much in my head." He looked up at Perley. "Have you got it all added up?"

"Nope," Perley lied. "I was too busy tryin' to keep it from bein' stolen." He wanted them to have the surprise he'd had when he'd figured it out.

Esther came back from the parlor with paper and pencil, sat down at the table, and began to total it. When she came up with a final figure of around eleven thousand, nine hundred dollars, there was a simultaneous whoop of surprise, followed by some question of the accuracy of Esther's figuring.

"No, that's about right," Perley confirmed, "and it's the reason it worried me to death till I could get home with it." He reminded them then that Grandpa had made him promise to take the gold home to his family, to help make up for having deserted them so many years ago.

"Well, for goodness sakes," Lou Ann exclaimed. "Go bring the rest of those sacks in the house. You can't leave them out there on the porch."

The crew at the Triple-G were all happy to see Perley back home. The days were already getting the chilly feel of autumn as the men prepared the cattle for the coming winter. Perley was pleased to find the youngsters, Jimmy Farmer and Rubin's oldest boy, Henry, eager to take charge of Link's orientation to life on a Texas ranch. Although Henry was a year younger than Link, Link was more than willing to learn from him. Since he had staked an aggressive claim to Grandpa's paint gelding, no one disputed his ownership of the horse. Jimmy, with Sonny Rice's help, taught him how to take care of the horse and they found a saddle for him to use. It was one that Sonny had used when he was not much older than Link.

Because of the family's general acceptance of Link, Perley was soon free of the responsibility for him. His days right after his return were spent preparing the cattle for the winter range. He noticed that the cattle were already starting to grow their winter fur, usually a sign of an early winter. After only a few days back at the ranch, he also noticed that, in spite of the trouble he had encountered on his trip to the Black Hills, it was a life far more suited to his nature than taking care of cattle. He wondered if he should be envious of Rubin's and even John's day-in and day-out monotonous routine of tending cattle. Not likely, he decided. He still wanted to see what was on the other side of the mountain. Thoughts of this nature made a trip into town a welcome break from the ranch.

One such trip was soon scheduled with his brother, John.

John's wife Martha caught Perley by the elbow as he passed through the kitchen on his way out to the barn where John was already hitching up the wagon. "I'm depending on you. I know darn well you two will stop in Patton's to have a drink of whiskey. Promise me you won't let John have more than one or two. The last time he went into town, he came home with a bloody nose and one eye swollen shut."

Perley shrugged helplessly. "I'll do what I can, but you know John ain't the easiest person to control when he gets a notion in his head that he wants to do something. I'll do my best to make sure he gets back home."

Unfortunately, his brother enjoyed a good brawl

like the one they'd had in Ogallala with those Kansas cowhands. To John, that was all just good clean fun.

"I'm depending on you," she repeated as he went out the door.

Perley shrugged. "I promise, I'll do my best."

As usual, the supplies they came to town to buy were loaded at Bill Henderson's store, and once they were secured, they drove the wagon up the short street to Patton's Saloon.

They were greeted by Benny Grimes. "Well, look who's back," he called out as the two Gates brothers walked in the door. "I heard you were up in the Black Hills, minin' for gold, Perley."

"Howdy, Benny," Perley replied. "Yep, I just got back last week, but I wasn't up there lookin' for gold. I was lookin' for my grandpa."

"Did you find him?" Benny asked as he poured two shots of whiskey.

"Found him, but he didn't come back to Texas with me." Perley glanced at John, who tossed his whiskey back and banged the empty shot glass on the counter for a second one. To Benny, Perley said, "I reckon I could stand another one, too, but that'll do it for me." He leaned over closer to John and whispered, "Martha told me to make sure you didn't have more than two."

"Is that a fact?" John replied. "Martha said I could have just two, huh?" The smug look on his face was one Perley had seen many times before when John was told he couldn't do something. "Well, maybe I might just have three, or four. That'd be all right, wouldn't it, Benny? What about that, Perley? Did she say anything about that?"

With a straight face, Perley answered. "She said I could shoot you."

"Well, that 'ud be one less drunk in town," a voice from a table in the back corner commented purposely loud enough to be heard at the bar.

Suddenly all the noisy chatter in the saloon went dead quiet.

John recognized the voice of Zach Taylor, a cowhand for the A-Bar-T—the man who had bloodied John's nose and blacked his eye. He was the man Martha had complained about to Perley.

"If he shoots you, that'll be one less blowhard in town, won't it?" John came back. He turned back to Benny then, willing to let it go at that.

"Is he the one Martha said gave you a black eye?" Perley asked.

John nodded.

"I'm guessin' he got worse than that."

John nodded again.

"How much worse?"

"I knocked all his front teeth out," John said.

Perley nodded.

Sensing a storm about to happen, Benny made a plea for sanity. "Your drinks are on the house, boys, if you'll leave right now. I still ain't replaced all the broken tables and chairs from the last fight."

"Now, Benny, you know I didn't start that fight, and I paid you for my part of the damages," John protested. "He started it. If you're gonna throw anybody out, it oughta be him and his two friends with him."

"Doggone it, John, I ain't throwin' you out. I'm just askin' you to leave, so we don't have another one of those fights in here."

"A reasonable request," Perley said. "We were just fixin' to leave, anyway. Come on, John." He knew his brother well enough to know that he was already heating up. "Thanks for the drinks, Benny." He took hold of John's arm and started toward the door.

John followed, but not willingly.

Too late, Perley thought when he heard the sound of a chair being pushed back from the table. A moment later, he heard the taunting challenge he'd hoped wouldn't come.

"You'd better slink outta here, Gates, or I'm liable to kick your ass. I ain't forgettin' you got in that lucky punch last time when I wasn't lookin'. All you Triple-G bastards are double-dealin' back shooters."

John turned to face his accuser. "I thought you learned something last time I did some dental work on you. Looks like I was wrong. You're gonna need another lesson."

Perley stepped between the two men, now only a few feet apart. "Looks like you nailed all of us double-dealin' back shooters that ride for the Triple-G. That's us all right. It's time we made a truce between the two outfits. No hard feelin's. Whaddaya say? You're man enough to forget about losin' your front teeth, ain'tcha? I know John ain't mad at you no more for his black eye and bloody nose." He nodded toward Taylor's two friends, now standing behind him. "Look at your two friends. They don't want any more trouble between our outfit and yours."

The two cowhands looked at each other with puzzled expressions.

Taylor was equally astonished, but was halted for only a couple of seconds before replying. "Feller, damned if you ain't been chewin' on locoweed or somethin'."

He and John started to square off with each other.

Perley had to think of something quick. One glance at Taylor's two friends told him he was going to be in it, too. "All right," he barked and held his hands up in the air, asking for everyone's attention. "I know John didn't want this to get out, but I ain't ready to see another man's skull crushed over nothin' more important than a little misunderstandin' between two hard-workin' cattlemen." When he was sure they were listening to him, he continued. "And I don't wanna see my brother go to prison for using his lethal right hand again." Giving Zach Taylor the best version of a sincere expression as he could create, he went on. "Not many folks outside our family know about John's right hand—maybe Benny, a few others—but not many know the Texas Rangers have it on record. They know that John can throw a punch that's the same force as a mule's kick, and they've warned him that the next time he throws a full punch and kills a man, he's goin' to prison." He paused to see if his yarn had any effect on the three A-Bar-T riders.

Their blank expressions told him they weren't sure if they were hearing a fairy tale or not.

"I know what you're thinkin'. You fought him last time and he only knocked your front teeth out. He told me about it. He said it was all he could do to hold back that skull-crushin' power when you bloodied his nose, but he kept on just givin' you little taps to keep from going to jail."

Skeptical expressions showed on all three of the A-Bar-T riders.

At the same time, Taylor had a hesitation to advance the fight. Finally, he said, "I ain't never heard such a tall tale in my life. I ain't never heard of such a thing."

"That's what that Texas Ranger said. What was that feller's name, John? I don't remember. All I remember is what a god-awful sight that man's skull was after that one punch."

"I ain't afraid of him," Taylor said, talking directly to Perley. "I ain't afraid of nobody."

"I can see that, and I admire you for it, but I can also tell that you're a smart man, too. Sometimes it pays to forget about little scrapes you've had with somebody, especially when we all work together durin' roundup. I don't blame you for doubtin' me, but I had to warn you, just to clear my conscience. But if you don't believe me, I reckon you can find out for yourself." Perley shrugged and stepped back. "Try to control that right hand, John."

John, as fascinated by the tale as anyone, did a poor job of keeping a broad smile off his face. He doubled up his fists and assumed a half-crouch as if ready to fight. Perley couldn't help thinking how formidable his brother looked. He was not alone in his thinking.

One of Taylor's friends spoke up. "I don't know, Zach. Maybe he's right. Us ranchers here in the valley oughta be more about helpin' each other."

It was all the incentive Taylor needed, and he used it to take an honorable retreat. "Well, I was ready to fight, but I reckon you're right. We oughta be tryin' to help each other, 'stead of fightin'."

They shook hands all around. The A-Bar-T men returned to their table. Perley and John started for the door, and as they passed by the bar they couldn't miss the wide grin on Benny's face.

He shook his head as if amazed and whispered low, "Damned if you ain't the biggest bullcrapper I've ever seen. You damn-near had me believin' that stuff."

"I promised Martha," Perley said.

CHAPTER 12

"You say that gunslinger that killed my nephew is named Perley Gates?" Clementine Cobb asked when Garland Wilson brought her supper and a second plate for her father, who was locked up with her.

When the town was left with a wounded old man, who was not guilty of any crime, they didn't know what to do about it. Dependent upon his daughter and grandson to meet him at the train station, he found himself alone and in need of help. The town council, which was made up in most part by the same men who had caused him to be shot, decided it was the Christian thing to do to at least have the barber dress his wound and find a place for him to recover. That last part was the hardest, for no one wanted to take the old man in. The council decided he could stay in Wilson's toolhouse with his daughter. That way, they figured, she could take care of him at least until Jim Little Eagle came back from Muskogee.

The couple of days before Jim returned had turned into a week with still no sign of the Choctaw policeman, however. Finally, Elvis Farrier took it upon himself to telegraph Fort Smith and request a deputy marshal be sent to pick up their prisoner.

"That was his name, all right," Wilson answered her question. "I don't think you could really call him a gunslinger. He just pitched in and gave us some help when we needed some."

"I don't know about that," Clementine said. "I know a gunslinger when I see one, and that feller was fast. Damn fast to beat Slick Dorsey. Slick was the fastest I'd ever seen until we ran into that Perley Gates. He was on his way to Texas is what I heard you say the other day." She had made it a point to get as friendly as possible with Garland Wilson, and he had become accustomed to making conversation with her whenever he brought food to her and her father.

Since she had no intention of being carted off to Fort Smith by a deputy marshal, she wanted to know all she could about Perley Gates. She didn't know how much time she had before a deputy showed up. She'd figured Wilson would get careless sometime, but much to her frustration, he had not slipped up so far. She glanced over at her father, who seemed to be getting worse instead of improving. Even if she got a chance to escape, how could she take him with her? She resigned herself to the fact that she might have to leave him, consoling herself with the idea that the people in Atoka would have to let him go eventually.

"Yep," Wilson answered. "He's a Texas man. I think his family has a ranch just below the Red River somewhere. He ain't no ordinary gunslinger—the kind you're talkin' about. He was takin' care of that little boy after your gang killed his parents."

"I hope you don't think I had anything to do with that business," Clementine said contritely.

"Oh, no," Wilson cooed sarcastically. "I wouldn't think that of a nice refined lady like yourself." He pulled his revolver from his holster and unlocked the door. "Now, if you'll be so kind as to step back against the wall, I'll set this bucket of water inside."

"I thought you'd know by now you don't have to hold a gun on me to get me to do what you want," she complained. "It makes me feel like a common criminal."

He couldn't suppress a chuckle for her remark. "Clementine, you are a common criminal. What else would you call somebody who murders a man and a woman, and leaves their little boy an orphan?" He chuckled again. "I have to say, though, it's been entertainin' to have you as a guest."

"I'm right glad to hear that, Garland, damned if I ain't."

He waited until she backed all the way against the rear wall before setting the bucket in. Had he been looking at her instead of where he was going to set the bucket down, he might have noticed her eyes opened wide with surprise. It was his fate to never know who struck him down, at least in this life, as his head was caved in with one mighty blow of his blacksmith's hammer. He collapsed, facedown, never to see the light of day again.

"Where the hell have you been?" Clementine demanded. "I've been locked up in this damn chicken coop for a week."

"I didn't know where you was," Junior Grissom replied. "And I had to lay low in the daytime, or they mighta seen me." He struck a foolish grin. "You ain't mad at me, are you?"

"Nah, I reckon not, but I figured you'd come after me before now." She had trusted that the simple giant would risk everything to rescue her. But she had begun to fear his wound was more severe than they'd figured, and that was the reason he hadn't come.

There was also concern about the money in the saddlebags belonging to her and Brice. The money from the bank robbery in Wichita, Kansas, was a sum large enough to require splitting it up to carry. Surely enough for most men in her business to take it for themselves and head for parts unknown.

It's a good thing Junior doesn't have enough sense to run off with it, she thought. *Like a faithful old hound, he came back to find his master.* "Have you got the horses?"

"Yes, ma'am. They're tied behind the store in them trees by the crick. I got your horse and my horse, and I took Brice's horse, too."

She started to ask why he didn't take all their horses, but decided to compliment him, since he took the horses carrying the money. "You done good," she said as she bent over Wilson's body to make sure he was dead. There was little doubt. She pulled the gun belt off his body and strapped it around her waist, then went through his pockets for anything of value. Finding very little, she picked up the pistol he had dropped. "Let's get the hell outta here."

"What about him?" Junior asked, pointing to her father, sitting propped up against the wall, trying to eat a biscuit.

He had remained silent to that point, watching the

assault upon Garland Wilson as it unfolded, unsure of his fate now that his daughter was free.

Clementine turned to face her father. "What about it, Papa? Can you ride?"

"I ain't sure," Clive Cobb rasped painfully as he tried to swallow, then choked up part of the biscuit. "But I'm damn-sure willin' to try."

"You don't look too good," Clementine said, shaking her head, concerned, "and we've got to do some hard ridin'. We've gotta be outta Injun Territory before a deputy from Fort Smith shows up here. We've gotta head for Texas and across the Red where the deputy marshals ain't got no authority. When we get to Texas, I need to get word to Coleman that Brice has been killed." Brice was her brother Coleman's eldest son, and her brother was not likely to take that news without demanding revenge. It was her intention to exact that revenge for him, if she could catch up with this Perley Gates.

"Well, I ain't plannin' to stay here," her father complained.

"Let's see if we can get you on your feet," Clementine said. "Gimme a hand here, Junior."

They took Cobb by his shoulders and lifted him to stand, causing him to grunt with the pain. Soon blood started from the wound in his side. As soon as they released him, he slid back down the wall, unable to stand on his own.

The old man groaned. "I ain't sure I can make it yet."

Anxious to get away from there before someone stumbled upon the escape, Clementine had to make a decision. "I reckon you ain't got much choice. I don't know what they would do with you after I'm gone. We can set you on a horse, but you'll have to be able to hang on. We can't stay here till you get better, and that's a fact." She thought about it a moment more before suggesting an alternative. "On second thought, if we *was* to leave you right here, they'd have to take care of you till you get well. Then they'd have to let you go."

The distress that suggestion caused was obvious in the old man's face. "Hell, the only reason I'm here is because you said you and Brice would take care of me. If you leave me here, even when I get well, I ain't got no place to go."

"Then I reckon you'll have to ride," Clementine said. "Pick him up, Junior, and let's get the hell outta here." The oversized simpleton bent down, easily picked up the wounded man, and led the way to the creek bank where the horses were tied.

"Put him on Brice's horse," she instructed, and watched while her father strained to throw his leg over the saddle.

By the time his body was seated, his trouser leg was saturated with fresh blood from the wound in his side.

"All right. Turn him loose," Clementine said and stepped back to watch him.

As soon as Junior released his arm, the old man remained upright for only a moment before keeling over to the side. He would have fallen to the ground had Junior not been there to catch him.

"He can't make it," she decided. "Lay him down over there against that tree. We'll have to think of some other way, Papa," she said to him. "Don't you worry." She went to the horses then to check her saddlebags to make sure all the bank money was just as it was the last time she'd checked it. It would be taken back to The Hole to be divided up as usual.

In a few minutes, Junior joined her. "I set him as easy as I could."

"I 'preciate it, Junior. It looks like he ain't gonna make it. That bullet musta tore his insides up, and I don't wanna leave him like this." She released a long sigh. "He's my papa. I don't want him sufferin', but we can't stay here. We've got to get the hell away from here before somebody comes lookin' for ol' Garland."

"I understand," Junior said. "I'll put him outta his misery." He drew the .44 handgun from his holster.

Clementine quickly stopped him. "Not with that, you damn fool. Everybody will hear that. Use your knife and do it fast, so he won't have time to know what's happenin'."

"Right, right," he stumbled. "I'm sorry, Aunt Clem. I reckon I didn't think about that."

"All right. Just do it and let's get goin'. And don't call me Aunt Clem. I ain't your aunt. Brice called me that because he was my nephew."

"Right," Junior said again. "I didn't think about that." He went at once to do her bidding.

When Junior got back to the tree, the old man looked up at him and said, "Tell Clementine I think I'm feelin' a little bit better. I think I just might be able to hang on if we try it again."

"That's good," Junior said. "I'll tell her." He paused a moment to consider that, then shrugged and walked around the tree so her father wouldn't know what he was about to do. Coming around the other side, he grabbed Clive from behind and drew his knife across the old man's throat, all in one motion. Junior held him tight against the tree until he ceased to struggle. The wild look of terror told the simple executioner that Clive knew what had happened to him. *I won't tell Aunt Clem,* he thought. *She might get mad at me.*

In the saddle then, the two outlaws rode down the creek until striking the road to Durant. They pushed the horses hard for about five miles before reining them back to an easy walk, riding another ten miles or so before camping for the night. With no more than a long day's ride left to the Red River, Clementine was confident that they had already left any pursuers behind them. She doubted the town council could get any volunteers to form a posse. If she had known that the telegraph to Fort Smith requesting a deputy marshal had not been sent until several days after her capture, she would not have worried at all.

"We ain't got much in the way of victuals," Clementine said as she looked through all the saddlebags, trying to find something to cook. She looked at her big partner as he brought a load of limbs to build a fire. "What did you eat while you were layin' low?"

"I killed a deer three days ago," Junior answered.

"What did you do with all the meat?"

"I et it," he answered.

"All of it? The whole deer? It must notta been a very big one."

He shrugged and grinned sheepishly. "It was a nice doe, about yea-high." He held his hand up even with his shoulder.

"It's a wonder you don't blow up one day. Well, you ain't gettin' nothin' but some moldy sowbelly tonight. We're gonna have to go shoppin' tomorrow."

He grinned, knowing that meant she was planning to rob the first store they came to.

The opportunity for Clementine to "go shopping" came after a ride of only about fifteen miles the next morning. Leon Shipley, clerk at Dixon Durant's general store, had just opened the door when he saw the two riders approaching from the north. He paused to give them a good looking over, but decided it was no one he had ever seen before. Two men, leading an extra saddled horse, they appeared to be heading for his store. He went back inside and prepared to receive them.

As he had speculated, they pulled up in front of the store and dismounted.

"Well, good morning," he greeted them cheerfully, just then realizing that it was a man and a woman, instead of two men, as he had originally thought. "You folks are traveling early. I just opened up." He was impressed by the size of the couple. The man was a massive brute with an expression suggesting an absence of intelligent thinking. The woman was large as well, not especially fat, but more brawny, much like her companion.

"Good mornin'," Clementine returned. "I'm glad we caught you openin' up. We need some things. Most of our supplies was stole yesterday in Atoka.

"Is that a fact?" Leon replied. "That's a piece of

bad luck. Do you know who stole your stuff?" He glanced at Junior, who was looking at everything on the shelves.

It was his usual custom in every store. Behind the counter or not, it made no difference to Junior. When he saw something he wanted, he put it on the counter. It obviously irritated Leon, but he was hesitant to complain.

Seeing the clerk's concern, Clementine chuckled. "You be sure you start writin' down all this stuff," she said, ignoring his question, 'cause we're gonna need a lot of other things. You got a coffee grinder?"

He said that he did, so she put him to work grinding a sack of coffee beans while she began picking things off the shelves with Junior.

"You got any dried apples?" Junior asked. "I like dried apples."

Leon pointed to a barrel at the end of the counter.

"One of these days you're gonna turn into a dried apple," Clementine said.

"I like dried apples," the simple man repeated.

She shook her head and sighed, amused. With no packsaddle on Brice's horse, they needed some sacks, as well. Seeing some heavy cotton bags on a shelf, she threw some on the counter. As she'd suggested, Leon kept busy writing each item down, his early concern having been eased by her constant reminders to make sure he tallied every item.

Finally, she said, "I reckon that's it," and she and Junior stuffed everything into the cotton sacks. "Junior, you start tyin' these sacks on the horses while

I settle up with Mister—" She paused. "I didn't get your name."

"Shipley," he replied with a wide smile. "Leon Shipley." He continued adding up the sizable sale.

"All right, Leon. I forgot, I'm gonna need a few feet of that rope yonder." She pointed to a spool of clothesline rope in the corner. He put his pencil down and went immediately to fetch the rope. When he started pulling some rope off, he asked how much she wanted.

"Just keep pullin' and I'll tell you when to stop." He pulled off about ten feet and she said, "That oughta do."

Leon went back to finish up his totals, thinking it a good way to start off the day, with an order of this size. Junior came in to pick up the last two sacks.

"Wait and I'll help you with those," she told him. "We need to settle up with Leon, here, first."

Leon started to show her the bill, but she didn't bother to look at it. Instead, she asked, "All right if we deal in lead?"

He didn't understand until she pulled the pistol out of her holster, cocked it, and stuck it in his face. Junior snickered. Stunned, Leon was too shocked to move.

"Take this rope and tie ol' Leon's hands and feet," she said to Junior. Back to Shipley, she said, "I like you, Leon, so I'm thinkin' about not shootin' you 'cause you've been mighty helpful."

When he was trussed up, hand and foot, Junior dragged him behind the counter.

Somewhat recovered from the initial shock, Leon, no longer fearing he was going to be shot, felt compelled to ask a question. "If you were planning to rob me all along, why did you want me to add up everything you took?"

"So you'd know how much you need to replace," Clementine answered. "It's been good doin' business with you, Leon. I hope the rest of your day goes a little better for you." His farewell glimpse of the two thieves was the foolish grin on Junior's face as the simple brute looked down at him while he chewed up a dried apple.

Outside, Clementine and Junior took their time securing their stolen goods, since there was no one on the street at the early hour. Knowing their normal routine would have been to jump on their horses and ride like hell to get away, Junior asked why Clementine was in no hurry. She explained that Leon wasn't going anywhere until someone happened to find him behind the counter. And from the looks of the deserted little town, that might be some time yet, so there was no sense in wearing their horses out. There appeared to be no law in the town, and even if they could scare up a posse, they couldn't catch them before they crossed the Red.

Junior considered that for a moment, then smiled in appreciation for her common sense. "What are we gonna do after we get to Texas? Are we goin' back to The Hole?" They had been gone from the Cobb family hideout, down near Tyler, Texas, for two months, but Junior preferred to continue their raids in Oklahoma and Kansas. Even after losing Slick, Shorty, and Brice, he had hoped that he and Clementine would keep on robbing banks and holding up stagecoaches.

"We're gonna track down that son of a bitch named

Perley Gates first," Clementine replied. "He killed Brice and Shorty and Slick and Papa, too. 'Least, he caused Papa to die. He might think he can get away with that, and run off to Texas to hide, but he can't hide good enough to keep me from findin' him sooner or later. That's all right with you, ain't it?"

"Yes, ma'am. Whatever you say is all right with me. Remember, he shot me, too." Junior smiled smugly to himself. He could understand Clementine's feelings about losing her father and nephew. He hadn't really known her father, but it was poor luck for Brice. Junior felt kinda sorry for Shorty and Slick, too, but he liked being the only one riding with Clementine. It was like he was her favorite, and in spite of what she had told him, when he thought of her, he would think of her as Aunt Clem.

As Clementine had figured, a ride of about twenty miles, following the MKT Railroad, took them across the Red River, and a few miles beyond to the town of Denison, Texas. They slow-walked their horses past the railroad depot until coming to a saloon with a sign that proclaimed it to be the Last Call Saloon. Clementine led them over to the hitching rail and dismounted, reading the name of the saloon out loud as she looked at the sign.

"Reckon why they named it that?" Junior asked.

Clementine shrugged, not really caring, then it struck her, and she explained it to her slow-witted partner. "If you're ridin' north, it's the last saloon before you cross the Red into Oklahoma Territory, where there ain't none. We're ridin' south, so it's the first call for us. Instead of jawin' about it, let's go in and get us a drink."

Her explanation pleased the simple man and he giggled with delight at her suggestion to get a drink.

Tommy Thompson looked up when the unfamiliar pair walked in, concentrating his gaze on the woman. The only women who frequented his saloon were the three that worked there. From the look of her, Tommy figured she could probably hold her own with the husky brute she was with. "Howdy, folks," he offered. "What'll it be? Whiskey for the gent and maybe a sarsaparilla for the lady?"

Clementine looked him in the eye and asked, "Do I look like I want a damn sarsaparilla?"

It brought a delighted chuckle from Junior.

"Two whiskeys it is," Tommy promptly replied and reached for two shot glasses. He poured their drinks and watched as they both tossed them down, then promptly ordered another. "Don't recall seein' you folks in here before," he commented. "Gonna be with us a while, or just passin' through?"

"We're on our way to see an old friend of mine," Clementine said. "Family's got a cattle ranch here-abouts somewhere. Trouble is, we don't know exactly where it is, and damned if I didn't forget the name of his ranch." She fashioned a smile. "I thought I'd go a few more years before I started losin' my memory. His name's Perley Gates. You don't happen to know him, do ya? He said his outfit ain't too far from the Red River."

"Perley Gates?" Tommy asked, not sure he had heard correctly. "Is that really his name?"

Clementine nodded.

"No, I'm sorry, but I ain't ever run into anybody by that name. I think I'da remembered it if I had.

There's some big cattle spreads all along the Red, east and west of here."

"Needle in a haystack, huh?" Clementine reacted. "I told him we'd find him, so I reckon we'll just have to keep lookin' till we run into somebody who knows him. How far is the next town from here, east or west?"

"Closest town from here would be Gainesville," Tommy said. "It's about thirty miles west. If you went back to the east, Paris is about sixty miles. It ain't near as big as Gainesville."

"Much obliged," Clementine said. "I reckon we'll try lookin' over Gainesville way."

"Most likely your best bet," Tommy said. "There's a sizable supply store in Gainesville that does a lot of business with the cattle drives that push up through Kansas. They might know your friend, if he's a cattle-man like you say."

"Thanks again," Clementine said and threw some money on the bar. "Gimme a bottle of that whiskey to take with us."

Tommy watched them until they went out the door. "Perley Gates," he mumbled to himself. "I doubt that's his real name, lady, and I expect when he sobered up and got a good look at you, he was damn glad he didn't give you his real name." *And whatever your real name is, Mr. Perley Gates, you sure as hell ain't gonna be happy when you see that ox she's bringing with her.*

With only thirty miles to Gainesville, and it still early in the afternoon, Clementine figured to make the town by nightfall, even with a stop to rest the horses and eat something.

They arrived about suppertime and went directly to Beck's Supply, which was easily the biggest store in the town. Clementine sought out the owner, John Beck, figuring that if anyone in the store knew Perley Gates, it would be the man who handled the money. She guessed right, for Beck did, indeed, know Perley Gates.

"Sure do," he replied when asked. "I've done a lot of business with the Triple-G since I opened this store. I started out with the old man, Nathaniel Gates. His sons run the ranch now. They drive their herds through here every year on their way over to strike the Western Trail."

Clementine cocked an eye at Junior and winked. "Well, I sure am glad to know we're finally gettin' close to the Triple-G."

Beck shrugged. "I reckon it depends on what you call close. The Triple-G is almost a hundred miles east of here, closer to the little town of Paris."

"Damn," Junior blurted, the first sound he had made since they'd walked into the store.

"It don't make no difference," Clementine quickly insisted. "We've got plenty of time and I'm sure we'll find him all right." Turning back to Beck, she asked, "You say Perley and his brothers run the ranch now? I don't recall him ever mentioning he had brothers. How many brothers has he got?"

Beck began to get a little leery of all the questions she was asking, and wondered if he was doing the Gates brothers any harm. The two people asking the questions didn't strike him as friends of any of the Gates family. He answered the question, however.

"There are three brothers, and the Triple-G is a big outfit, with a big crew of cowhands."

"Well, I reckon we'll be on our way, then," Clementine said, sensing that Beck seemed to be getting a little guarded in his answers. "I'm lookin' forward to meetin' all the Gates boys, if we do run across 'em. Come on, Junior."

Outside, Junior felt inclined to comment. "We picked the wrong direction to ride, back there in Denison. We shoulda rode east 'stead of west. Now we got a two-day ride back to that other town he told us about."

"Paris," Clementine said. "If that Triple-G is as big as this feller says it is, somebody will sure as hell know where it is. We ain't in no big hurry. We'll find Mr. Perley Gates and he'll pay up for the killin' he's done."

"He needs to pay up for this slug in my leg, too," Junior reminded her again. "I'm still limpin' when I walk."

"I ain't forgot about that," and she hadn't. She just didn't think it was that important. Reminded now of his childlike brain, she said, "No, sir, I ain't forgot about that. He's gotta pay for shootin' you in the leg."

The childlike grin on his face told her that pleased him.

What she had just found out from Beck caused her to reconsider her immediate plan to take her revenge, however. Perley Gates alone was one thing, but Perley Gates with two brothers and a large crew of cowhands might pose a far more difficult job for her and Junior. She thought of other things to consider, as well. One man had killed three other men who'd ridden with her. In retribution, the Cobb family needed to take the lives of all three Gates brothers. And to do that, it made more sense to wait for her brothers, Coleman and Beau, and maybe one or two additional gun hands to make it right.

The more she thought about it, the more the idea of wiping out the Gates family appealed to her. She thought about telegraphing her brother Coleman to tell him to come at once, and bring help, but she knew he'd never get the message. There was a telegrapher at Tyler, but he wouldn't ever find Coleman to give him his message.

CHAPTER 13

When none of the Gates brothers wanted to go into town to pick up supplies, Sonny Rice volunteered to drive the wagon and take the youngsters with him. They were all excited over a trip to town, and Sonny didn't mind taking them. He wasn't interested in visiting the saloon like most of the men, so Martha and Lou Ann didn't worry about sending the children with him. They knew Sonny to be dependable to take care of them.

Although still pretty young, he had shown enough maturity to take on the responsibility of managing the remuda on the past summer's cattle drive. And according to all three brothers, he had done an impressive job as a wrangler. Going to town was a holiday for the young children on the Triple-G Ranch. Rubin's two sons, John's daughter, Link Drew, and Jimmy Farmer made up the party for the five-mile trip. Henry, Robby, Betsy, and Link were all given a penny for a peppermint stick. Jimmy, at thirteen, considered himself too old for penny candy. And since he chose not to go in the wagon with the younger children, he decided to ride his horse to town. Eager to take his horse on a ride of that length, Link asked to take the paint gelding he had laid claim to. Sonny consented, since Jimmy was taking his.

It was a chilly autumn morning when Sonny drove his wagon load of bundled-up children into the little settlement of Paris. Followed by Jimmy and Link on their horses, he pulled up before Henderson's Store and his three passengers were out of the wagon and running to spend their pennies before he could tie the horses.

"Mornin', Sonny," Bill Henderson greeted him when he walked in.

"Mornin'," Sonny returned and handed him a list. "Here's some things we need to pick up, if you've got 'em all. 'Course, that's after you take care of those big orders ahead of me."

Ben laughed. "Shirley's taking care of the peppermint business." He nodded in his wife's direction. She was busy handing out the candy. Ben glanced briefly at Sonny's list before saying, "I think we're got everything you want here." He started pulling the items off his shelves and placing them on the counter while Sonny amused himself watching the kids work on the peppermint sticks.

It served to quiet the children as their attention was occupied with the slow sucking of the candy sticks, the object of which was to make them last as long as possible. It resulted in a sharpening of one end of the peppermint until it broke off. Once that was chewed and swallowed they started on the stump until it was sucked into a sharp point, and so on until the stick was totally consumed.

It was a new experience for Link and he was enjoying it as much as the other kids. Although his father had run a trading post, he had never had any call for candy of any kind. Among his usual customers, he'd seldom seen any children.

While Sonny and Jimmy loaded the supplies in the wagon, Link stood near the door, working on his peppermint stick with the Gates children, each one trying to make his candy last the longest. Link saw right away that seven-year-old Betsy was going to be tough to beat, for she was simply licking the candy so ladylike. His piece of peppermint was already worn down to an inch or two. The kids paused in the competition to move out of the way when two adults came in the door.

"You might as well give up," Henry said to him. "Nobody ever beats Betsy. I don't think she even likes candy."

Robby and Betsy laughed at the remark, but stopped, astonished when Link stood staring as if frozen. His peppermint dropped from his hand and he made no move to catch it, standing like a statue, with his eyes like saucers. Then, without a word, he suddenly ran out the door.

"Link!" Henry called after him, but Link didn't respond, so they ran after him. With no word to Sonny or Jimmy, he ran by the wagon and climbed on his horse, then wheeled the paint and galloped away toward the road to the Triple-G.

"What in the world . . . ?" Sonny asked, startled. "What's eatin' him?"

"I don't know," Henry said. "Just all of a sudden, he went crazy. Like a bee or something stung him."

Surprised, but not as shocked as the others, six-year-old Robby bent down and picked up the small stump left of Link's peppermint stick. When Betsy screwed up her face in disgust, Robby put the sticky piece of candy in his pocket. "Link might still want it," he explained.

"Come on, young'uns," Sonny told his charges. "We'd best get on our way back home." Since he was responsible for the children, he worried about Link's strange behavior, and was anxious to find Link. At least he had raced off on the road to the Triple-G. Maybe they would catch up with him along the way. Sonny was especially concerned about the way Link had whipped that horse into a gallop, not certain how well the boy could ride. He hustled the children again. "Come on. We gotta get goin'."

"We ain't even walked around the whole town yet," Jimmy complained. "I thought we were gonna stay a little while before we started home."

"You mean so you can peek under the saloon door to try to get a look at some of them painted ladies that work there?" Sonny accused. "We ain't got time for that mischief. Get ready to ride."

"I didn't think no such a thing," Jimmy insisted, even though that was on his list of things he wanted to do. It was plain to see that Sonny wasn't going to give in on the issue, so he went to his horse while the younger kids climbed into the wagon.

Inside the store, one of the customers who had walked in just before the children filed outside, asked Ben a question. "You got any dried apples?"

"You're gonna turn into a dried apple," the gruff-looking woman with him declared, a prediction she voiced often.

Junior looked at her and grinned. "I like dried apples, Aunt Clem."

"What'd I tell you about callin' me that?" Clementine responded.

"I forgot," Junior quickly replied. "I didn't mean to do it."

"I've got dried apples," Henderson said. "How many you need?" He realized right away that the huge man's brain was nowhere near the size of his head.

"Give him a pound of 'em." Clementine watched Henderson as he weighed out a pound from the barrel of dried apples, paused to let her see the scale, then dropped a couple more in the bag. Clementine nodded to acknowledge his gesture of fair measure. "Maybe you can tell us somethin. We met a feller in Atoka that claimed his family was in the cattle business near here. Me and Junior are just passin' through town, but if I knew where to find him, I'd like to say hello. 'Course we had all had a few drinks, so he mighta been japin' us about his ranchin' business. His name's Perley Gates."

"Perley?" Ben replied at once and broke out a wide smile. "Sure, Perley's in the cattle business, all right. The Triple-G is one of the biggest outfits in this part of Texas. Him and his brothers run it."

"Well, I'll be . . . ," Clementine started. "Whaddaya know, Junior, ol' Perley warn't japin' us a'tall. Ain't that somethin'?" Back to Henderson, she said, "I was gonna ask the sheriff about Perley, but it didn't look like there was anybody in there when we rode by."

That brought a chuckle from Henderson. "No, I reckon not. We don't get to use that little jailhouse very often. Once in a while there'll be some drunk who needs to sleep it off, so the sheriff will put him in the cell and let him go the next morning. I'm proud to say we don't need one too often, so we've only got a part-time sheriff. Paul McQueen took the job. He's the blacksmith, but he does a pretty good job when we need a sheriff."

"Sounds like you got yourself a peaceful little town here," Clementine said. "We might be seein' you again before long. Which way would I ride to find the Triple-G?"

"The ranch house is about five miles north of town. It's not hard to find. Just follow that trail that leads out between the stable and the barbershop. Matter of fact, that fellow driving the wagon with the young'uns in it is going to the Triple-G. They just left when you folks walked in."

"Much obliged," Clementine said. "Maybe we'll catch up with ol' Perley for sure."

Outside the store, Clementine said, "Don't look like we're gonna have any trouble findin' Perley Gates a'tall."

When Junior asked if they were going to kill him right away, Clementine took the time to explain. She was much more patient with the slow-witted gunman, now that she thought her prey was at hand.

"First, we're gonna take a look at the Triple-G and see how many men we might hafta deal with. If I know Coleman Cobb, we might put the Triple-G outta business for good."

Brice had been Coleman's pride and joy. He would

demand a big price in dead bodies to pay for the loss of his son. The thought of it caused the pitiless woman's heart to beat with excitement, but it would take some time before she and her brothers could get ready to plan the destruction of the Triple-G. It was two days' ride from Paris to the family's hideout northwest of Tyler—four days in the saddle before they could return.

She would like to start home right away, but thought it important that she and Junior scout the Triple-G to see what the Cobbs would have to deal with. She wanted to be able to tell Coleman and Beau where the headquarters was located and where they grazed their cattle.

"Get on your horse," she said to Junior. "Let's catch up with that wagon."

Unable to think of anything beyond the shock of seeing the monsters who had murdered his mother and father yet again, Link's only reaction was to find Perley as fast as he could. He held the paint to a full gallop for almost two miles before his terrified mind reminded him that he was running the horse to death. Reluctantly, he reined the rapidly tiring horse back to a walk, dismounted, and led it, walking as fast as he could. He was not really sure how long he should let the horse walk before he could push it again. He remembered Jimmy telling him that the horse would let him know when he was rested enough to trot, and that he could go a long distance at a trot.

Link didn't want to hurt the horse—the paint was his. Perley had said it was. He arrived at the barn at a trot. As soon as he slid off the paint's back, however, he ran as fast as he could into the barn, looking for Perley.

"What is it, boy?" Fred Farmer asked, seeing the look of panic in Link's eyes.

"Perley!" Link blurted. "Where's Perley?"

"He ain't here," Fred answered. "What's wrong? Where's Jimmy and Sonny?" When Link seemed unable to reply, he tried to calm him. "Take it easy, boy. Did somethin' happen? Are the other kids in trouble?"

"I've gotta tell Perley," Link insisted. "Where's Perley?"

"Perley's down near the river, lookin' for strays," Fred said. "Now, why don't you calm down a little and tell me what happened, and maybe I can help you."

After a few moments, Link began to calm down. Now that he had reached the safety of the ranch, he began to recover from the initial shock of seeing the demons who'd killed his parents. "It's them!" he said to Fred. "They're in town right now. I need to tell Perley."

"Who's in town?" Fred asked.

"Those people that killed my ma and pa!" Link answered.

Fred wasn't really sure what to do about the situation. Like Link, he wished Perley was there. Maybe the boy just saw somebody who looked like the ones that killed his folks. Perley had told them that the one member of the gang who had escaped had probably put as much distance as he could behind him after he got shot. The leader of the gang was the woman,

Clementine, and she was locked up in Atoka, waiting for a deputy to take her to trial.

Fred decided he'd best tell Rubin and let him deal with it. He had started to take Link up to the house when Sonny and the other kids rolled into the barnyard. His first thought was relief upon seeing his son riding in beside the wagon, then he noticed that there seemed to be no urgency on Sonny's part as he pulled up beside the barn.

"What in the world got into you?" Sonny exclaimed to Link.

Feeling somewhat safer in the bosom of the Triple-G, Link repeated the story he had just told Fred.

When he had finished, Sonny asked, "Are you sure you saw those same people?"

Link assured him that the two he saw in Henderson's store were two of the murderers. He told Sonny that he would never forget the woman.

"Maybe he's right. Maybe we'd best go find Perley. I'll saddle a horse. I know where he might be—down there where Muskrat Creek runs out to the river. There's a mighty soft bottom right there that cows get stuck in once in a while. Perley always checks that out."

"That's a good idea," Fred agreed. "Perley will know what to do." He paused when he thought about it, then added, "If we oughta do anything about it, might be, Paul McQueen's who we oughta tell. He's the sheriff. Give him somebody to put in that jail besides drunks."

"What would he arrest 'em for?" Sonny asked, "Unless they were robbin' the store." He lowered his voice, so that only Fred could hear him. "Link could be wrong. Those two he saw in the store might be somebody that looks like those two he remembers."

Fred shook his head, uncertain, then shrugged. "You'd best go find Perley. He might be able to make some sense outta this. You go ahead and saddle up. I'll take care of the wagon."

Watching from a low hummock, some distance from the barn, Clementine Cobb lay at the foot of a stunted pine, her long glass focused on the people gathered around the wagon. She had no notion that she and Junior had been recognized by the young boy she had orphaned. She had never gotten a look at him. "They act like they're all excited about somethin'," she said to Junior. "Now the feller drivin' the wagon jumped on a horse and hightailed it outta there." She watched until she could determine what direction he was heading. "I wanna see where he's goin' in such a hurry. Come on."

Back in the saddle, she led Junior in a direction tangent to the one Sonny took until they had circled the headquarters buildings, then she struck his trail. They followed him at a safe distance until they started passing through grazing cattle. When Sonny slowed almost to a walk, she motioned Junior to stay back. The range they rode through had very little cover, so they couldn't trail Sonny as close as she might have wanted.

She reined her horse back hard when he suddenly threw up his hand to signal someone. "We need to find us a place to hide. At least we know where their range starts, 'cause it looks like there ain't no cattle on the other side of this creek."

She and Junior led their horses down near the creek where they couldn't be seen by the man they had been following, who was now waiting while another rider came up to greet him. Clementine pulled out her long glass again and focused on the two men.

"Damn!" she exclaimed when she recognized the face of Perley Gates. "It's him! It's the son of a bitch we're chasin'!"

"Who?" Junior asked.

"Perley Gates," she answered, so surprised to see him that she didn't bother to chastise Junior for his stupid question. Her initial impulse was to draw her rifle from her saddle sling and settle his hash once and for all. She pulled the rifle halfway out, but stopped when she reminded herself that she had a war in mind for the Gates family. If she took her revenge out and killed Perley, she and Junior would have no choice but to run. If she shot at him at that distance and missed, the Triple-G would be forewarned. She decided not to risk it. She wanted Perley and his two brothers and was confident she would take a lot more from the Triple-G before she was through. Perley was home, working his cattle. He wasn't likely to be anywhere else for a while. She and her brothers had time to make their plans before they moved against the Triple-G.

Watching her actions, Junior was puzzled. When she slid the rifle back in the sling, he asked, "Ain't you gonna shoot him?"

"Damn right I'm gonna shoot him. I'm gonna shoot his brothers and his wife and young'uns, if he's got any, and his cows and his horses. He's gonna regret the day he ever messed with the Cobbs. I ain't ready to shoot him right now. It would spoil the party I'm plannin' for him, so what we're gonna do right now is start ridin' south. I wanna be home in two days.

As he had suspected, Sonny found Perley herding half a dozen cows away from the creek, working alone, as he most often did. He wasn't particularly happy to hear the news Sonny brought. Clementine was locked up in Garland Wilson's shed, if she hadn't already been picked up by a U.S. deputy marshal. At least, that's where she was supposed to be. If it was her, he was well aware of why she wanted to settle her score with him.

Still, he wondered how she knew where to come looking for him. "I'd best talk to Link," he decided. The boy might have been seeing ghosts. "Help me turn this bunch away from the creek," he said to Sonny.

The two of them started the little group of strays toward the main part of the herd. Once they joined it, the cowboys left them to stay out of trouble on their own.

By the time they returned to the barn, both John and Rubin had joined Fred and the children. In the midst of the group, Link stood tight-lipped, waiting for Perley. When Perley and Sonny rode into the barnyard, he ran to meet him.

"It was them, Perley!" he declared before Perley could dismount. "They were in the store in town!"

Perley stepped down off the roan gelding he had been working that morning. "You sure it was them you saw?"

"Yes, I'm sure," Link insisted. "It was that big ol' mean woman—don't no woman look like that ol' witch. And that big man was with her."

There was still a chance that Link was mistaken and might have let his imagination build a picture that wasn't true. A lot of farmers and cattlemen lived in Lamar County, and some of them had some pretty tough-looking wives.

"Did you hear them talkin'?" Perley asked.

Link nodded.

"What did they talk about?"

"I don't know," Link replied, confused. "They were talkin' to Mr. Henderson about somethin'." He shook his head slowly, trying to remember. "I don't know. I was scared."

"That's all right, Link," Perley said calmly. It was hard not to have doubts about who Link actually saw, but he decided it best to be sure. *I hope to hell he's wrong.*

Perley glanced at his brothers standing there, both waiting for him to explain. "I expect I'd best take a little ride into town and talk to Henderson," he finally concluded. "Jimmy, can you cut ol' Buck outta those horses in the south pasture for me? You can take this one to the pasture." He pulled his saddle off the roan and Jimmy hopped up on the horse and turned it toward the south pasture. Rubin sent the kids to help unload the wagon, Link included. No hesitation on the part of the children. They all feared the stern, always serious man who was the head of the family since his father's death. A casual suggestion from Rubin was akin to a commandment from God, or Moses at the least.

With the children off to the barn, Rubin turned to

Perley. "You think that boy knows what he's talkin' about? And if he does, does it mean any trouble for the Triple-G?"

"Maybe I'll find out when I talk to Henderson," Perley said. "If it is the two Link thinks it is, then I'd have to believe that the one I just shot in the leg musta come back and sprung the woman. I hope nobody in Atoka got hurt if he did."

"You're too damn softhearted," John spoke up, halfway in jest. "If you had a clean shot at the son of a bitch, you shoulda shot him in the head."

Perley ignored John's remark and continued. "What I wonder about is, how did they know to come to Paris?" He paused, then added, "If it really is Clementine and that big fellow that got away . . . and if they really are lookin' for me."

"See what you can find out," Rubin said. "We need to know if there's some trouble headed our way, so we can be ready."

"That's right, Perley," John piped up again. "I hope all that fuss you caused up in Atoka ain't comin' home with you. You know what I've always said about you. If there wasn't but one cow pie—"

That was as far as he got before Perley interrupted. "I know, I know. Save your breath," he said, causing John to laugh and Rubin to shake his head as if exasperated.

The discussion was ended then with the arrival of Jimmy Farmer returning from the pasture, leading Buck.

John couldn't pass up the opportunity and called out to Jimmy. "Whaddaya doin' walkin' back? Why didn't you ride Buck back?"

"The same reason you don't jump on his back," Jimmy replied, knowing John was japing him. "'Cause I ain't wantin' to get throwed." He handed the reins to Perley.

Perley placed his saddle blanket on the big bay's back, then threw his saddle on. "They just don't understand you, do they, boy?" He patted the horse's neck affectionately. "You don't tolerate anybody on your back that you don't approve of." He stepped up into the saddle then and said to Rubin, "I don't know how long I'll be. If it's late, I'll most likely eat supper in town."

"Tell Lucy Tate all the men at the Triple-G said hello," John said with a wide grin.

"I'll tell her *you* said hello," Perley came back, no longer touchy when it came to jokes about the flirtatious waitress.

Rubin stepped up beside his stirrup. "John and I will get everybody on their toes here and be on the lookout for them. If they show up, we'll see that they get a warm welcome. You be careful, Perley. It could be a coincidence those two showed up here, if it turns out that's who Link really saw. But I don't believe in coincidences, so you be careful."

"I will," Perley said and wheeled Buck toward the road back to town.

"Howdy, Perley," Bill Henderson greeted him. "I was just talking about you earlier today."

"That so?" Perley replied, already thinking that was a bad sign.

"Yep, there were a couple of folks asking about you."

"Man and a woman?" Perley asked.

"Why, yeah, matter of fact it was. How'd you know that?"

"Just a lucky guess, I reckon," Perley said. *Link was right.* He'd said it was Clementine and the big ox that hobbled away with a bullet in his leg.

Perley was not really surprised. He had not been a hundred percent sure the boy was wrong. Still, to be absolutely certain, he asked Henderson why they were talking about him.

"As I recollect, he called her Aunt Clem, which she objected to. She called him Junior, I think, and they said they met you in Atoka, up in Indian country, and you told 'em you were in the cattle business down here." He paused to chuckle. "They said they thought you mighta been japin' 'em, on account you were all drinking a little. I told 'em you weren't the kind to talk big, that you were in the business of raising cattle, all right, and had one of the biggest ranches in the county." He paused again, because of the look of concern on Perley's face. "I told 'em how to get to your place, and I think they started out that way when they left here. I'm surprised you didn't run in to 'em if you just came from the ranch."

"I'm surprised, myself," Perley said, thinking back over the road he had just ridden, and the many places where an ambush would be an easy thing to set up.

Now that he definitely knew Clementine and Junior were searching for him, they could have only one thing in mind. The question was, why didn't they take a shot at him? Maybe they were planning something bigger than just his death. He decided he should tell Paul McQueen about it, since he was the acting sheriff, just in case there might be some trouble heading for the town.

"Thanks, Ben," he said and started to leave, then paused when he thought it best to warn him. "You need to know those two people that were askin' about me are what's left of a gang after a shoot-out in Atoka. They're bad people. If they come in here again, you'd best watch yourself and make sure you don't turn your back to 'em."

His comment had a sobering effect on Henderson. "Damn . . . ," he drew out, his eyes wide with the realization that he had given the man and woman all the information they asked for about Perley. "Damn," he repeated. "I didn't have any idea. I mean, when they asked me all those questions about you, I never thought to keep my mouth shut. I'm sorry, Perley, I swear."

"No reason you would have," Perley said. "Just be on the lookout if they show up in here again." He turned to leave and saw that Ben's wife Shirley was in the doorway and had evidently heard the last part of the conversation.

"I'll darn-sure keep my shotgun handy," she said, making no attempt to hide her distress. "And to think those two were in here while I was handing out peppermint sticks to those children."

"Just be real careful if they come back," Perley warned her. "That little fellow named Link that was with the other kids was orphaned by that woman and her gang—killed both his parents. It's best not to give 'em any trouble. I'm goin' now to talk to Paul McQueen, so he'll know to be on the lookout for 'em. I'm sorry to have to bring you bad news, but I figure it's better for you to know." He left them looking fearfully at each other.

He found Paul McQueen shoeing Raymond

Patton's chestnut gelding. Patton was watching the process. They both greeted Perley when he entered Paul's shop.

"Howdy," Perley returned. "I reckon it's a good thing you're here, Mr. Patton. You need to know what I'm fixin' to tell Paul." He went on to warn them of the possible threat to the town with the appearance of the two outlaws. "I know, after talkin' to Bill Henderson, that it's me they came here to find, but you folks in town oughta be ready in case they've got anything else on their minds."

The warning was taken very seriously by both men, especially Paul, since he would be called upon to enforce the law. Patton was concerned as well, considering he was the owner of the only saloon in town.

"I have to tell you," Perley continued, "I don't know where they are right now. They asked Ben how to find the Triple-G and he thought they headed that way, but I ain't found no sign of 'em anywhere between here and there." He didn't know what else he could tell them, except that he suspected the trouble, if it came, would be directed toward the Triple-G.

"'Preciate the warnin', Perley," McQueen said. "I'll keep a sharp eye tonight. Make sure ain't nothin' goin' on."

"Right," Perley said in parting. "Just be careful, Paul, and don't take that woman lightly. She's straight outta hell. And they ain't greenhorns in the killin' and robbin' business."

He left the blacksmith shop and started for his horse, thinking he should hurry back to the ranch, but he reconsidered. What if that evil pair was still hanging around town somewhere? Maybe they might have seen him ride in and were waiting for the right opportunity to bushwhack him. John and Rubin would have the men on alert at the Triple-G to handle any trouble Clementine and Junior might bring. On the other hand, Paul McQueen was not an experienced lawman and might need the help of Perley's gun.

He gave it more thought for a few minutes then decided to do what he had originally told Rubin—stay in town long enough to have some supper.

"Well, hello stranger," Lucy Tate sang out sweetly when Perley walked in the door. "I was beginning to think you weren't ever comin' back to see us."

"I've been outta town for a while," he said and took a seat at the long table in the center of the dining room.

Lucy seemed to sense a sober disposition in him that was not usually present. "You want coffee?" she asked and he nodded, but said nothing.

She thought she detected a coolness in his attitude toward her. It bothered her, because he used to shine up to her like every other bachelor in town. He'd even worked up the nerve to ask her if he could come calling one time. She'd rejected him then, but she hadn't thought that would really stop him from trying. It hadn't stopped other men from coming back.

"You ain't very cheerful tonight," she said.

"I'm just hungry, I reckon," he replied and watched his cup while she filled it.

She stood there for a moment longer, waiting for something more in the way of flirtatious banter.

There was none, so she shrugged and went to the kitchen to fill a plate.

At the other end of the table, Becky Morris stood, fiddling with some silverware, pretending to be busy while she listened to the conversation between Perley and Lucy. *Good for you, Perley,* she thought smugly, long since hoping that Perley would someday realize how fickle and insincere Lucy was.

She went to the kitchen and intercepted Lucy, who had just filled a plate with stew. "Want me to take that for you?" Becky asked.

"Yeah, if you want to," Lucy answered. "It's for Perley. He's a regular ray of sunshine tonight."

Becky smiled and took the plate, walked back to the stove, put another ladle of stew on top of the portion Lucy had ladled, and went back to the table. "Evening, Perley," she said as she placed the stew before him. "It's nice to see you again."

"Evenin', Becky," he returned and managed a smile to match the one on her face. "How have you been doin'?"

"Oh, about the same as always." She picked up the empty bread plate. "I'll get you some bread. You can't eat stew without bread." Then she was away to the kitchen.

One of the men sitting near the middle of the table looked at him and joked. "I'm glad you sat down, mister. I've been waitin' for one of them gals to put some more bread on the table." His remark brought a laugh from a couple of customers at the other end of the table.

When she returned, she held the plate for Perley before placing it back on the table.

Perley looked up at her smiling face and thanked her, and for a moment he forgot the trouble that caused him to be eating in the diner on this night. But it was only for the moment, for he immediately returned his thinking to what his next step should be if he was going to stand in the way of any harm Clementine might be planning.

Becky left him then to fetch more coffee for another customer. She wasn't able to get back to him before he was finished, but headed him off as he started for the door. "Was everything all right?" she asked, concerned.

"Everything was fine," he answered. "I'd like to stay a while and drink some more of that coffee," he paused, "and visit with you, but I've kinda got a lot of things on my mind." He gave her a smile. "I've got to go, but it was nice to see you again."

"Maybe next time you come in there'll be time to visit," she said and stood in the doorway to watch him leave.

Behind her, she heard Lucy comment. "Something's really got a hold on him. He acts like he's half dead.

"Yeah," Becky said as she thought *he acts like he isn't fooled by your flirting anymore.*

Perley decided to make one more stop before heading back to the Triple-G, and that was in Patton's Saloon to talk to Benny Grimes. Benny greeted him with the usual friendly hello.

Perley said no when Benny asked him if he wanted a drink. "I just wanted to ask you if you've seen a couple of strangers in here this afternoon or this evenin'." Perley said.

"I ain't seen them two you're lookin' for," Benny replied. "Mr. Patton was in here a little while ago and he told me about that man and woman you were worried about. I don't look for no trouble I can't handle. I set my shotgun and my .44 right here under the bar where I can reach 'em real quick. If it's just one man and a woman with him, I don't see how I couldn't handle 'em."

"That's good you're prepared," Perley said, "but don't sell the woman short. She's a genuine handful, maybe tougher than the big ol' jasper she rides with."

"Is that so?" Benny replied, giving it some thought, his bravado turned down a notch. He was a smallish man to begin with, and he had assumed he could shoot the man, and the woman wouldn't do much more than scream and cry. "How 'bout you, Perley? You gonna stick around for a while this evenin', in case they show up here?"

"Reckon not, Benny. I'm fixin' to ride on back to the ranch in a little while. Like I told Paul and Mr. Patton, I think these two are lookin' for me."

CHAPTER 14

The five-mile ride from town to the Triple-G headquarters seemed more like ten on this night, as Perley constantly peered into the darkness all around him. Most of the trail was across open prairie, but there were plenty of hummocks and ridges, some with clumps of trees wherever a small stream found a way through. It was dark, but not a hard dark. No moon to light the way yet, but a man could see well enough to aim a rifle. Perley figured to reach the ranch before the moon came up and he just barely beat it, for he saw it rising over the distant hills as he rode into the barnyard.

Rifle in hand, Fred Farmer stepped out from behind the open stable door to meet him. "Glad to see you back, Perley," he called out. "Rubin said you'd be back and to make sure I don't take a shot at you." He laughed in appreciation of his little attempt at humor. Getting serious right away, he asked, "You think that man and woman will show up here?"

"I swear, I don't know, Fred," Perley answered as he stepped down from his saddle. "I know for sure they were in town and they asked Bill Henderson where they could find me. I can't figure out why they didn't try to ambush me between here and town. From what little bit I know about that woman, I'da thought she'd come after me first thing, but for some reason she ain't. Beats me." He led Buck into the stable.

"I reckon I'd best stay out here," Fred said. "Rubin's got us lined up to stand lookout all night, just in case somebody comes sneakin' around here durin' the night. Two hours at a time, just like the army."

Perley smiled. That sounded like Rubin. "It's probably a good idea, at least till we find out what those two are up to." He pulled the saddle off Buck and let him go to the watering trough in the corral while he measured out a ration of oats for him.

He found both of his brothers and their wives seated around the kitchen table when he went to the house. He had nothing he could tell them beyond the fact that Link had not been mistaken and the two people he'd identified were definitely looking for Perley.

"Well, I don't know what we can do different," Rubin said. "I've got the men takin' turns standin' guard tonight. I might keep one of 'em back here tomorrow. I don't like to take a chance there'll be any time when the women are alone. Maybe you oughta stay close to the house, too." His thought was to take advantage of Perley's skill with a firearm.

"I'm pretty sure those two are after me," Perley said, "so it seems to me you'd rather have me away from here."

"Maybe he's right," John said. "You know how he attracts trouble." He was not joking, and when everyone paused after he said it, he tried to undo it. "I'm just sayin' it happens to him more than most folks, that's all. No offense, Perley."

Perley just grunted in response.

Rubin pointed out that it wouldn't put the ranch out of danger if he did leave. "Those two would come to the Triple-G to look for you, anyway, so you might as well stay and help defend the Triple-G."

Thirty miles south of the Triple-G, Clementine Cobb and Junior Grissom sat before a campfire by a shallow creek. They had driven their horses hard to put that much distance behind them. Clementine was anxious to reach her family hideout five miles north of Tyler, and she figured they still had a day and a half ride ahead of them. Much to Junior's surprise, Clementine had changed her thinking on how best to deal with Perley Gates, and that was the reason they were racing to get to the Cobb hideout.

He still couldn't understand why she hadn't simply shot him and been done with it. *That's the best way to even a score*, he thought. *When you see him, shoot the son of a bitch.* But she kept saying they were going to take the whole family down, kill every one of them, and that was something he could understand and enjoy.

They were in the saddle early the next morning, passing Sulphur Springs well before the sun had risen halfway toward noon. They camped that night on the Sabine River, less than a half day's ride from The Hole, as Clementine's family called the family hideout.

Late the next morning they struck the wide creek that wound its way through almost a hundred acres of thick forest. They left the river and followed the creek until it passed through the trees to a clearing several acres wide. In the center of the clearing stood a barn and a large log house. It was surrounded by four smaller cabins and several outbuildings of various sizes.

Jesse Cobb sat on the porch of one of the small cabins, his chair tilted back against the wall and resting on its back legs. Idly whittling a green branch from a laurel bush to a sharp point for use as a toothpick, he was distracted when the two riders appeared. Until he could get a better look, he eased the chair back down to rest on all four legs, drawing the .44 Colt he wore as a matter of habit. When the riders cleared the opening in the trees, he let out a whoop. "It's Aunt Clem!" He jumped off the porch and fired two shots in the air to announce their arrival, then ran to meet them.

Jesse's shots almost emptied the cabins, as everybody in the compound came out to greet the travelers, expecting to welcome Clive Cobb home from prison. The explosion of raucous laughter and cheering stopped almost as soon as it started when they realized there were only the two of them returning home.

"What the hell?" Coleman Cobb bellowed. "Where's Pa?" Looking back at the opening in the trees, expecting to see other riders appear, he bellowed again. "Where's Brice?" Confused, he turned to his sister. "Clementine?"

"I'm damn sorry to have to tell you this, Coleman, but me and Junior are the only ones comin' back."

Amid a sea of disbelief, she tried to explain. "The people in Atoka hired 'em a gunslinger that damn-near got all of us." She motioned toward Junior. "Junior got shot and they was holdin' me prisoner." Junior nodded his confirmation as Clementine continued. "That gunslinger shot Brice and Shorty and Slick. There was a helluva lot of shootin' goin' on, and Papa caught a bullet in his side, and there weren't no reason for that. He didn't even have a gun."

Coleman tilted his head back and howled like a wolf when Clementine said Brice's name, wounded gravely by the loss of his son, even more than that of his father.

Clementine's brother Beau could not seem to understand what she was saying. He just swayed his head back and forth for a few moments as if trying to sort it all out in his brain. "Where was all this shootin' goin' on?" he finally asked.

"At the train station," Clementine said, "when Papa got off the train."

"All you was supposed to do was meet Papa at the train," Beau went on, still finding it hard to believe. "Why did they come after you? Did you hold up a store or somethin'? That woulda been downright dumb."

"No, damn it," Clementine responded, starting to heat up over the line of Beau's questioning. "We never did a thing in that town, did we, Junior?"

The big simpleton shook his head slowly several times to emphasize the truth in Clementine's statement.

"We were only in that town to meet Papa, stick him on a horse, and bring him here." Witnessing the doubtful reactions from everyone, and especially her two brothers, she finally told them about the man and woman they'd killed at the trading post. "Somehow, that damn gunslinger knew about it, so that's the reason they laid a trap for us at the train station."

"Damn," Coleman swore, still finding it hard to believe Clementine's story. "That son of a bitch is gonna hafta pay for takin' Brice's life." He paused, then remembering, he added, "and Papa's." He looked then at the porch behind him and the frail little gray-haired woman holding on to the corner post for support. "Mama, you don't need to be out here." He motioned to his wife then. "Clara, take Mama back inside the house. She'll take a chill out here."

He waited until his wife put her arm around the frail little woman and led her back into the house. In the yard, they could still hear her pitiful question. "Where's Clive? You said my husband was comin' home." Clara hurried her inside and closed the door behind them.

Back to Clementine then, Coleman asked, "What about that bank up in Wichita you were so hot to rob? What happened to that big plan of yours?"

"Kiss my ass, Coleman," she blurted. "I went up there to rob it, so I damn-well robbed it."

Unimpressed by her bluster, he asked, "Where's the money?"

"In my saddlebags and Brice's," she replied. "Twenty-one hundred dollars, easiest job we've ever done. They was so scared, they couldn't hand us the money fast enough. Ain't that right, Junior?"

"That's right, Coleman," Junior answered dutifully. "Easiest job we've ever done."

"Well, that's some better," Beau said, "but it don't make up for Papa and Brice."

"No, it don't," Coleman stated. "I mean to kill that son of a bitch that shot my son." His nostrils flared in anger as he glared at Clementine. "Do you know where to find him?"

She met his glare with a sly smile. "Yeah, I know where to find him and I coulda shot him two days ago, if I'd wanted to." She glanced around the little circle of men that had crowded in so as not to miss anything.

"Well, why in the hell didn't you?" Beau demanded.

"Because I've got bigger plans for Mr. Perley Gates than just shootin' him."

"Who?" Beau asked, thinking he had not heard correctly.

"Perley Gates," Clementine repeated. "That's his name." Warming up to her subject then, she laid it out for them. "If we go about this the right way, we can wipe out his whole family and end up with a helluva lot of cows. He's got two brothers and I say 'an eye for an eye.' He killed Papa and Brice. We kill him and his two brothers and anybody else that gets in the way. Cut out half his herd and drive 'em down to Houston and sell 'em." She winked at Beau. "'Course, I don't know if you've got what it takes to be in the cattle business."

Coleman hadn't interrupted while his younger brother and sister were bantering with each other. He was accustomed to his sister's brash boldness when suggesting holdups and rustling, but he was thinking that maybe she was talking sense this time. She had been right about the bank in Kansas. Maybe he wasn't giving her credit for her brains. "You might have a good idea," he finally said. "Let's go in and get something to eat and we'll talk about it." Remembering, he said, "Bring those saddlebags in and we'll count that money out."

Clementine took the saddlebags into the kitchen and dumped the money in the middle of the table. Everyone gathered around while she counted it, waiting expectantly to see what the individual payday would be. No one ever questioned her figuring, since she was the only one of them who had a bent for numbers. Since she had already counted the money several times after the bank robbery, she knew what the splits would amount to—considerably more with the loss of Brice, Shorty, and Slick.

"Before I divide this up, I'm takin' two hundred dollars off the top that goes to Junior for his part." She counted it out on the table before him. "He's earned it. If he hadn't come to get me, wouldn't none of us be gettin' anything."

Junior grinned in stupid appreciation for her words of praise.

"Two hundred dollars, Junior," she teased him. "That'll buy a lot of dried apples. That's good pay for takin' a little ride up Kansas way, ain't it?"

He picked up the stack of bills and fanned them, the grin on his face almost reaching from ear to ear.

With the oversized simpleton taken care of, Clementine started dealing the rest of the money in four equal stacks. When the last ten-dollar bill was placed on the stack nearest her, each of the four shares totaled four hundred and seventy-five dollars. Although no one announced the total, they all had added it up as Clementine dealt it. Junior, content to that point, couldn't help noticing that the other stacks of money were considerably taller than the stack Clementine had given him. He looked at Clementine, his grin turned upside down.

"What's the matter, Junior?" Clementine asked.

"It looks like my cut ain't nowhere near as big as everybody else's," he complained.

"Ours is a little bit bigger than yours," she said, "'cause we're family. This is a family business. But your share is twice what it woulda been if Shorty and the others hadn't got shot. Besides, I wanted to give you that extra hundred 'cause I know I can always count on you. I made sure you got that first before anybody else got anything."

"Oh," he said, the simple grin reappearing. "I understand now."

Coleman and Beau exchanged glances of disbelief at the simple giant's stupidity. His acceptance of Clementine's explanation for his small share of the bank money was proof of his devotion to her. Neither Shorty nor Slick would have willingly settled for an unequal share. They recognized Junior's usefulness to the family, however, for he was powerful and fearless, and never hesitated to obey a command, especially if that command came from Clementine. Besides that, Coleman thought it a good idea to have someone like Junior in the event there was a need for a sacrifice to save a family member.

After the money was split, Coleman and Clementine got down to the business of planning the war on the Triple-G. He was adamant that it would, indeed, be a war, and not a simple raid. Both were in agreement on that point, for both were passionate for revenge. Beau was long in the habit of going along with whatever his older brother decided to do, so he was content to let Coleman and his sister decide how the war would be handled.

Beau's son Jesse would drive the wagon needed to carry a small tent and a full load of supplies, not unlike an army unit going into battle. Operations would stem from a camp they'd establish on the Red River. Jesse, generally recognized as the gang's fast gun, wasn't pleased with the job of driving the wagon. He didn't complain, however, since he was by far the youngest of the Cobb men.

They would likely be encamped for several weeks while methodically rustling the Triple-G range and eventually killing the three Gates brothers and any of their crew who got in the way.

Also, they needed to stock ample supplies for the wives, who would be left behind to take care of their mother. Clara and Dixie were up to the task, having been left to care for themselves on many occasions.

When they were through with their planning, they began their preparations.

When all was ready, the expedition saddled up and Coleman led his party of assassins out of The Hole and set his course to strike the trail that Clementine and Junior had ridden down from Paris. Astride a flea-bitten gray gelding, Coleman looked the part of a general as he sat rigidly upright in the saddle, his hands holding the reins close to his midsection, with his elbows out. When observing the ragged bunch that made up his command, he seemed hugely out of place, but it had been many a man's misfortune to assume Coleman was not mongrel enough to lead them to pillage, plunder, and kill.

As Clementine had promised, it took two days to reach Paris. Coleman pulled up about one hundred yards short of the small gathering of stores and shops. Since Clementine and Junior had been in the town, Coleman didn't want to risk the possibility that they would be recognized, but he wanted to get a look at the town. When Clementine pulled her horse up beside his, he asked, "Is there a sheriff?"

"Nope," she replied. "They got a feller that acts like the sheriff sometimes. He's the blacksmith and he ain't nothin' to worry about."

Coleman stared at the town for a few minutes longer before commenting. "It's a nice peaceful little town, ain't it?" He cast a thin, evil smile in her direction. "For now, though, we'll ride around it." He heard a groan behind him from Beau, who had already spotted Patton's Saloon.

"They'll get to know us when we're ready to let 'em know us," Coleman said to him. "We need to get ourselves set up in a camp first, start thinnin' out that Triple-G bunch. Then when we're ready, we'll take what we want outta the town. That'll be after all three Gates brothers are dead, and what cattle they've got left will be scattered all over Texas."

"You always were a big talker," Beau remarked. "Why don't we hit this town the same way we hit any town this size? Ride in and take what we want, and anybody who don't like it gets a .44 slug for his trouble, startin' with that damn blacksmith."

"Because, when we hit a town like this, we hit it fast, before they know what hit 'em. We take what we want and get gone before anybody can get word to the Texas Rangers," Clementine answered for Coleman. "You've already forgot the main reason we're here. That's to clean out the Triple-G. We'd be damn fools to go shootin' this town up before we go to work on that ranch. The damn Rangers would be up here before we got started good."

Beau paused and let that sink in. "I reckon you're right. I reckon I worked up a powerful thirst ridin' up here and I wasn't thinkin' straight."

"I was thinkin' the same thing as you, Aunt Clem," Junior piped up, proudly. "You know, about not shootin' up the town first."

"Damn it, Junior!" Clementine railed. "I ain't your aunt."

"I forgot again," he was quick to apologize.

Beau laughed at the bungling simpleton. "That's right, Junior. Clementine ain't your aunt. Your aunt is a lop-eared mule and your uncle is a split-hoof ox." They all laughed at that, including Junior, who wasn't sure if it was an insult or not. "Don't matter, anyway," Beau went on. "There's a bottle in the wagon. Let's ride around this town and find somewhere to make camp. I'm hungry."

Clementine led them along Muskrat Creek to the place where she had discovered the western boundary of the Triple-G range. It was decided to make camp there for the night, then move to a more permanent camp across the Red River the next day.

While Clementine and Jesse gathered wood for a fire, Beau walked up to stand beside Coleman as he looked out toward the east and a small group of cattle that had strayed from the herd.

"I think I'm cravin' some fresh beef for supper," Beau remarked.

Coleman grunted. "That suits my taste, too. Why don't you pick us out a nice one and we'll send Junior to fetch it."

"You reckon they'll have anybody nighthawkin'?" Beau asked.

"Maybe. I hope they do, then we'll have one less to worry about, after we settle with him." Perley Gates was responsible for his son's death and the sooner he saw an opportunity to send some of the Triple-G riders to hell, the better.

While the horses were still being taken care of, Beau told Junior to go cut out one of the cows in the small bunch of strays.

When Junior returned with the cow, Beau set him to work killing and skinning it. Handy with a skinning knife, Junior was soon slicing prime steaks from the carcass and handing them to Clementine to roast over the fire.

"I swear," Beau offered, "ol' Perley Gates and his brothers sure raise some tasty cows." His comment brought an appreciative chuckle from the others, even Coleman.

They saw no sign of a nighthawk long after they had enjoyed their fill of the freshly slaughtered cow. By the time everyone was ready to call it a day, they'd made no effort to disguise their fire or their camp. In fact, Coleman welcomed a visit from a Triple-G rider, and insisted that, in that event, he deserved the privilege of striking the first blow in honor of his son Brice. To his disappointment, however, the night passed peacefully enough.

In the morning, after a breakfast provided by the late Triple-G heifer, they left the remains of the carcass where it could be easily found, and crossed the river to Oklahoma Territory. The first order of business was to find someplace that was not so easy to spot.

Charlie Ramie sought out Rubin as soon as he came in to headquarters that morning. He found Rubin and John in the barn. "Somebody killed one of our cows last night," Charlie said, which captured their attention at once. "Didn't just shoot it. They cut it up and cooked some of it, then just left the rest of it to rot. I found it on my way in from ridin' nighthawk. Found their camp, too."

"Indians?" Rubin asked, knowing an occasional cow was stolen by some renegade Indians, usually to keep from starving to death.

"I don't hardly think so," Charlie answered. "When it's Injuns, they usually take everything they can use. Whoever did this just cut off enough to eat for supper and left almost the whole cow." While Rubin and John exchanged glances of suspicion, Charlie continued. "I didn't see no sign they was Injuns around their camp. Tracks were from shod horses and boots, and they had a wagon."

"Damn," John uttered. "Which way'd they go?"

"Looked like they crossed the river and headed north," Charlie said.

"Sounds like a bunch of outlaws headin' into Indian Territory to hide out," John said. "Decided they'd have a little supper on us, I reckon."

"Maybe," Rubin allowed, "and maybe not." He was thinking of the pair Perley had told them about, especially the woman. She had come looking for Perley, and when she'd found him, she'd disappeared for a few days. He believed, like Perley, that the woman, not wanting to give up her quest for revenge, was up to something. He had a bad feeling that the incident with the dead cow was connected to the vengeful woman and it was a sign that she was planning to cause the Triple-G a hell of a lot of trouble. "I'm thinkin' this might be Perley's lady friend come to visit, and she's brought some of her friends with her. Go on and get yourself some breakfast, Charlie. Make sure you keep your eyes open all the time you're workin' the cattle."

The two brothers went at once to the forge behind the barn where Perley was fitting Buck for new shoes. Actually, Perley was watching Ralph Johnson shoe Buck. Ralph was a good blacksmith, so that was practically all he did, only occasionally working with the cattle. He saved the crew from having to go to town to get their horses shod.

Hearing about the butchered cow near Muskrat Creek, Perley reacted much the same as Rubin had. "I got a feelin' Clementine had something to do with it. Did you say Charlie said they didn't go to any trouble to try to hide the carcass or their camp?"

"That's right," Rubin replied.

"Kinda like they wanted us to know about it, ain't it?" John said. "I expect we'd best ride up there to the river before they start killin' more 'n one cow at a time."

Rubin nodded in agreement, but Perley differed. "I don't think that's a good idea," he said. "I'm thinkin' they're hopin' to draw us up there and they're sittin' in an ambush somewhere ready to cut us down."

Rubin nodded again as he considered that possibility.

Perley continued. "The best thing to do is for me to slip up that way tonight and scout along the river before it gets light enough to see me. It'll be easier for one man to do that without attractin' attention."

"I don't know," John protested. "That river runs close to fifteen miles along our north range. They could be anywhere."

"They're gonna be where our cattle are bunched," Perley replied, "and right now, that's in the wide bend about three miles from Muskrat Creek." He put his hand up when both of his brothers started to protest. "Ain't no use. Me and Buck are better at slippin' around than you two ol' married men, and I'm the one who brought all this trouble down on the family, so it's settled. I'll head out tonight right after supper, but we need to tell all the men to be careful every day now, till we get this thing finished."

Although they still protested mildly, both of his brothers knew he was right. They left it at that and went to inform the men of their intention and caution them to be careful.

* * *

After supper was finished, Perley walked down to the barn to find Rubin staring at the sky.

He turned when he heard Perley coming up behind him. "I ain't so sure you picked a good night to be lookin' for those people. It ain't gonna be long before that"—he pointed toward a low mass of dark clouds over the distant hills—"moves this way. It's gonna be a helluva night to go scouting along the river. It's makin' a little noise, too," he said, referring to a faint rumble of thunder.

"Yeah, I noticed it." Perley held up his rain slicker. "I figured I might need this." Actually, he wasn't disappointed to see a thunderstorm moving across the Triple-G range. It might provide additional cover for what he had in mind. Maybe allow him to get closer in the event he did find Clementine and her gang.

John soon joined them and he and Rubin walked back in the barn to watch Perley saddle Buck.

"Damn it, Perley, you be careful," Rubin exclaimed. "Don't go takin' any chances, just because you think you ought to. You couldn't have helped any of this trouble."

"What are you plannin' to do if you find this bunch of outlaws?" John asked. "I hope to hell you've got better sense than to try to take them on by yourself."

"Don't worry about that," Perley assured him. "I'm just interested in findin' their camp, see if it is Clementine, and try to see how many she's got with her. Then we'll figure out what to do about it."

"All right," Rubin said. "Just remember to let us all decide what to do."

He and John walked with him to the front of the barn, still watching the sky while Perley climbed up into the saddle.

"Be careful," Ruben said again when Perley rode out into the yard.

The storm was approaching rapidly with frequent flashes of lightning that lit up the whole barnyard.

Clearly concerned for his brother's safety, he called after him. "Never mind the damn outlaws. You'll be lucky if you don't get hit by lightning." A loud clap of thunder sounded then to emphasize his words.

"Maybe," Perley replied with a chuckle, "but I figure it'll be harder for them to see me. I don't expect to see them doing much in this storm but hunkerin' down and trying to stay dry." He pulled his rain slicker up tighter and nudged Buck. "I'll see you in the mornin', or maybe before if I find 'em right away."

CHAPTER 15

With a steady rain beating against his face, Perley rode along the banks of Muskrat Creek until coming to its confluence with the Red River. It was hard dark by then, but he had no trouble finding the tracks Charlie had told him about. If the rain continued they would soon be washed out, but he easily spotted the wagon tracks where the outlaws had entered the water. He also found their tracks where they'd come out of the river on the other side. The fact that their tracks led east along the river from that point, instead of heading deeper into Indian country, tended to enforce his suspicions that it was Clementine.

He hurried to examine what tracks they had left before the downpour erased them. She had obviously come back with more men. In addition to the wagon and the horses pulling them, he saw tracks of four horses carrying riders, plus one with no rider—the fellow driving the wagon, he assumed. He was confident in his count because they had spread apart when they crossed the river instead of crossing single file.

He peered out at the single-file line the tracks had become, confirming they had followed the river east.

With no more trail to follow, Perley was left to rely on his own idea of a camp that would offer cover and be hard to find. With that in mind, his first thought was to ride up from the river about a hundred yards to the low ridge that ran parallel to the river for about half a mile. Many gullies and ravines ran through those hills that would hide a camp. He had one in particular in mind, a deep, narrow gulch he had often wondered about when seeing it from the Texas side of the river. The problem, however, was they would have to hide their wagon somewhere. That gulch was not wide enough to drive a team of horses and a wagon up. Those hills offered about as good a place to make a more permanent camp as any, though. And if the party was who he suspected it was, that's most likely what they had in mind. Deciding to check that ravine out, anyway, he turned Buck in that direction and pulled his slicker up over his hat as the rain pelted his face.

After riding a few hundred yards along the base of the ridge, he thought he recognized the entrance to the ravine. But with the storm and the absence of light, he couldn't be sure. Riding a little way in, it became so dark it was almost totally black. He found out at once that he was going to have to be cautious.

Afraid he might injure his horse, he dismounted when he came to a point where the ravine made a sharp turn. He left Buck there, giving him some protection. The floor of the ravine began to rise from that point on, forcing Perley to be even more careful, lest he stumble on the uneven path. Suddenly, a gust of wind from above forced a downdraft that stopped him in his tracks, for he was sure he smelled smoke.

Almost immediately after, Buck whinnied behind him and far up the ravine he heard another horse answer. He knew at once that he had guessed right. Someone was camped near the top of that ravine.

The question before him was whether or not to proceed any farther up the ravine to get a closer look. He thought that over for a few seconds before deciding he needed to know how many were in the camp. He had gone that far, maybe he could get just a little farther, he decided, and took a few dozen more cautious steps.

"What was that?" Beau Cobb asked. "I thought I heard a horse whinny."

"I heard one of our horses snort," Coleman said.

"I mean, I thought I heard one down the ravine," Beau insisted. He turned to Jesse. "You got younger ears than me. Did you hear a horse down there?"

"Nope," Jesse answered. "This storm's makin' so much noise, you can't hear nothin'."

"How 'bout you, Clementine. You hear a horse whinny down that way?" Beau asked.

When she said she had not, Jesse volunteered to go down the ravine to see if his father was hearing imaginary sounds.

"You be careful," Beau warned him. "There might be some of that ranch crew snoopin' around. They mighta found our wagon."

"In this weather?" Clementine had to ask. "I damn-sure doubt it. We're the only ones sittin' out here tryin' to keep our behinds dry." She reached up and pushed on the canvas over her head to empty a puddle that had formed. "Besides, they ain't got no business over here in Oklahoma. We ain't on their damn range, and they'd 'a had to be snoopin' around the backside of these hills to run across that wagon."

"I'm tired of settin' around this little fire, anyway," Jesse declared. "I'll go take a look down there. I hope there is somebody sneakin' up that ravine. I'll give 'em a real good welcome." He was anxious to limber up the .44 on his hip, even if it was just to shoot a horse or a cow. The stormy camp was a little too crowded for his taste, especially with Junior Grissom taking up most of the space. The big simpleton always made an effort to stay as close to Jesse's Aunt Clementine as possible.

The problem wasn't helped by the fact that there was not enough room at the head of the narrow ravine to set up the tent they had brought. Consequently, they had to simply drape the canvas over the five of them huddled together. The raid on the Triple-G had sounded better back in The Hole. Jesse would have preferred a shoot-out in the middle of the street in Paris. He was faster with a six-gun than either his father or his uncle, and he never missed an opportunity to demonstrate his talent.

The rain seemed to come down harder when he left the cover of the tent. He pulled his rain slicker all the way over his hat to keep the rain from beating him in the face. Pitch-black darkness in the narrow ravine was made even worse by the fact that his eyes had not yet adjusted after staring into the fire for so long. As a result, he almost stumbled a couple of times as he made his way down.

Suddenly a flash of lightning illuminated the path before him as bright as day, and in that few seconds, a ghostlike figure was revealed, no more than twenty feet from him. Then it was gone as quickly as it had appeared, leaving him stunned for the moment. Terrified, he pulled his pistol and fired as fast as he could, round after round, shooting blindly, until he emptied the weapon.

Equally stunned when the lightning had flashed, Perley fell back against the side of the ravine, hugging the wall while .44 slugs zipped and whistled all around him as Jesse tried to cover every inch of the narrow opening. In a frantic effort to get his own pistol out of an entanglement with his rain slicker, he didn't free it until Jesse had fired all six shots. Still unable to see clearly in the dark confines of the gulch, he nonetheless was able to hear the metallic clicking of Jesse's empty gun.

Using that sound as his target, Perley fired a couple of shots in that direction and heard his assailant grunt and fall. Not certain what his next move should be, he paused to decide. In a few moments, he heard voices from up above him sounding the alarm and knew he had to do something. *First, I'd better see if that one is dead.*

In the dark ravine, he could barely see the body lying in the middle of the path. He moved cautiously up closer to it, his .44 ready to fire until he could see that the man was dead. Bending close over the body, he knew he had never seen him before. It was not Clementine or the big ox he had wounded at the railroad depot in Atoka. Concerned with the voices he had heard above him, could he expect a charge down that ravine? His common sense told him they would be foolish to do so, since the ravine was so narrow they would have to charge single file. It amounted to a temporary standoff—they couldn't come down, and he couldn't go up. To get to him, they would have to go out the top of the ravine and circle back down the ridge to trap him inside.

Those thoughts were interrupted when he heard a shout from above him.

"Jesse!" Beau Cobb yelled. "Are you all right?" There was a brief pause, then, "Jesse! Answer me, boy!"

In anticipation of what might follow when Jesse failed to answer, Perley eased back down the ravine to a point where a slight turn in the path provided a little bit of protection.

"He ain't answerin'," Beau said and turned to Coleman for help.

"He's dead," Coleman declared. "Walked right into an ambush. Ain't nothin' we can do about it, Beau." He was already thinking fast, trying to decide what their options were, and the only thing he could think of was for them to go out over the top of the ridge.

"We're trapped in this damn pocket, like a rat in a hole," Clementine said, thinking the same as her brother. "We've gotta go out the top." She had no fear in her voice, only anger, for she felt certain Perley Gates was at the bottom of this. "There ain't no tellin' how many is down there. There was a helluva lot of shootin', but we'd best give 'em a little somethin' to think about." She drew her pistol and prepared to shoot down the ravine. Following her lead, Junior drew his pistol as well.

"Hold on!" Beau exclaimed. "You might hit Jesse!"

Drawing his own pistol, Coleman said, "Beau, Jesse's dead." He fired the first shot that ignited a hailstorm of .44 slugs down the dark, narrow ravine.

Below them, Perley lay flat on the floor of the ravine as it filled with flying lead, praying that his luck would hold. Even with sudden death only inches above his prone body, he couldn't help thinking that he had managed to step in the biggest cow pie of his life. He hoped that would not be his final thought. After a barrage of three or four minutes, which seemed eons longer, the shooting finally stopped. It occurred to him then that he had not seen proof that the people shooting at him were Clementine's gang— and he had killed one of them. That thought was replaced by one that was more urgent, as his mind formed a mental picture of half of the party above him spilling out of the top of the ravine in a hurry to circle around behind him. Thinking he needed speed more than caution, he jumped up and ran recklessly back down the ravine, hoping when he turned the sharp curve near the opening that his horse would still be standing.

His luck was holding. Buck was still there, although stamping nervously from all the shooting that had occurred. The big bay did not have to be told that it was time to depart. As soon as Perley jumped up into the saddle, Buck wheeled and headed for the opening.

Out of the mouth of the ravine, Perley headed toward the river, aided by a flash of lightning to show him the best approach. His one objective at the

moment was to find a place to hide where he might
be able to hold off an attack if he had to. Not certain
about the number of his enemies, he assumed there
were four left . . . if he had read their tracks correctly.
He figured they would surely split up, with two going
out the top of the ravine, and two staying put, hoping
to trap him between them.

In the cramped camp, the outlaws were reacting
exactly as Perley had figured, although Beau had to
be restrained from rushing blindly down the ravine
to take his vengeance.

"Don't be a damn fool!" Coleman reproached him.
"Just because they didn't shoot back, don't mean we
killed all of 'em. They might be hopin' you'll come
chargin' down there to get shot."

"They killed my boy," Beau lamented. "I ain't
gonna just set here." His need for vengeance was
almost choking him.

"They killed my son, too," Coleman reminded him,
"and I damn-sure mean to make 'em pay for it. We
don't know how many's down there. We'd best get
outta this hole before they split up and trap us in
here before we can get to our horses."

"I know how many's down there," Clementine declared after rethinking her original thoughts and
relying on a gut feeling that had suddenly struck her.
"There ain't but one man down there and I aim to
get in behind him before he has a chance to get out.
Maybe one of our shots got him and maybe it didn't,
but if he's still holed up in there, I aim to get him.
You two stay right here. I'm going out the top and get
down the hill behind him. I'll drive him up the ravine
to you." In her mind, she still saw Perley emerging

like a demon out of hell from the railroad depot trapdoor to shoot Brice down. It fed the flames of her hatred for him to intensity. Not waiting to hear any argument from her brothers, she threw the canvas back from over her and climbed up to the top of the ravine.

"What if you're wrong?" Coleman called after her. "What if it ain't just one man?"

"I ain't wrong," she called back. "It's that one son of a bitch."

"I'll go with Clementine," Junior announced at once, to no one's surprise. Like a faithful hound, he shuffled his huge body out in the rain after her. With little choice, Coleman and Beau situated themselves in position to fire at the first person to appear in the ravine below them.

Finally, Perley noticed a lessening of the rain as the wind moved the storm farther along the river, so he moved Buck a little farther into the stand of trees on the bank. Holding his Winchester under his slicker to keep it dry, he ran in a crouch along the low bluffs to a spot where he could see the opening to the ravine he had just vacated. While he waited to see if his assumption would prove to be true, he pulled his railroad watch from his pocket.

Shielding it with one hand to protect it from the rain, he could just barely make out the time. It would be at least two hours until daylight and he hadn't figured out what he was going to do when that occurred. Already exasperated with himself for bungling his scouting mission, he wondered if he had made matters worse. His objective, as he had told Rubin, was to see if he could find the outlaws' camp so he and his brothers could plan their attack on it—and that was only if the outlaws showed they intended to stay on Triple-G range. He hadn't counted on running smack-dab into one of the party in the middle of that dark ravine.

Thoughts of his misfortune were immediately forgotten when something caught his eye farther along the line of hills. He stared hard at the spot for a few moments before he realized something was moving down the slope toward the foot of the hill. Thinking at first that it was maybe a deer, he was jolted when he could see it was two people. As he had figured, they were headed to the ravine, moving cautiously, rifles in hand.

What to do? He wasn't sure. At that point, they weren't on Triple-G range. They weren't even in Texas. He hadn't seen them stealing Triple-G cows, so he couldn't lay the front sight of his rifle on them and just blaze away. When he thought about it, he realized that they might be in the right, merely protecting their camp from attack. *And he had shot one of them.*

Rubin's words came to mind again. *If there wasn't but one cow pie . . .* and then he recognized them. Clementine and her big sidekick—no mistaking the pair.

She was big as most men—the reason he didn't know it was her until she turned to look back the way she had come to caution the brute to be careful.

Perley just then noticed the man still limped from the slug he had put in his leg. All his suspicions were confirmed. By identifying Clementine and Junior, there was no longer any doubt about the party's purpose in showing up on Triple-G range. They had come for him and evidently intended to do critical damage to his home and family, as well.

Knowing he was totally responsible for bringing this misfortune down upon the family, he felt it was up to him to protect them from the lawless murderers. The trouble was, he wasn't quite sure he could get the best of four hardened outlaws. The plan had been for him to locate them, and if they were still lingering around Triple-G range, his brothers and some of the cowhands would join him in driving the outlaws out of the territory. The natural thing to do was to ride like hell back to the house to sound the alarm, but that was not to his liking. While he was riding back to headquarters, Clementine and her gang might decide to thin the herd out and start shooting cows at random. The only other option he could think of was to get them to chase him. That way, he might at least lead them away from the cattle.

All he could do was sit and wait.

Clementine edged up to the side of the opening of the ravine and waited until Junior moved up close behind her. "Go over to the other side, and when I give you the signal, we'll rush in there at the same time."

With no hesitation, he went to the other side of the mouth of the ravine while she stood ready to react in the event Perley was inside and shot Junior when he walked across the opening. When Junior reached the other side without incident, she could still not be sure Perley wasn't in the ravine. He just might be too far up it to see Junior when he'd crossed the opening.

With that in mind, she whispered across to him, "When I say go, we'll charge in there together, all right?"

"All right," he whispered back.

"Ready, set, go!" she sang out, then hesitated just a moment to make sure the big ox ran into the ravine ahead of her. As narrow as the ravine became, she felt sure his huge body would be enough to protect her from any gunshots Perley might fire down at them. She need not have worried. Junior charged recklessly up the dark, narrow gulch with no sound of gunfire, until he suddenly went down to land hard on the gravel path. Clementine dropped to her knee immediately, ready to fire, but she had not heard a shot when he went down, and still there were none.

In a moment, Junior grunted. "What the hell?" He began to get up.

When Junior got to his feet, she saw a lump on the floor of the ravine and realized he had tripped over Jesse's body. They were too late. Perley had fled. She moved up beside Junior and knelt down beside the body of her nephew to make sure it was him. Then she yelled to her brothers waiting above. "Coleman! He ain't here no more. I found Jesse. He's dead." She heard a wailing like that of a coyote and recognized the voice of her brother, Beau.

She shrugged, thinking they had already figured that Jesse was dead. She had never been especially fond of Jesse, anyway. She had always liked Brice best, and that thought reminded her of her intention to settle with Perley Gates on that account.

"We'll bring the horses around," Coleman yelled down. "Then we'll find that bastard."

Perley waited, watching the mouth of the ravine a hundred yards away. There was no sign of the outlaws for more than half an hour, then two riders showed up leading two extra horses. It had finally stopped raining, but Perley was not aware of it. His watch on the ravine had been intense. He saw Clementine and Junior come out of the ravine to take the reins of their horses, then the four of them seemed to be deciding what to do. It was a fair guess that whatever their plan, finding him was number one.

When Clementine and Junior mounted up, Perley retreated back along the bluff to the trees where Buck was tied. He remained there, where he could see them through the trees, wondering if they could see the tracks he had left when he'd bolted from the ravine.

It appeared that they were not interested in scouting his retreat, for one of them, a man riding a flea-bitten gray, started straight toward the river. The other three followed him to cross over to the Texas side.

Now I'm in Oklahoma and they're in Texas, Perley thought. *That's just the opposite of what I need.* It occurred to him then that they may have decided to take their attack straight to the ranch. He had no doubt that Clementine knew how to lead them there. He couldn't let that happen.

As early as it was, the four killers would catch the family before they could finish breakfast.

His next move was dictated by a sudden fit of retaliation by Beau Cobb.

When the four riders came out of the river, they found themselves riding through some cattle bunched together. Unable to control his temper, Beau drew his rifle and started shooting cows as fast as he could. Perley felt he had no choice. He steadied his Winchester against a tree trunk and drew a bead on the shooter probably one hundred and fifty yards away.

Riding beside Beau, Clementine was startled when she heard a dull thud and he suddenly threw his arms up in the air and dropped his rifle. By the time she heard the report of the rifle that killed him, he was already falling out of the saddle. Stunned for a moment, she wasn't sure which way to turn until Coleman wheeled his horse and pointed toward the opposite bank.

"There!" he shouted while raising his rifle in a frantic attempt to get off a shot before the shooter disappeared.

Excited, the gray provided an unsteady platform to shoot from and his shot was nowhere close to his target.

"Look out!" Clementine shouted at her brother. "That son of a bitch can shoot! Get to some cover!" She was all too familiar with Perley's skill with a firearm, having encountered it at the railroad depot in Atoka.

Coleman ignored her warning, firing two more shots in Perley's direction. When no more shots came from Perley, Coleman kicked the gray hard and charged toward the river, his anger driving him on.

Across the river, Perley climbed into the saddle when he saw Coleman galloping toward him, undecided whether to take a shot at him or not. It would be easy to simply wait to see if the man was angry enough, or fool enough, to keep charging straight toward him. If he did, Perley could hardly miss.

Then Clementine and her big sidekick took off after the man on the gray, causing Perley to hesitate. If they started out to chase him, at least he could lead them away from Triple-G cattle. Had he shot the man on the gray, they might have pulled back deeper into the herd for cover, making it risky for him to shoot at them without hitting the cows. In spiteful intention to harm the Triple-G, they would likely continue to kill his cattle on their own.

That made sense. Giving Buck his heels, Perley galloped out of the trees and followed the river west with all three in pursuit.

With nostrils flaring, the big bay's hooves pounded the sandy riverbank in a steady beat that maintained a sizable lead on his pursuers. He held the willing horse to the pace for longer than he normally would have, but when Buck began to strain after a couple of miles, he knew he was going to have to let up on him. The flea-bitten gray chasing him was proving to be a stout horse, but he figured it had to be near spent as Buck. He had to assume that the man riding the gray would push it even harder if he let up on Buck, maybe even killing the horse in order to catch him.

Knowing that he wasn't going to chance foundering Buck, Perley looked for a spot to take his stand.

At a trot now, he decided on a grove of cottonwoods where a narrow stream emptied into the river, even as his pursuer closed the distance between them. Pulling Buck into the trees, he grabbed an extra cartridge belt then slid out of the saddle and released Buck to go down to the river for water, figuring the horse would take care of himself. If it happened that one of the outlaws found Buck, they would not likely shoot him, and if they tried to ride him, Buck would throw them.

Perley gave the bay a slap on the rump to encourage him to trot upriver a little way. *No sense in making it too easy for them*, he thought while he crouched down behind a low knob in the stream bank. It wasn't the best of defensive ramparts—not much cover from the river if one of them came up from there— but it would give him plenty of cover from a head-on attack. Whether it had been his intention or not, it looked like he was in a war.

With his anger a little more under control, now that he had galloped over two miles along the river bluffs, Coleman was able to think more sensibly. When he saw that Perley had taken cover, he realized that he was galloping straight into an ambush. He had already seen the man's accuracy with a rifle. He reined the gray back and turned to wait for Clementine and Junior to catch up to him.

When they pulled up beside him, he pointed and said, "He's gone to cover up yonder in that creek, behind that hump in the bank 'bout a hundred yards."

"Whaddaya figurin' on doin'?" Clementine asked. "I thought for a while back there that you was hell-bent on gettin' yourself shot like Beau did."

"I thought about it," Coleman admitted, "but I wanna make sure I kill that son of a bitch. He's tore our family all to hell. He's gotta die!"

She could see that he was getting himself all worked up again, so she repeated her question. "Whaddaya figurin' on doin'?"

"Hit him on three sides."

"That makes sense to me. He ain't got much cover on either side of him." She stared at the hummock her brother had pointed out. "It don't look like there's a helluva lot of cover for us on either side of him." She met his gaze then. "Who's goin' to sneak around on the sides and who's gonna take it from the front?"

"Maybe me and Junior oughta work our way in on the sides," Coleman said. "You can get yourself set up here where there's cover, you bein' a woman and all."

"Horsefeathers!" She reacted in disgust. "I'm as good a shot as either one of you. I'll work my way in a lot closer to that knob he's hidin' behind. I can make it plenty hot for him, and he won't have time to worry about you two."

"Maybe he's right, Aunt Clem." Junior spoke for the first time since they had caught up to Coleman. "Might be better if you stayed back here where it's safer."

"Shut up, Junior," she scolded. "Damn you. I ain't your aunt." She turned to Coleman and ordered, "Let's quit pussyfootin' and get down there and kill that son of a bitch before he wipes out our whole family. If we get goin', we can trap him in that little ditch he's holed up in. Coleman, you go on down the river. Might be a good idea to cross over to the other side, else you might find yourself too close to him when you get even with that creek." Without pausing for his comments, she instructed Junior. "Junior, you circle around thataway till you strike that creek. Then work your way back along the creek till you can get a shot at him. And don't take too long to get there."

"Yes, ma'am," Junior said with a grin, and started out immediately, heading north to take a wide circle back to the creek.

Clementine looked at Coleman, her expression needing no words to convey her question as to what he was waiting for.

He wasn't comfortable with the way she had taken charge of the situation. Though always brash, she had never been so bold as to take command over him, and he didn't like it a bit. He didn't take the time to argue with her because he couldn't think of a better way. "All right. I reckon that's about what I was fixin' to do." He left his horse there, thinking it better to go on foot, ran toward the river, and waded across.

After they settled with Mr. Perley Gates, he intended to have a little talk with his sister about who was the boss in this family.

She waited and watched until he made it to the other side of the river before she nudged her horse forward, carefully picking a way through the trees that would give her the most protection from a shot from the stream. She wanted to get as close as possible and lay enough fire down to keep Perley busy, too busy, she hoped, to watch his flanks.

While his pursuers were making their plan of attack, Perley was making plans of his own. With his knife and his hands, he was busy digging away at a rifle rest in the sandy bank from which to fire. As soon as he was satisfied with that, he started digging away at the bank behind him, making a big enough hole to back out of the stream without having to stick his head up. Since the stream curved on both sides of the spot he had settled on, if they intended to come at him from the sides, they wouldn't have a clear shot until they got pretty close to him. The hole he was digging behind him might come in handy if it got too hot for him in the creek.

He had just about finished it when the first shot from Clementine's rifle snapped a laurel branch over his head. He pressed up close against the bank, peeking through the slot he had carved in the dirt for his rifle. In less than a moment, he saw the muzzle flash as a second shot rang out. In quick succession, he answered with two shots from his Winchester. They were answered, in turn, with two more from a location a few feet to his left. Even so, he felt sure all those shots were from one rifle, convincing him that what he suspected was accurate. Two others would be coming at him from the sides.

My first two must have been too close for comfort. He shifted his aim to the left.

More shots went back and forth for a little while until he decided the other two outlaws had probably had enough time to circle around to sneak up the stream and come at him from the sides. As a couple more shots threw dirt flying from the stream bank, he backed into the notch he had dug behind him and crawled back under the bushes that lined the stream. Hidden by the bushes, he lay flat on the ground and waited and listened.

Across the river, Coleman waited, too, straining to

see up the stream in the first rays of light. Although the rain had stopped, a blanket of heavy dark clouds hung low over the river valley, still making eyesight a little difficult. When he felt sure Clementine had stopped shooting, he waded into the river at the mouth of the stream, ready to shoot at the first sign of Perley.

A couple dozen yards above the trapped man, Junior made his way down the stream, closing on the spot where the shots had come from. His rifle at the ready, he plodded impatiently along the bed of the stream, anxious to be the first to sight Perley. With nerves set on hair-trigger anticipation, both men converged on the spot in the stream from which Perley had fired. Nervous fingers rested on triggers as they closed on their target, ready to fire before he had time to react.

Suddenly, they saw a shadowy figure in the morning gloom and reacted immediately, firing at the same time, only to feel the impact of a rifle slug as it tore into their bodies. Coleman was knocked backward to land in the shallow stream, while Junior was dropped to his knees, both men fatally wounded, stunned, not realizing they had shot each other.

A surprised witness to the double execution, Perley couldn't believe the scene he had just witnessed. Lying flat under the boughs of a large laurel bush, his Colt .44 in his hand, his plan had been to get a shot at the first one to close on his position in the stream. With his .44 still ready to fire at the first sign of movement, he inched forward until he could see down into the stream. The first body he saw was Coleman's, lying flat on his back. When he turned to look upstream, he fired without thinking, for he discovered

Junior on his knees, facing him. His shot slammed into the huge man's chest and he keeled over to fall facedown in the water. Perley realized then that Junior was already dead before he'd shot him.

Still shocked somewhat by the unbelievable ending of two of the three stalking him, Perley had to remind himself that the third member was still out there in the trees somewhere—and that third member was the woman Clementine. His natural reluctance to cause harm to a woman did not enter his mind when he formed the picture of an angry Clementine and the ruthlessness with which she regarded the death of young Link Drew's mother and father. *I'll be just as dead from a bullet from her gun,* he told himself as he returned to his original position in the stream. What would she now do, he wondered?

She immediately told him. "Coleman!" she called out, maybe some forty or fifty yards away. "Coleman, are you all right?" She called out again. "Junior?" It didn't appear that she was going to advance toward the stream until she knew for sure she wasn't walking into a trap.

Perley decided to answer. "Yep, we got him. Come on in." He got a reply immediately.

"To hell with you!" she shouted in reply, not fooled a moment by Perley's attempt to disguise his voice.

As soon as he heard her, he ran to the river for his horse, wondering if she would run now that she no longer enjoyed the advantage. Even so, he cautioned himself to be wary of running into an ambush. It would be a mistake to underestimate the woman's determination to kill him. She had relentlessly dogged him, making her seem more determined than before to settle with him.

Once in the saddle, he guided Buck carefully through the trees until he sighted her crossing a ridge over two hundred yards away. She was evidently pretty sure her companions were dead, because she was leading their horses behind her. It was then Perley discovered a more apparent reason for her flight. He turned to see his two brothers, followed by Ralph Johnson and Sonny Rice, riding up from the river.

"Looks like we got here too late for the party," Rubin said when he pulled up beside Perley. "I knew when we heard the shootin' that you didn't wait till you talked to us before you jumped right into 'em."

"I didn't have any choice," Perley said. "I don't think they were willin' to wait for you boys to get to the party." He wasn't prone to admit that he had started the shooting by accident when he ran into Jesse in that dark ravine.

"Where are they now?" Rubin asked.

"There ain't but one of 'em left," Perley answered. "That crazy woman, and she just disappeared over that ridge yonder, leadin' two horses." He pointed to the last place he had seen her. "I reckon she took off when she saw you comin'."

"How many were they?" John wanted to know, surprised that the woman was the only one left. "Did you kill the rest of 'em?"

"Nope, two of 'em shot each other," Perley replied. When his answer called for an explanation, judging by their blank expressions, he told them how it had happened.

Rubin shook his head, amazed, when Perley recounted the whole encounter with the outlaw gang. "So there's nobody left but that crazy woman, and she took off for Indian Territory, it looks like. The question now is what to do about her. Chase her, or decide she's had enough?"

They talked it over for a few minutes, and the general opinion was that she most likely wanted no more contact with the Triple-G.

"If she's got any sense at all," Rubin concluded.

Perley went along with the conclusion, even though he wasn't quite comfortable with the thought of Clementine giving up on her determination to seek vengeance for the destruction of her gang.

With the decision made, there were the outlaws' horses to round up and drive back to the Triple-G.

"There's also a wagon back yonder somewhere on the other side of the ridge," he said. "I reckon you saw the cows they shot down. I didn't get a count, but that one fellow musta shot at least half a dozen before I stopped him."

With a word of warning for everyone to keep a sharp eye just in case Clementine decided to try something foolish, Rubin sent Ralph and Sonny to search for the wagon, while he and John went with Perley to drag the two bodies out of the stream. Perley told his brothers who the large man was. The other was a stranger to him, but had appeared to be the boss. They stripped them of their weapons and ammunition, but found little else of value on them.

"This one's got his pockets full of dried apples," John said as he searched Junior's body.

They recovered the horses and once the wagon was found, they hitched the horses up and took it back across the river, where the butchering of a couple of the dead cows was in progress.

"Might as well save a little bit of the meat," Rubin

decided. "With the weather as cool as it is, it'll keep if we throw some of it in that wagon and take it back to headquarters." Thinking it best to leave two men to watch the herd, Rubin told Ralph and Sonny to stay and he would send two other men to relieve them. Ralph volunteered to butcher one of the other carcasses and smoke it. All done then, the three Gates brothers rode back to the ranch, with John driving the wagon.

CHAPTER 16

Clementine's horses were bearing the brunt of her fury at having once again been beaten by Perley Gates. She drove them relentlessly along Boggy Creek. Finally, she realized she was going to have to rest them before they foundered, so she reluctantly reined them to a halt. With rifle in hand, she stood watching her back trail, not knowing if the riders she had seen were coming after her, or not.

After a while, with no sign of anyone in pursuit, she began to have hope that they had elected not to follow her. A little while longer and she felt sure they were not after her. Maybe they didn't follow because she was in Indian Territory, she speculated as she shifted her mind toward more mundane thoughts.

The first that struck her was a feeling of hunger. Although it was still early, she was hungry, now that she was no longer consumed by the feeling of being chased. She thought it not too risky to take the time to eat, but the trouble was she had no food to cook and no pan to cook it in. All her supplies and cookware had been left behind in the wagon. That thought caused her anger to flare again. The nearest town was possibly Durant, but she dared not go there since she and Junior had robbed the store on their way to Texas. Cursing her luck, she climbed into the saddle again and continued to follow the path beside the creek.

She felt the loss of her brothers and her nephew, but not because of her affection for them. Her regret was in having lost members of her gang who'd enabled her to rob and murder at will. But most of all, she regretted her failure to settle with Perley Gates. She was alone now. She even missed Junior, maybe more than Coleman and Beau, for Junior obeyed blindly. Her brothers always thought they should be running the show.

"Well, where the hell are you now?" she roared. Finding it ironic and kind of funny, she chuckled to herself. "I'm the one still breathin'."

A few miles farther, when approaching the fork that divided into Muddy Boggy Creek and Clear Boggy Creek, she caught the smell of smoke drifting along the creek. She pulled her horses to a stop while she sniffed the air, deciding at once that she also thought she detected the aroma of roasting meat. Starting again, she continued along the path until she caught a glimpse of a campfire through the trees.

Close enough to see the camp, she realized that her luck was holding as she heard a horse whinny. Hers answered, causing the two men seated by the fire to quickly reach for their rifles.

"No need for alarm," Clementine called out and continued at a slow walk until the men could see her clearly. "It's just me and I can't do you no harm."

Jed Hackett got up, his rifle ready to fire, while he craned to look beyond the single rider. "Keep your eye on 'em, Wormy. They might be up to somethin'." To Clementine, he called out, "Where's your partners? I see you're leadin' two horses, but there ain't no fannies in the saddles."

"These horses belonged to my two brothers," she said in as pitiful a tone as she could create. "We were attacked by outlaws on our way to Durant. My brothers tried to hold 'em off, but they were shot down. They died so I could get away."

"I swear, that's sorry news," Jed replied. "Left you all alone."

More concerned about a gang of outlaws, Wormy asked, "How many outlaws was there, and which way was they headed?"

"I reckon you don't have to worry about them outlaws," Clementine said. "They was headed to Arkansas." That seemed to relieve the sudden tension that had arisen at the mention of outlaws. "I wonder if I might have a little bite of that meat on the fire?" she asked meekly. "I haven't et in a long time."

Only then realizing that their surprise guest was a woman, Jed exclaimed, "Why, of course you can, miss. Come on in and let me help you step down. Set yourself down by the fire and I'll get you some coffee. We kilt a nice doe this mornin'—I'm the one that shot it—so we've got real fresh meat a-cookin'. Ain't that right, Wormy?"

"Yes, sir. Jed shot it. I didn't have no clear shot." He dumped his coffee on the ground and filled his cup for her. "That's real sorry news about your brothers. You just make yourself comfortable."

Troubled by the fact that both of them hung on to their rifles, she sat down by the fire and took the plate Jed offered her. Like his partner, he dumped the half-eaten piece of venison on the ground and pulled another chunk off the fire for her. Then both men sat across the fire from her, their rifles resting across their thighs, staring at her in fascination while she devoured several pieces of meat.

"You've got a fair-sized appetite for a woman," Jed remarked. "I like a big woman, myself. Always been partial to 'em."

"Why, thank you, sir," Clementine replied in an effort to be ladylike. "I owe you gentlemen for your kindness. I feel ashamed to say I have no way to repay you."

"Ain't no need to worry 'bout payin' us," Wormy was quick to respond.

Jed's mind was working on a different possibility. Judging by the way the woman was dressed, wearing britches and a heavy coat, her hair pulled up under a Montana Peak hat, she was a rough-looking woman— but she was a woman. And he had an idea that she was not as refined as she tried to sound, so he thought it was worth a try.

If he was wrong, he didn't have anything to lose, so he took a shot. "No, ma'am, Wormy's right. Ain't no need to worry 'bout givin' us no money. 'Course, if you feel like you owe us for feedin' you, there's other ways to pay for food. I mean, you bein' a woman and all." He winked at Wormy and waited for her response.

She didn't respond immediately as she looked from one grinning face to the other. She took her hat off and shook her hair out to hang about her shoulders. "I think I know what you're talkin' about, but I don't know . . ." She hesitated, her head bowed modestly.

"We'd be willin' to do a lot more to help you," Jed quickly assured her. "We'd even take you to Durant, wouldn't we, Wormy?"

"Yes, sir," Wormy said, "all the way to Durant."

Trying to be as coy as possible, Clementine fiddled with her hands, her head still bowed as if making a decision. Finally, she spoke. "I reckon as long as nobody else would know about it, and it's the only way I have to pay you . . ."

"Hot damn!" Jed crowed. "No, ma'am, won't nobody but us know about it. I reckon I'll be first, since it was my idea."

"You mean right now?" Clementine asked, still faking shyness.

"Good a time as any," Jed replied and started to unbuckle his belt.

"All right," she said, "but put those rifles away. It don't seem right to have us makin' love with a rifle layin' by your side." To show her sincerity, she unbuckled the gun belt she wore and laid it carefully beside her, then she started unbuttoning her coat.

"You're right." Jed responded, eager to get on with it before she changed her mind. "That ain't no problem." He handed his rifle to Wormy and dropped his trousers. "Lay this over there by my saddle."

Grinning in anticipation of his turn with the woman, Wormy took the rifle and laid it by Jed's saddle along with his own. He turned in time to take a .44 slug in his chest that dropped him to the ground. When the horrible realization that they had been duped struck Jed, he panicked. Clementine calmly cocked her pistol while he tried to run for his rifle. With his pants down around his ankles, however, he could only shuffle his feet back and forth. He was halfway there when the bullet struck him in the back. He staggered several steps farther before going down flat on his face. She got up and put her gun belt back on before she walked over to see if they were still breathing. Standing over Jed, she saw that he was still alive, but barely, so she cocked her pistol and put another bullet in him, this one in his head.

Wormy, lying faceup, was trying desperately to breathe. When her shadow fell across his face, he strained to focus on her. "You've kilt us, you ugly bitch," he gasped.

"I sure as hell have," she replied and pumped another round into his chest. Finished, she took a look at both bodies and uttered in contempt, "Men." She sat down again to finish her breakfast before she took an inventory of their possessions. Although still in somewhat of a state of shock and disbelief over the destruction of the men in her family, habits of an outlaw were ingrained in her. So she was interested to see what the murder of the two men had profited her. In her mind, the acquisition of food supplies and cooking utensils was enough to justify the killings, but there was very little else of value aside from two horses of questionable worth and two cheap saddles.

By the time she had finished all her business at the deer hunters' camp, and was ready to move on, it occurred to her that there was no question now as to whether or not the Triple-G riders were chasing her. She was no longer in a hurry. She had the rest of her life to extract payment from Perley Gates, even though every day he still walked on this earth was like a sharp thorn in her side.

She climbed on the flea-bitten gray Coleman had ridden. "I reckon I'm the big dog in the Cobb family now," she announced to the two bodies lying there, and left the campsite at the fork of the creek, leading her horse and three others behind her. If possible, she would prefer to sell the extra horses, since they would be a bother to her with what she had in mind.

Her plan was to circle back down into Texas to finish the job she had started out to do. Once again, her primary target was Perley Gates, since she had little hope of destroying the Triple-G family by herself. First, she had to rid herself of the horses. She didn't even want to bother with a packhorse, and since Durant was out of the question, she decided to try in Denison. When she and Junior had stopped at the Last Call Saloon on their way to Texas, she remembered seeing a stable of sorts. Maybe they might be in the market for horses.

Roy Wallace looked up to see a single rider leading four horses head straight toward his shop, He put aside the wagon wheel he had been in the process of repairing, and waited.

"Howdy," he greeted the rider when she pulled up to the corral between the forge and the stable. He was taken a bit by surprise when Clementine stepped down and he discovered the rider was a woman. In those parts, it was unusual to see a woman riding alone, even one as rugged-looking as this one. "Somethin' I can help you with?"

"Howdy," Clementine returned. "Maybe there is and maybe there ain't. I've got a couple of horses for sale, includin' the saddles, and some guns, too. The last time I passed through here, I was talkin' to Tommy Thompson and he said that you were sometimes in the market for horses and tack. I was on my way down to Fort Worth to sell 'em, but I've been away from my home near Tyler for a long time, and I just decided I'd sell 'em cheap if I found a buyer, and then go on home. What about it? You interested?"

Roy couldn't help being curious. First off, they were brought in by a woman alone, and all four horses she was leading were saddled. He wondered what had happened to the riders. "Well, I don't know. How'd you come by these horses?"

"I came by 'em in a sorrowful way," she answered. "These horses was all owned by members of my family that was killed in a church fire up in Oklahoma City. I reckon you ain't heard about it down here in Texas. I don't know how many folks died in that fire. You sure you ain't heard nothin' about it?"

Roy shook his head slowly.

She continued. "Anyway, there wasn't nobody left in my family but me to go up and get their horses and belongin's. It was just a terrible thing to see." She paused for effect. "I ain't out to make a profit on their things. I just would like to get a fair price." She hoped that he would interpret that to mean he might be able to steal them from a grieving family member.

She was accurate in guessing his reaction to her story, for he couldn't help thinking this might be a chance to drive a hell of a bargain for himself. He didn't regard himself as a man to take advantage of another person's hardship, but business was business. "Well," he said, "I ain't really in a position to buy horses right now. I do a little business with the folks movin' in around here, but it don't amount to a whole lot. Wouldn't hurt to look at what you've got, though. Why don't you step down and rest a while? I can offer you a drink of water, that's about all. The dipper's in that bucket yonder."

"Thank you, sir," Clementine said graciously while Roy inspected the horses.

He looked them over thoroughly, then inspected the weapons. "You sellin' the gray you're ridin'?"

When she said she wasn't, he asked, "What kinda price are you askin' for the other four?"

"Whatever you think they're worth. I don't really know what horses are worth."

That was what he was hoping to hear. "Well, to tell you the truth, horses in this shape generally sell for twenty dollars apiece. I reckon I could come up with that much—eighty dollars for the four."

When she replied that that didn't sound like much money for four horses, he upped his bid. "'Course, if you throw in the saddles and the rifles in the saddle slings, that'd make 'em worth a little more. Say thirty-five dollars apiece."

She wavered again, but when she left they had settled on a deal for the horses, saddles, and weapons for two hundred even, which was a bargain for Roy and enough to satisfy Clementine. She was free of the care for the extra horses and could concentrate on the mission most important in her life. *If I'd known he kept that much money on hand,* she thought as she rode away, *I'd have just shot the son of a bitch and took every bit he had.*

Then she remembered then that her main objective had been to rid herself of the extra horses. *And left the horses to the undertaker.*

An uneasy air swirled about the Triple-G ranch for the next couple of days, but after no sign of any more trouble, things got pretty much back to normal. As it often did that time of the year, the weather seemed to have difficulty making up its mind, and suddenly, it decided to head into winter. Work on the Triple-G turned to preparations for winter range.

Perley was helping Charlie Ramey stock up supplies for the line shack. Charlie had spent the prior winter in the shack near the river, found that he'd enjoyed the lonely task, and had volunteered to do it again. Short on some of the supplies he would need right away, they decided to go in to town to get them. Perley was about to step up into the wagon and sit beside Charlie when he heard someone behind him. He turned to find Link Drew running to catch him.

"Miss Lou Ann said for you to pick up a sack of bakin' soda for her," the boy said.

"We'll do that," Perley said, then paused when Link remained standing there as if there was something else on his mind. "Was there something else she needed?"

Link shook his head, but continued staring as if pleading.

"What is it, boy? Something botherin' you?"

"What if that woman is in town again?" Link asked. "Do you think she'll be back in town?"

"Is that what's on your mind?" Perley replied. "I don't think she'll be back around here again, so don't trouble yourself worrying about that." He thought the youngster would have forgotten about Clementine, but it was beginning to appear that he was never going to let it go. Perley thought about the terrifying image the nine-year-old must be carrying in his brain. It would take a long time to get that image out of his head. "Don't worry. If she shows up in town again, we'll have Paul McQueen throw her in jail." He gave Link a great big smile and climbed up beside Charlie.

Charlie gave the horses a slap with the reins across their rumps, and they pulled out of the yard with Link watching them. "I believe that boy's tryin' to adopt you as his daddy."

"You think so?" Perley asked. "I reckon it's just because I'm the one who found him and brought him here." He thought about it then, and had to admit that Link always came to him when he wasn't sure what to do about something. "He gets along all right with the rest of the young'uns, doesn't he?"

"As far as I've seen," Charlie said. "He's always in the middle of the bunch when they're playin' around the barn. Seems like the only time he ain't playin' with 'em, he's tendin' to that paint you gave him."

Perley looked back behind them, but Link was no longer standing in front of the barn. *Good*, he thought. He really didn't want the boy to become too attached to him. Perley really didn't expect to be at the ranch all the time. It seemed that things almost always worked out for him to have to go somewhere, like the trip he made that summer to Deadwood. He had really hoped that John and Martha would adopt Link, since they seemed to be having trouble having a boy, or a baby of any kind for that matter, ever since Martha had had Betsy.

Perley and Charlie continued on for another mile or so when they heard a horse come up behind them.

"Would you look at that," Charlie said as both men turned to see Link's paint loping to overtake them. Charlie hauled back on the reins to let him catch up, thinking something must be wrong. "Maybe Lou Ann thought of somethin' else she needed."

"What's the matter, Link?" Perley asked when the boy pulled his horse up beside the wagon.

"Nothin'," Link answered. "I just wanted to ask you if I could go to town with you."

"Well, I'll be . . ." Perley started. "Did you tell any-body you were gonna come after us?"

Link shook his head.

"You can't just saddle up a horse and take off like that," Perley started again, thinking the boy should be scolded. When Charlie laughed, Perley couldn't keep a stern face. After a moment, he gave up and laughed with Charlie. "I reckon since you're already halfway there, you might as well go along with us, but you might have some explainin' to do when we get back home."

Link rode the rest of the way to town beside the wagon, content to be riding a horse that belonged to him, and beside the man he admired more than anyone except his late father. He didn't care if he was punished by Aunt Lou Ann for disappearing without telling anyone he was going. He reasoned that if he had told her what he was going to do, she might not have permitted him to go. Besides, Aunt Lou Ann seldom gave a real whipping, and a good scolding was worth a trip to town with Perley any day.

Taking care of business first, they drove the wagon down the street to Henderson's to buy the things Charlie needed for the line shack. The transaction didn't take long, but the conversation with Ben and his wife took enough time for Link to enjoy the peppermint stick Perley bought him. Henderson was naturally concerned about the possibility of a return visit from the scary woman and her gang, so Perley told him what had taken place on the northern border of the Triple-G range.

"There ain't any gang left," Perley said. "At least not any of the men she brought with her. She's the only one that got away when the shootin' was over, and the last time I saw her she was hightailin' it over a low ridge, headed for Indian country."

"What's gonna keep her from coming back?" Shirley asked, clearly still concerned. "That woman is crazy."

Perley hesitated, then answered. "Well, you're right. She's crazy all right, but I can't believe she's crazy enough to show her face here again. In the first place, there ain't nobody but her now. Maybe she's got some more family or other men she can round up, but I expect the four she brought with her was the best she could do." When Shirley still looked doubtful, he said, "I don't think you've got any worry about your store. It's me and my family she's at war with."

"Perley's right," Ben said. "That woman's mean as they come, but she ain't likely to try a holdup in our store."

"I guess so," Shirley finally conceded. "I worry about everything because you men don't have enough sense to worry about anything." Nodding toward Link, sitting outside on the step while he finished the last of his candy, she said, "I have to make sure nothing happens to our supply of peppermint."

"I reckon that's right," Perley replied. "And I reckon I shoulda told him he couldn't eat it till after dinner. I'm thinkin' it wouldn't be bad if we stopped at Beulah's place as long as we're in town. That'd be all right, wouldn't it Charlie?"

"I could be persuaded," Charlie replied, obviously pleased by the suggestion and knowing it would be Perley paying for it. "I wouldn't worry about ruinin' Link's appetite, either. He's a little undersized for his age, anyway, He needs to eat." With that settled, they bade the Hendersons good-bye and left the store.

Charlie was right on his assessment of Link's appetite. He was delighted to hear that they were going to have dinner at the Paris Diner. He led his horse up the street, following the men in the wagon. It was early yet, so the breakfast customers were gone and no one else was inside the diner.

They were met with a big welcome from Lucy Tate as she came from the kitchen. "Howdy, boys. Come on in." She guided them to one end of the long table in the center of the dining room. "I'd best tell Beulah we've got three fine-lookin' men from the Triple-G dinin' with us today. She'll be honored." Lucy placed her hand on Link's shoulder and asked, "What are you wantin' to drink, cowboy? I know your two partners want coffee."

Perley shook his head slowly, thinking Lucy had no age limits when it came to her flirting. When Link looked to him for permission before answering Lucy's question, Perley said, "I reckon he'll have whatever he wants today." He knew the youngster would like to drink coffee, just like the men.

"Coffee," Link said to Lucy, and she laughed delightedly, then went to the kitchen to fetch it.

Having heard the conversation in the dining room, Becky Morris looked up when Lucy came into the kitchen. *Why is it he only comes in the diner when I'm back here in the kitchen?* she thought. It did seem that Lucy always happened to wait on Perley.

Almost as if she knew what Becky was thinking, Lucy said, "Perley's out there. You wanna take him his coffee?"

"Why?" Becky replied, making an effort to seem disinterested. "Aren't you waiting on him?"

"I kinda thought you'd like to," Lucy said, displaying an impish smile. "You're kinda sweet on him, ain't you?"

Becky flushed red. "Why, whatever gave you that idea? I've always thought Perley was a nice man, but I wouldn't say I was sweet on him."

"Well, I would," Lucy insisted. "He's out there with Charlie Ramey and that little kid Perley brought back with him. Go take 'em three cups of coffee. I need to go to the outhouse." Without waiting for Becky to feign a protest, she walked out the back door.

"Maybe Lucy ain't the bitch she likes to act like," Beulah Walsh commented, having heard the words passed between her two waitresses. She favored Becky with a wide grin, causing the shy girl to flush once again. "Don't keep the customers waiting."

Becky immediately picked up the coffeepot and hurried out to the dining room. She admitted to herself that she was always glad to see Perley. She was disappointed to hear that he was with Charlie and the boy, because the last time he was in, he mentioned something about having the time to stay and visit a little longer.

"Good morning, Perley, Charlie," Becky said when she set three coffee cups in front of them. "I've heard about you, Link. I'm very pleased to meet you." She filled the cups. "I guess you came for dinner, since it's kinda late for breakfast, but dinner is almost ready."

"Whenever it's ready will be fine," Perley said. "We ain't in a big hurry, anyway, are we Link?"

The boy's smile was answer enough.

It occurred to Perley that it was only recently that he'd seen Link smile at all. It was a good sign that the boy was beginning to deal with the tragic turn his young life had taken. He nodded to himself, thinking it a good thing Link had ridden after Charlie and him this morning.

In a small stand of trees on the banks of the stream that ran behind the buildings of the town, Clementine Cobb trained her long glass on the Paris Diner. She saw a young woman come out of the outhouse behind the diner and go back inside. Then she trained the glass on the wagon and horses tied out front. She had followed that wagon ever since it had left the Triple-G that morning after a constant watch on the ranch headquarters for the past two days, waiting for a chance to catch Perley riding out alone. She was determined to kill him but was not willing to risk being chased afterward. It seemed, however, that she was never going to find him alone, so she had followed him into town, hoping for any opportunity to get a clear shot at him, even if he wasn't alone. The hatred for him burning inside her could not be denied much longer, making her more willing to take desperate chances.

Thinking of the pleasure it would bring her to see his face when he realized he was about to die made Clementine so anxious for the actual moment that she felt she could wait no longer. It was now or never, she told herself.

No one noticed the solitary figure leading a horse out of the trees behind the hotel and heading past the outhouse toward the back door of the diner. Only a few people were on the street in town, and no one would likely have thought much about it if they had seen her.

She led her horse up to the back stoop and tied it to the corner post. Pausing only to make sure her pistol was fully loaded, she opened the door carefully, so as not to make a sound, and only far enough to see into the room.

No one in the kitchen but one woman, and she was standing at the stove with her back to Clementine.

Beulah was too busy making sure her fried corn cakes didn't burn to notice the big woman tiptoeing through her kitchen to pause at the door to the dining room.

It was all Clementine had hoped for. There he was, sitting at the end of the long table with his back to her. The other man was sitting to the side, also facing away from the kitchen door, as was the little boy who had followed the wagon in. Two women were busy setting the tables along the side of the room. She wanted him to see who killed him, but she was not willing to give him the chance that Slick Dorsey had given him at the train depot in Atoka.

To make sure she did not become a victim of his speed with a handgun, she cocked her pistol and aimed it straight at him. "Perley Gates," she slurred contemptuously.

"Perley!" Charlie shouted as she pulled the trigger.

Perley acted instantly, keeling over to the side, trying to pull his .44 as he did, but it was too late to keep from being hit in the shoulder by her bullet. He hit the floor hard, losing his gun when it slid under the table.

The attack stunned everyone in the dining room. Charlie, who wore no handgun, backed away helplessly, his rifle behind the little table by the front door.

Clementine, set to finish him off seconds before, hesitated when she realized Perley's helpless position. Still stunned by the shot in his shoulder, he struggled to try to get to his feet. She couldn't resist the pleasure of taunting him as she cocked her pistol again. "That was just to get your attention, Mr. Gunslinger. This next one's gonna be right in your belly, so you can think about what it's gonna be like in hell. Then I'll put one in your head." She flipped the pistol in Becky's direction for a moment when she made a move as if to get to Charlie's rifle. "Go ahead, Missy, make a try for it."

"Becky, don't!" Perley shouted. "She'll kill you!"

"That's right, Becky. I'll kill you." Aware then that Beulah had run to the door when she heard the shot, Clementine ordered her out of the kitchen. "You get your ass out here where I can see you, or you're gettin' the next one." Confident that she was in control of the diner, she smiled as she waved her gun back and forth casually. "Now, you're all gonna get the treat of watchin' Mr. Perley Gates pay for his sins against the Cobb family."

Looking down at Perley again, she said, "This is for what you done to my brothers and my pa. I hope they're all waitin' for you in hell." She leveled the .44 at him.

The sound of the fatal shot caused everyone in the room to jump. The smile on her face turned into a shocked look of surprise when the bullet struck her breast, forcing her to take a couple of steps backward. Still she tried to raise her pistol to fire, but staggered again when a second shot struck her in her gut and she collapsed to the floor.

There was not a sound in the room for a long moment when it seemed as if time stood still, everyone stunned by the sight of the nine-year-old boy standing frozen, both hands holding Perley's .44 still aimed at the evil woman.

The first to move was Becky, who hurried to Perley. She was followed quickly by Charlie, who went first to Link's side and gently took the weapon from the stunned boy's hands then helped Becky lean Perley against the wall. Beulah stepped up then and put her arms around Link's shoulders to calm him. He stared wide-eyed at Perley as if in a trance. Lucy picked up the chairs that had been toppled.

While the women hustled to take care of the wounded man, Charlie glanced at the body lying halfway in the door to the kitchen. "Damn! If that ain't one of them demons outta hell, then there ain't a cow in Texas."

When Becky and Lucy had stopped the bleeding in Perley's shoulder and it was plain to see that he was going to be all right, Link walked over and sat down next to him.

Perley put his good arm around his shoulders and said, "I reckon you saved my life. I wanna thank you for that. We don't have to worry about that witch anymore." Link didn't say anything, and Perley hoped the boy wouldn't be scarred mentally by what he had been forced to do. Only time would tell.

Charlie went out the front door to get Bill Simmons, but Simmons was already in the street with a small crowd attracted by the gunshots. He was a barber by trade, but also the only person in town to treat a gunshot wound. Charlie told him his doctor services were needed, and he ran back to his shop to get his medical tools.

"It ain't that bad. I can walk down there," Perley said.

"You'll do no such a thing!" Becky ordered. "I'll not have you aggravating that wound."

The forceful statement from the usually shy, soft-spoken woman surprised everyone standing around the wounded man, Lucy more than most. She couldn't suppress a wide grin that broke out on her face. She turned and gave Beulah a wink.

When Bill Simmons returned with his instruments, the patient was already prepared for him. With Charlie's help, Becky had gotten Perley's shirt off and water was already boiling on the stove.

After a quick look, Bill said, "It ain't a bad one, at all. You were lucky, I reckon. It looks like you were turnin' away when you got shot, and the bullet missed the bone. You want me to dig it outta there? It wouldn't hurt you none to leave it in. It'll heal right over."

Those standing around nodded their heads in agreement, all save one.

"He certainly will not!" Becky exclaimed. "No telling if that thing might get infected. He doesn't want to carry any souvenirs around from that vile woman, anyway."

Recognizing her apparent authority, Simmons went right to work probing for the lead slug in Perley's shoulder without waiting for Perley's preference.

It didn't take long to extract the bullet, and when he was finished, Becky took over the job of cleaning and bandaging the wound. In the meantime, Paul McQueen, with a couple of volunteers from the street, dragged Clementine's carcass from the diner, and Lucy and Beulah started cleaning up the mess. When it was all over, Perley walked out to the wagon, his shoulder heavily bandaged. Becky was right beside him, giving him instructions on what he should do to make sure it healed properly.

Watching from the front steps, Beulah said to Lucy, "I ain't ever seen that spark in Becky before."

"She's just not wantin' you to lose a customer," Lucy replied facetiously, and they both laughed.

Becky stood beside the wagon while Link tied the paint's reins to the tailgate and climbed up inside to sit behind Perley. When Charlie pulled away, Becky came back to stand with Lucy and Beulah, both with wide grins on their faces.

"What?" Becky asked, seeing their silly expressions.

"Nothin', honey," Lucy replied. "Let's go inside and get ready to serve dinner."

CHAPTER 1

When Joe Buckhorn emerged from the livery stable
and spotted the town marshal striding in his direction, he couldn't suppress a twinge of apprehension.

Looked like trouble was coming his way already.

Buckhorn had only just arrived in the town of
Forbes, Texas. With the sun hanging low in the afternoon sky and the place looking peaceful and sort
of welcoming from the knob of a distant hill, he'd
decided he would ride in for a good meal and a
cold beer, maybe a bath, and then a night's sleep in
a soft bed before moving on in the morning. He
wasn't wanted for anything and wasn't looking for
trouble.

But the lingering memory of times past, when
his business and the interests of the law had often
been at cross-purposes, tended to make him leery
whenever he saw somebody wearing a badge headed
his way.

Not that the badge-toter in this case looked particularly menacing. He was on the short side, had

more than a few years on him, was potbellied and bespectacled, and sported a high-crowned, cream-colored Stetson that appeared at least one size too large so that it rested on the tops of a pair of jug ears.

As if in acknowledgment of his mild appearance, the man walked with somewhat tentative steps rather than the bold, clear-out-of-my-way strides that marked the bullying tactics of too many law enforcers in small settlements across the West. And, if Buckhorn wasn't mistaken, it sounded as if the man was humming a soft tune as he came down the street.

Buckhorn was still trying to decide what to make of this vision when the livery proprietor, a fellow named Hobbs, came out of the barn and stepped up to stand beside him. Chewing on a long piece of straw that poked out one corner of his mouth, Hobbs said, "Okay. Here comes Elmer now."

"Elmer?"

"Elmer Dahlquist. Our town marshal."

"I see the badge. You expectin' him?"

Hobbs cut Buckhorn a sidelong look.

"Well, yeah. I sent my boy to fetch him right after you rode up."

Buckhorn looked puzzled for a moment before working that expression into a scowl.

"You sayin' you called the law on me?"

Hobbs felt the heat from those narrowed eyes and cleared his throat, then said, "No, sir. Not like that, not the way you make it sound—I just let Elmer know you'd showed up, the way he asked some of us business owners to keep an eye out for."

Buckhorn was growing more confounded and annoyed by the minute.

"The marshal had business owners around town on the lookout for me to show up?" he asked. "What the hell for?"

"Probably be simpler," Marshal Dahlquist said as he drew closer to the two men, "if you just went ahead and let me explain, Mr. Buckhorn. You *are* Joe Buckhorn, ain't that right?"

"That's right," Buckhorn said, still with the scowl in place. "But I don't understand what makes you so doggone interested in me."

A wan smile came and went on the marshal's round face.

"Me, personally? I got no special interest in you at all. Not as long as you behave yourself and don't cause no trouble while you're in town. My interest in you is strictly on account of this telegram I got a couple days ago."

Dahlquist produced a folded piece of paper from his shirt pocket, unfolded it, held it out to Buckhorn. In the dimming light of early evening, Buckhorn saw that it was from a man named Tolliver, addressed to Dahlquist.

BE A FAVOR IF YOU'D STAY ON THE
LOOKOUT FOR A JOE BUCKHORN WHO
MIGHT BE PASSING YOUR WAY. HIRED
GUN, BUT NOT WANTED BY THE LAW.
PART INDIAN. WEARS A BOWLER HAT.
RANCHER HERE NAMED DANVERS HAS
NEED OF HIS SERVICES. LET ME KNOW IF
HE COMES AROUND. I'LL HAVE DANVERS
WIRE HIM THERE DIRECT. THANKS.

When Buckhorn lifted his eyes after he was done reading, Dahlquist said, "Thad Tolliver is a sheriff farther west and south some. Good man. Works out of the town of Barkley. Don't know this Danvers personally, but I've heard the name. Runs a big ranching operation in that area."

"Big enough to have the local sheriff acting as a messenger boy for him, it seems," observed Buckhorn.

"Don't know about that. Like I said, Tolliver has always been a good man, so I got no problem doing him this favor. You familiar with him or Danvers, either one?"

"Can't say I am."

"Well, at least one of 'em seems to know something about you. Enough to describe you and want to hire your, ah, 'services,' as the message says."

"I've been doin' what I do for a while now," Buckhorn replied. "Long enough for folks to have heard about me and long enough for me to know how to stay on the right side of the law. As far as the description . . . how many big, ugly Indians do you run across wearing a bowler hat and packing a six-gun they look like they know how to use?"

"You make a point there," Dahlquist said.

There was no denying that Buckhorn's appearance tended to leave a lasting impression. Tall, lean, solid looking; crow's wing–black hair and skin bronzed to a deep reddish-brown hue that spoke clearly of the Indian blood in him; hawklike facial features that most would consider to be on the homely side although a surprising number of women seemed to find them intriguing. All decked out in a brown suit jacket and matching vest, neatly knotted string tie, and topped off with a rakishly tilted bowler.

At first glance he might be mistaken for a whiskey drummer or some such—but nobody would maintain that assessment for very long. Not after closer consideration of the hardness around his eyes or the way the Frontier Colt .45 pistol hung loose and ready in the well-worn holster on his hip.

"I guess the only question left now," Dahlquist went on, jabbing a finger to indicate the paper Buckhorn was still holding, "is how you want to respond to that? I'm sure Virgil Holmes, who runs our telegraph office, has closed up shop for the day. But he's a pretty amenable fella, especially after he has a good meal in him. Once I know he's finished supper, I could ask him to send a response to Tolliver and probably have something direct to you from Danvers back in the morning. Unless none of it is any interest to you, then we can just forget the whole thing."

Buckhorn didn't have to think on it for very long. His last job, moneywise, hadn't worked out nearly as well as he'd expected. So if a big Texas rancher had a new proposition to make, he was willing to hear the man out.

As far as Dahlquist's friendly offer to help speed things along by providing a little extra go-between service, there was a part of Buckhorn that wanted to take him up on it. But at the same time there was also part of him that stubbornly hated being beholden to anybody. He had wrestled with that pride many times in his life, and pride usually won.

So his response was, "I'd be obliged for the chance to hear what this Danvers has to say, Marshal. But I sure hate to step on your telegraph man's suppertime, not to mention yours. I can wait until morning to respond to this message from the sheriff myself, then see what Danvers comes back with."

"Nonsense. I still got my evening rounds to make and it won't take Virgil but two shakes to send that telegram. You wouldn't be stepping on our time to amount to nothing. You see, Mr. Buckhorn, folks in and around Forbes are real friendly that way—to each other and to strangers passin' through alike." Here the marshal showed another brief smile, this one a bit toothier than before. "And when it comes to hired guns like yourself passin' through—meaning no disrespect to you personally, mind you—I figure our best chance to keep things that way is for me to help move situations like this along."

Now it was Buckhorn's turn to smile as he said, "You know, Marshal, I think that was about the most pleasant get-your-ass-out-of-town speech I ever heard."

Dahlquist held up an admonishing finger.

"Nobody said anything about kicking anybody out of town. Just helping to move the situation along, like I said, that's all."

"Well, I guess I can't hardly blame you for that. And since all I ever intended was to stop for the night anyway, reckon we're both aimed in the same direction." Buckhorn handed back the telegram. "If you'll contact that sheriff over in Barkley, I'd appreciate it. Suppose I can count on you lookin' me up in the morning when you've heard something back?"

"Bright and early."

Buckhorn gestured toward one of the buildings across the street.

"Sign over there says Hotel and Restaurant. That's where you'll find me."

"Fine place. I recommend it. See you there in the morning."

CHAPTER 2

In the Star Hotel dining room, Buckhorn enjoyed a fine meal of steak with all the trimmings, washed down by a couple of cold beers and then followed by coffee and a generous slice of just about the best peach pie he'd ever tasted.

When he was done eating, he was directed to a back room on the hotel side where a tub of fresh, hot water was waiting. While he soaked and scrubbed, his clothes and boots were taken for a good brushing.

If anyone had an issue with him being part Indian, Buckhorn saw no sign of it. No sidelong glances or veiled, hostile stares. It appeared Marshal Dahlquist had it right about the folks in his town being real friendly.

In his second-floor room, Buckhorn hung up his freshly brushed outer clothes. He'd changed to clean socks and long johns downstairs and now he took a fresh shirt from his war bag, which he hung with the other garments he'd dress in tomorrow. The dirty items he stuffed down at the bottom of the war bag, telling himself that he'd have to remember to look up a laundry service in Barkley or whatever the next town was that he landed in for any length of time.

Early in his profession as a hired gun, Buckhorn had done some bodyguard work for a rich man whose attention to grooming and attire had left a lasting impression. Buckhorn decided he would pattern his own way of dressing after much of what he'd seen practiced by that wealthy man and others in his circle.

As the son of a "tame" Indian father and a white-trash mother who'd abandoned them both when Joe was only six years old, his beginning had been a shabby one. The years that followed with his remaining parent were grim, as Albert Buckhorn took to drink and feeling sorry for himself until he staggered into the middle of the street and got trampled by a runaway freight wagon.

That left Joe facing almost a decade of abusive, filthy living on the reservation where his father's people didn't want any more to do with an orphaned half-breed than the white folks in town did.

As a young man, he had left that miserable existence behind and soon discovered that he was good with a gun, but people still regarded him as little better than a cur. If he wanted to climb to a better station in life, he told himself, then he would start by dressing the part. And he'd adhered to that goal ever since.

Tonight, settled into his room at the Star Hotel, Buckhorn was feeling pretty good. Full belly on the inside, boiled and scrubbed clean on the outside, the prospect of a new job on the horizon. The big, soft-looking, fresh-smelling bed beckoned him, and he could hardly wait to stretch out. But first, he decided, he wanted to let in some cool night air.

The room's single window was tall and narrow, opening onto an elongated balcony that ran across the front of the hotel building. After first dimming the bedside lantern so he would not be silhouetted against a background light, Buckhorn went to the window and prepared to crack it open a few inches.

Looking down on Forbes's main street, softly illuminated by a series of oil lanterns hung on posts at well-placed intervals, he saw Marshal Dahlquist strolling unhurriedly along on the opposite side, stopping to check and make sure the front doors of each of the buildings he came to were securely locked.

Buckhorn made a little bet with himself that, when he got the window open, he'd be able to hear the marshal softly humming a tune as he went along. It wasn't very often you ran across somebody who seemed so content in his work.

Buckhorn pushed aside the window's gauzy curtains. An instant before he twisted the lock tab that would allow the bottom half of the window to be raised, the roar of a heavy-caliber gun split the night. Buckhorn jerked back a half step. The sound of the gunshot came from somewhere very close—outside and directly under the balcony, the way it sounded.

Across the street, Elmer Dahlquist's oversized hat flew off and went spinning one way while the marshal made a dive in a different direction. Buckhorn watched the little man hit the ground and go scrambling with surprising nimbleness toward a thick-walled water trough. As he squirmed in behind the tank, he grabbed his pistol.

Two more shots boomed. One slug tore a deep gouge in the dirt, throwing up a geyser of dust and grit right behind where Dahlquist's heels had been digging a moment earlier. The second one *whapped!* loudly against the side of the trough.

After spinning and snatching his Colt out of the holster and gunbelt he'd hung on a bedpost, Buckhorn turned back and used the noise of those latest blasts to cover the sound of him throwing the window open wide. He slipped over the sill and onto the balcony, creeping shadow-quiet in his stocking feet.

Below, somewhere in the blackness beyond the reach of the streetlamps at the mouth of an alley running beside the hotel, a voice called out.

"I've got you right where I want you, Dahlquist, you son of a bitch! I've got seven years of payback built up in my craw, and now it's time to settle accounts for what you did to me and my little brother Varliss. I ventilated your stupid hat and now I'm gonna do the same to your damn head!"

"Who is that talking, you ambushin' skunk?" Dahlquist wanted to know. "You got something to settle with me, let's step on out in the street and do it face-to-face. Like men!"

"The hell with that! I like things just the way they are," the gunman in the alley called back. To emphasize his words he fired again and sent another round hammering against the water trough.

Dahlquist popped out long enough to reach around one end of the tank and snap off two shots, shooting blindly into the inkiness of the alley.

"Stretch out like that again, you old bastard, and see what it gets you," the ambusher mocked.

Having crept to the end of the balcony, Buckhorn eased forward to peer over the railing. It took his vision a moment to adjust, but then, in the murkiness below, he could make out the man shooting at the marshal. He was hunkering behind an enormous rain barrel, an angular specimen clad in a pair of one-strap overalls, lace-up work shoes, and a slouch hat. He was doing his shooting with a long-barreled rifle, a modified Spencer carbine turned into a buffalo gun, probably .56 caliber.

Ordinarily, Buckhorn made it a point never to stick his nose in a situation unless his life was in danger or he had been hired to get involved. But there were times, like now, when a fella had to make exceptions. Elmer Dahlquist had gone out of his way to be fair and friendly, something a half-breed rarely ran into. On top of that, Buckhorn loathed ambushers and back shooters.

Another exchange of shots crackled back and forth across the street. Once again the water trough took a hit, and its contents sloshed and slopped over the edges. Many more impacts like that from the buffalo gun and the tank was liable to rupture wide open, Buckhorn knew.

"Mighty good shootin' to be able to hit this big ol' tank from clear across the street. You must've been target practicin' for those seven years," Dahlquist taunted. Then: "Wait a minute. Seven years? And a brother named Varliss . . . Is that you over there, Clyde Byerby?"

"Give the man a great big see-gar!" crowed the shooter in the alley. "Too bad you ain't never gonna get the chance to enjoy it, Dahlquist, 'cause I'm gonna blow apart your smoke puffer like a melon dropped from a church steeple."

Buckhorn could have easily leaned over the balcony and fired down on the ambusher before the man ever knew he was there. Could have killed him with one shot. But the varmint's own words about dropping a melon from on high gave Buckhorn another idea—one he had a hunch Marshal Dahlquist would be far more approving of.

"You blamed fool, Clyde," Dahlquist called. "You couldn't have got out of prison more'n a couple weeks ago. So now you're gonna shoot me and land yourself right back in?"

"They'll never put me in the pen again," Clyde said. "If I can't make it across the border after I've done for you, they'll have to cut me down. But no matter, however it turns out, at least I'll have squared things with you!"

While this exchange was taking place, Buckhorn was silently on the move. A row of brightly painted clay pots holding cactus rose plants sat along the railing of the balcony. Buckhorn hefted the nearest of these and found it to have what he judged to be sufficient weight.

Setting his Colt aside, he picked up the potted cactus and carried it over to the end of the balcony. Held at arm's length, it was almost directly above Clyde Byerby. When the man snugged the buffalo gun to his shoulder again and braced very still, getting ready to trigger another round, Buckhorn released the pot.

He scored a direct hit.

The pot struck the top of the target's head with a dull *clunk!* and, mashing flat the slouch hat, broke apart like flower petals opening. Clay shards fell away, spilling clumps of dirt and pieces of cactus down over the ambusher's shoulders and back. Byerby went limp, arms falling loosely to his sides, rifle slipping from his grasp, body sagging against the big rain barrel like a pile of soiled laundry.

When Buckhorn was satisfied he had knocked the man cold, he straightened up behind the railing and called across the street to Dahlquist, "War's over, Marshal. You can come claim your prisoner now."

Dahlquist peeked cautiously above the edge of the water trough, and then he, too, stood up. He still held his pistol at the ready. The front of his clothes were soaked and there was a smudge of mud on one cheek. Lifting his chin to gaze up at the hotel balcony, he said, "Is that you, Buckhorn?"

"None other."

Now that the shooting had stopped, lights started appearing in the windows of living quarters over some of the businesses lining the street. Two or three men emerged tentatively from the front of the saloon down in the next block, and Buckhorn thought he could hear a sudden scurry of activity downstairs in the lobby of the hotel.

"What did you do to Byerby?" Dahlquist wanted to know.

"He found out he was allergic to cactus rose plants.

You'd better get over here and slap some cuffs on him before he regains consciousness. I'll be down as soon as I get some pants on."

By the time Buckhorn made it down through the lobby and out to the street—after donning not only his pants but also his boots and gunbelt—quite a crowd had gathered in front of the alley next to the hotel. There was an edge of annoyance in Elmer Dahlquist's normally mild tone as he tried to answer jabbering questions as politely as he could while alternately barking orders in an attempt to keep the scene under control.

When he spotted Buckhorn shouldering his way through the crowd, the marshal's frown fell away. Smiling, he said, "Here's the man of the hour now. Ladies and gentlemen, I give you Joe Buckhorn—not only a hired gun of wide renown, but well on his way to becoming one of the most feared potted-plant-slingers in the West."

There was actually a smattering of applause from some of those present, thinking the marshal was truly being serious. Most of the others just looked a bit puzzled.

Unruffled by the good-natured rib, Buckhorn came to stand before the marshal and said, "I may quit carrying a six-gun altogether, soon as I've perfected a brace of holsters so's I can pack a potted plant on each hip."

Dahlquist's expression turned serious.

"Well, you sure got the job done with one tonight,"

he said for everybody to hear. "And you just may have saved my life in the process. For that I'm mighty grateful."

"Trouble is," Buckhorn said, gesturing to the shredded Stetson Dahlquist had retrieved from the middle of the street and now stood fidgeting with, "I wasn't in time to save that fancy hat of yours."

"This old thing?" Dahlquist said, continuing to worry the Stetson between his hands. "It was a gift from my late wife, just before she passed on. Special ordered from some fancy haberdashery in Dallas." A lingering sadness touched his face for a moment before he realized it, and he quickly covered it with a wry twist of his mouth. "Anybody could see the blamed thing was a mile too big, but I didn't have the heart to hurt her feelings by not wearing it. And after she was gone, well, I just kept on wearing it. Reckon I've got cause to buy one that fits proper now."

"Reckon so," Buckhorn agreed in a somber tone. "The right hat's a serious thing for a man."